W9-CBG-833

Through THE WOODS

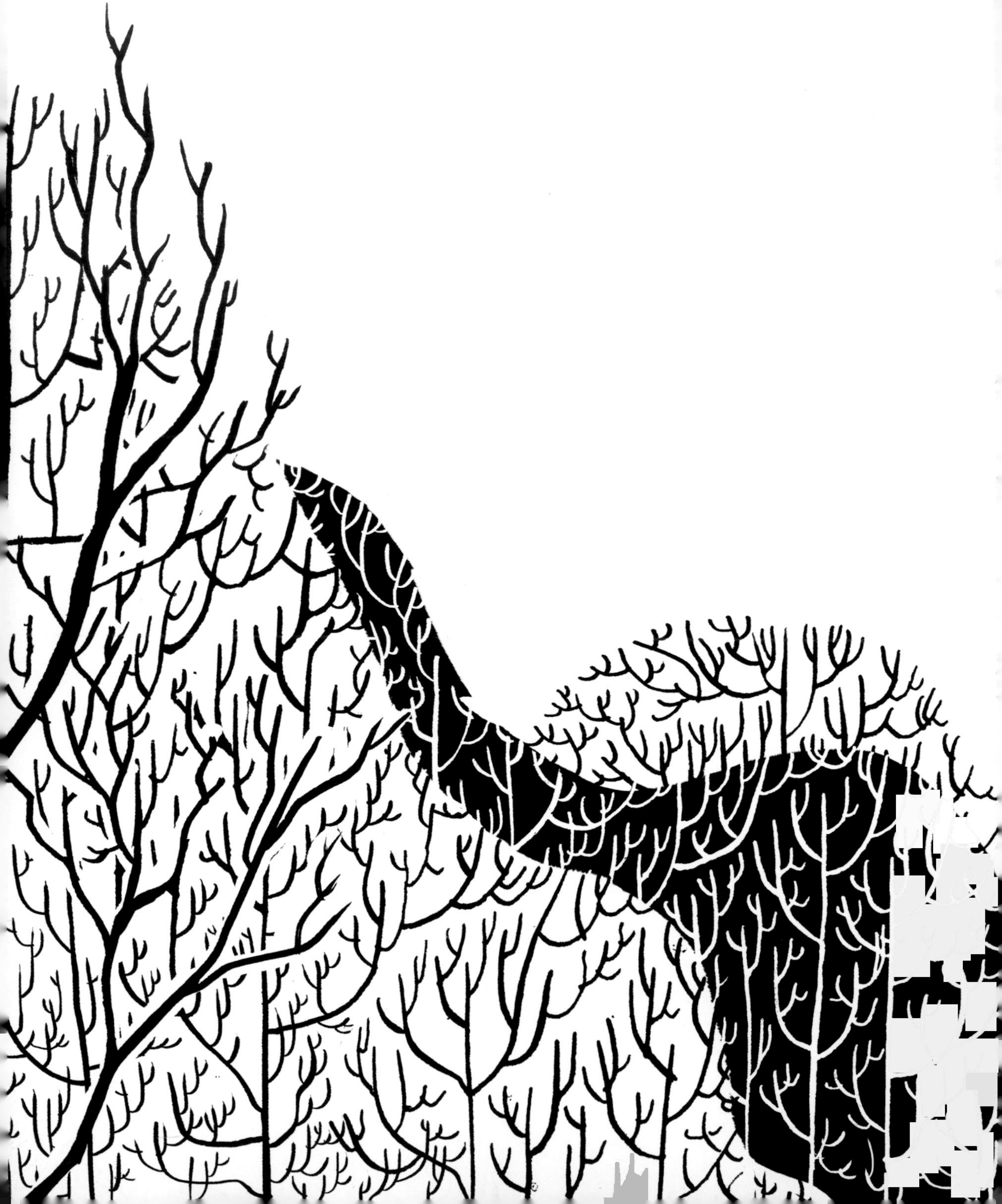

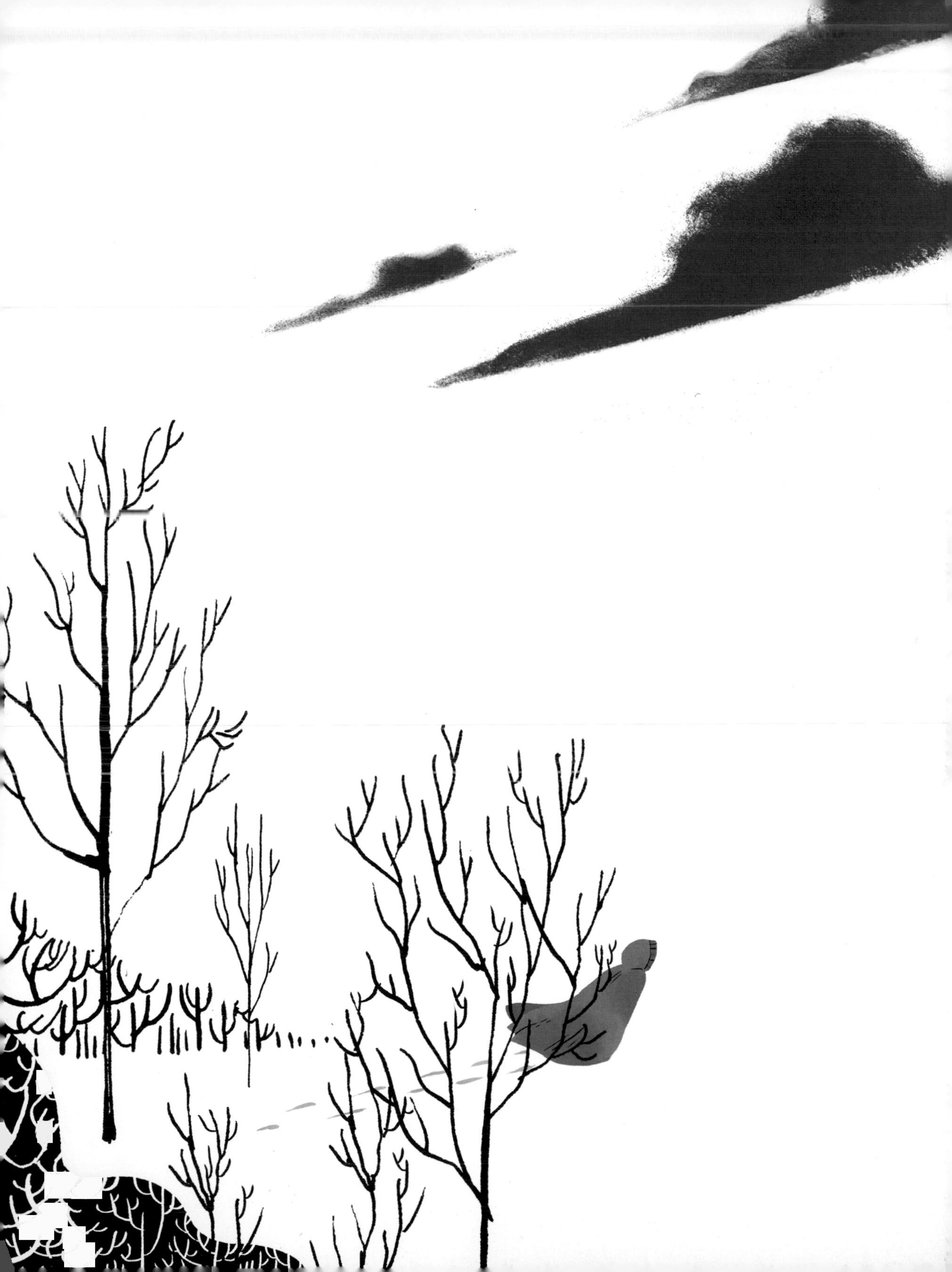

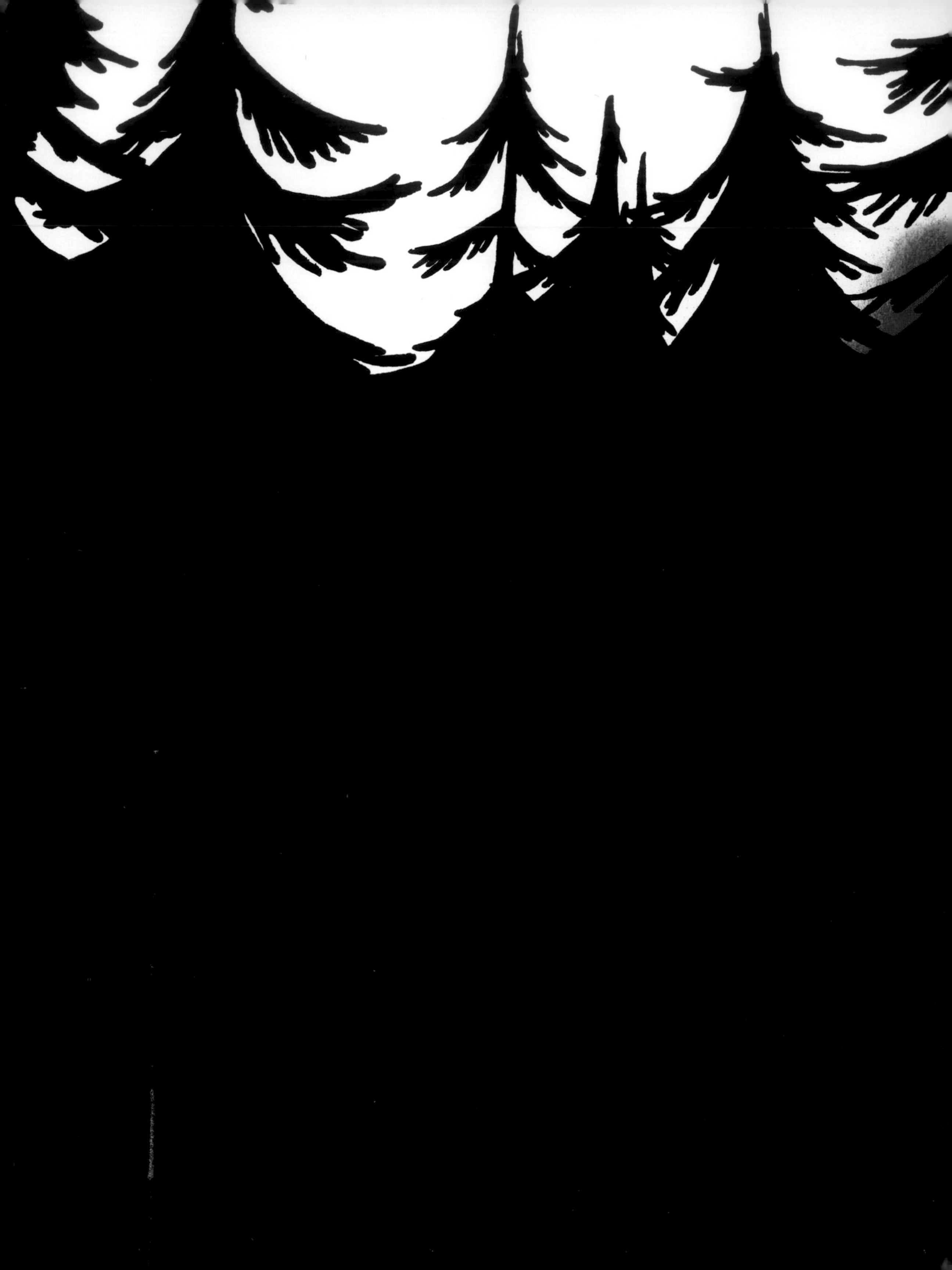

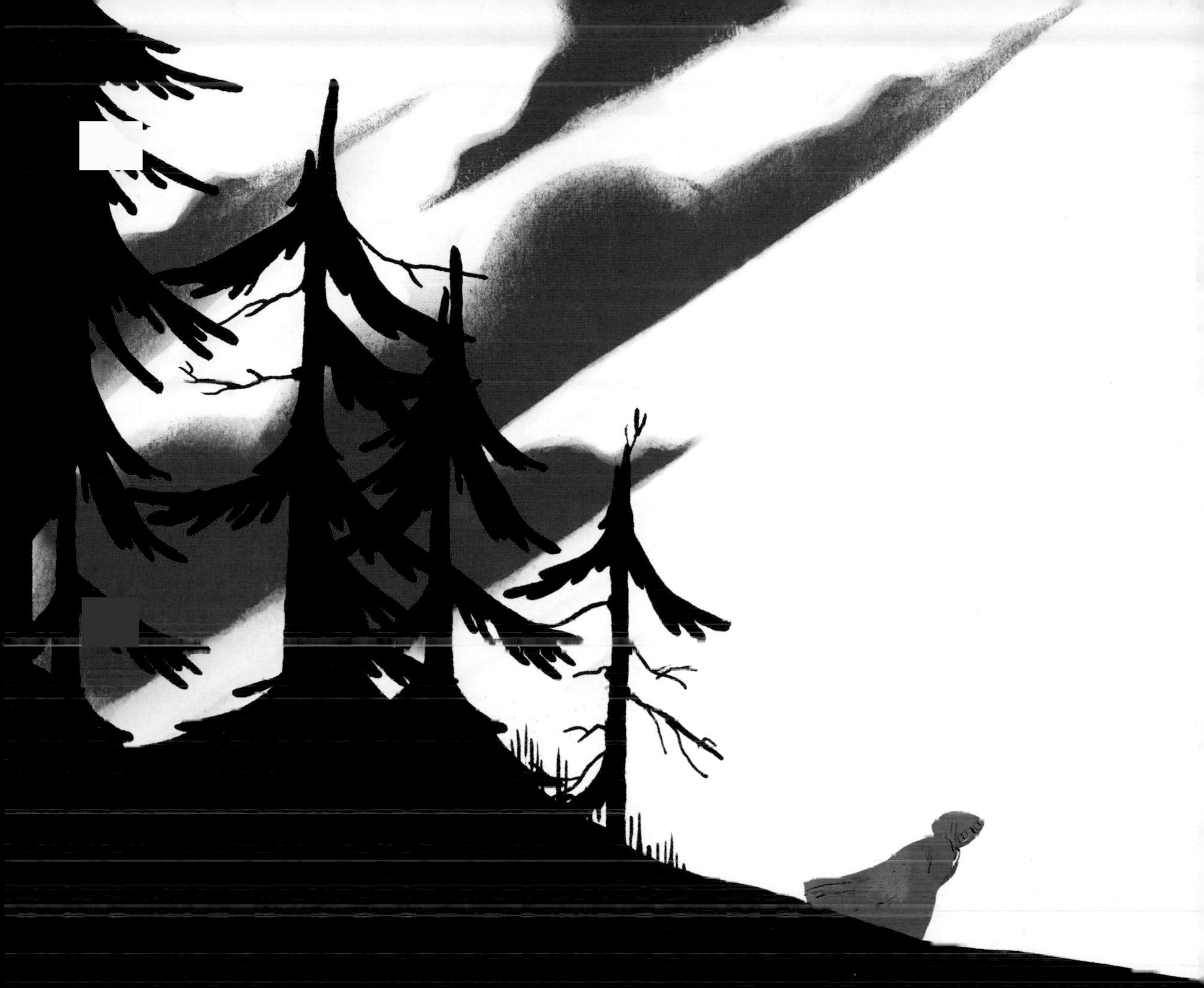

THROUGH the WOODS

stories by

EMILY CARROLL

Margaret K. McElderry Books
New York London Toronto Sydney New Delhi

MARGARET K. McELDERRY BOOKS
An imprint of Simon & Schuster Children's Publishing Division
1230 Avenue of the Americas, New York, New York 10020

This book is a work of fiction. Any references to historical events, real people, or real places are used fictitiously. Other names, characters, places, and events are products of the author's imagination, and any resemblance to actual events or places or persons, living or dead, is entirely coincidental.
Copyright © 2014 by Emily Carroll
All rights reserved, including the right of reproduction in whole or in part in any form.
MARGARET K. McELDERRY BOOKS is a trademark of Simon & Schuster, Inc.

For information about special discounts for bulk purchases, please contact Simon & Schuster Special Sales at 1-866-506-1949 or business@simonandschuster.com.
The Simon & Schuster Speakers Bureau can bring authors to your live event. For more information or to book an event, contact the Simon & Schuster Speakers Bureau at 1-866-248-3049 or visit our website at www.simonspeakers.com.
Book design by Sonia Chaghatzbanian
The text for this book is hand-lettered.
The illustrations for this book are rendered in ink and graphite on Bristol board and then digitally colored.
Manufactured in China
6 8 10 9 7
Library of Congress Cataloging-in-Publication Data
Carroll, Emily.
[Graphic novels. Selections]
Through the woods / Emily Carroll.—First edition.
p. cm.
Summary: "A collection of five spine-tingling short stories"—Provided by publisher.
ISBN 978-1-4424-6595-4 (hardcover)
ISBN 978-1-4424-6596-1 (Pbk.)
ISBN 978-1-4424-6597-8 (eBook)
1. Horror tales, Canadian. 2. Graphic novels. [1. Graphic novels. 2. Horror stories. 3. Short stories.] I. Title.
PZ7.7.C369Th 2014
741.5'973—dc23
2013030969
0416 SCP

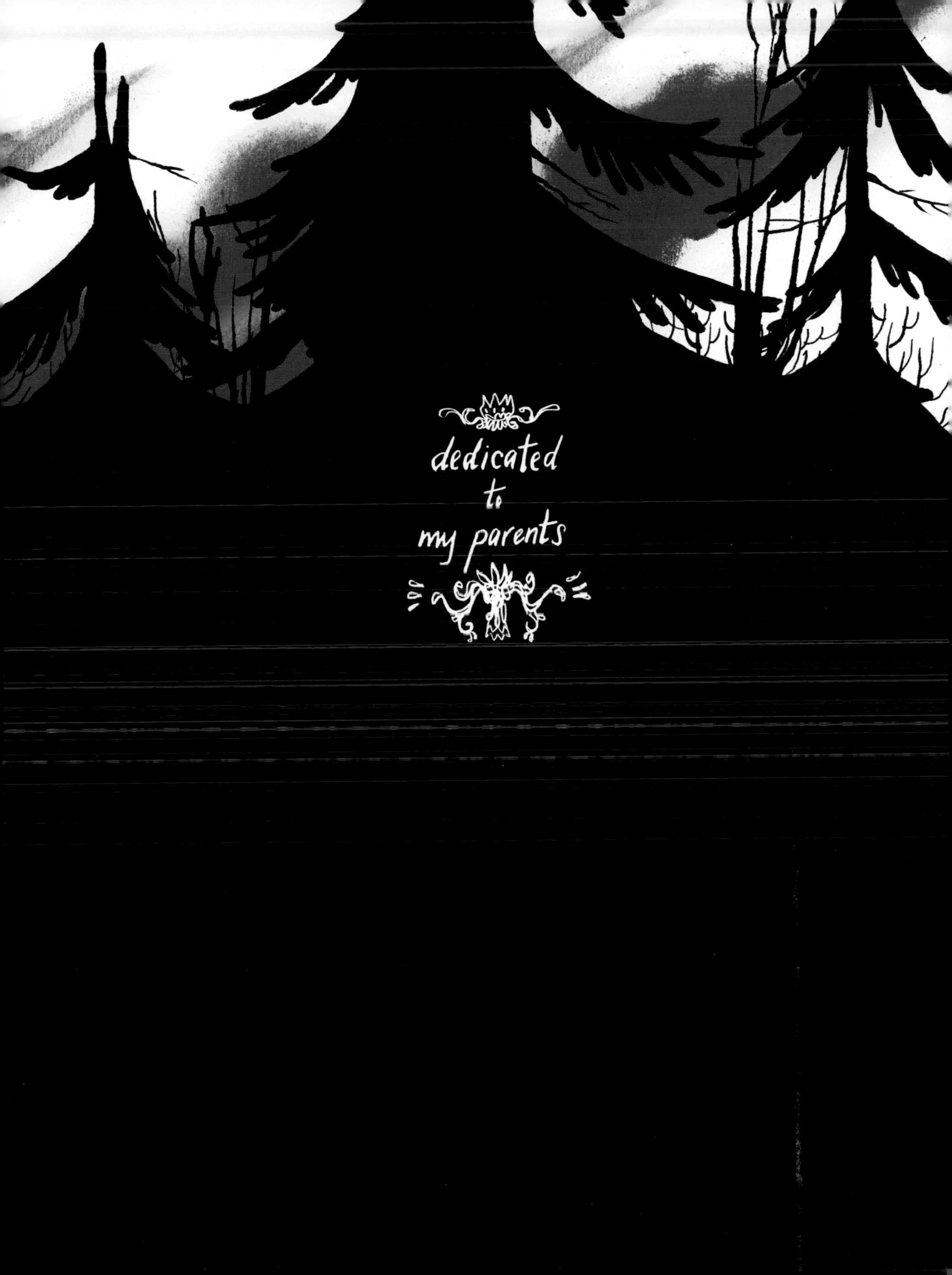
dedicated
to
my parents

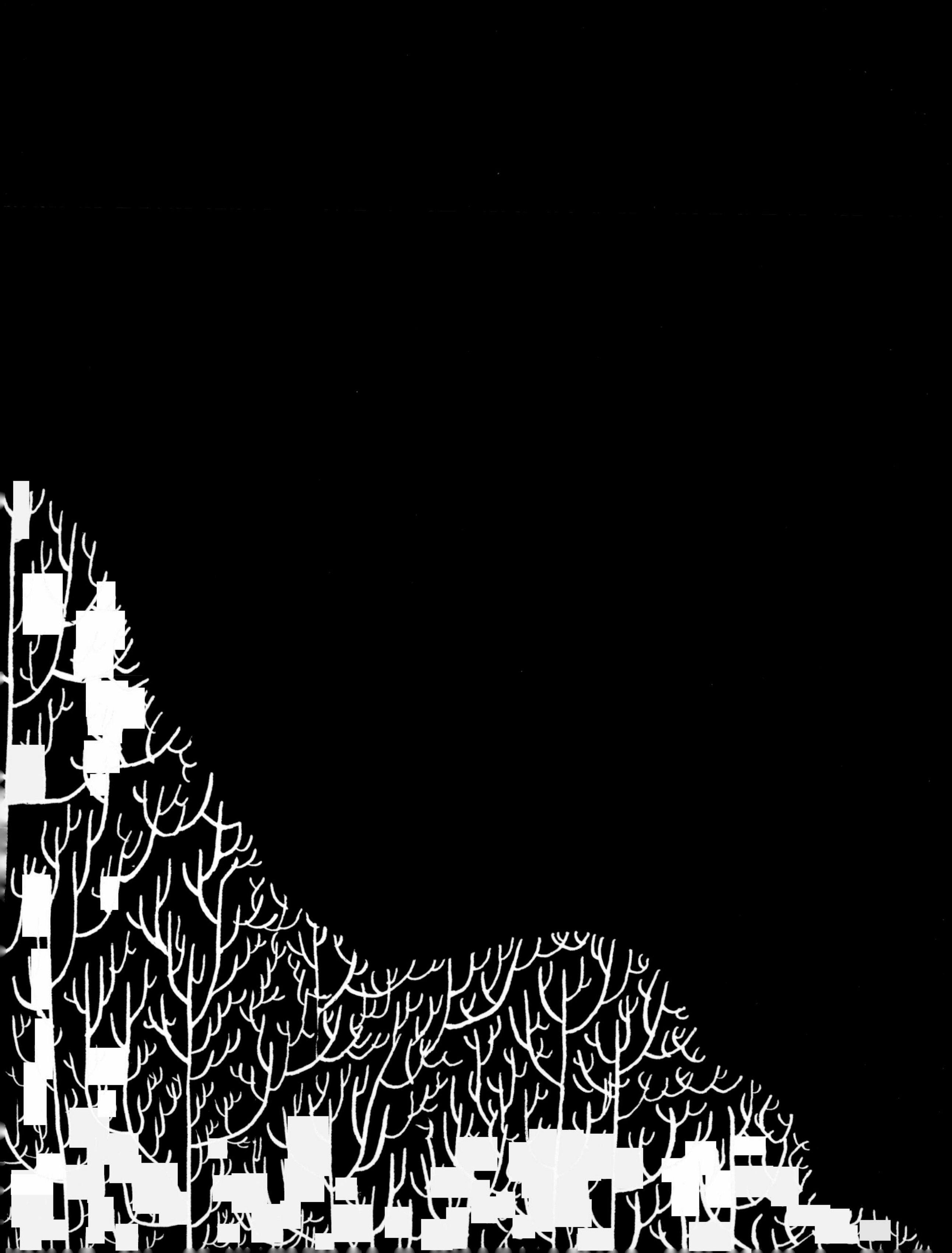

TABLE of CONTENTS

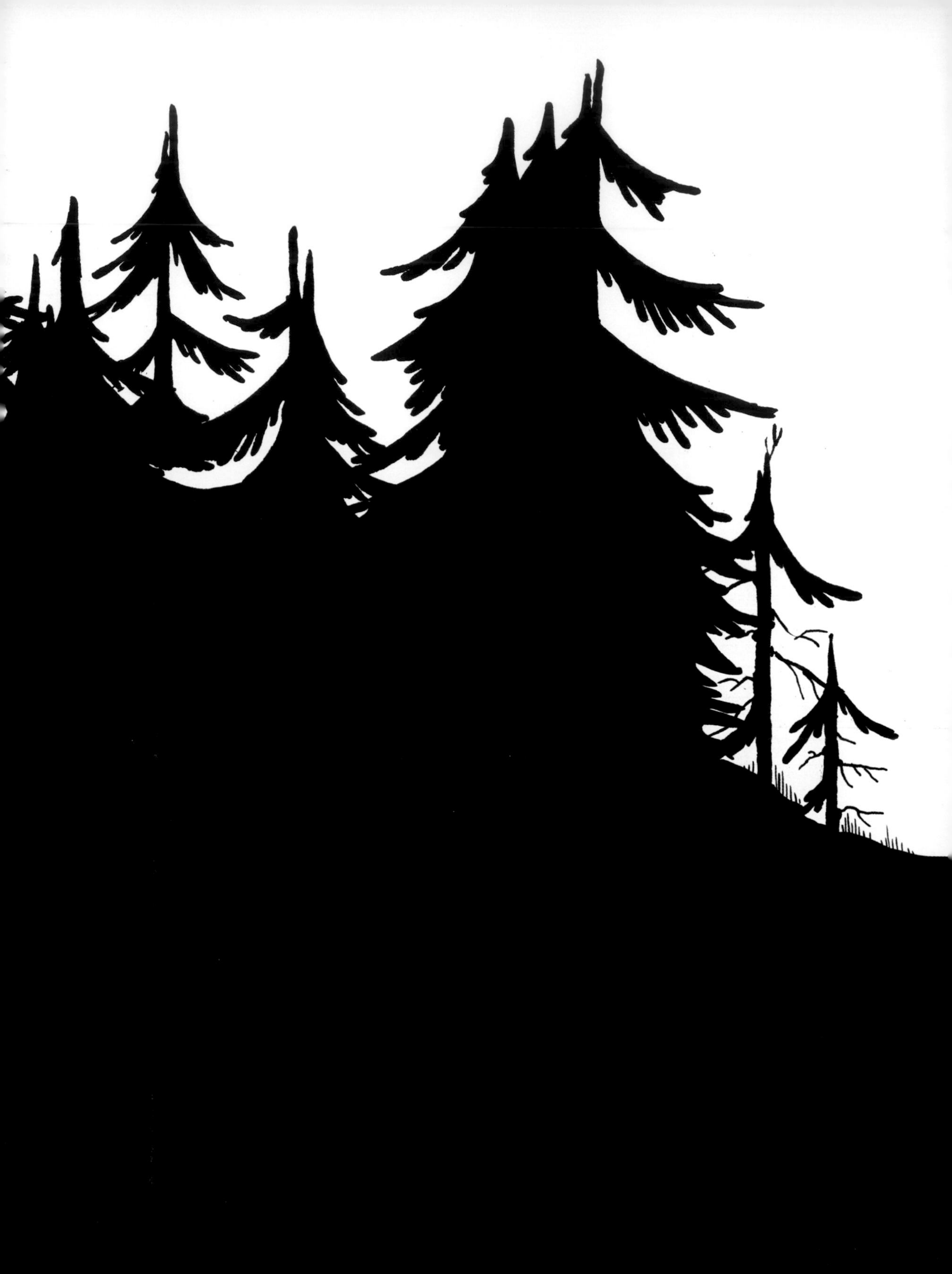

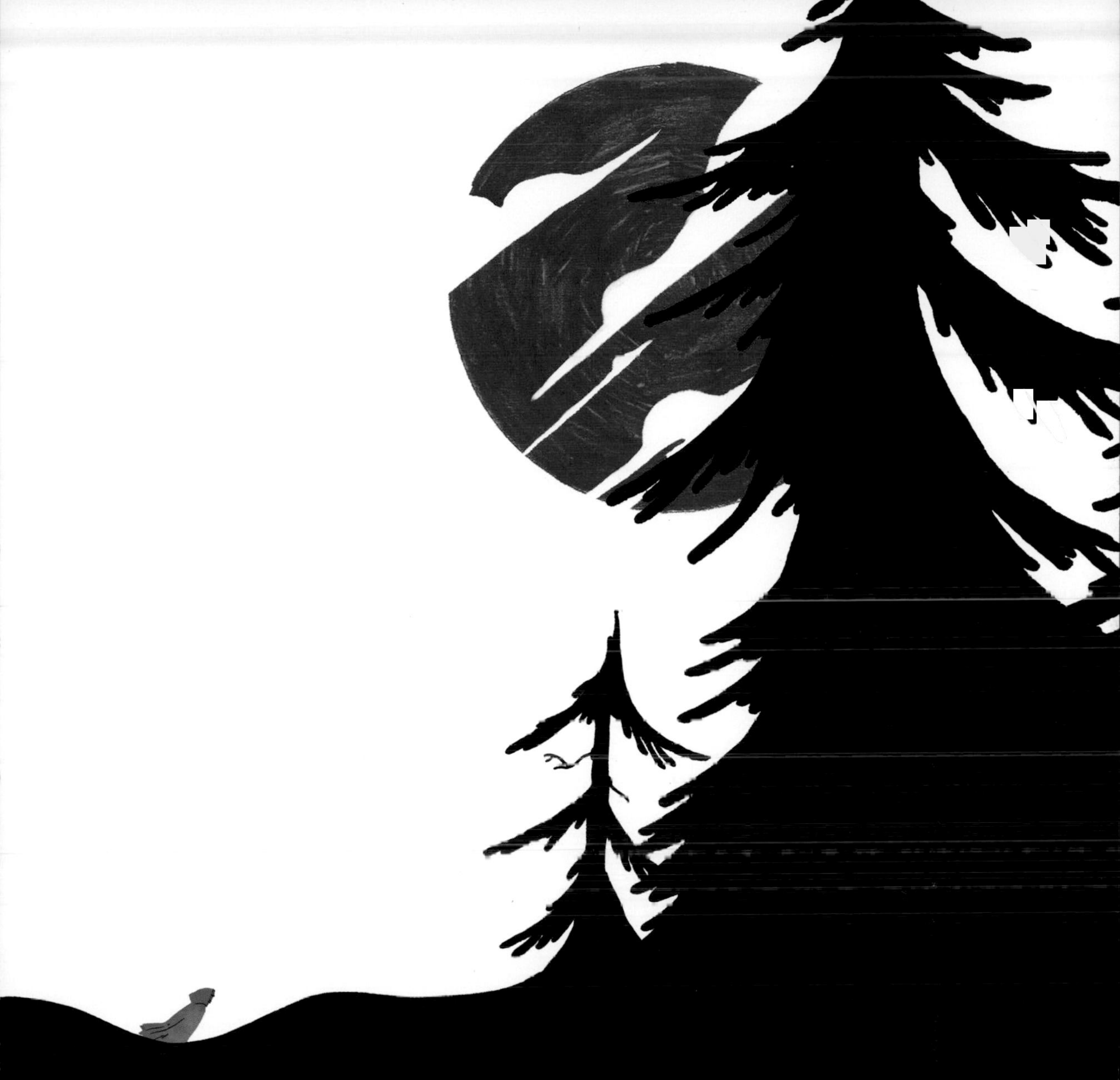

AN INTRODUCTION

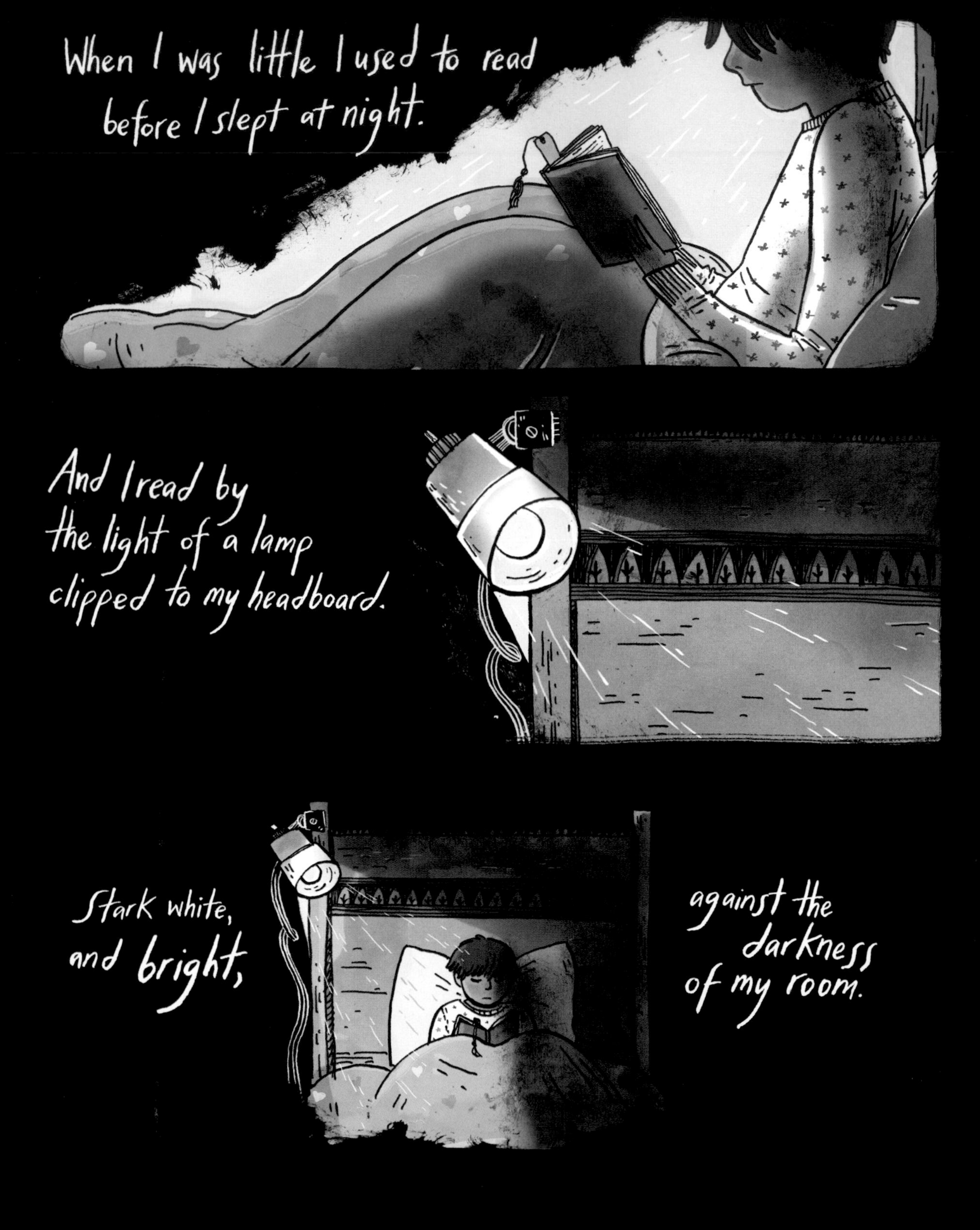
When I was little I used to read before I slept at night.
And I read by the light of a lamp clipped to my headboard.
Stark white,
and bright,
against the darkness of my room.

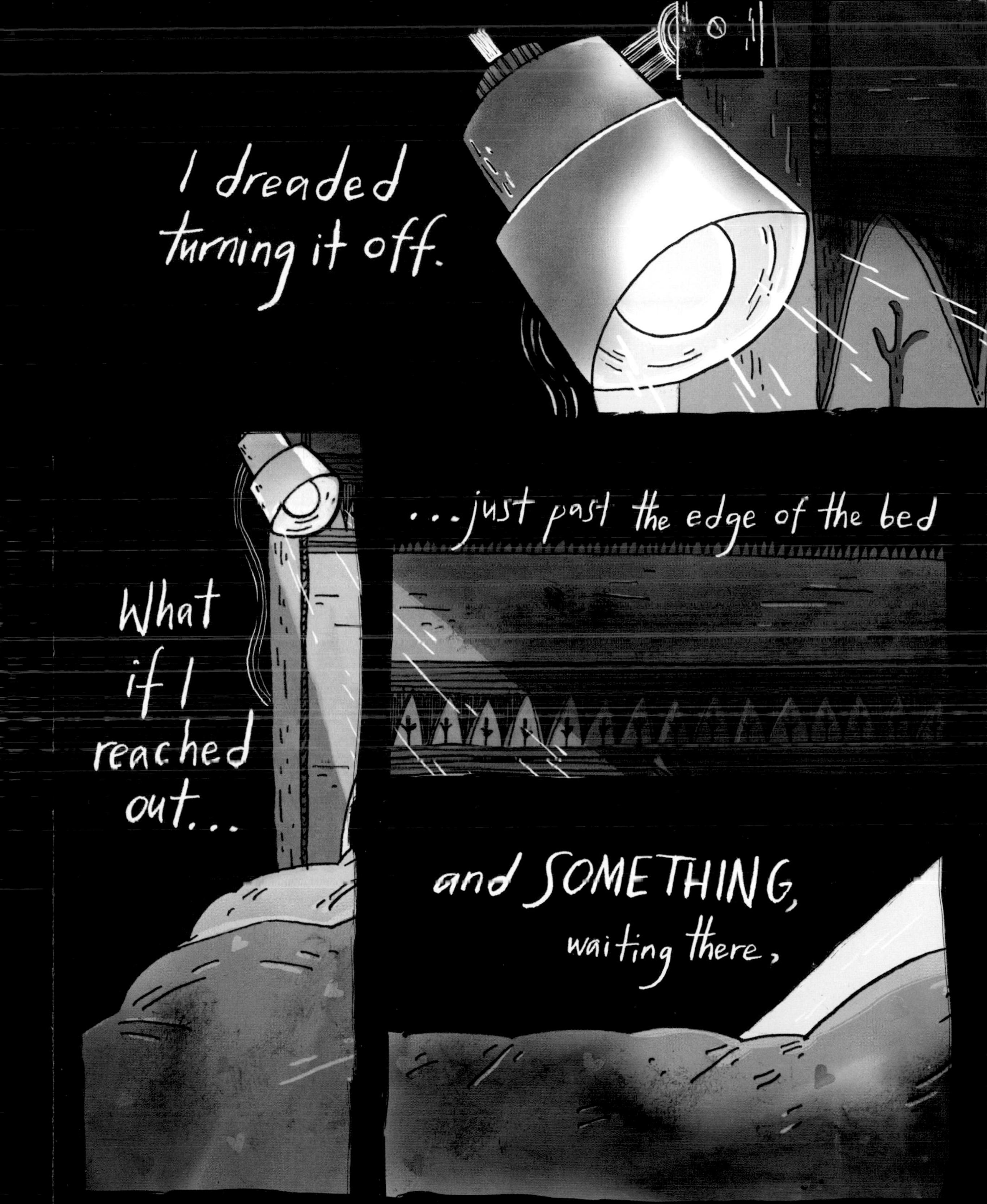
I dreaded turning it off.
What if I reached out...
...just past the edge of the bed
and SOMETHING, waiting there,

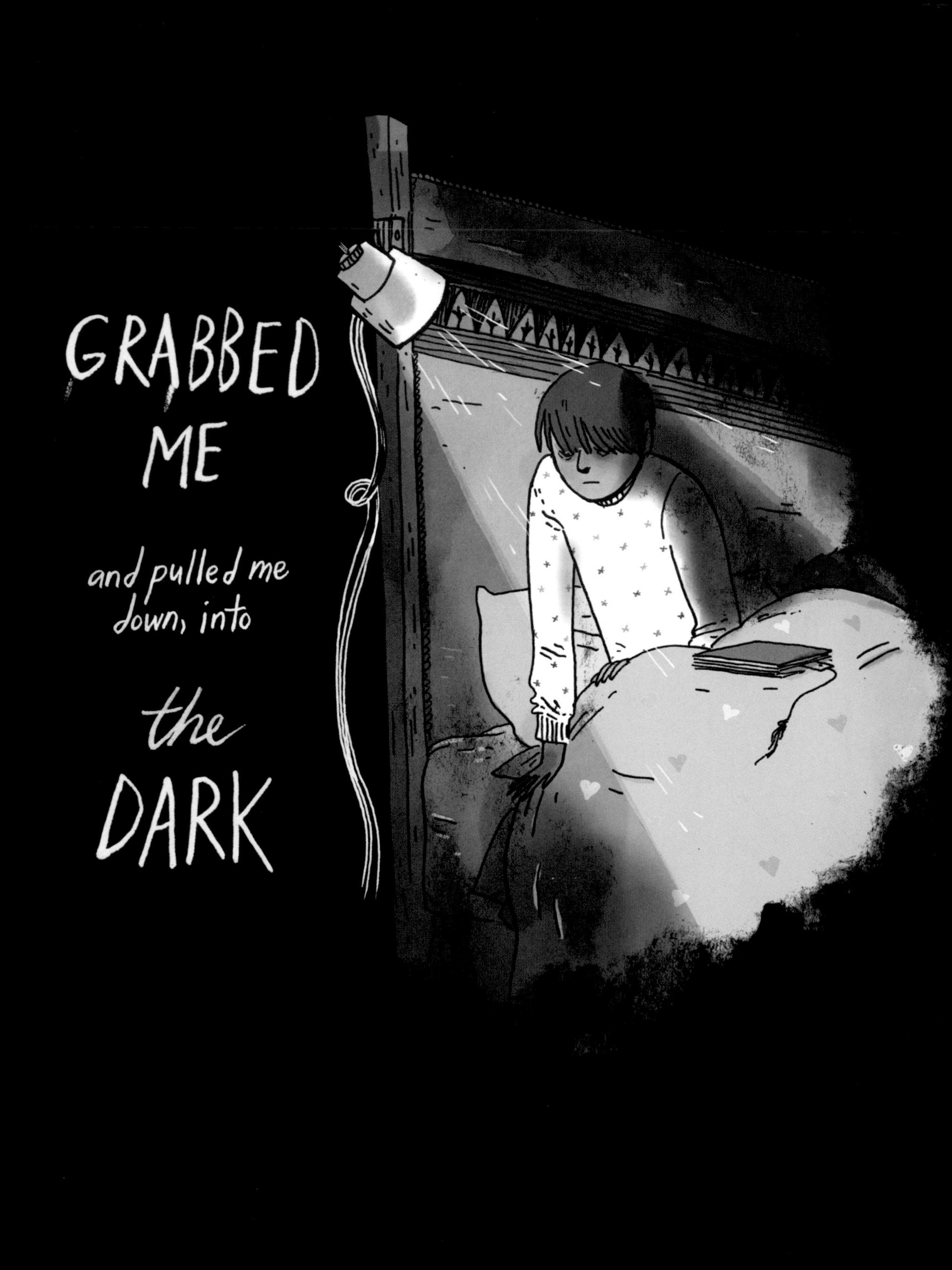
GRABBED
ME
and pulled me
down, into
the
DARK

OUR NEIGHBOR'S HOUSE

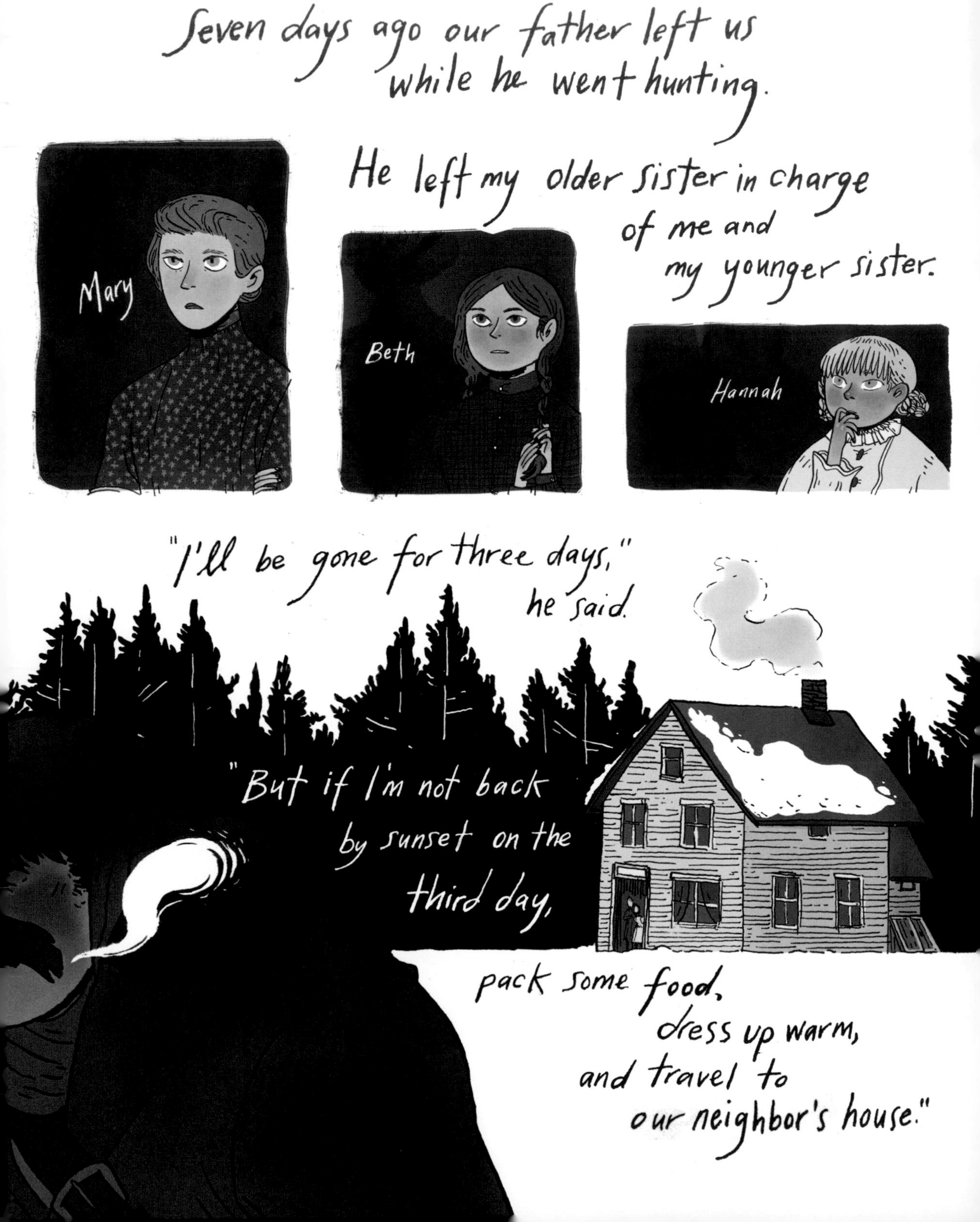
Seven days ago our father left us while he went hunting.
He left my older sister in charge of me and my younger sister.
Mary
Beth
Hannah
"I'll be gone for three days," he said.
"But if I'm not back by sunset on the third day,
pack some food, dress up warm, and travel to our neighbor's house."

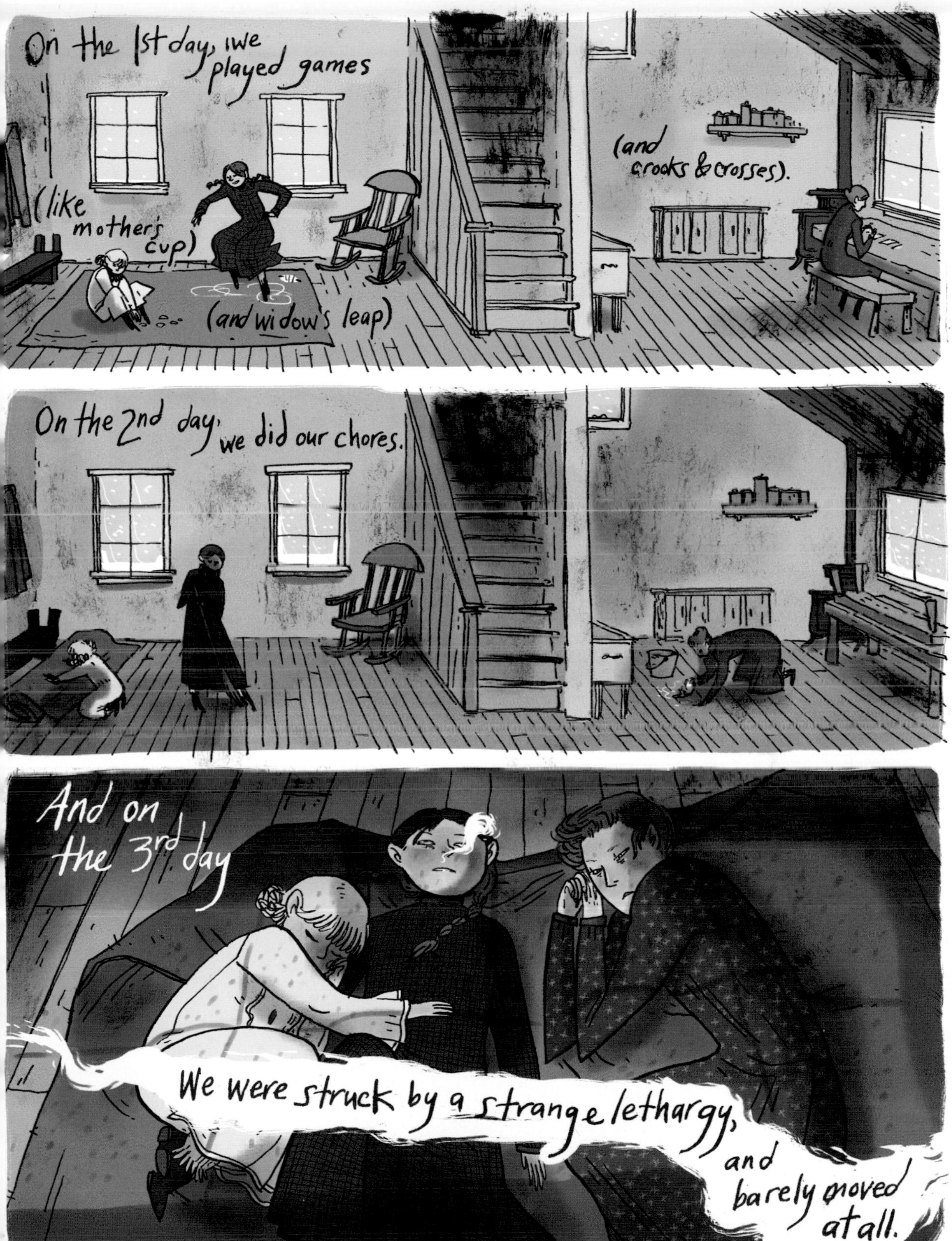
On the 1st day, we played games
(like mother's cup)
(and widow's leap)
(and crooks & crosses).
On the 2nd day, we did our chores.
And on the 3rd day
We were struck by a strange lethargy,
and barely moved at all.

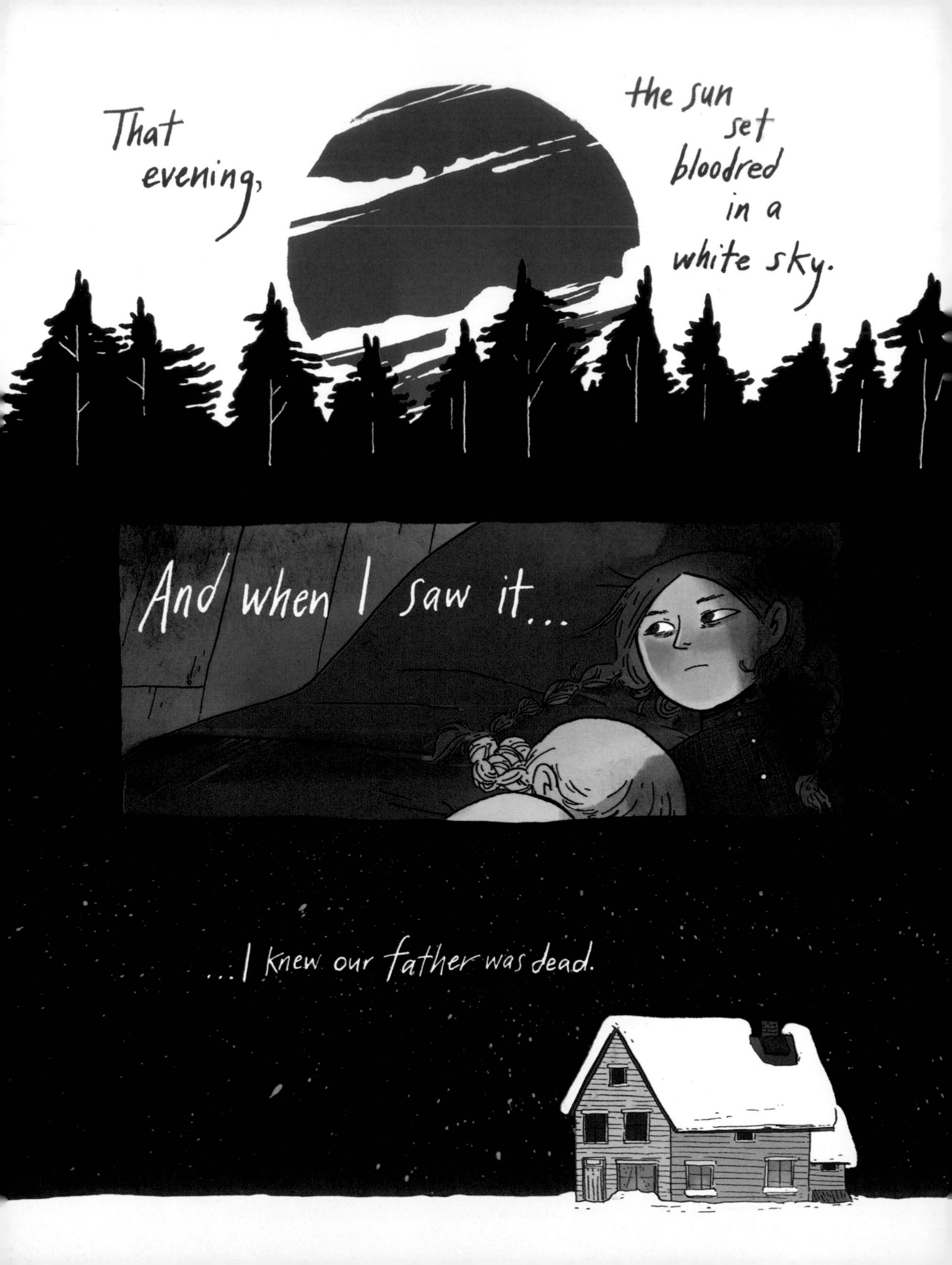
That evening,
the sun set bloodred in a white sky.
And when I saw it...
...I knew our father was dead.

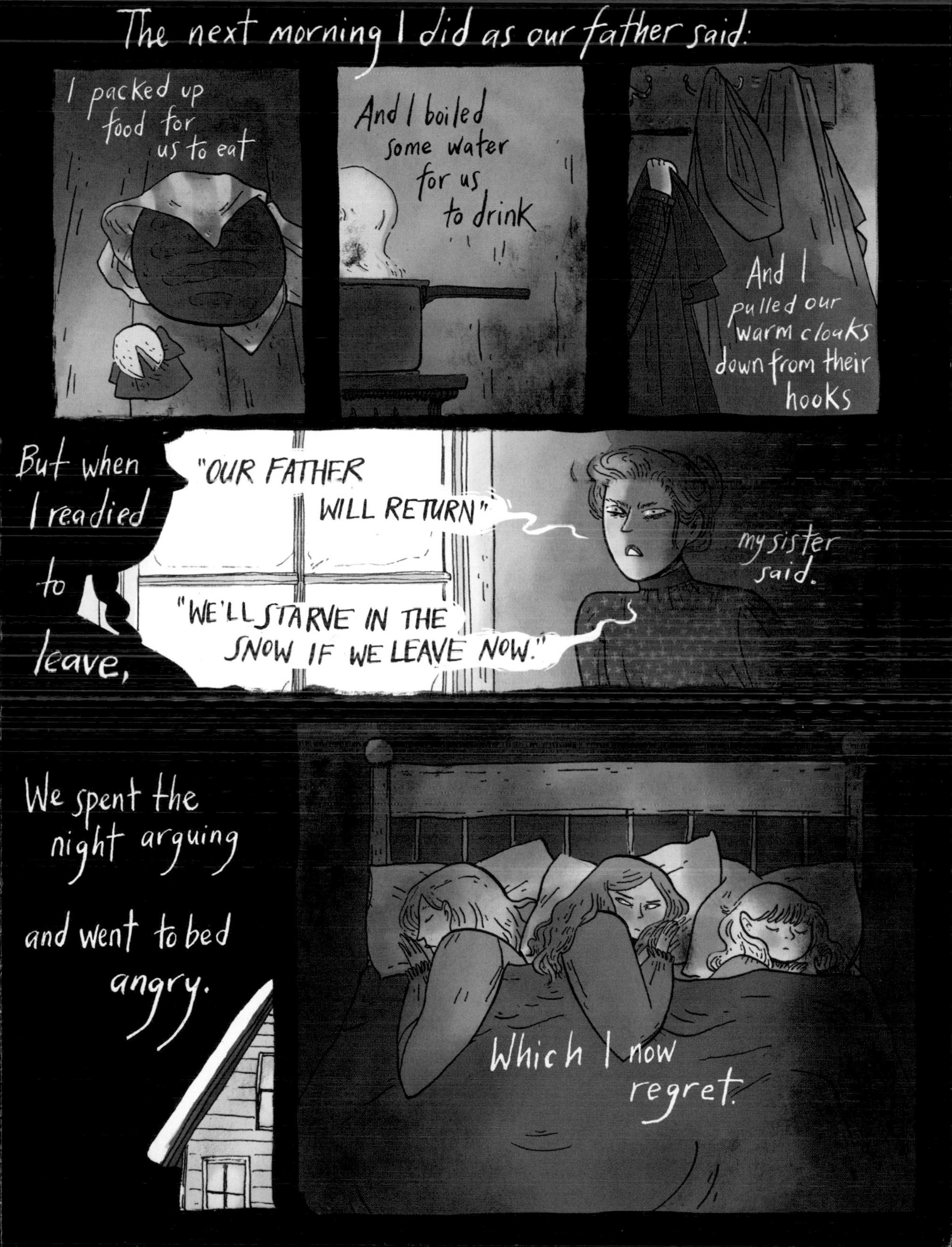
The next morning I did as our father said:
I packed up food for us to eat
And I boiled some water for us to drink
And I pulled our warm cloaks down from their hooks
But when I readied to leave,
"OUR FATHER WILL RETURN"
"WE'LL STARVE IN THE SNOW IF WE LEAVE NOW."
my sister said.
We spent the night arguing
and went to bed angry.
Which I now regret.

We didn't leave the next day either.

But my sister was different.

No longer angry.

She was **happy.**

She said a man had come to the door in the night.

(Yet I had heard no knock).

(And there were no footprints in the snow outside).

She said,

"He was a tall man, in a wide-brimmed hat, with a smile that showed all his teeth."

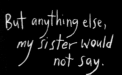

But anything else, my sister would not say.

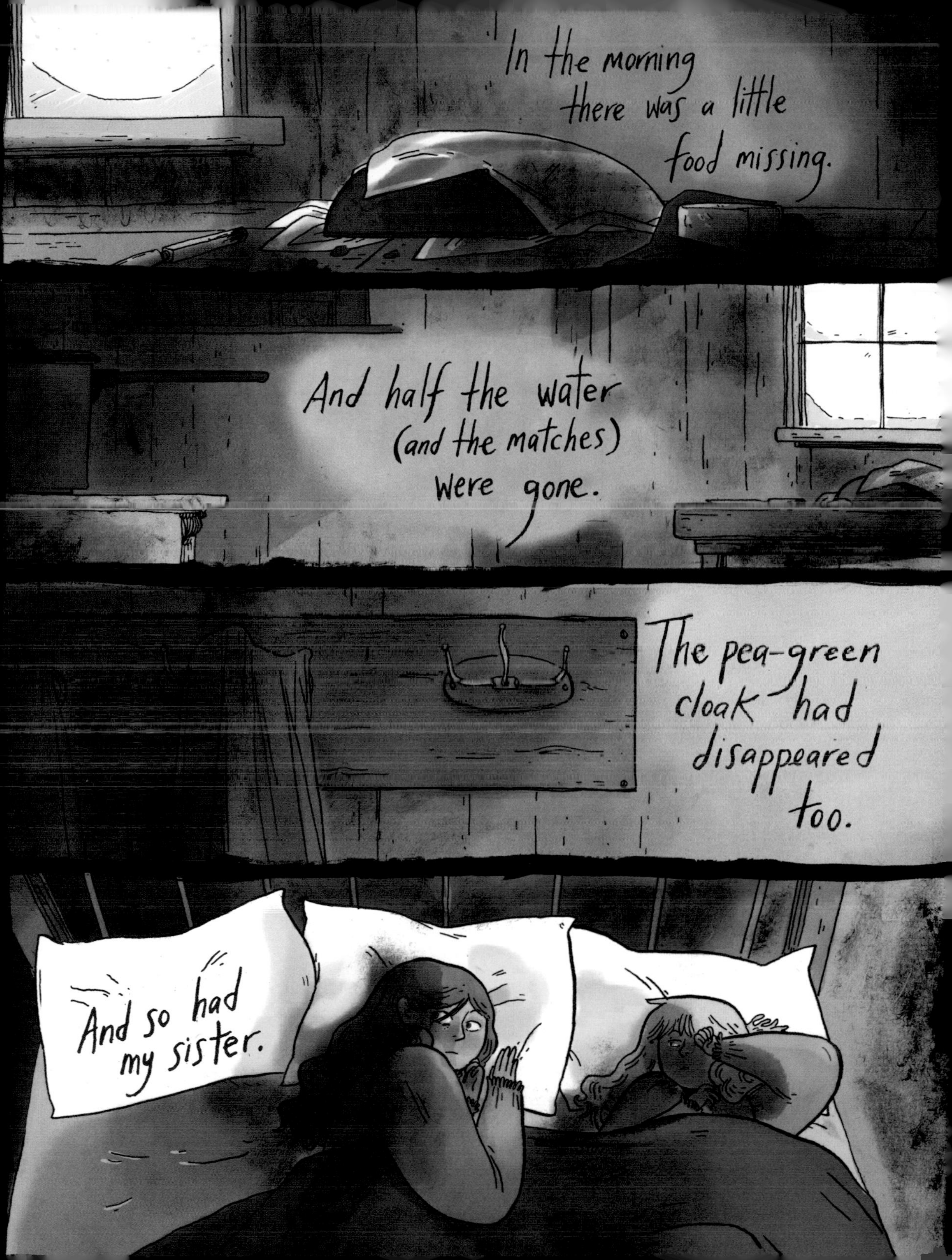
In the morning there was a little food missing.
And half the water (and the matches) were gone.
The pea-green cloak had disappeared too.
And so had my sister.

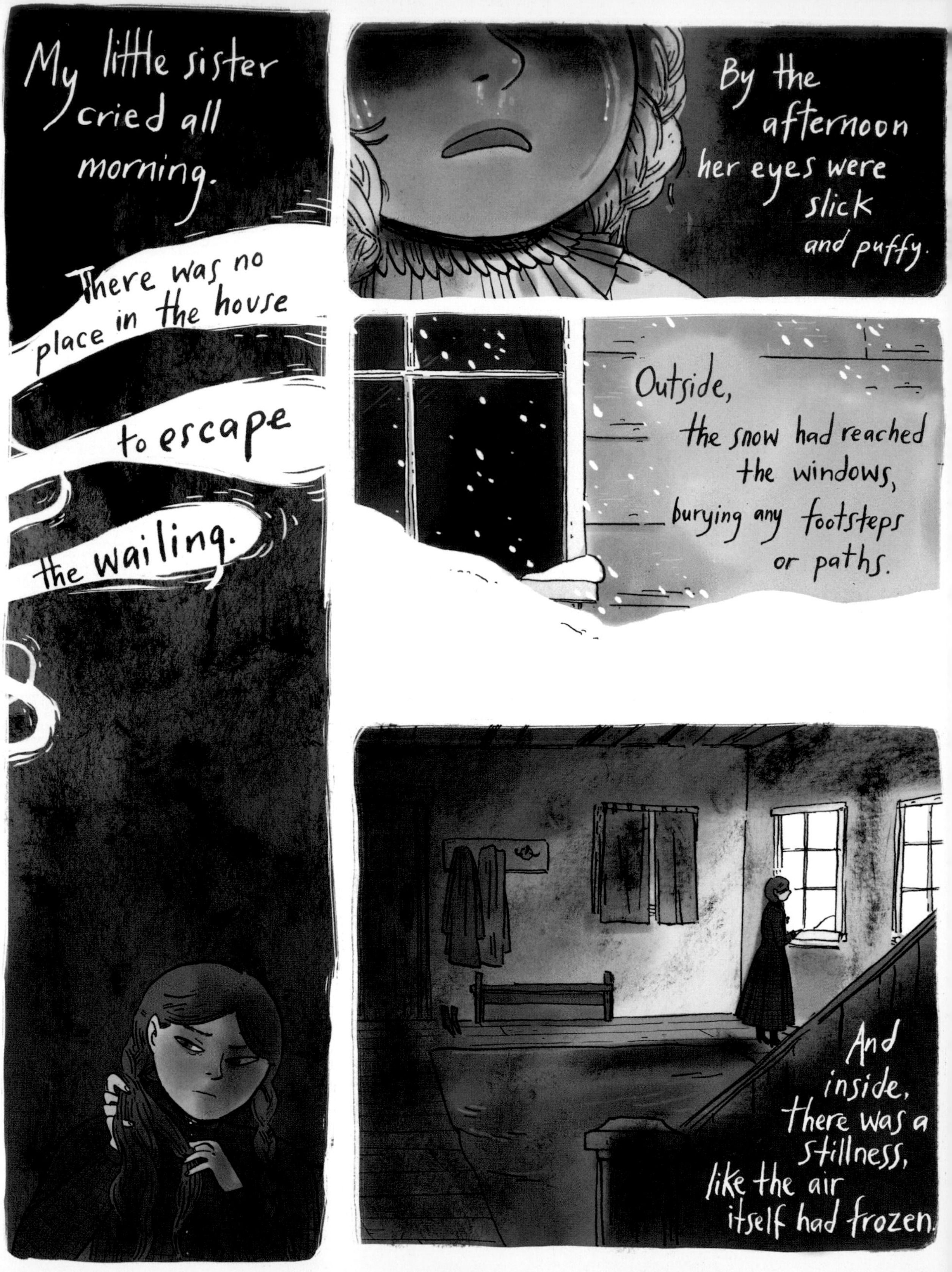
My little sister cried all morning.
There was no place in the house
to escape
the wailing.
By the afternoon her eyes were slick and puffy.
Outside, the snow had reached the windows, burying any footsteps or paths.
And inside, there was a stillness, like the air itself had frozen.

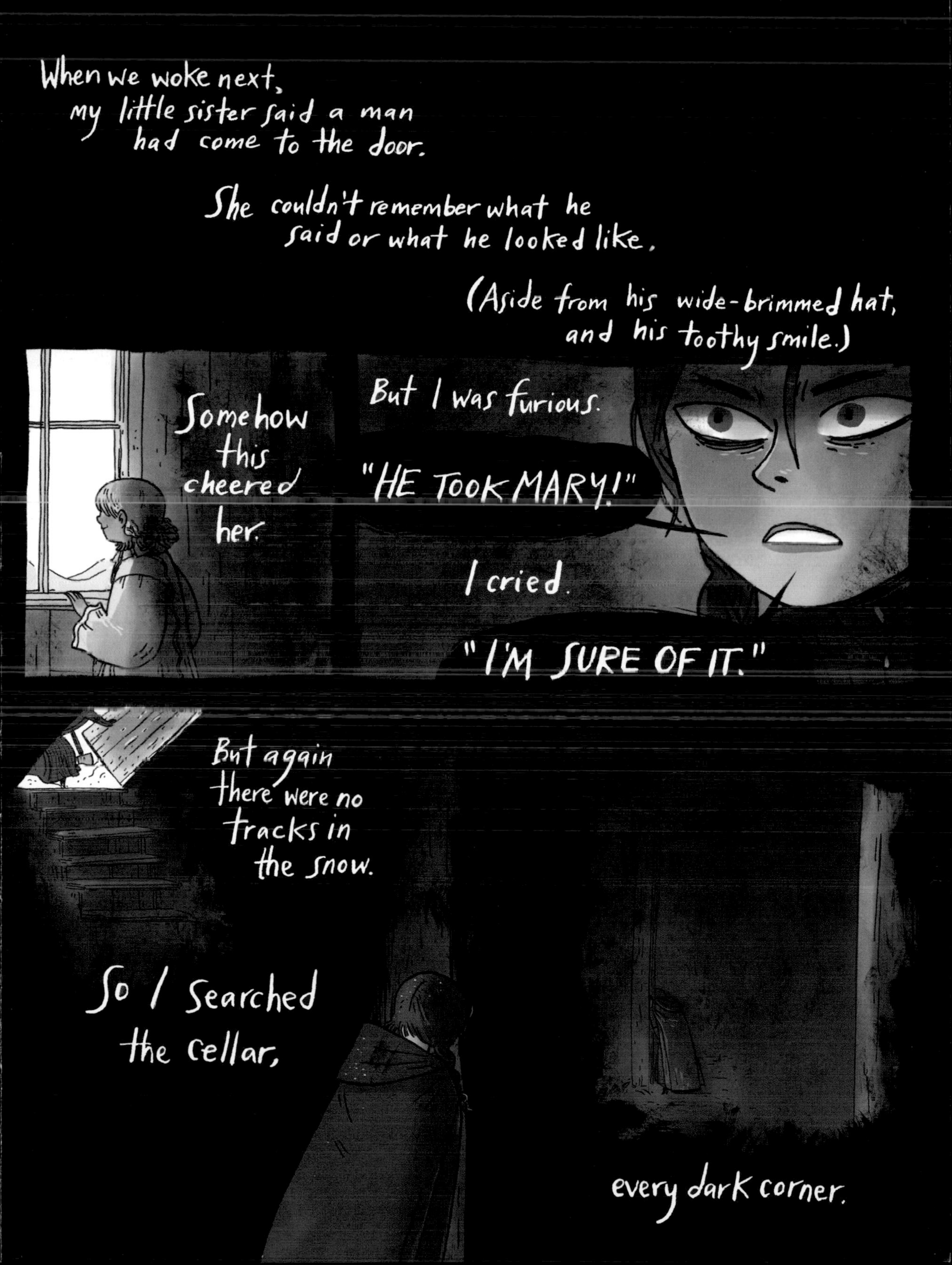
When we woke next, my little sister said a man had come to the door.
She couldn't remember what he said or what he looked like.
(Aside from his wide-brimmed hat, and his toothy smile.)
Somehow this cheered her.
But I was furious.
"HE TOOK MARY!"
I cried.
"I'M SURE OF IT."
But again there were no tracks in the snow.
So I searched the cellar,
every dark corner.

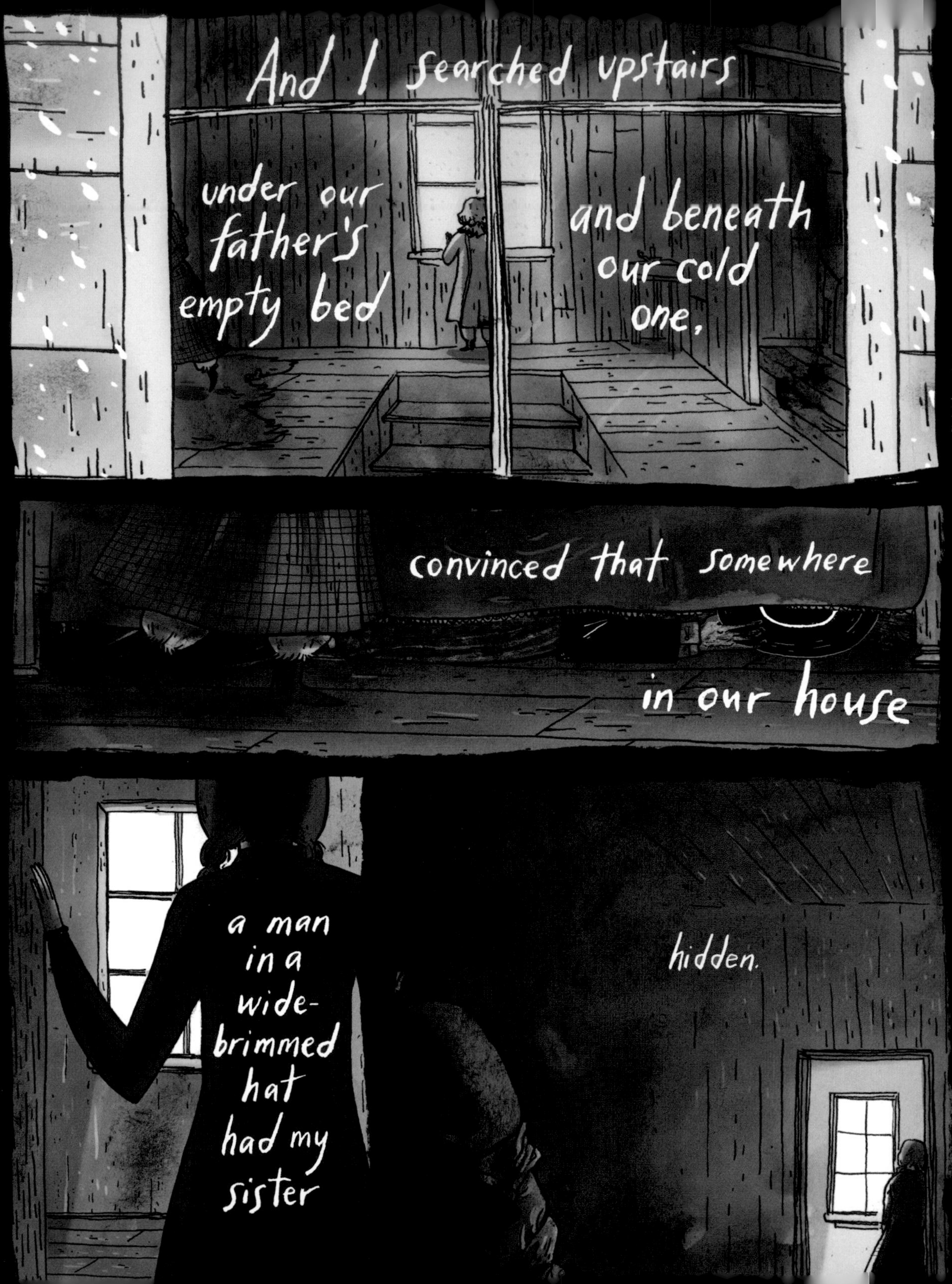
And I searched upstairs
under our father's empty bed
and beneath our cold one,
convinced that somewhere
in our house
a man in a wide-brimmed hat had my sister
hidden.

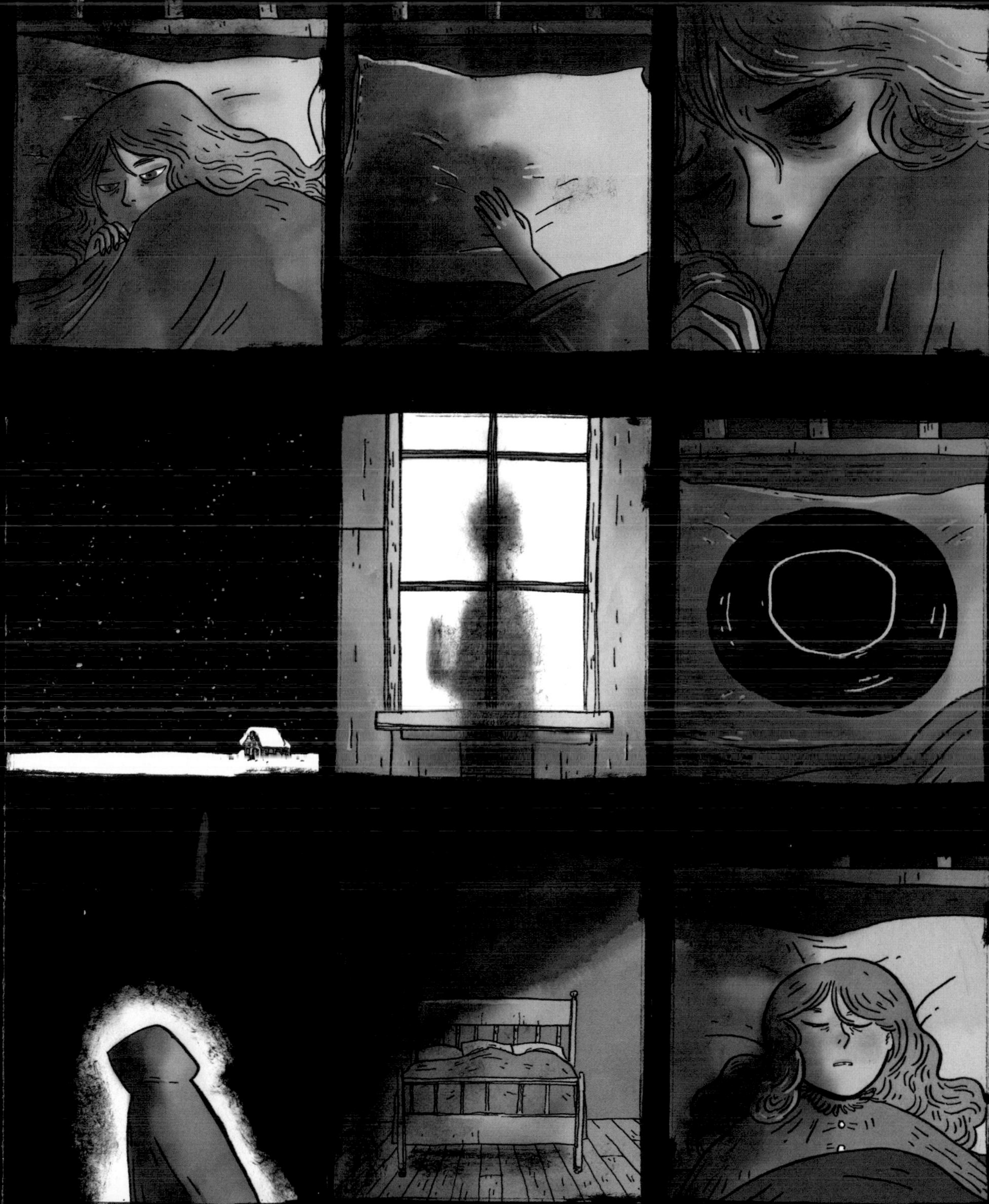

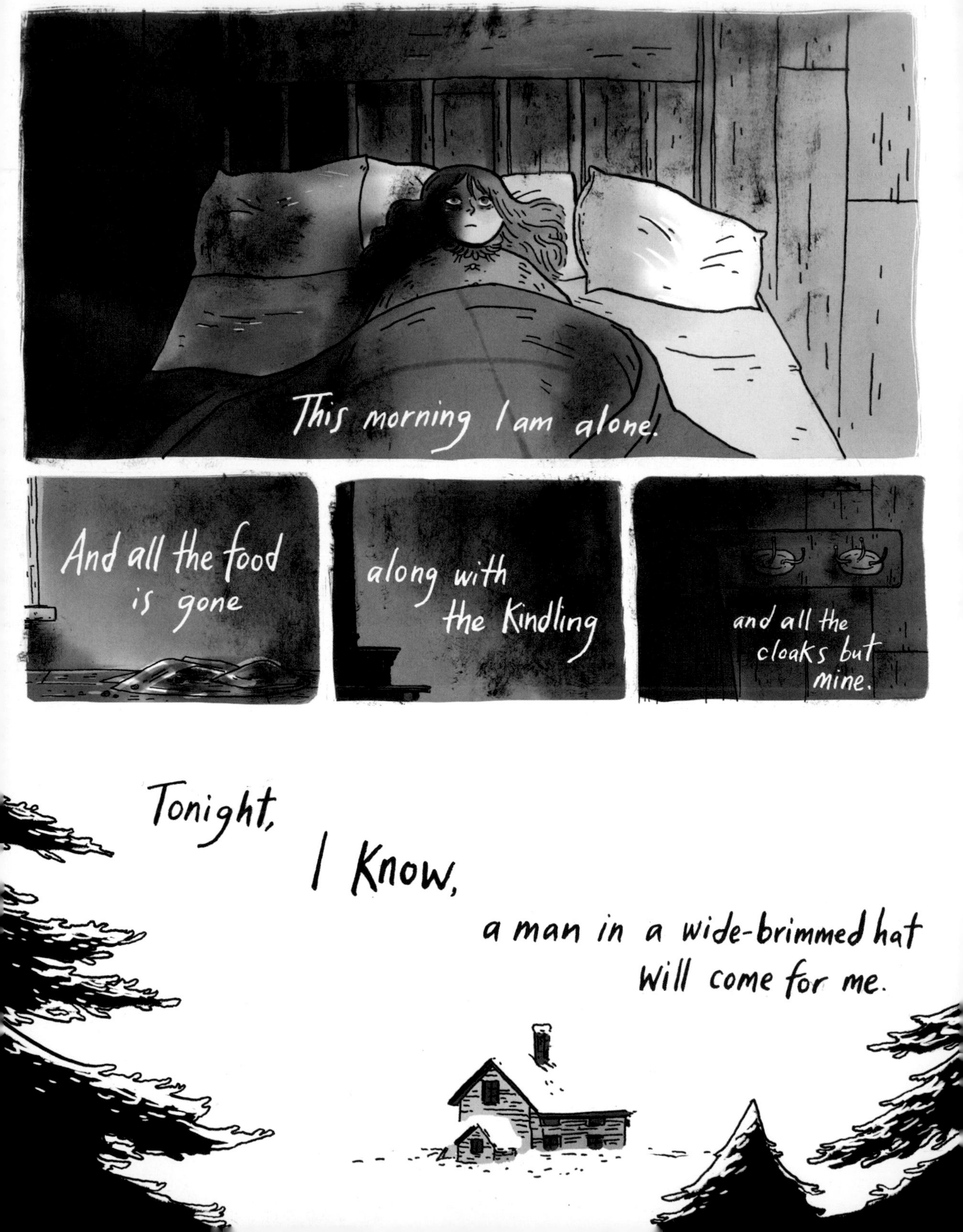
This morning I am alone.
And all the food is gone
along with the kindling
and all the cloaks but mine.
Tonight,
I know,
a man in a wide-brimmed hat will come for me.

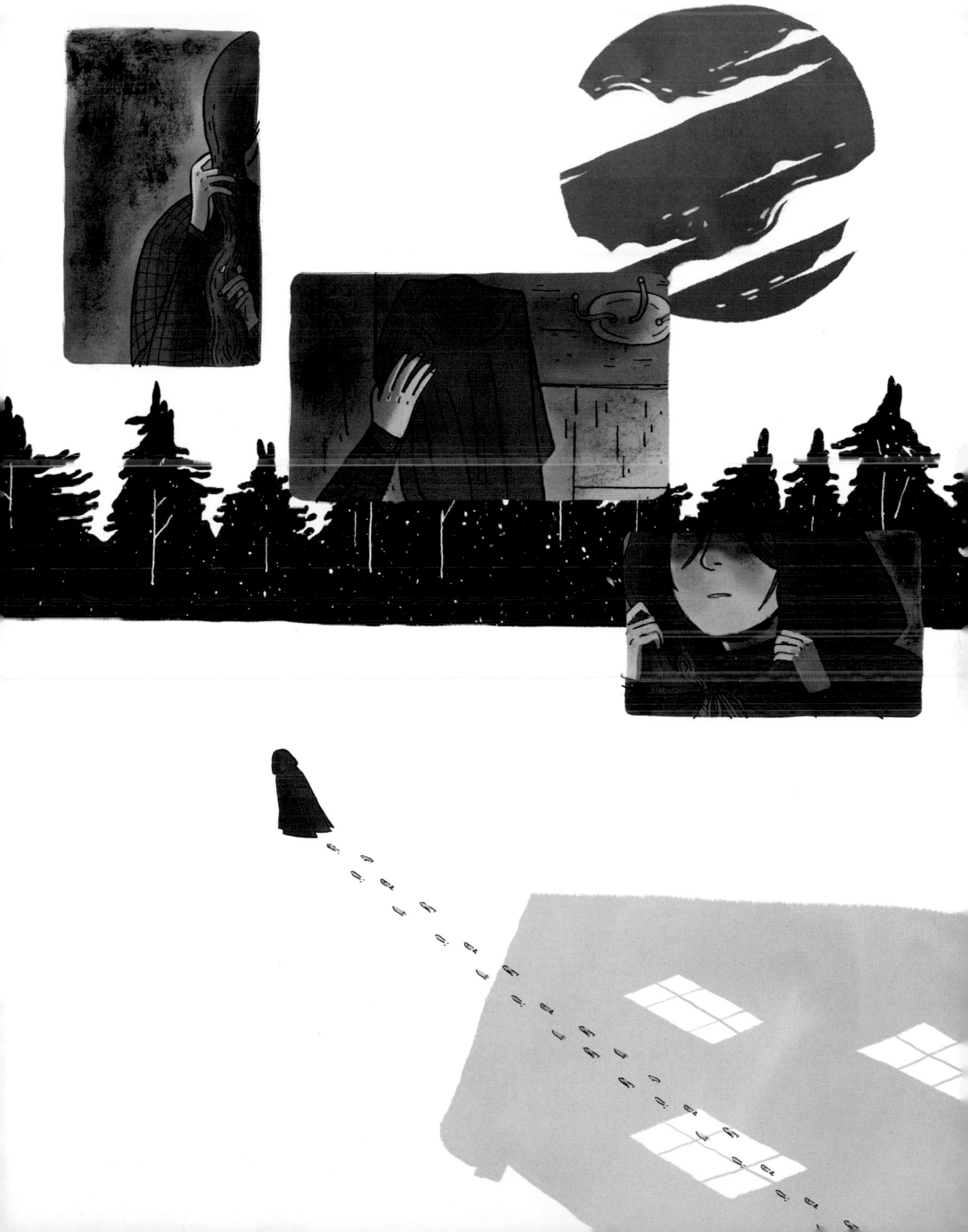

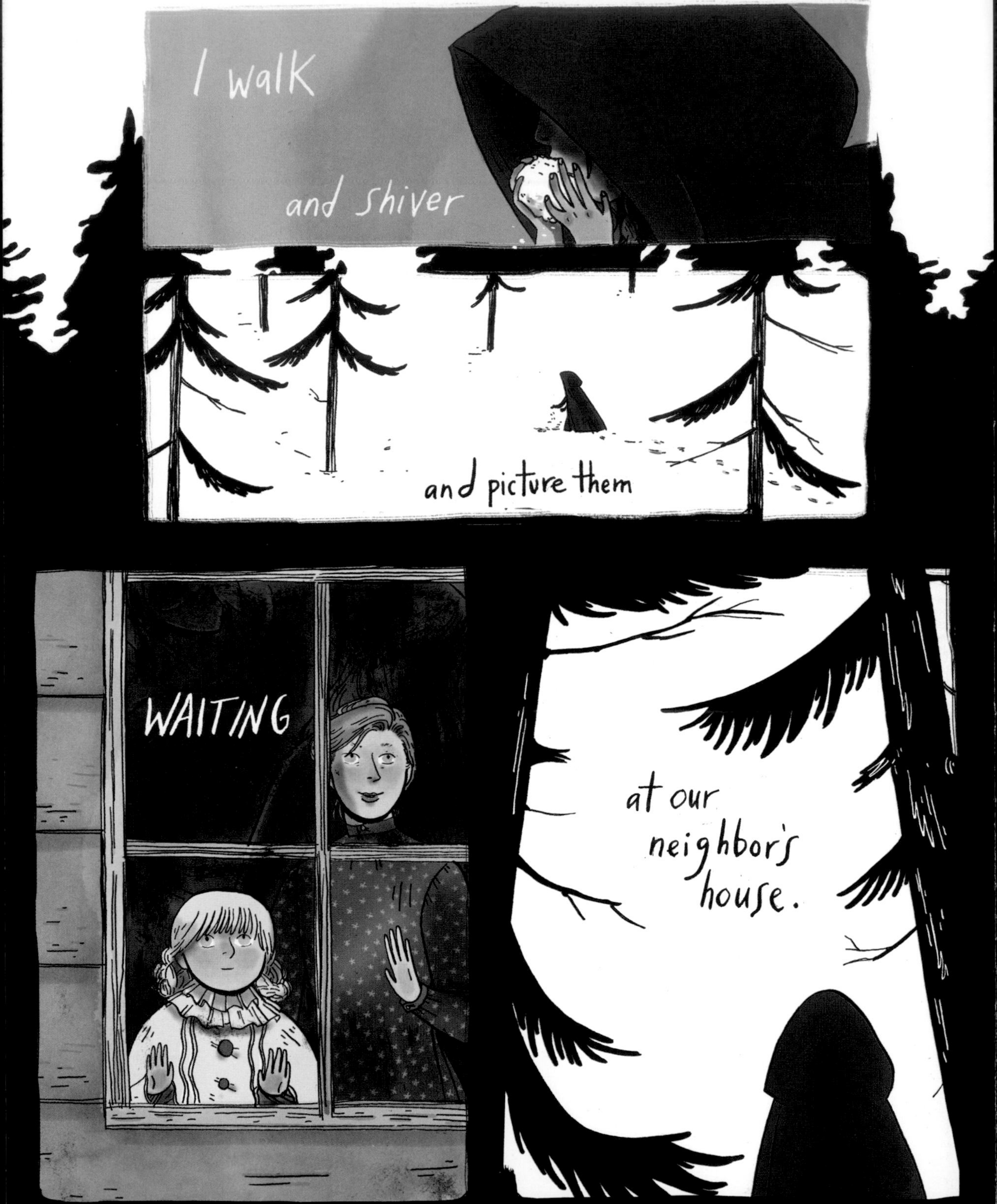
I walk
and shiver
and picture them
WAITING
at our neighbor's house.

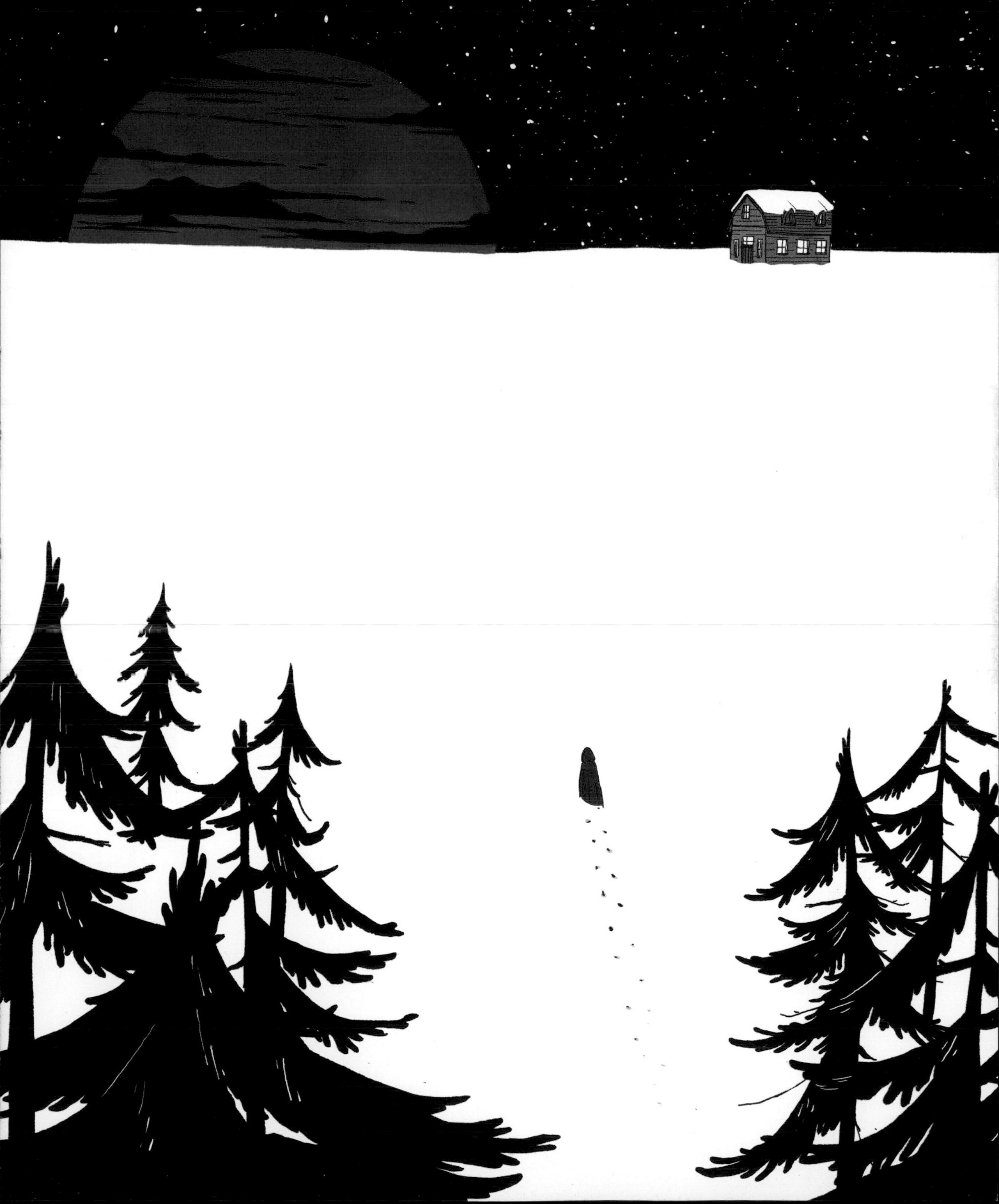

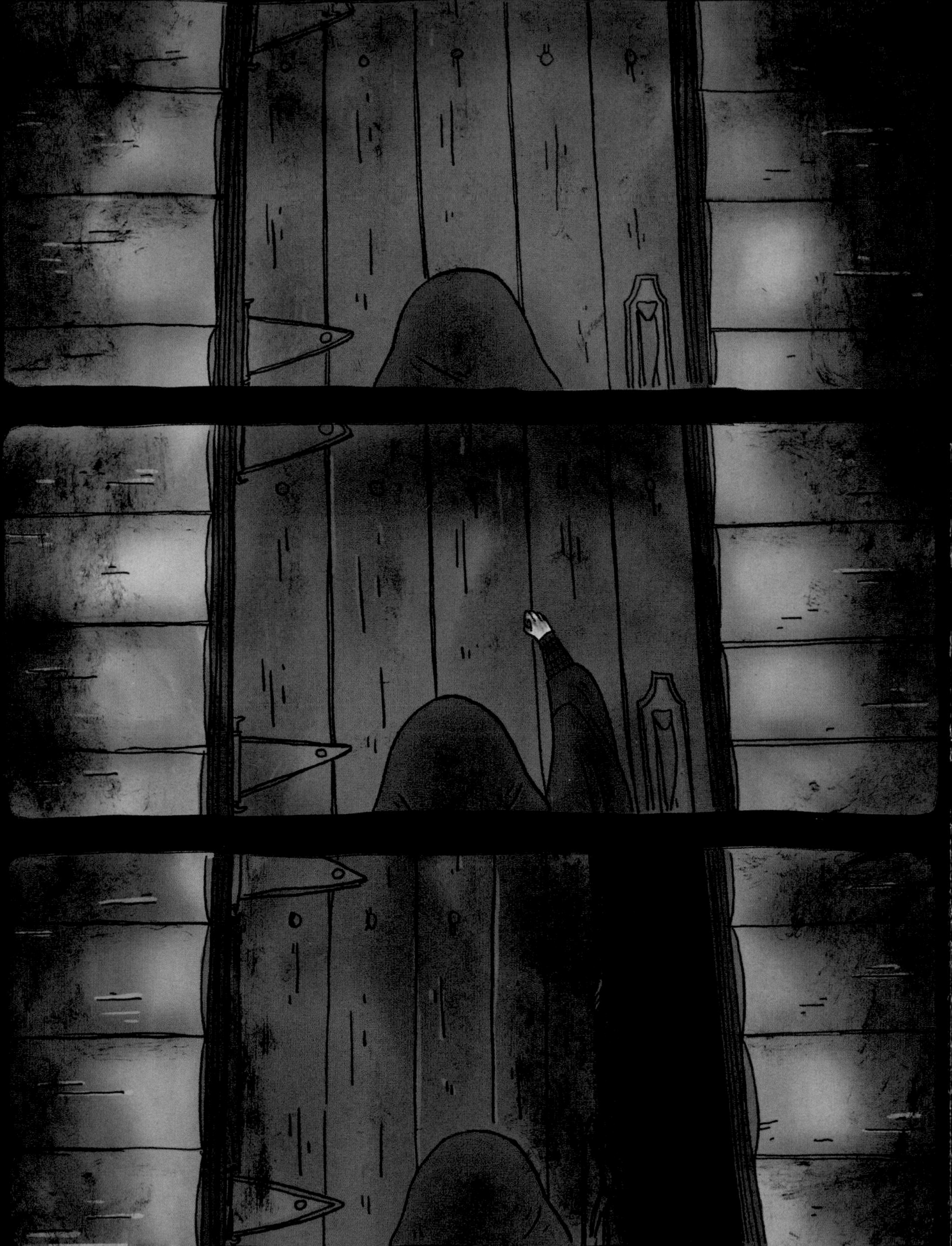

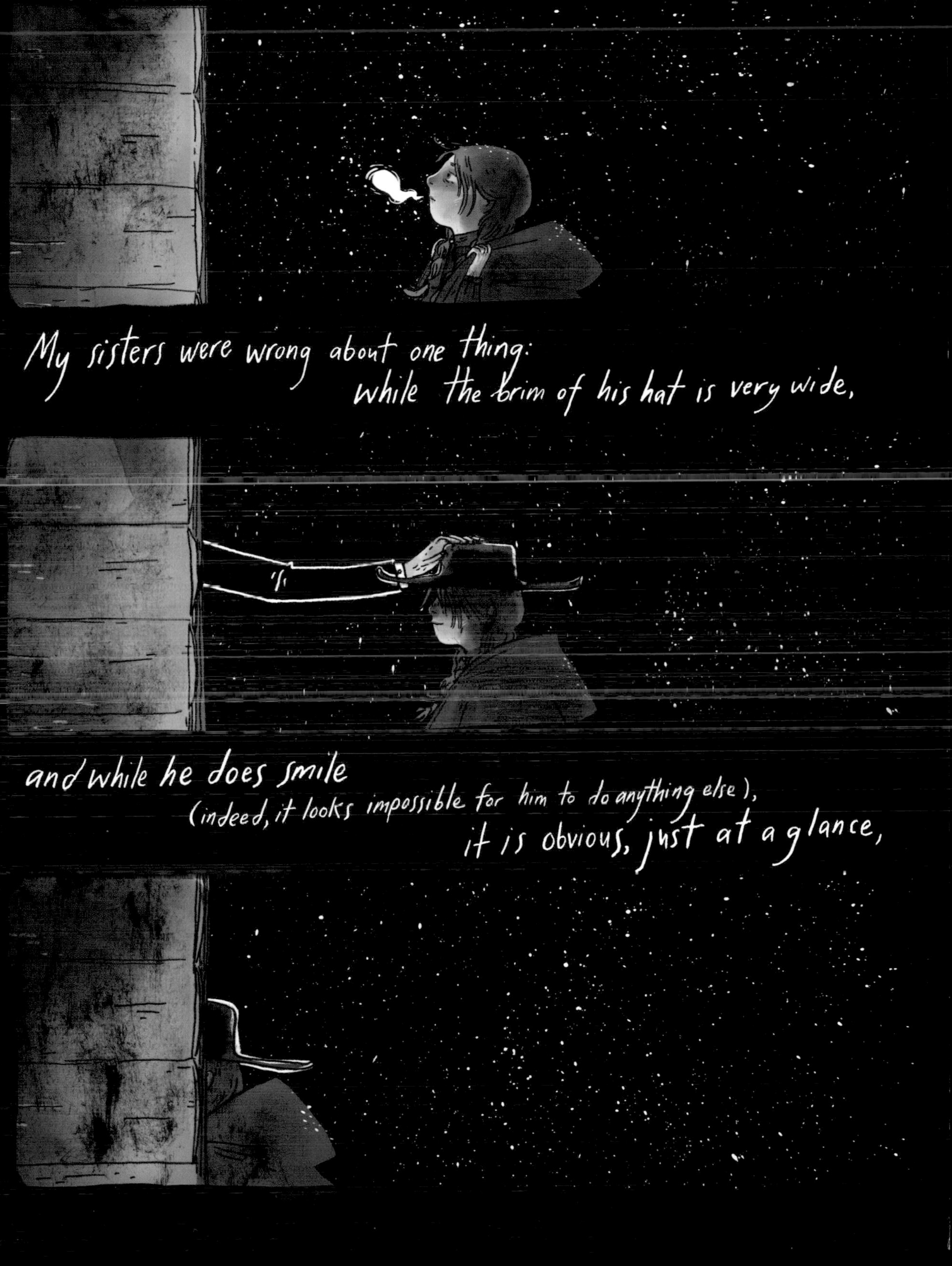
My sisters were wrong about one thing:
while the brim of his hat is very wide,
and while he does smile
(indeed, it looks impossible for him to do anything else),
it is obvious, just at a glance,

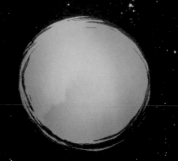

HE IS NO MAN.

A LADY'S HANDS ARE COLD

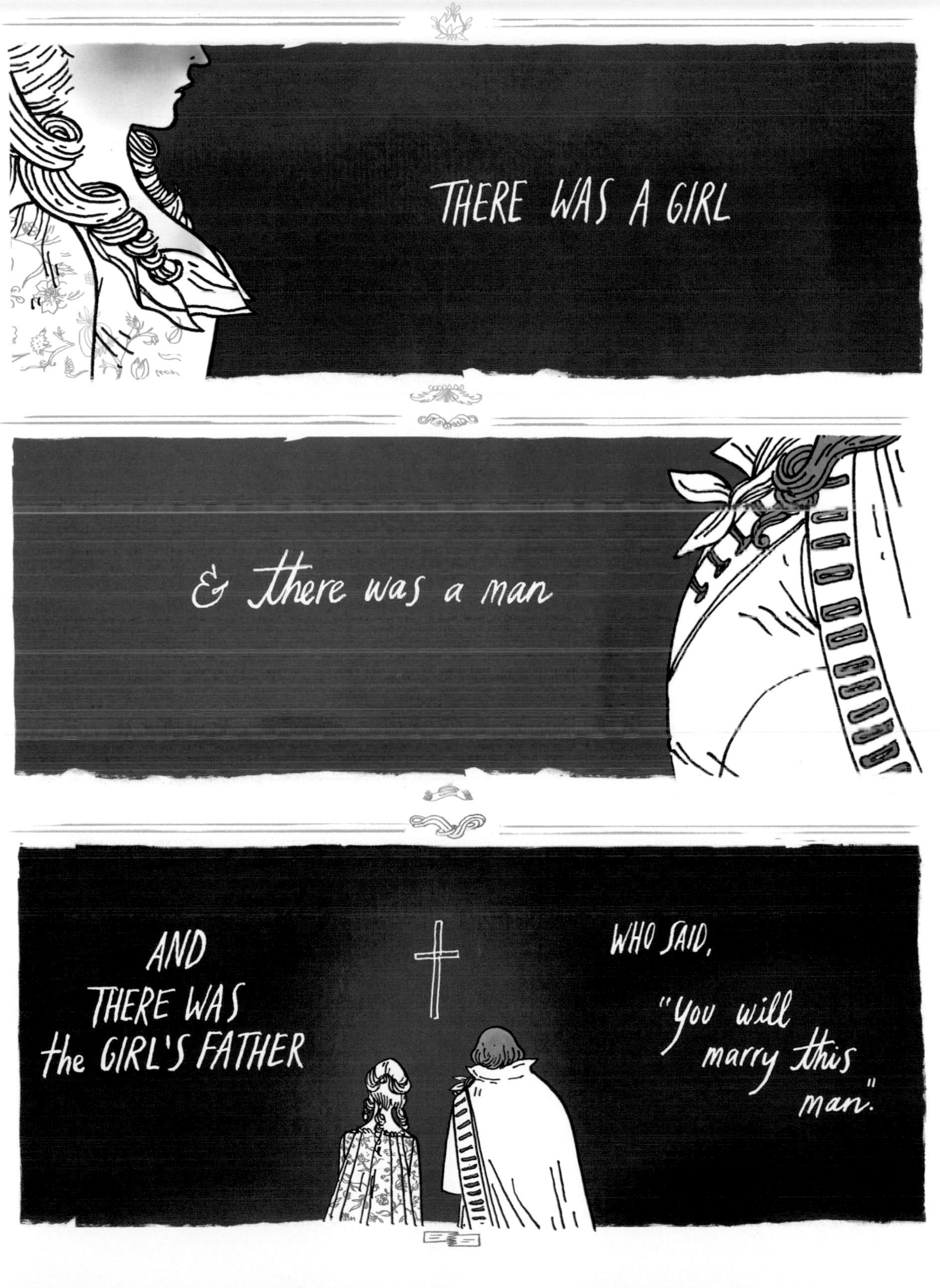
THERE WAS A GIRL
& there was a man
AND THERE WAS the GIRL'S FATHER
WHO SAID,
"You will marry this man."

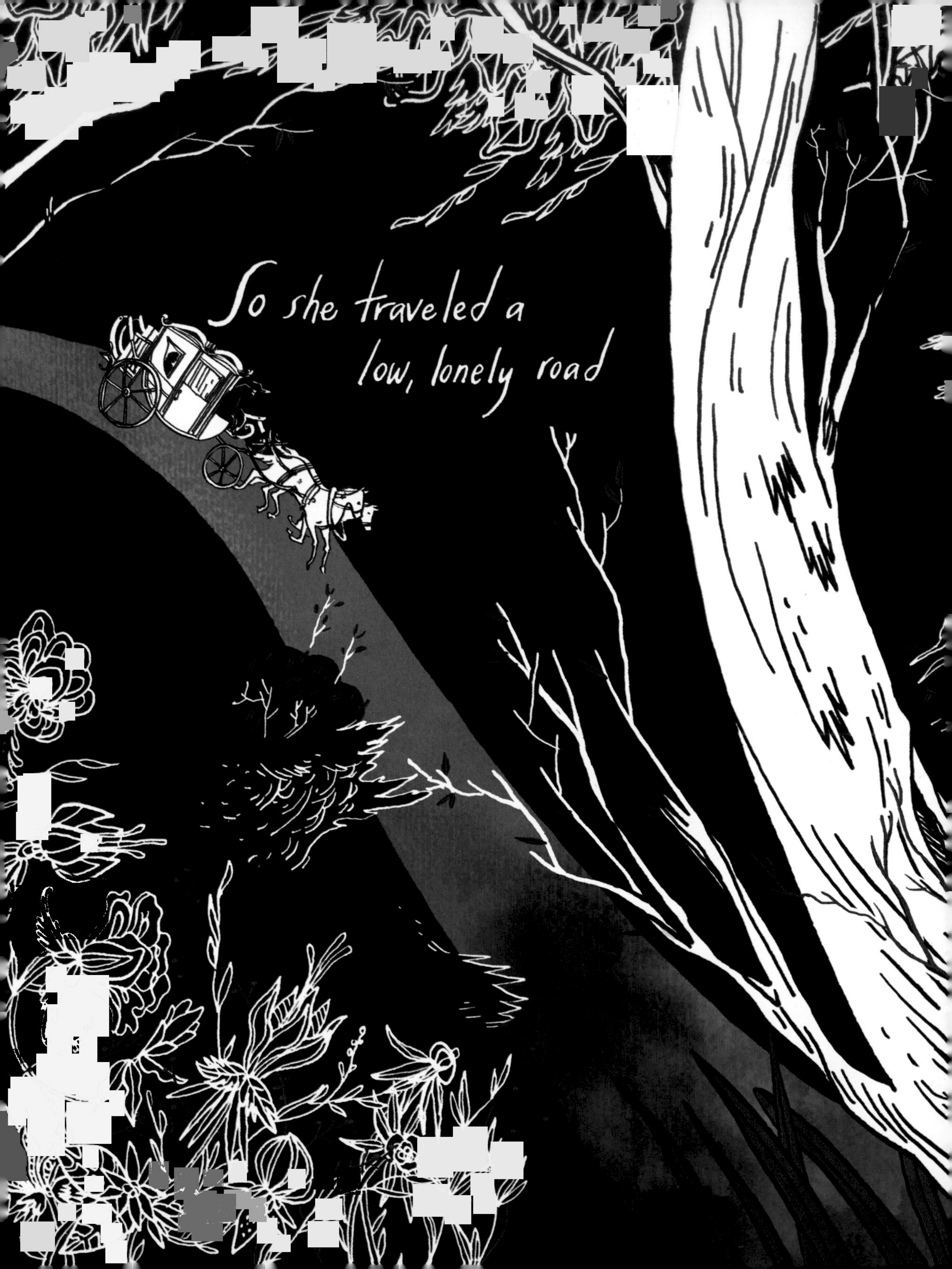
So she traveled a
low, lonely road

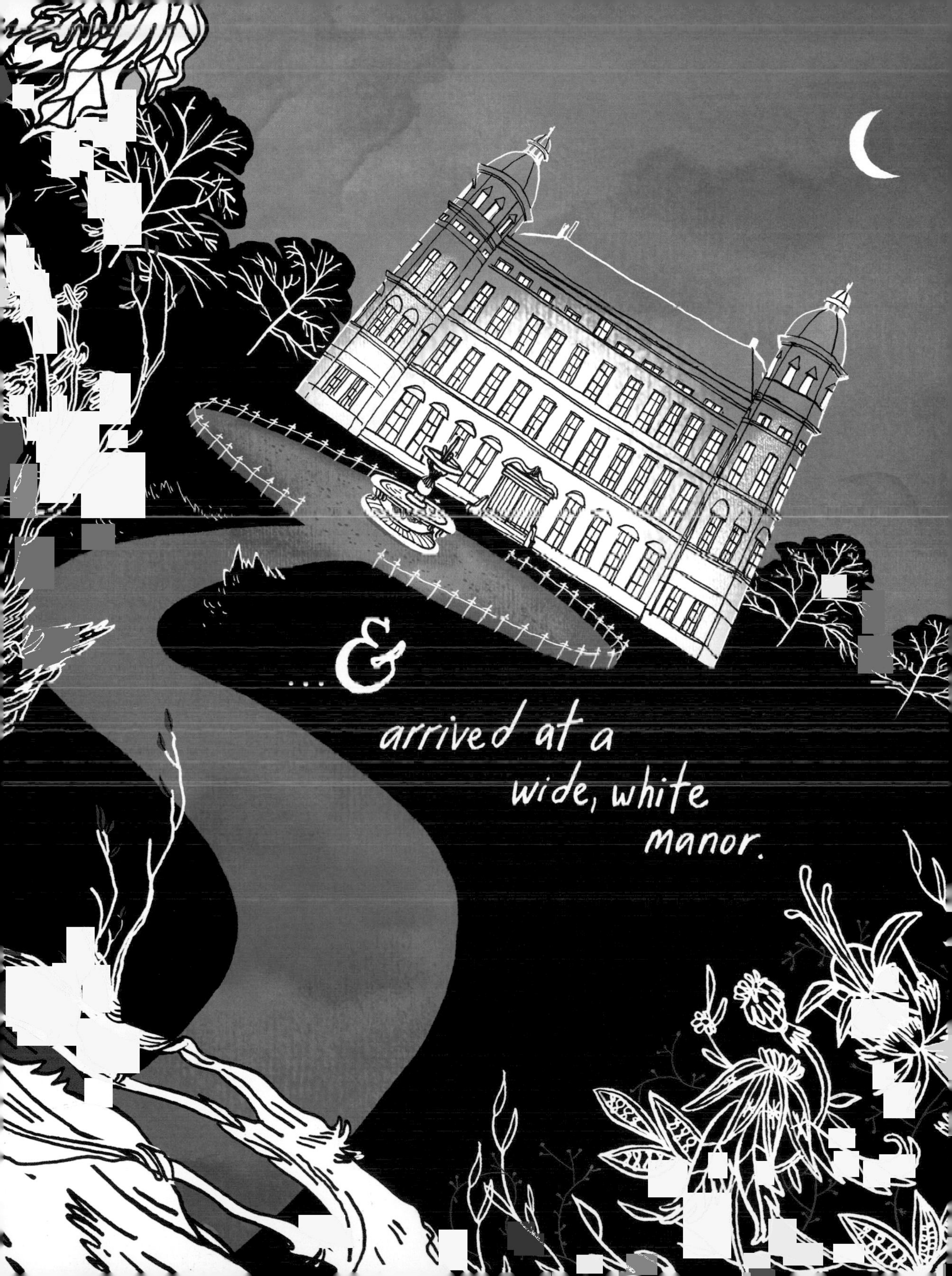
... &
arrived at a
wide, white
manor.

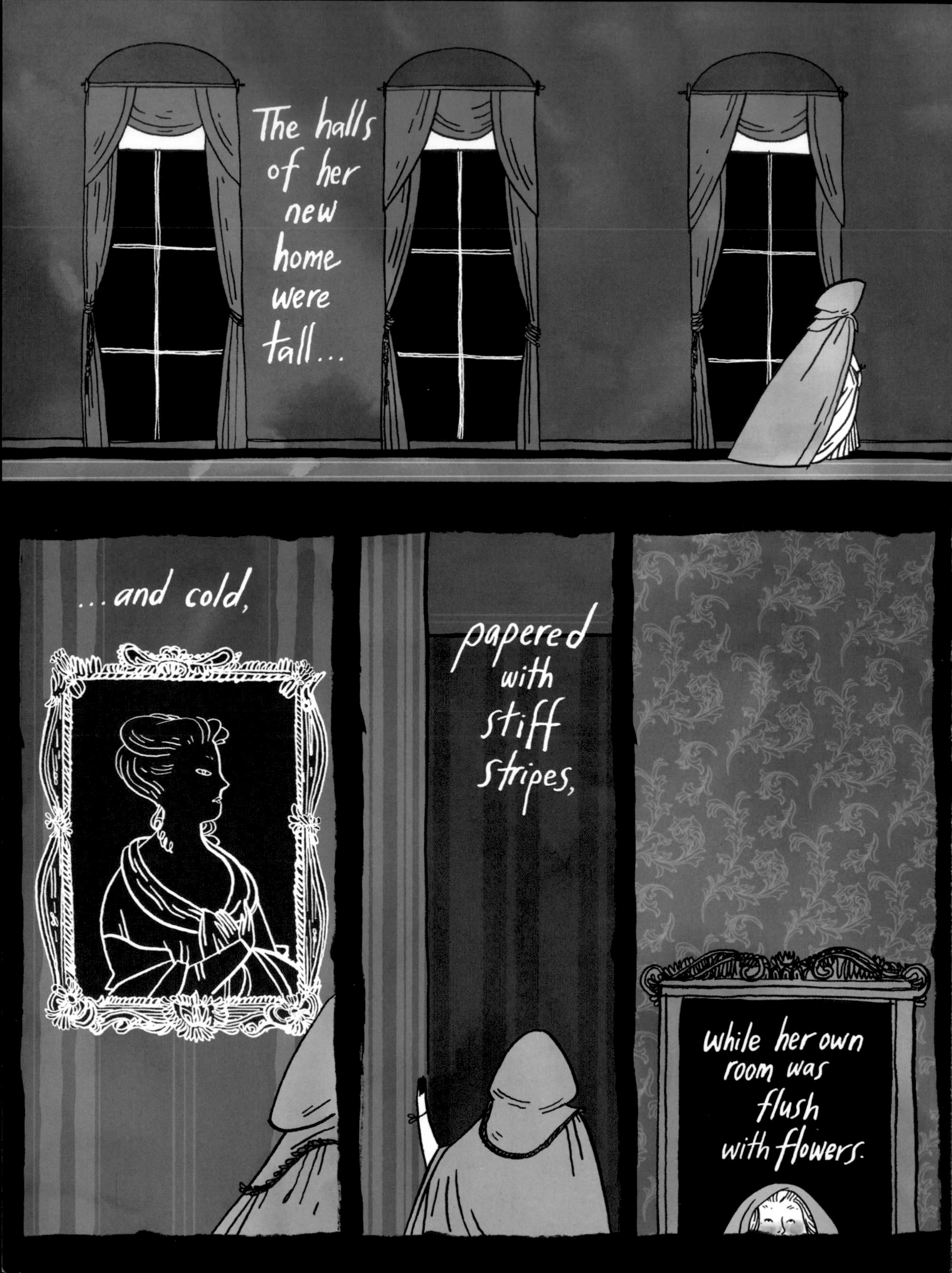
The halls of her new home were tall...
...and cold,
papered with stiff stripes,
while her own room was flush with flowers.

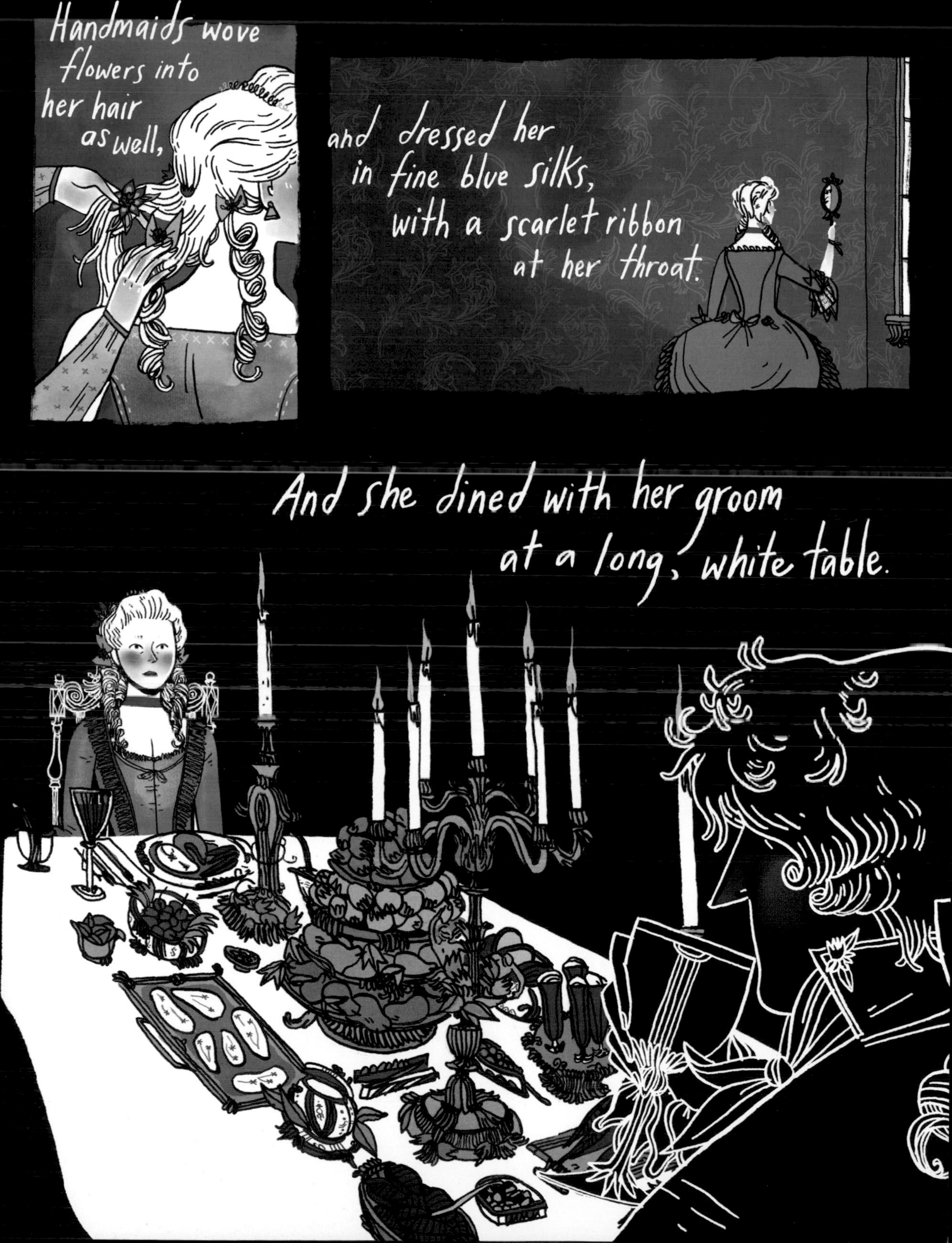
Handmaids wove flowers into her hair as well,
and dressed her in fine blue silks, with a scarlet ribbon at her throat.
And she dined with her groom at a long, white table.

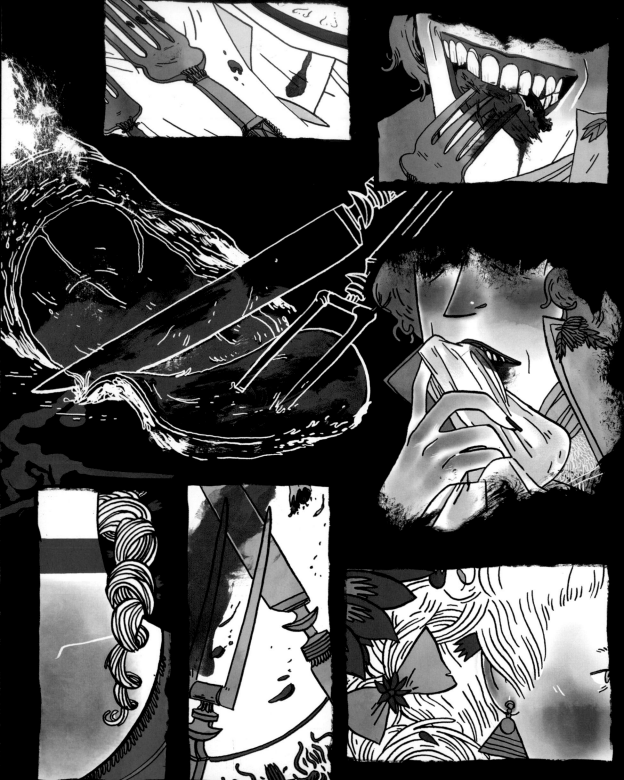

THAT
NIGHT...

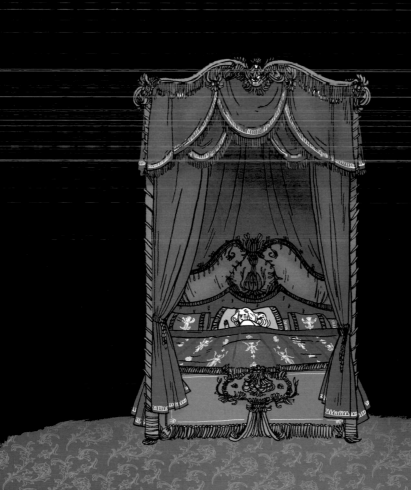

. . . she was awoken by a soft, sad song.
I MARRIED MY LOVE in the SPRINGTIME,
BUT by SUMMER HE'D LOCKED ME AWAY.
HE'D MURDERED ME DEAD by the AUTUMN,
& by WINTER I WAS NAUGHT BUT DECAY.

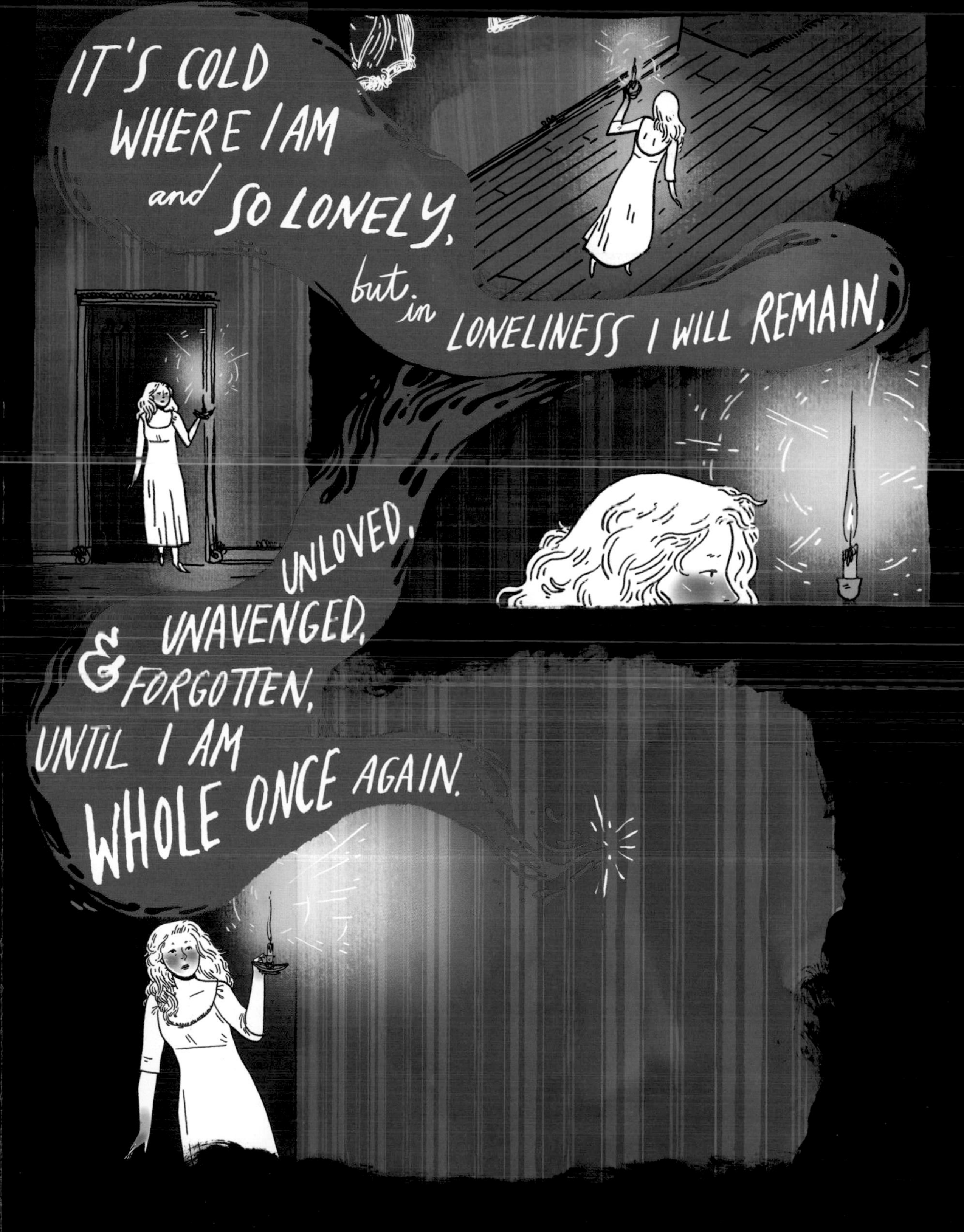
IT'S COLD
WHERE I AM
and SO LONELY,
but in LONELINESS I WILL REMAIN,
UNLOVED,
UNAVENGED,
& FORGOTTEN,
UNTIL I AM
WHOLE ONCE AGAIN.

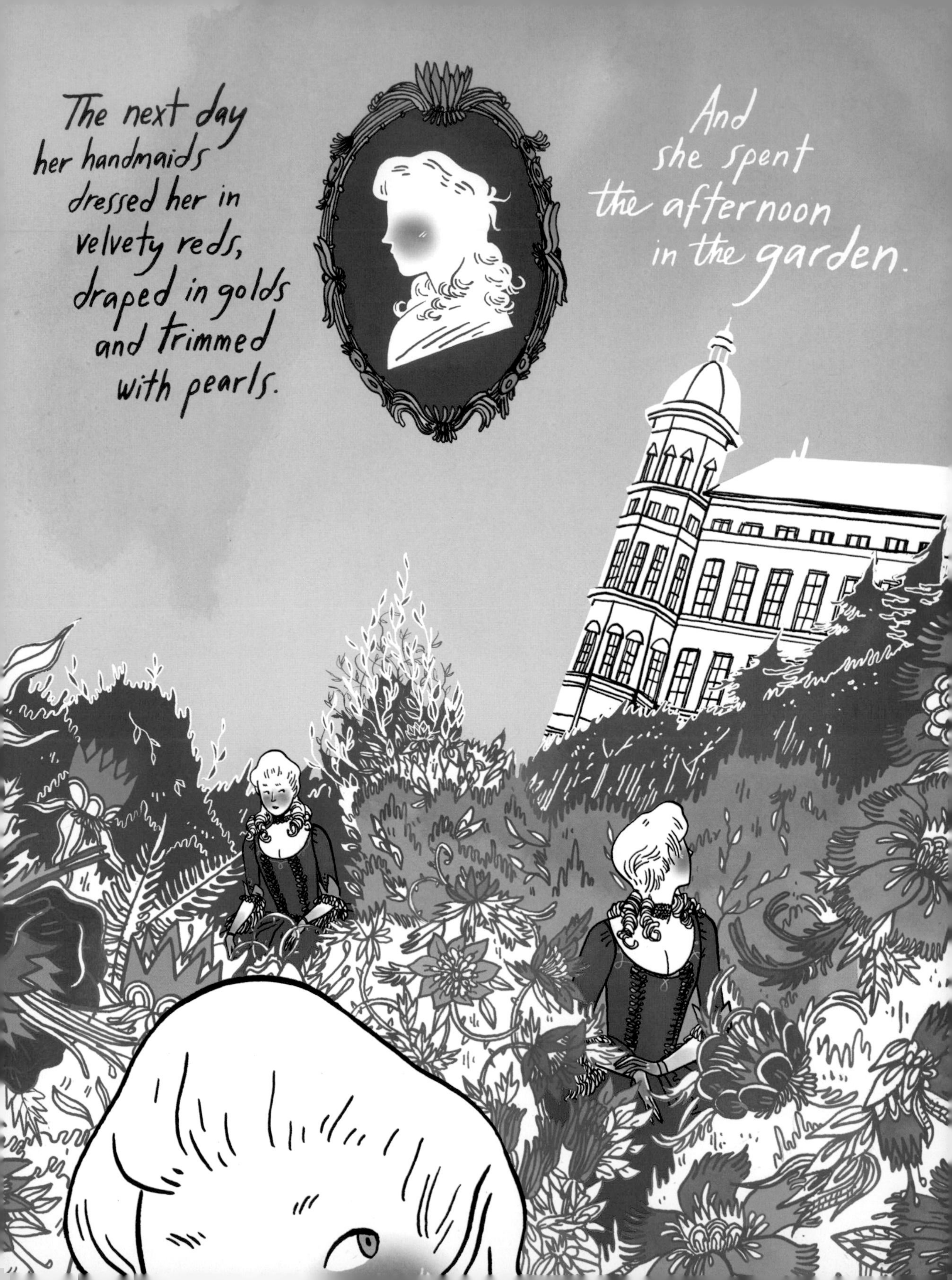
The next day her handmaids dressed her in velvety reds, draped in golds and trimmed with pearls.
And she spent the afternoon in the garden.

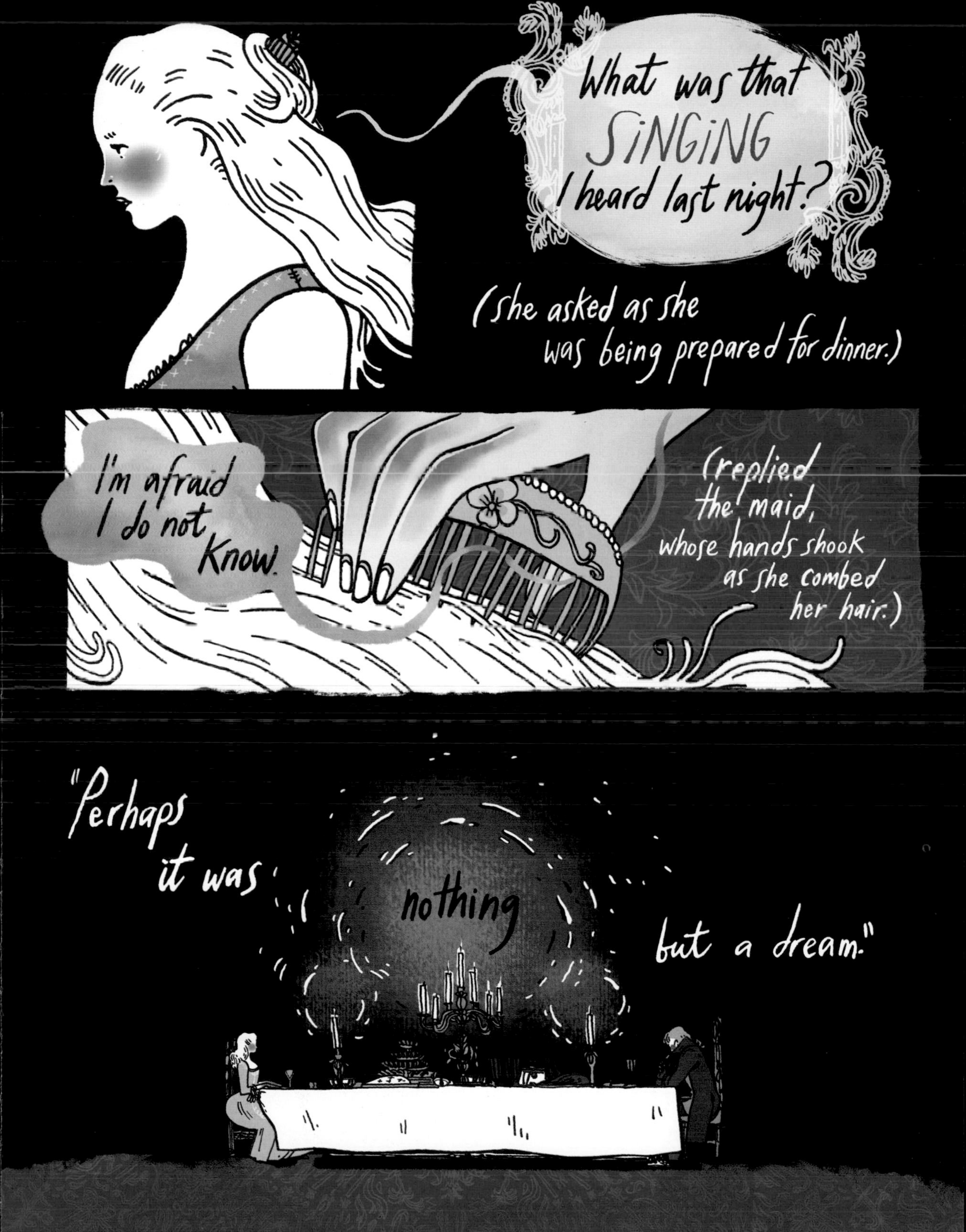
What was that SINGING I heard last night?
(she asked as she was being prepared for dinner.)
I'm afraid I do not Know.
(replied the maid, whose hands shook as she combed her hair.)
"Perhaps it was nothing but a dream."

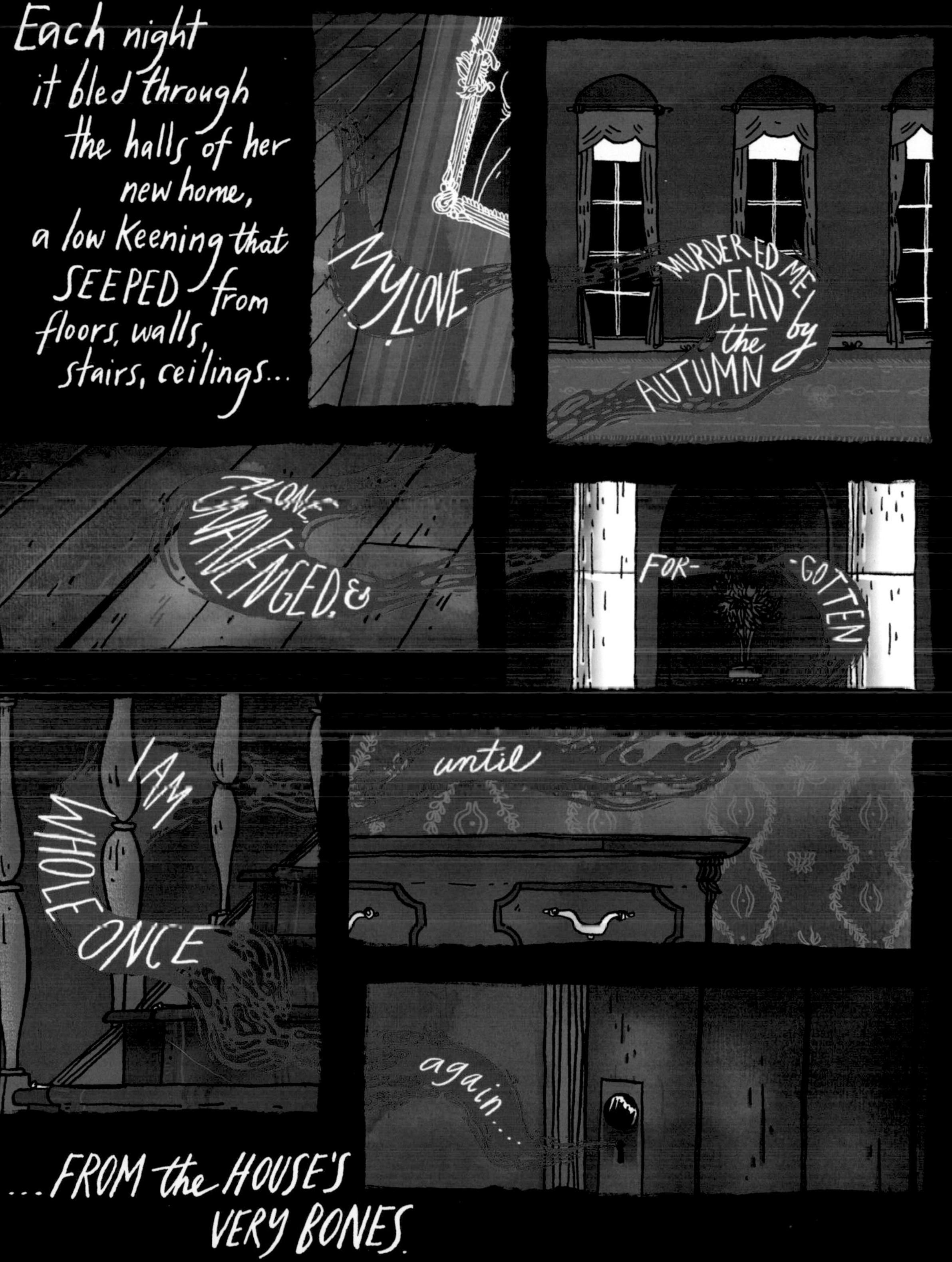
Each night it bled through the halls of her new home, a low keening that SEEPED from floors, walls, stairs, ceilings...
MY LOVE
MURDERED ME DEAD by the AUTUMN
ALONE
UNAVENGED &
FOR-
-GOTTEN
I AM
WHOLE ONCE
until
again....
...FROM the HOUSE'S VERY BONES.

& then it settled into HER bones.
EVERY NIGHT, THAT SONG (THAT WAIL) until the girl's insides were clotted with cold HEARTACHE.

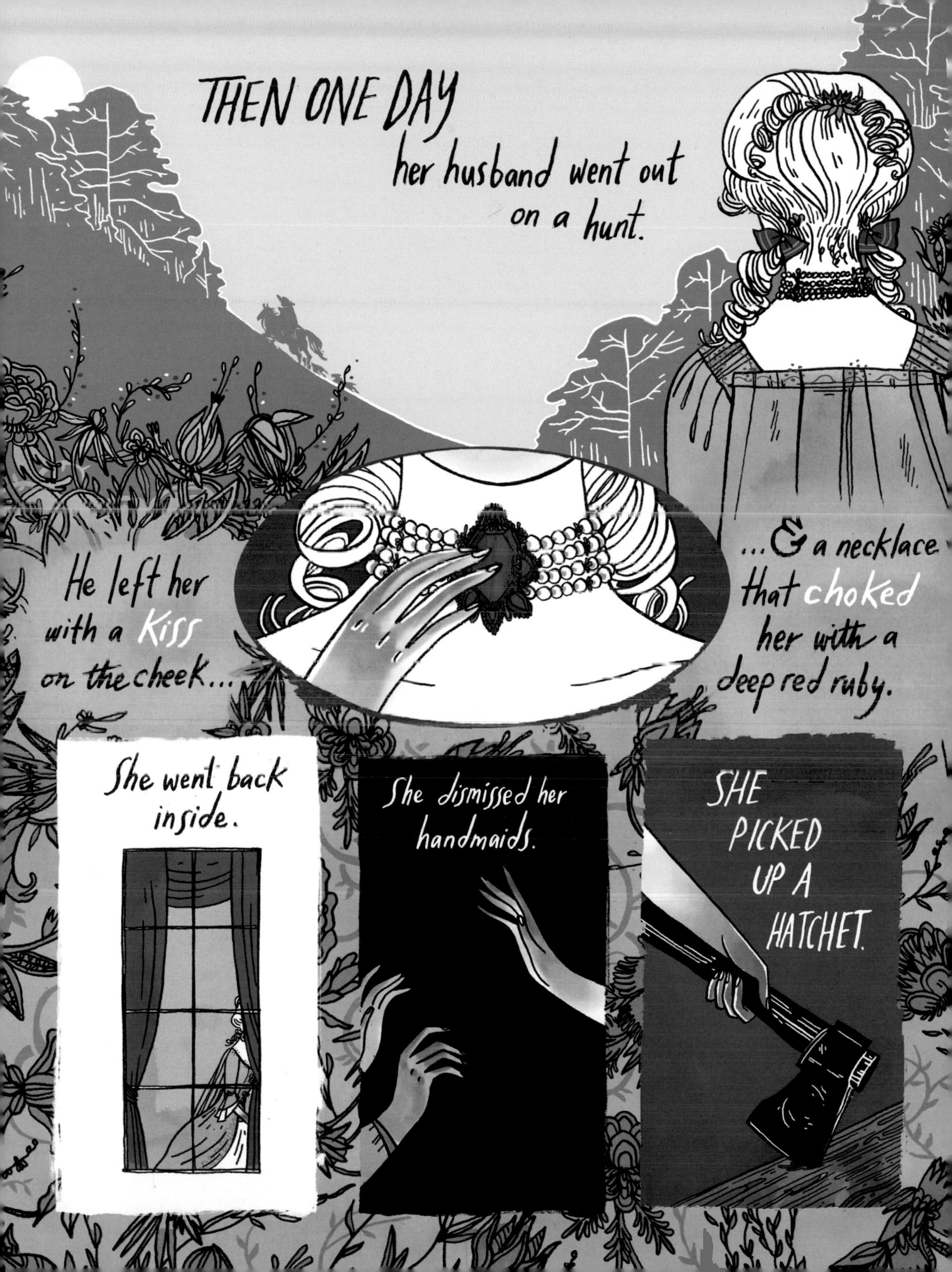
THEN ONE DAY
her husband went out on a hunt.
He left her with a KISS on the cheek...
...& a necklace that choked her with a deep red ruby.
She went back inside.
She dismissed her handmaids.
SHE PICKED UP A HATCHET.

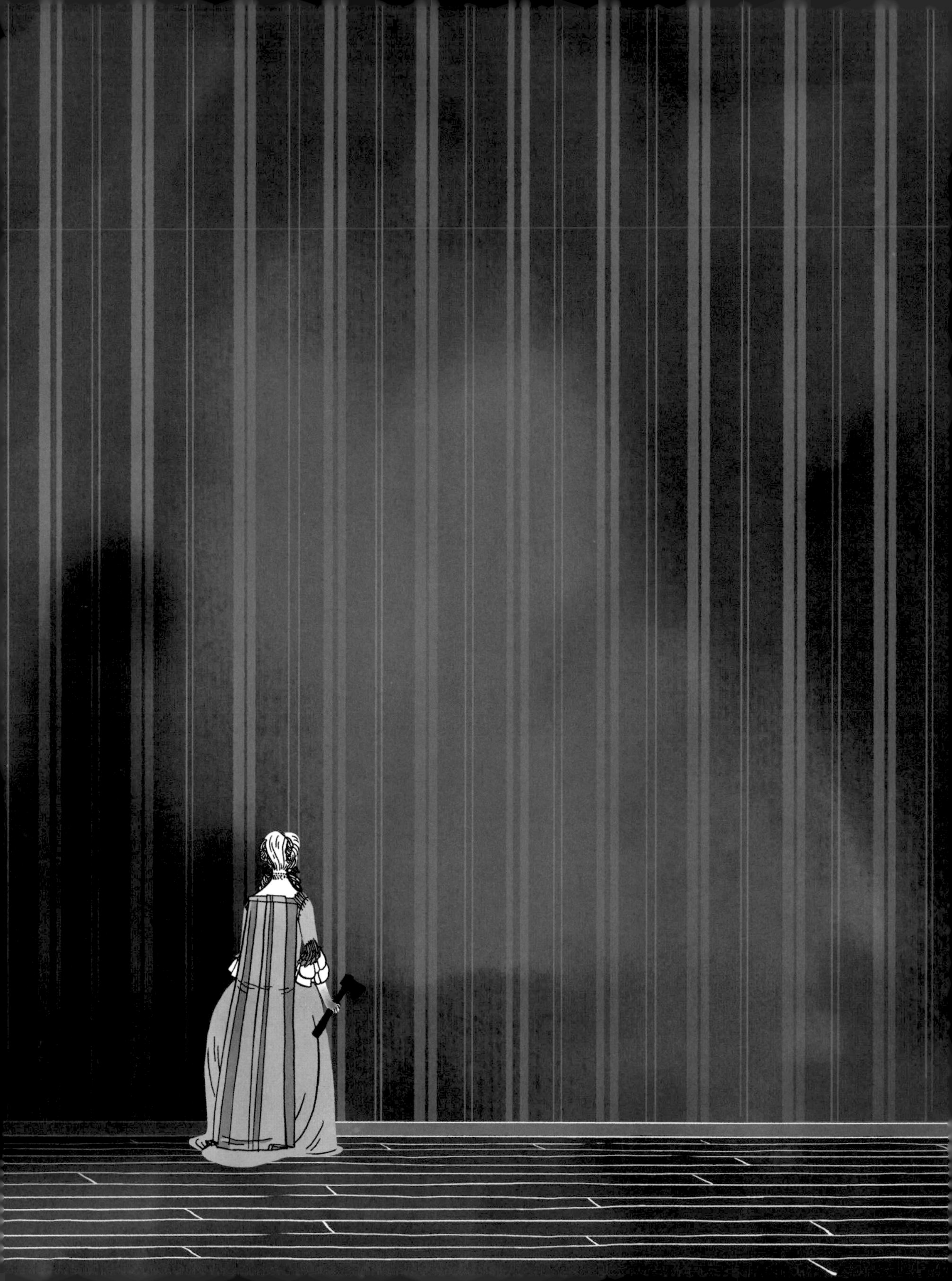

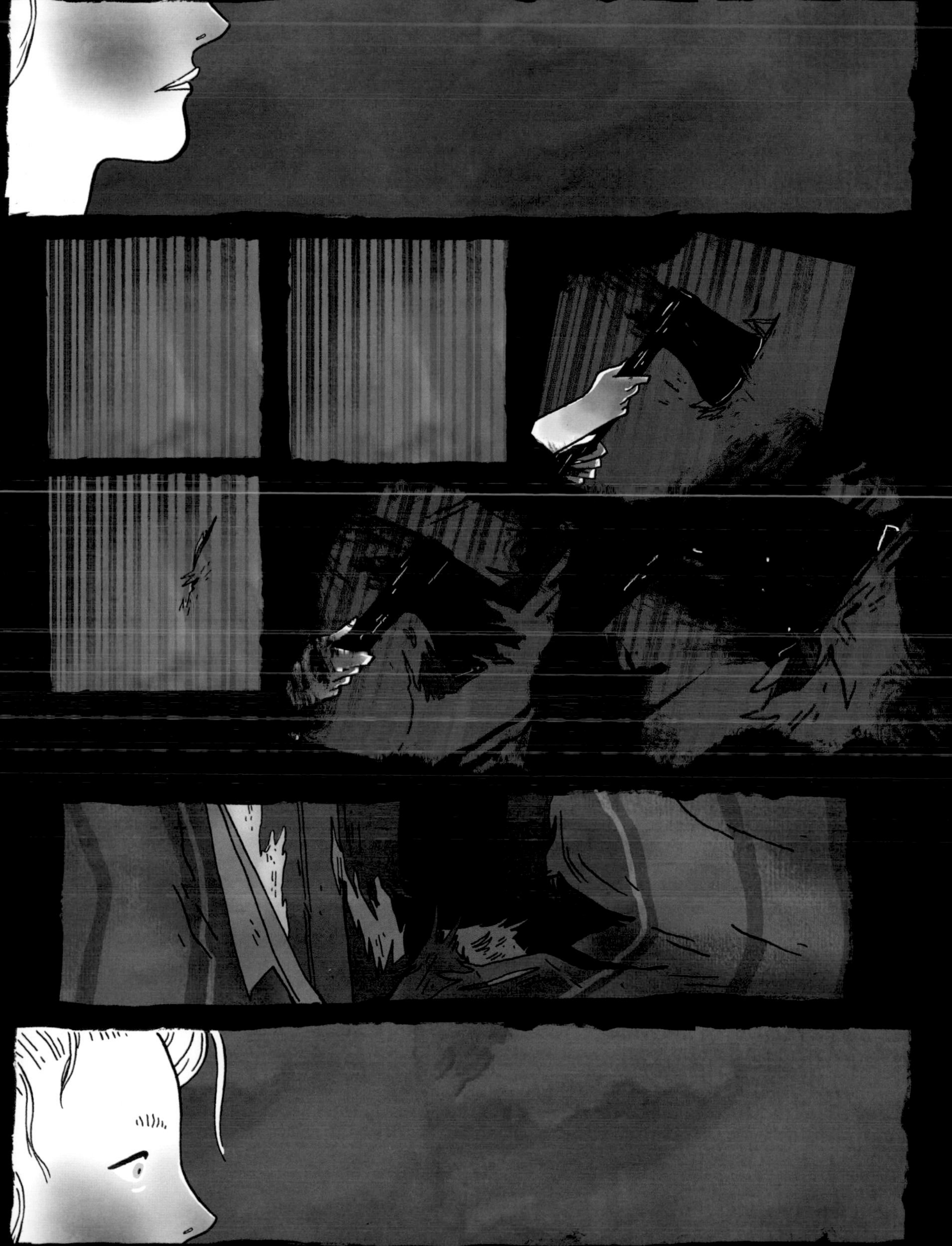

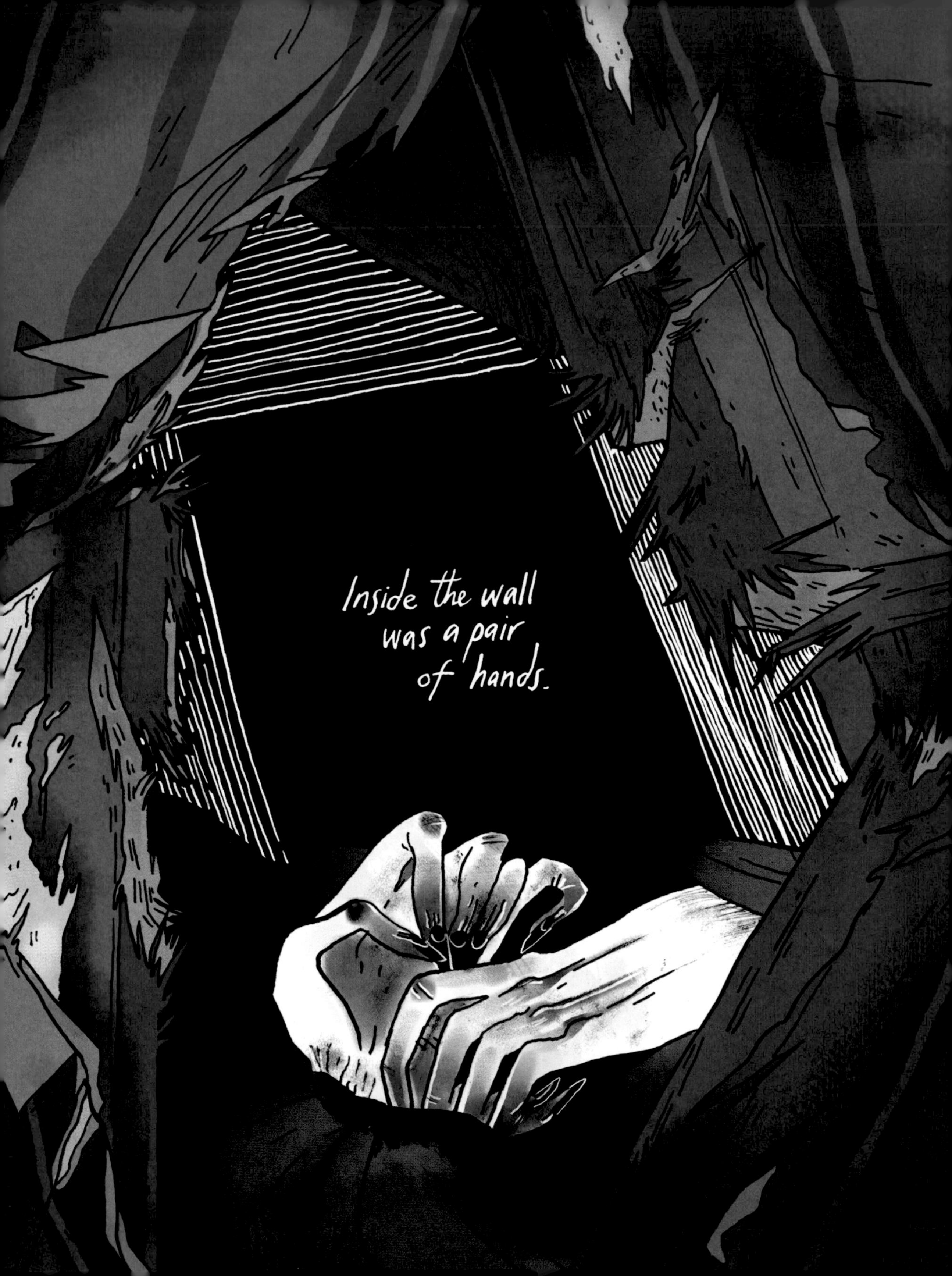
Inside the wall was a pair of hands.

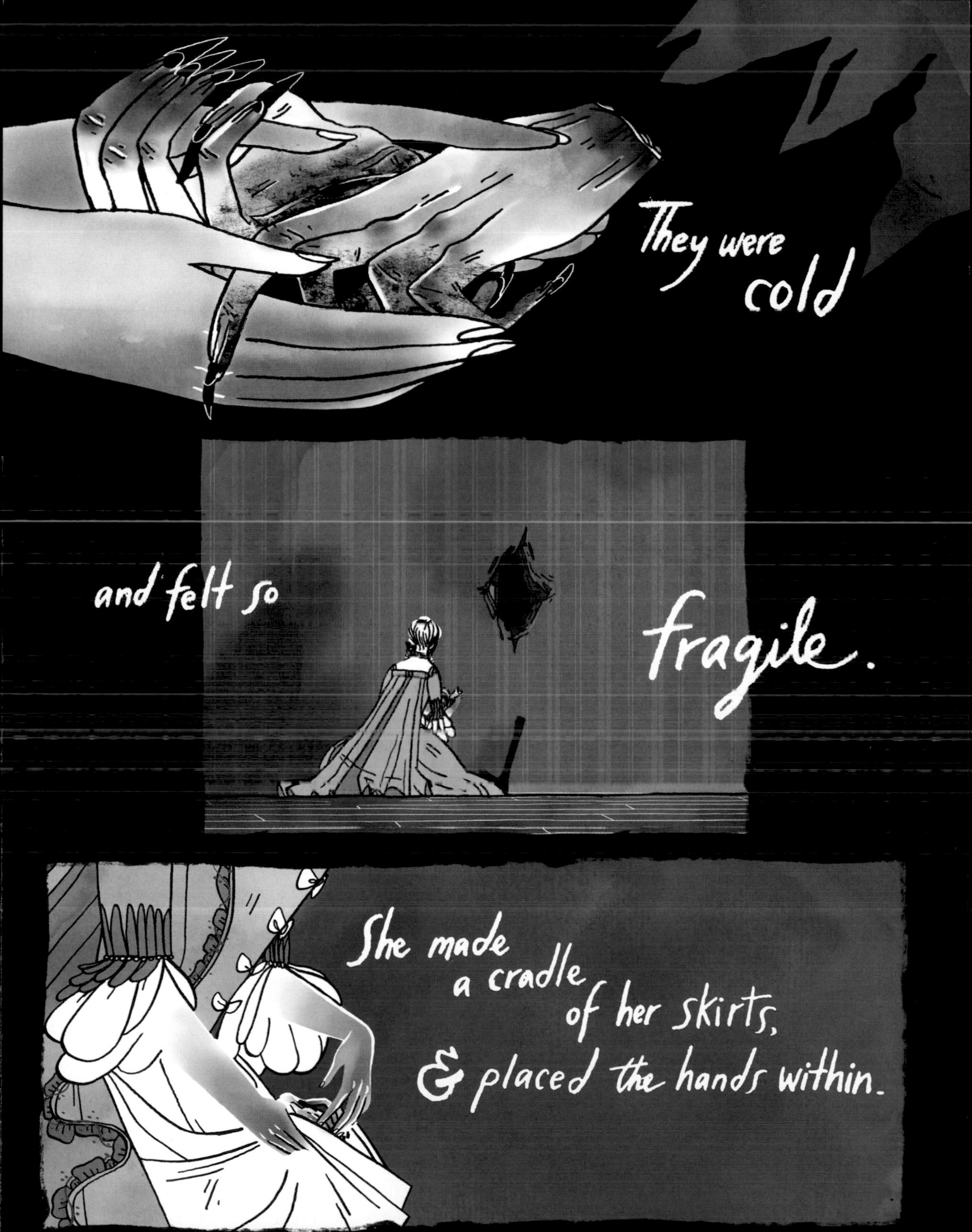
They were cold
and felt so
fragile.
She made a cradle of her skirts, & placed the hands within.

She found a leg
in the hallway floor,

& two arms,
linked at the elbows,
beneath a
portrait.

One foot was lost
under a
chest of drawers,
& its opposite was
discovered within
a closet.

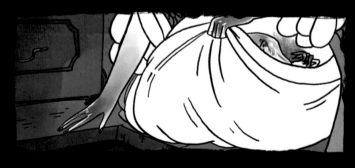

A torso,
wrapped in a stained gray gown,
lined the bottom of the stairs,

& after much digging, another leg was discovered
between two dusty columns.

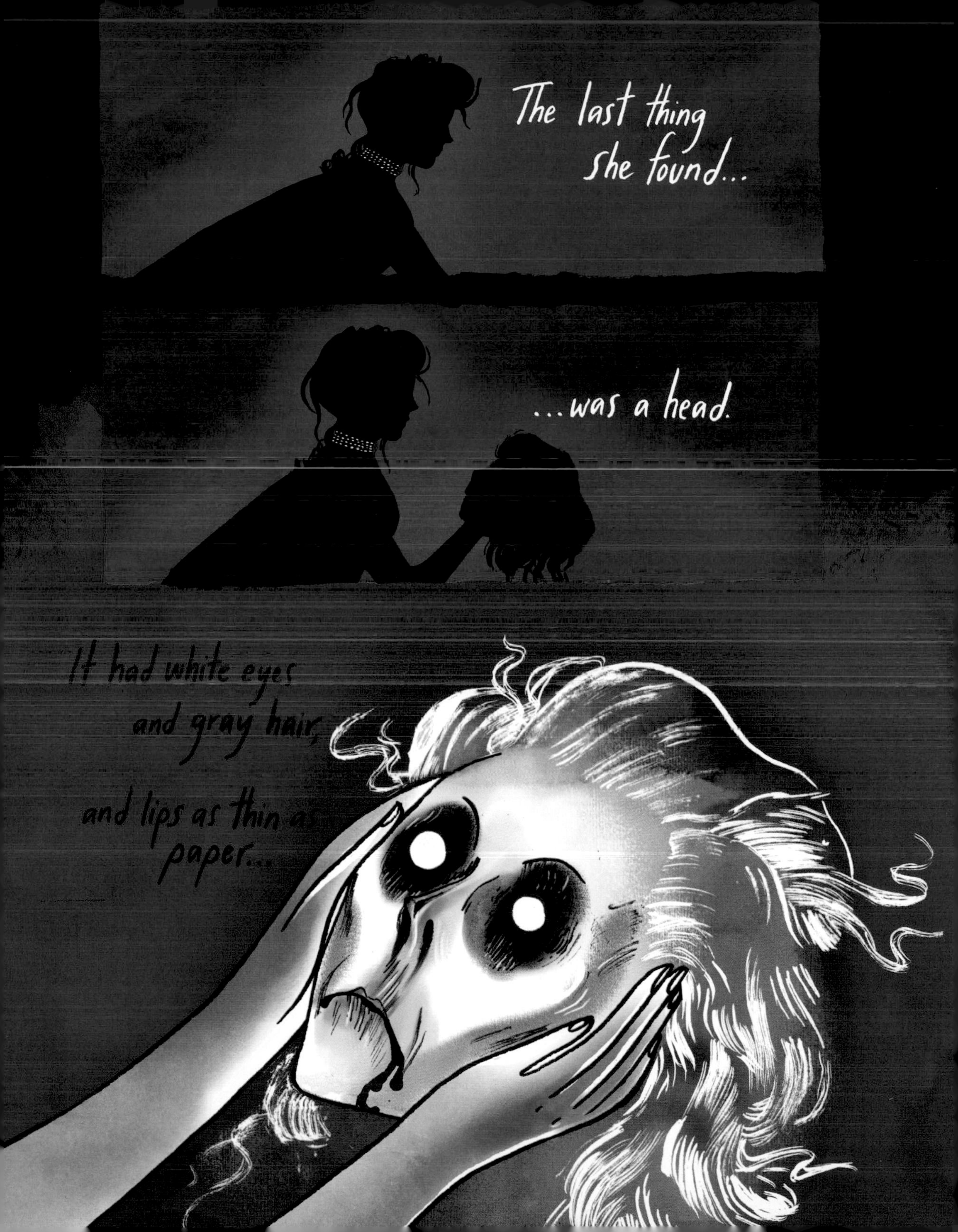
The last thing she found...
...was a head.
It had white eyes and gray hair,
and lips as thin as paper...

...WHICH SANG:
I MARRIED my LOVE in the SPRING-TIME,
but by SUMMER
HE'D LOCKED ME away.
HE'D MURDERED me dead
by the AUTUMN,
& by WINTER
I was NAUGHT BUT decay.

IT'S COLD where I am
SO
& LONELY, but in LONELINESS
I will REMAIN,
UNLOVED,
UNAVENGED,
&
forgotten,
UNTIL I AM
WHOLE
once
again

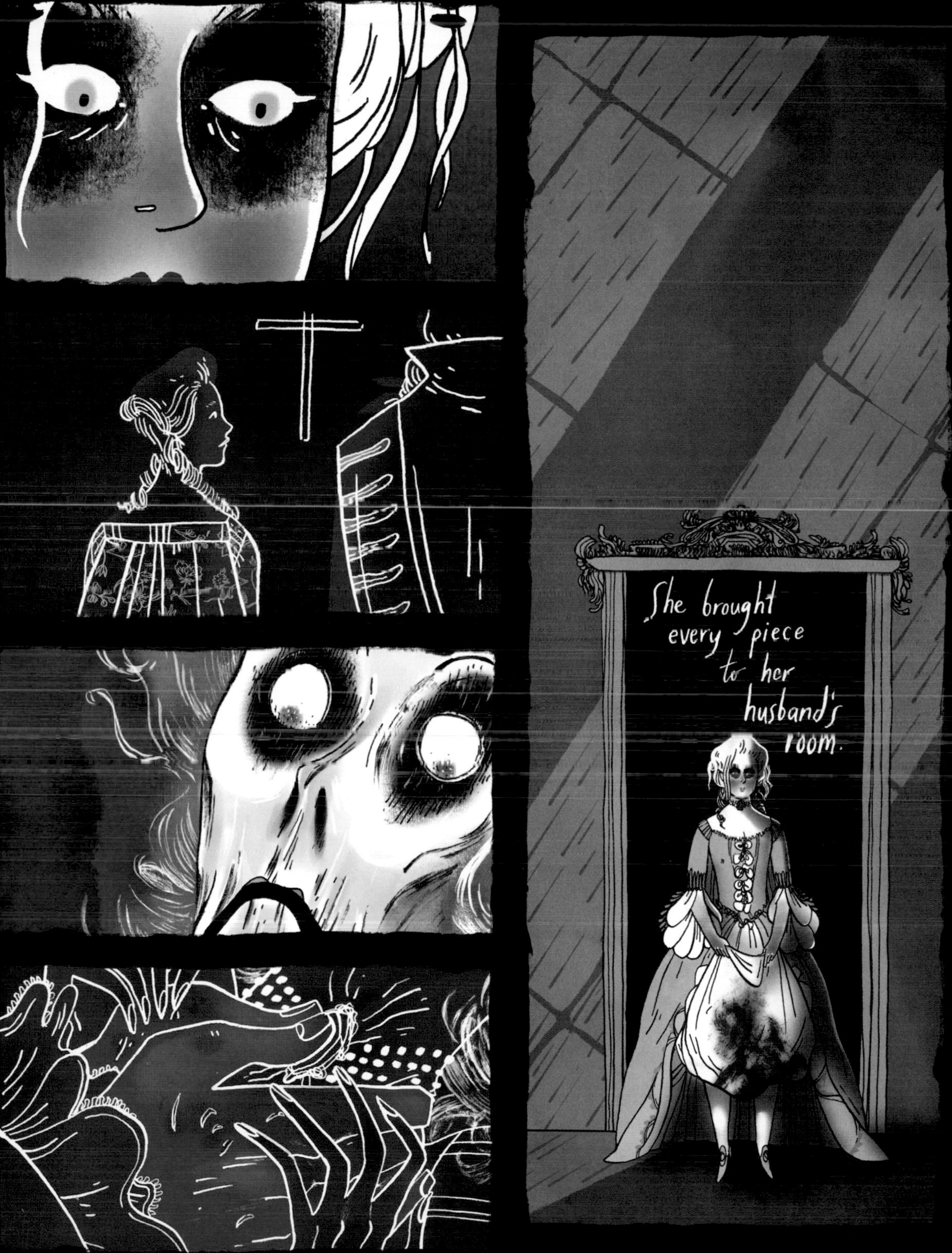
She brought every piece to her husband's room.

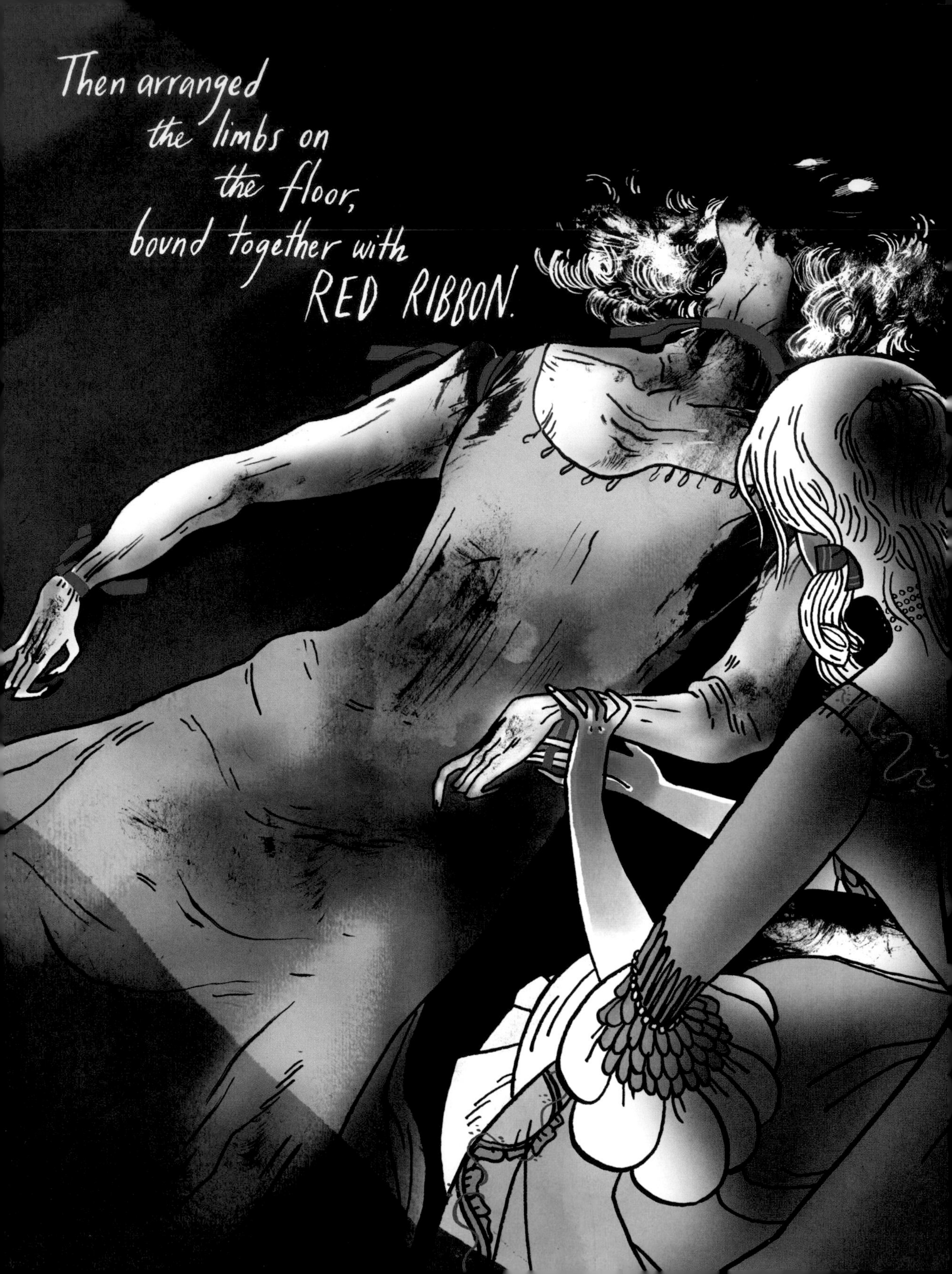
Then arranged the limbs on the floor, bound together with RED RIBBON.

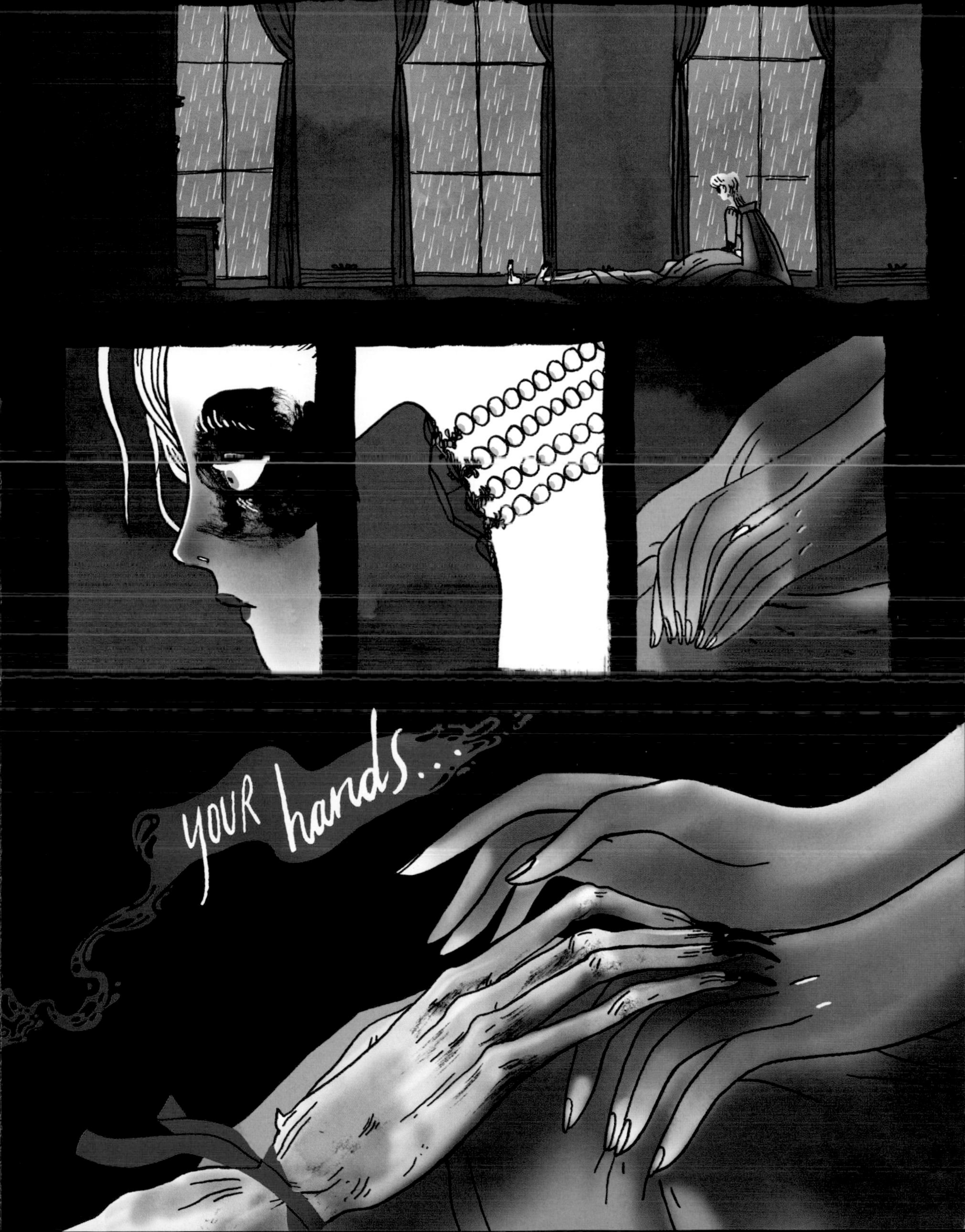
YOUR hands...

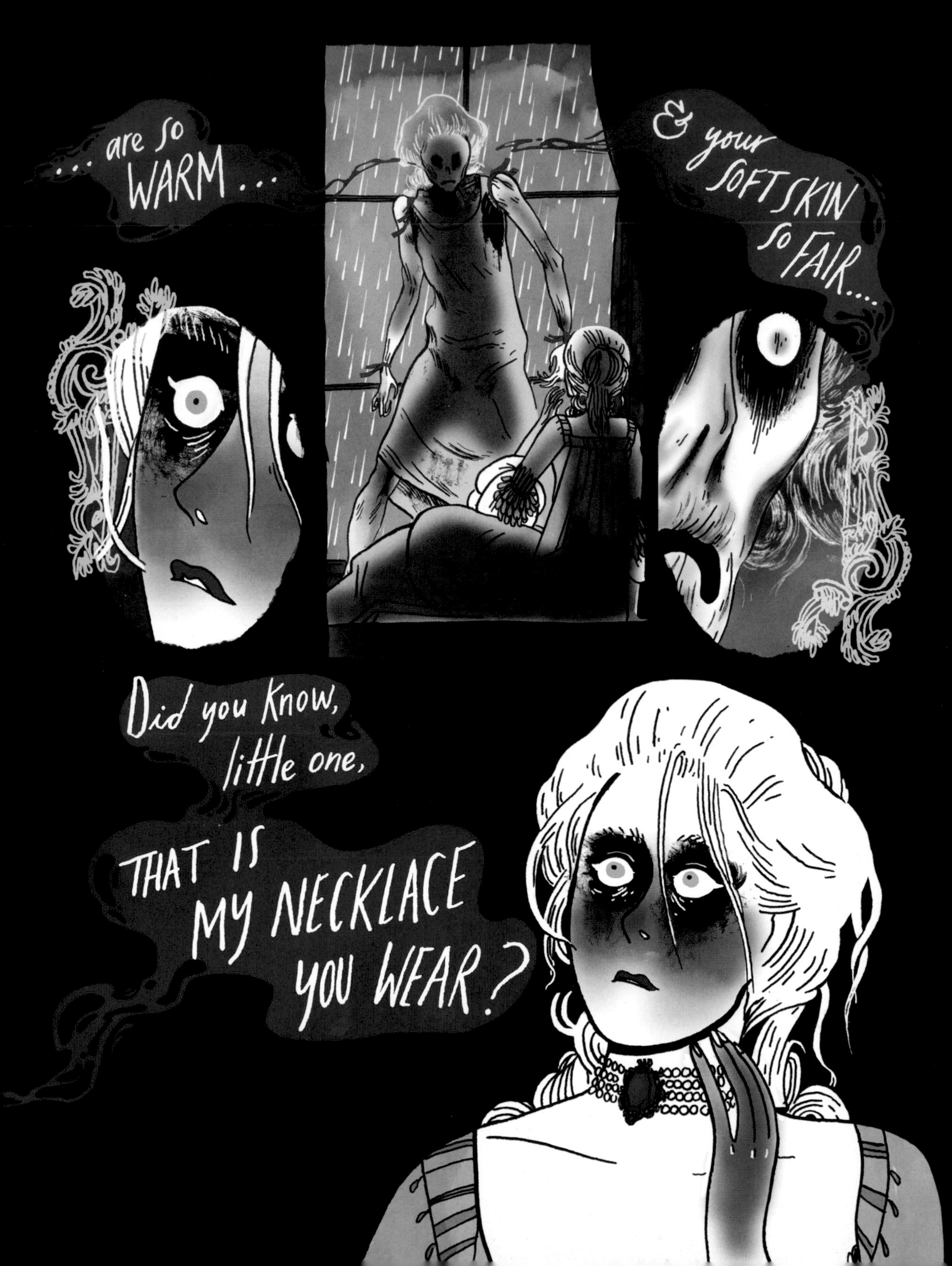
... are so WARM ...
& your SOFT SKIN so FAIR....
Did you know, little one,
THAT IS MY NECKLACE YOU WEAR?

& MY BED that you sleep in?
MY MANSION? MY LANDS?
I gave my LOVE everything...
...AND HE CUT OFF MY HANDS.
Do you think he loves you now?
THINK you've usurped MY role?
WHEN I'VE TORN YOU TO PIECES, GIRL,
THEN I'LL BE WHOLE.

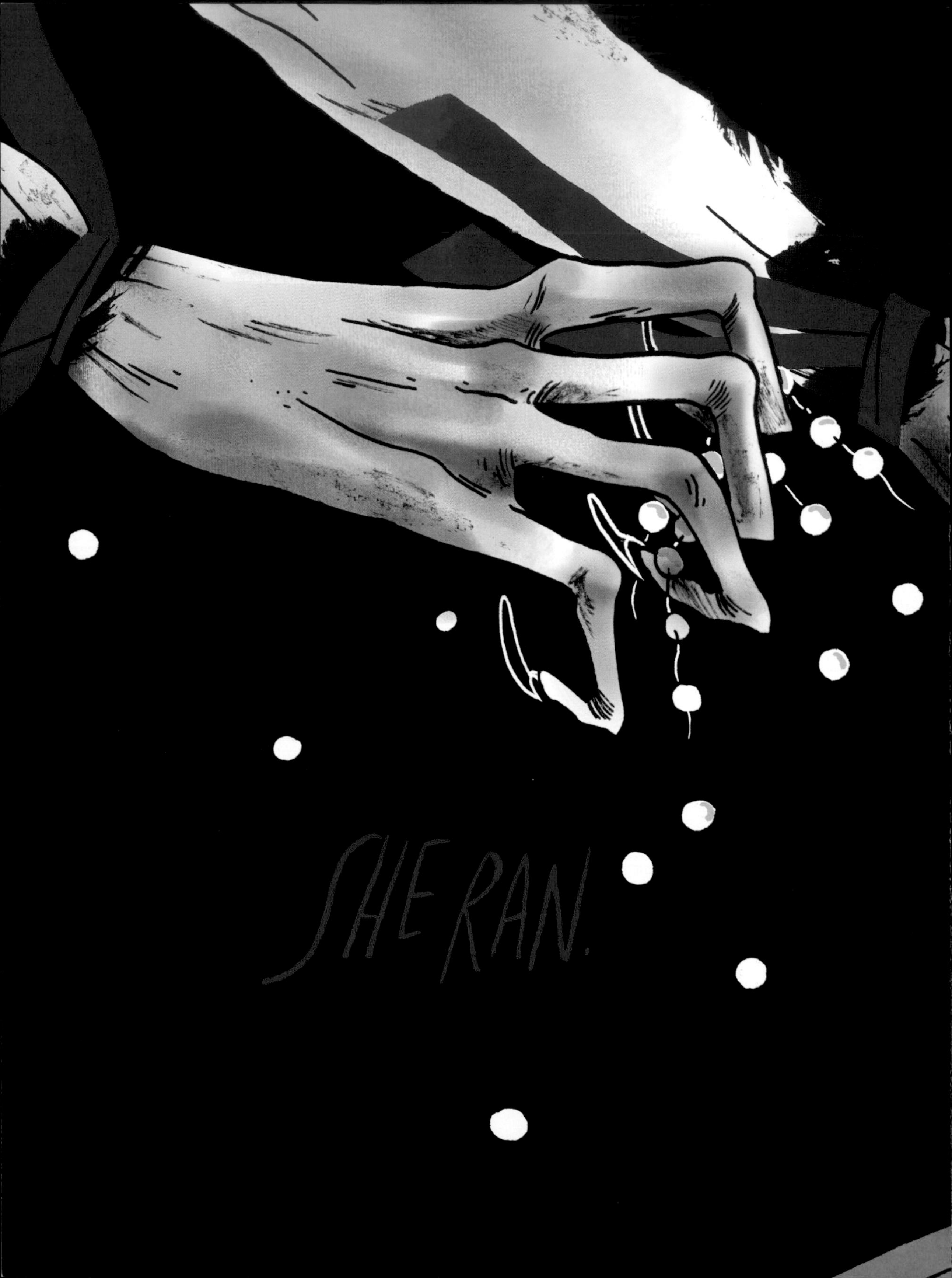
SHE RAN.

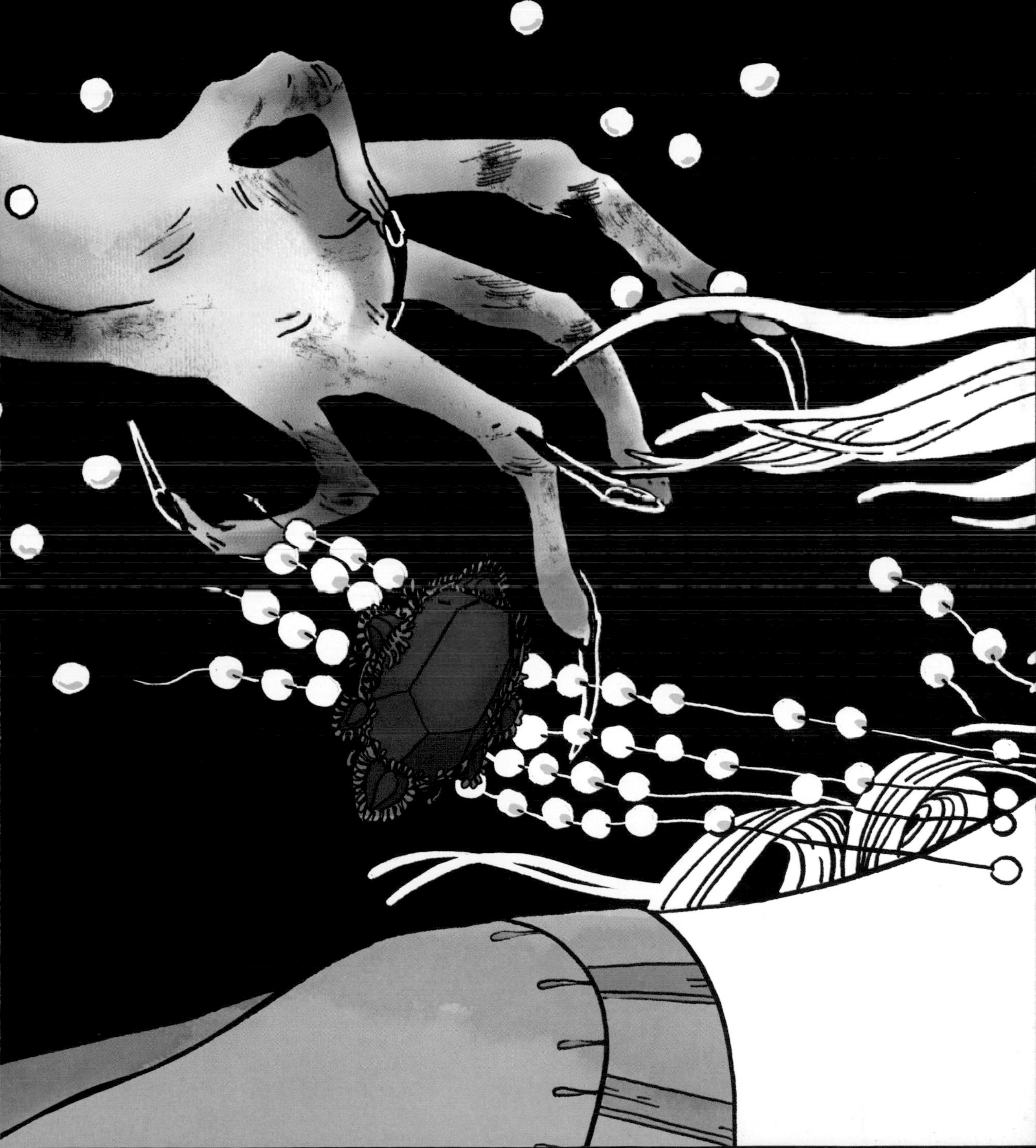

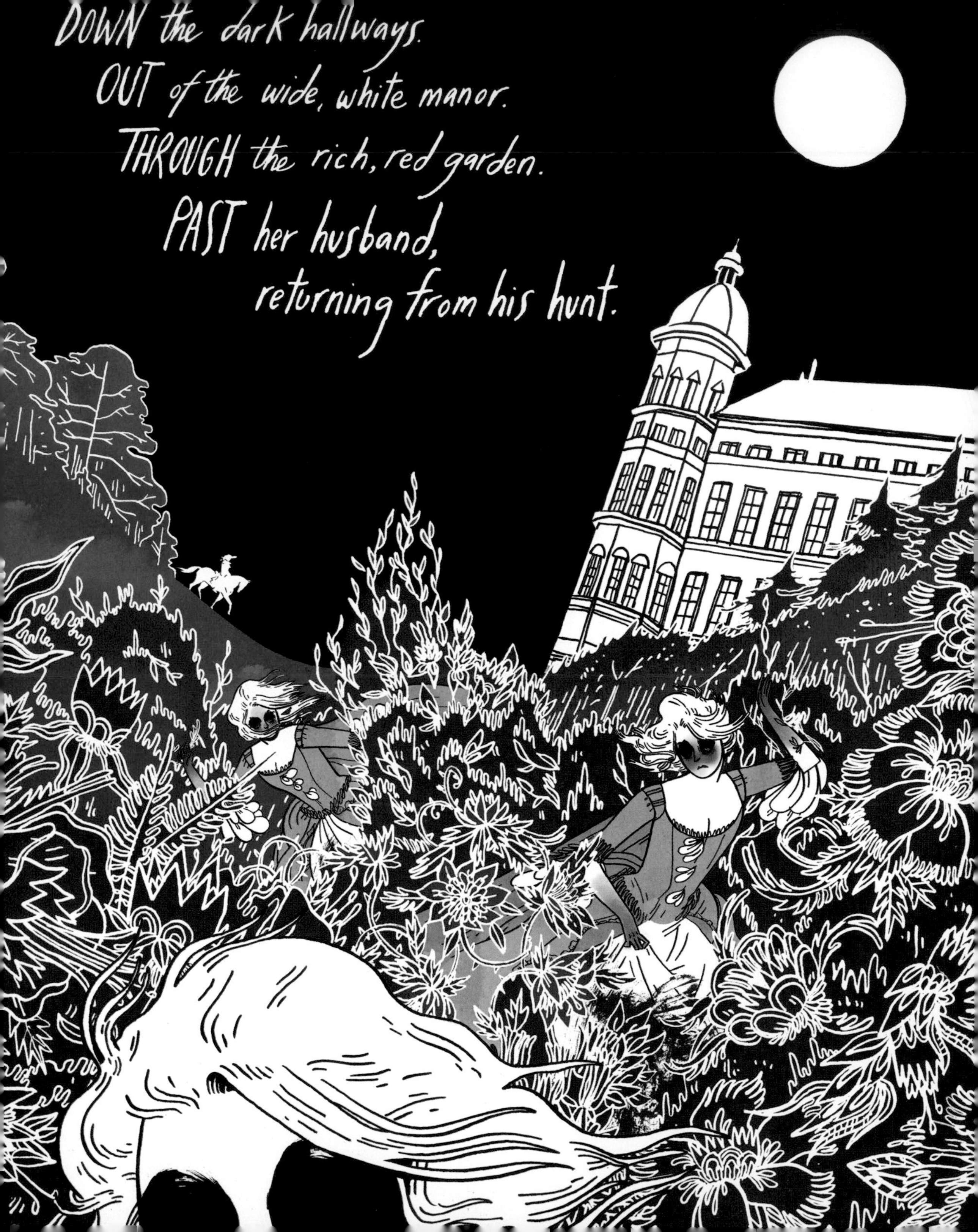
DOWN the dark hallways.
OUT of the wide, white manor.
THROUGH the rich, red garden.
PAST her husband,
returning from his hunt.

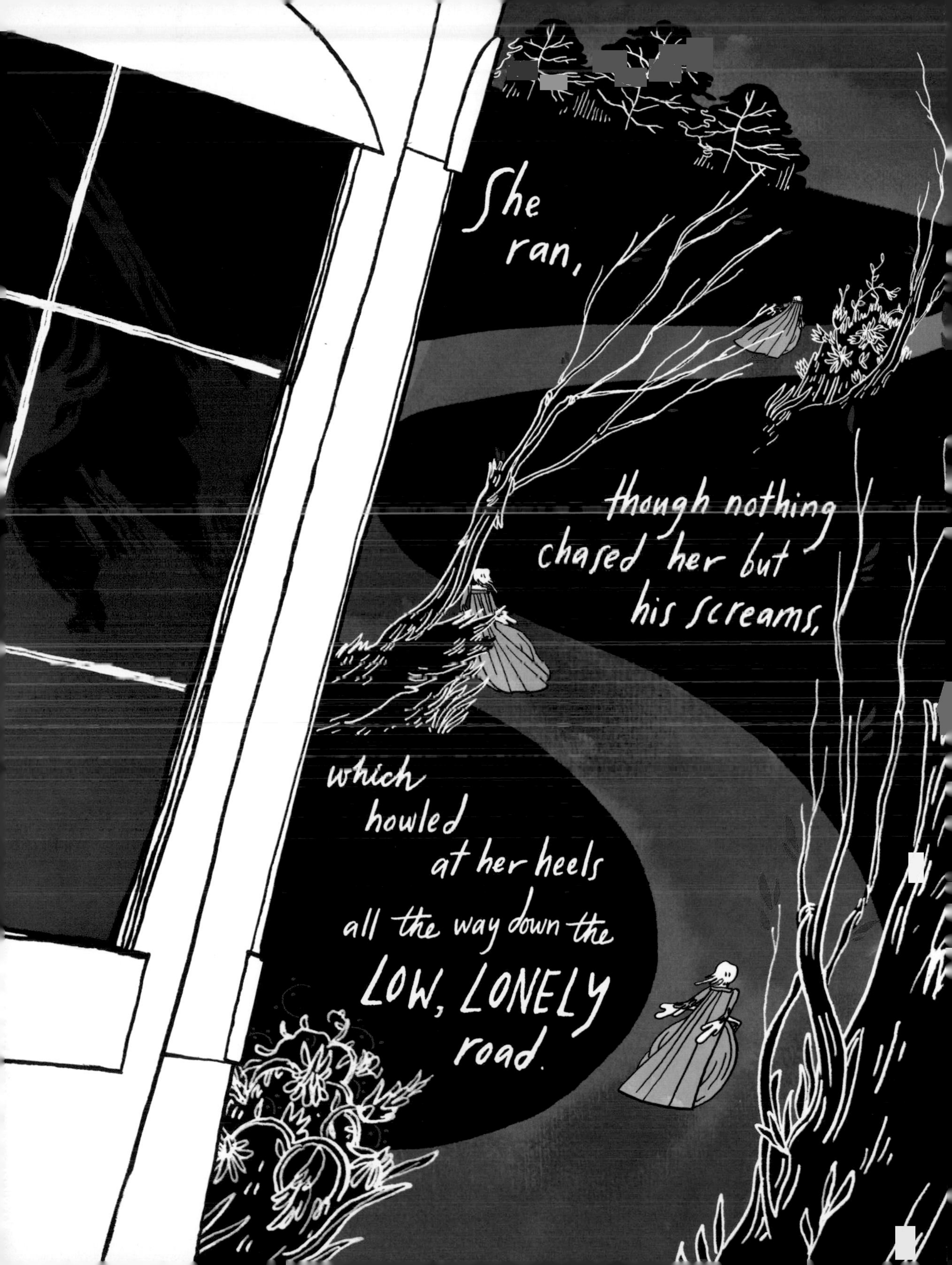
She ran,
though nothing chased her but his screams,
which howled at her heels all the way down the LOW, LONELY road.

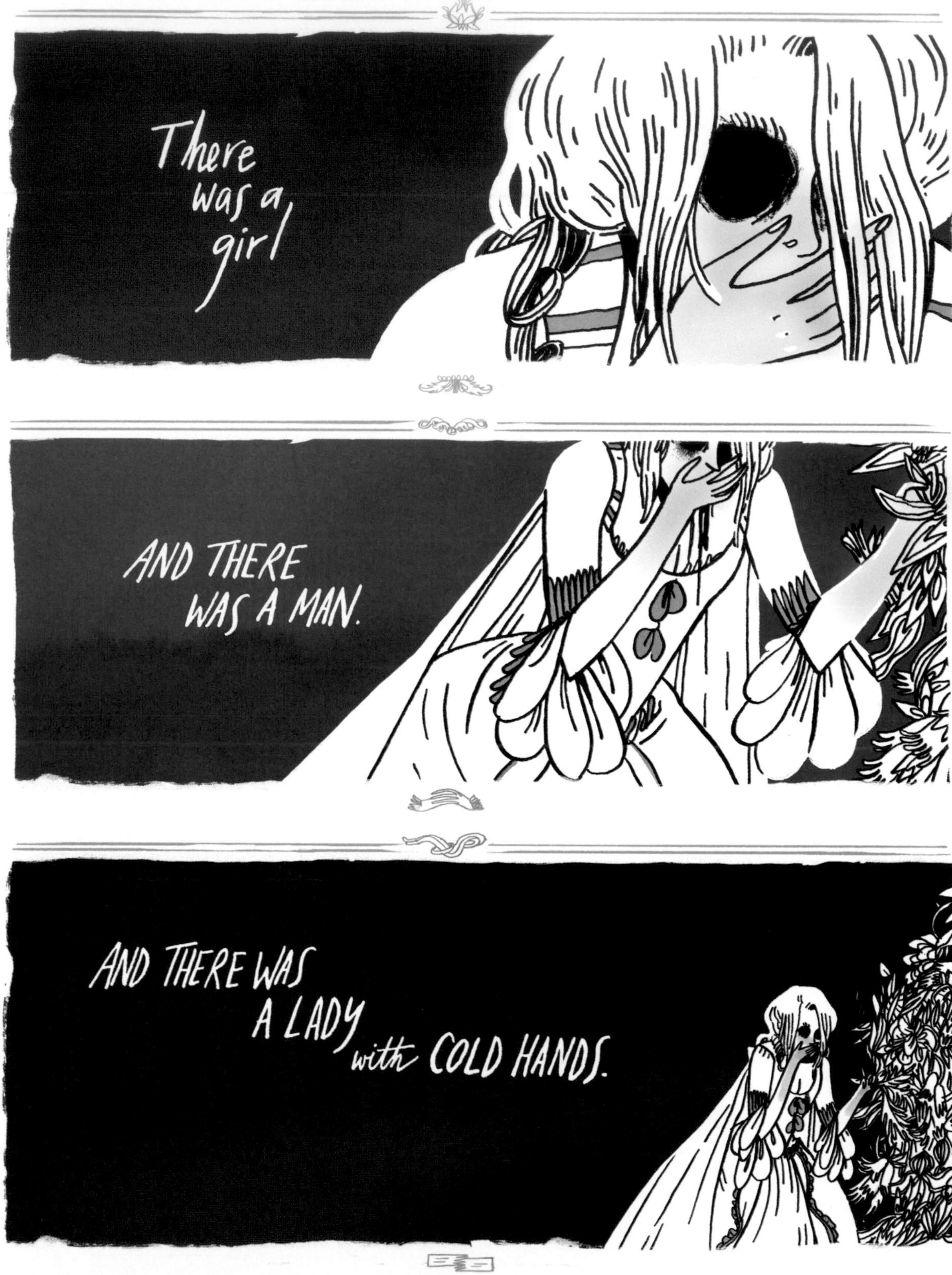
There was a girl
AND THERE WAS A MAN.
AND THERE WAS A LADY with COLD HANDS.

HIS FACE ALL RED

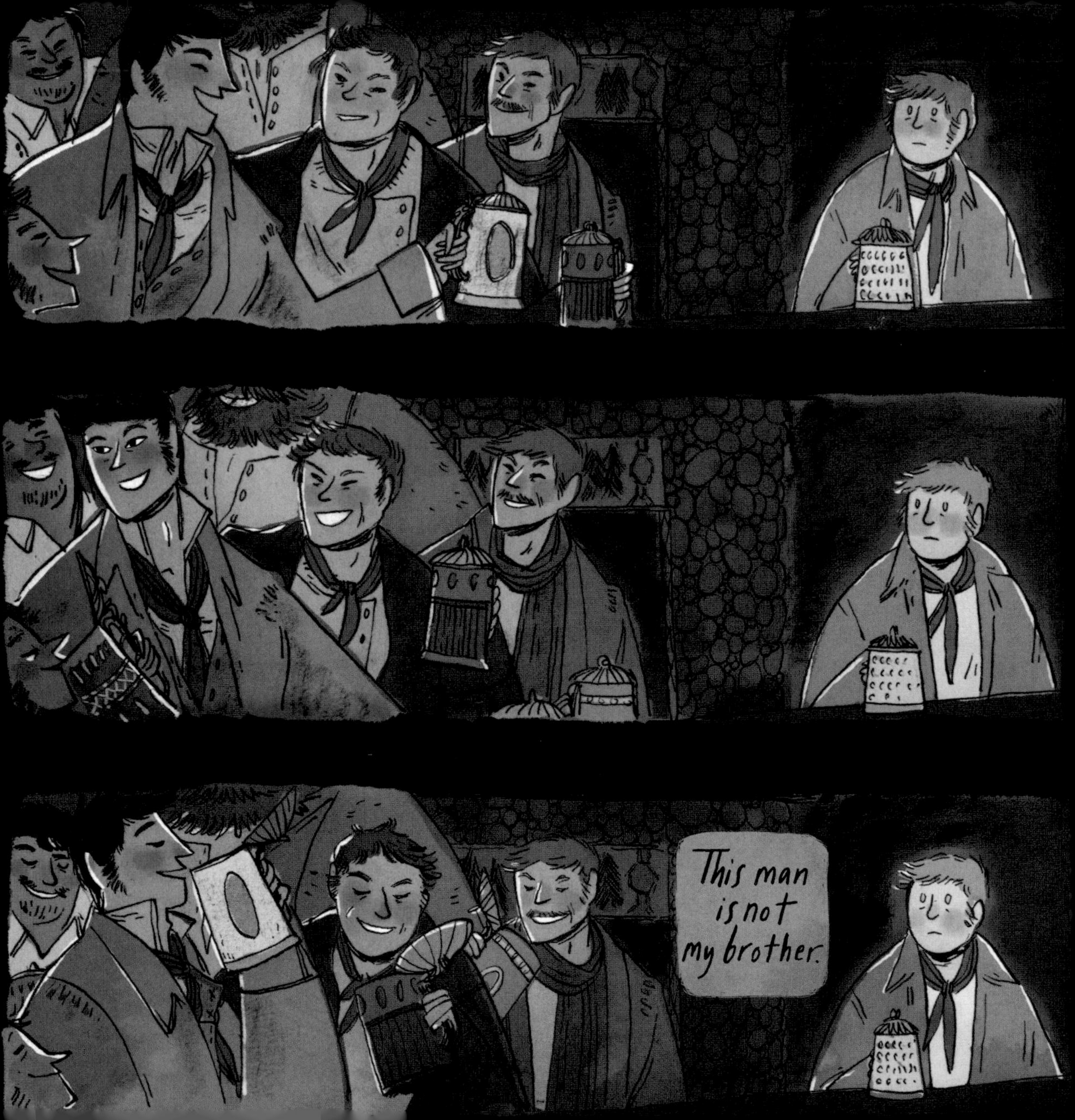
This man is not my brother.

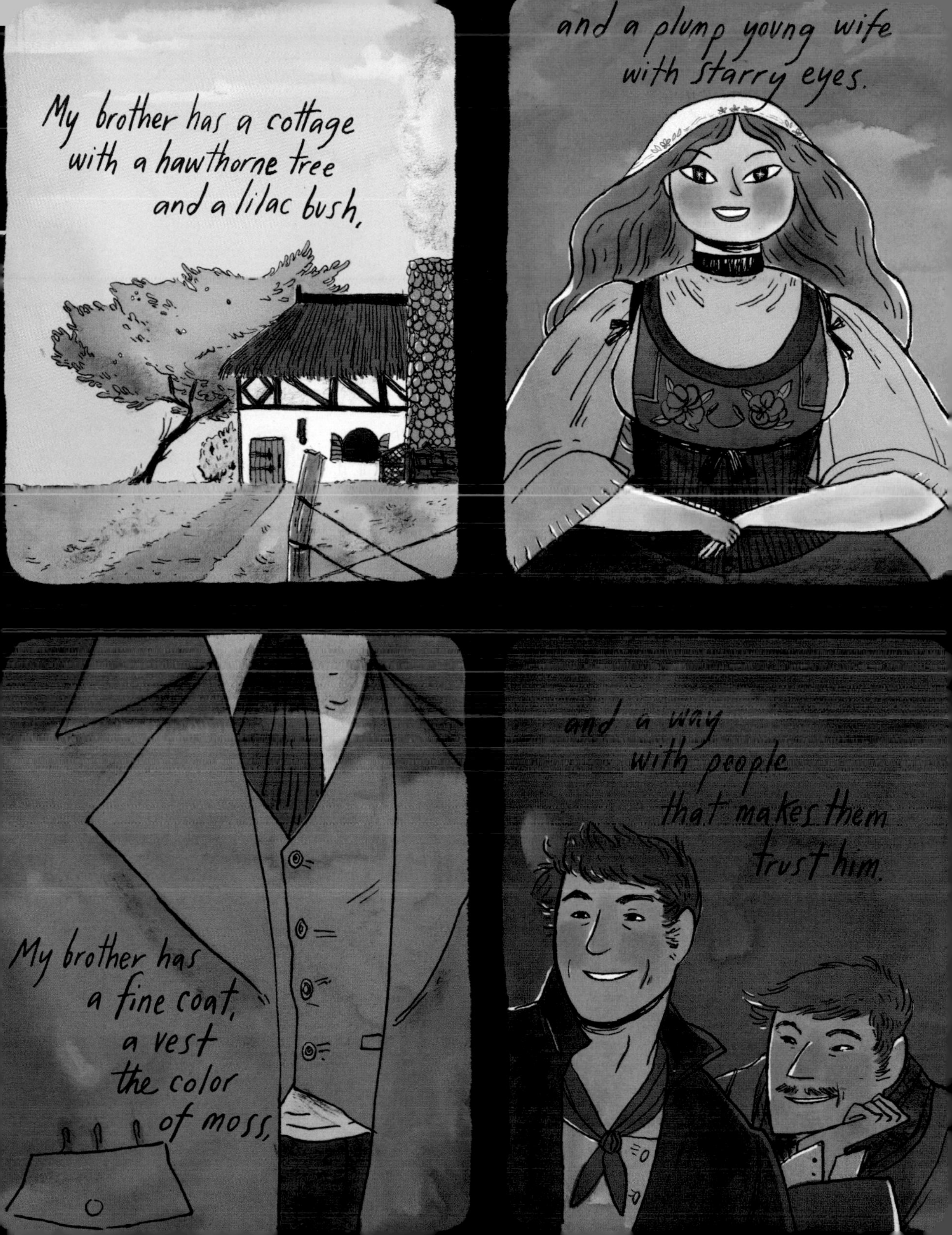
My brother has a cottage with a hawthorne tree and a lilac bush,
and a plump young wife with starry eyes.
My brother has a fine coat, a vest the color of moss,
and a way with people that makes them trust him.

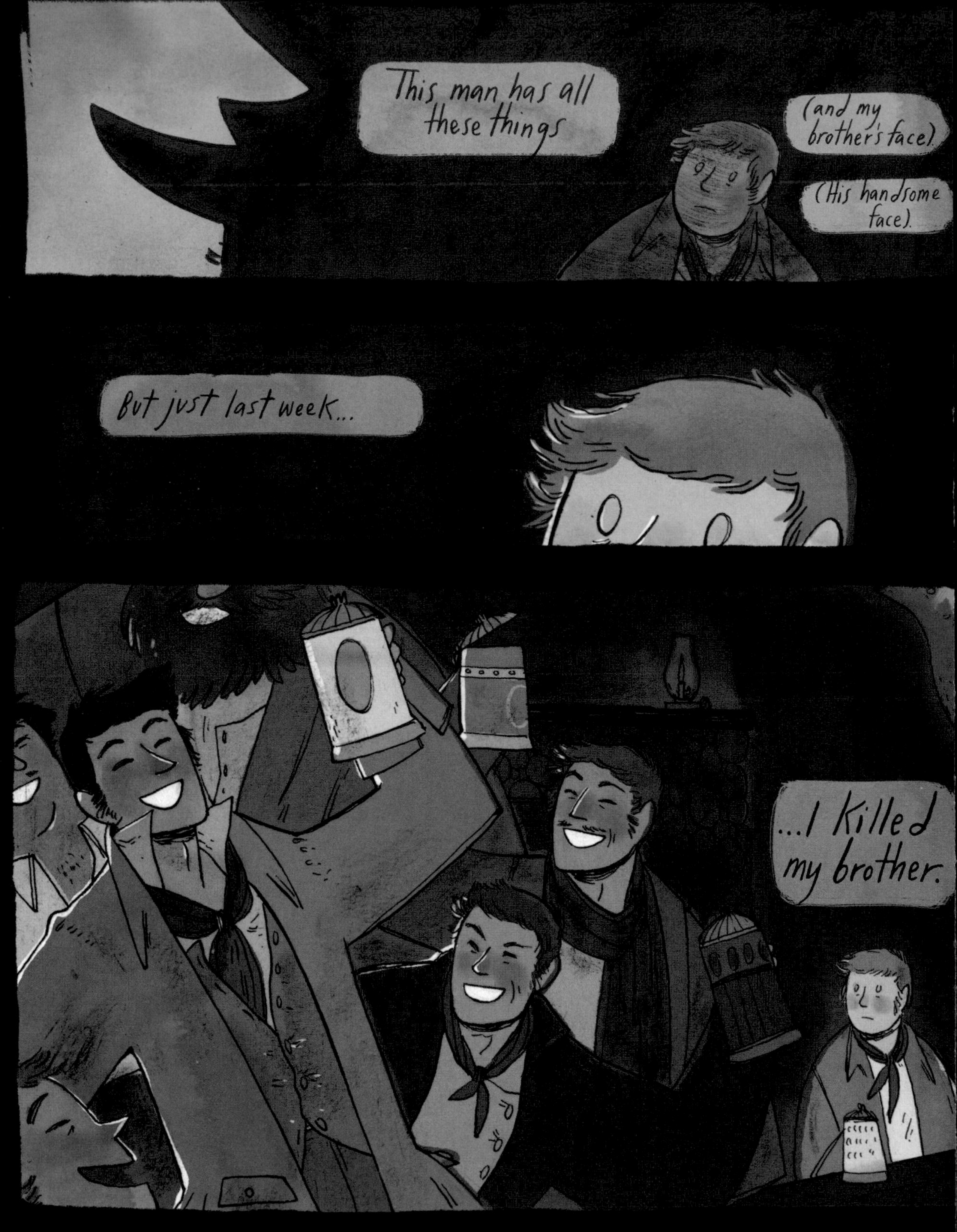
This man has all these things
(and my brother's face).
(His handsome face).
But just last week...
...I killed my brother.

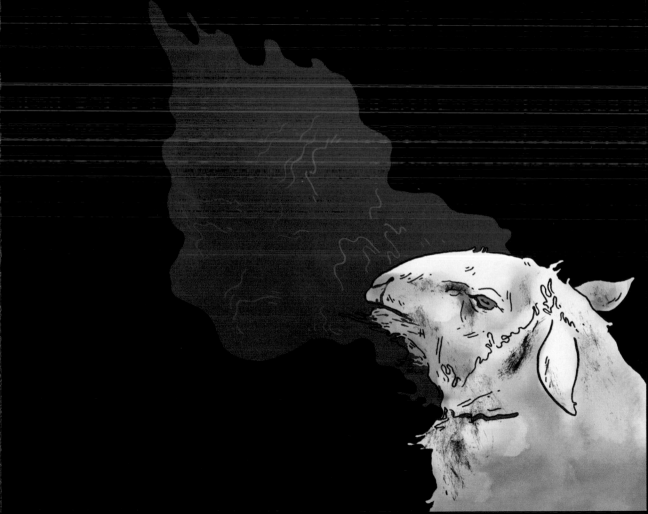

For a month,
our village had been
plagued by an unknown beast.

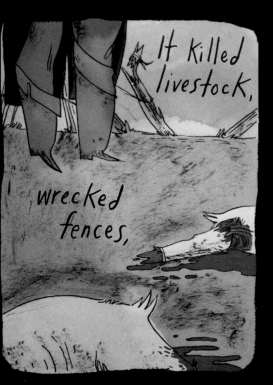

It killed
livestock,

wrecked
fences,

came from
the
woods

(most
strange
things do).

My brother lost three sheep in one night.

(I was safe.)
(I have no animals)

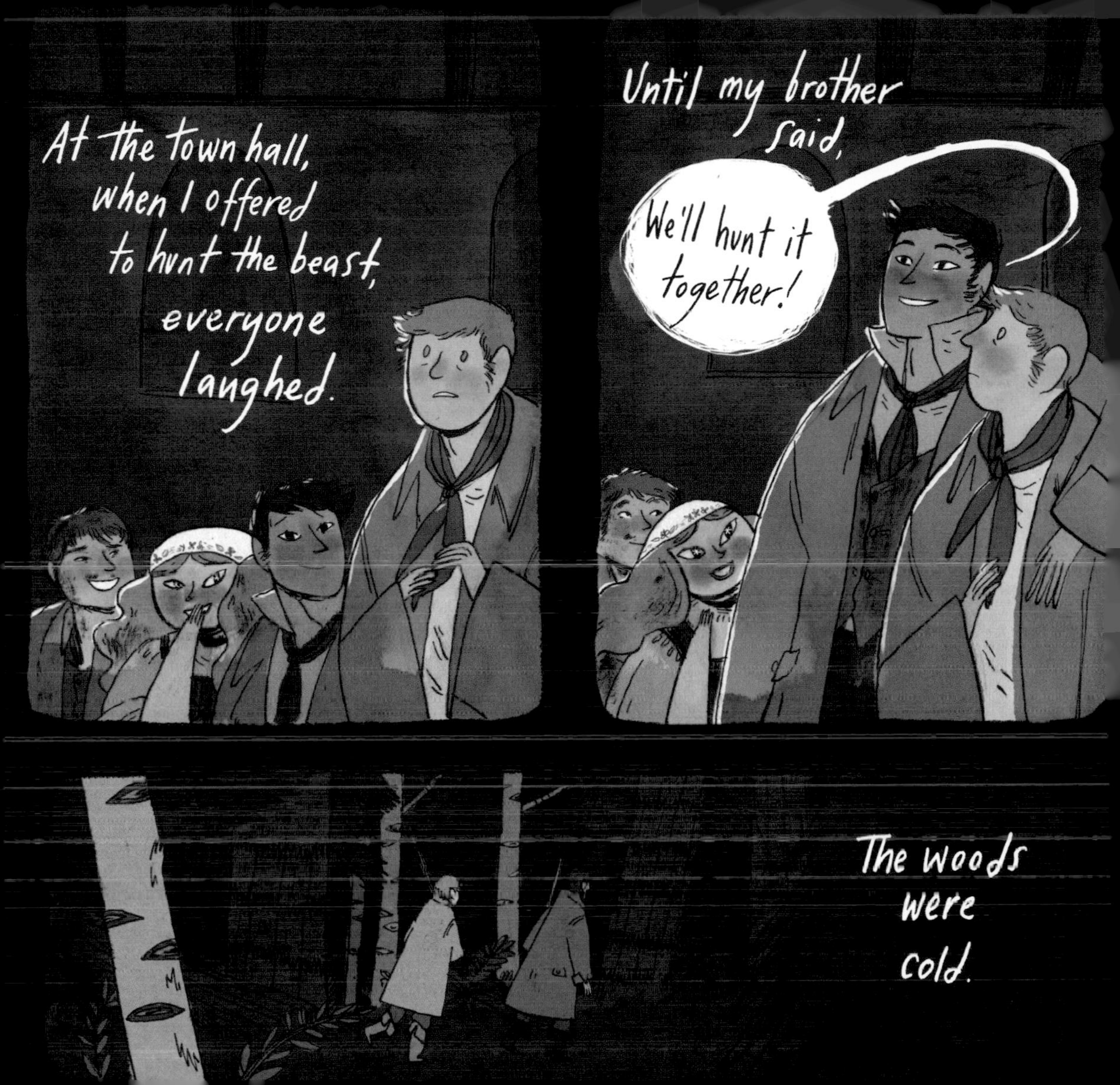
At the town hall, when I offered to hunt the beast, everyone laughed.
Until my brother said,
We'll hunt it together!
The woods were cold.

We passed a [tree] with leaves [that looked] like a lady's hands.

A common oak!

And a stream that sounded like dogs growling.

A babbling brook!

And a hole deep full of black

How curious!

that smelled of lilac.

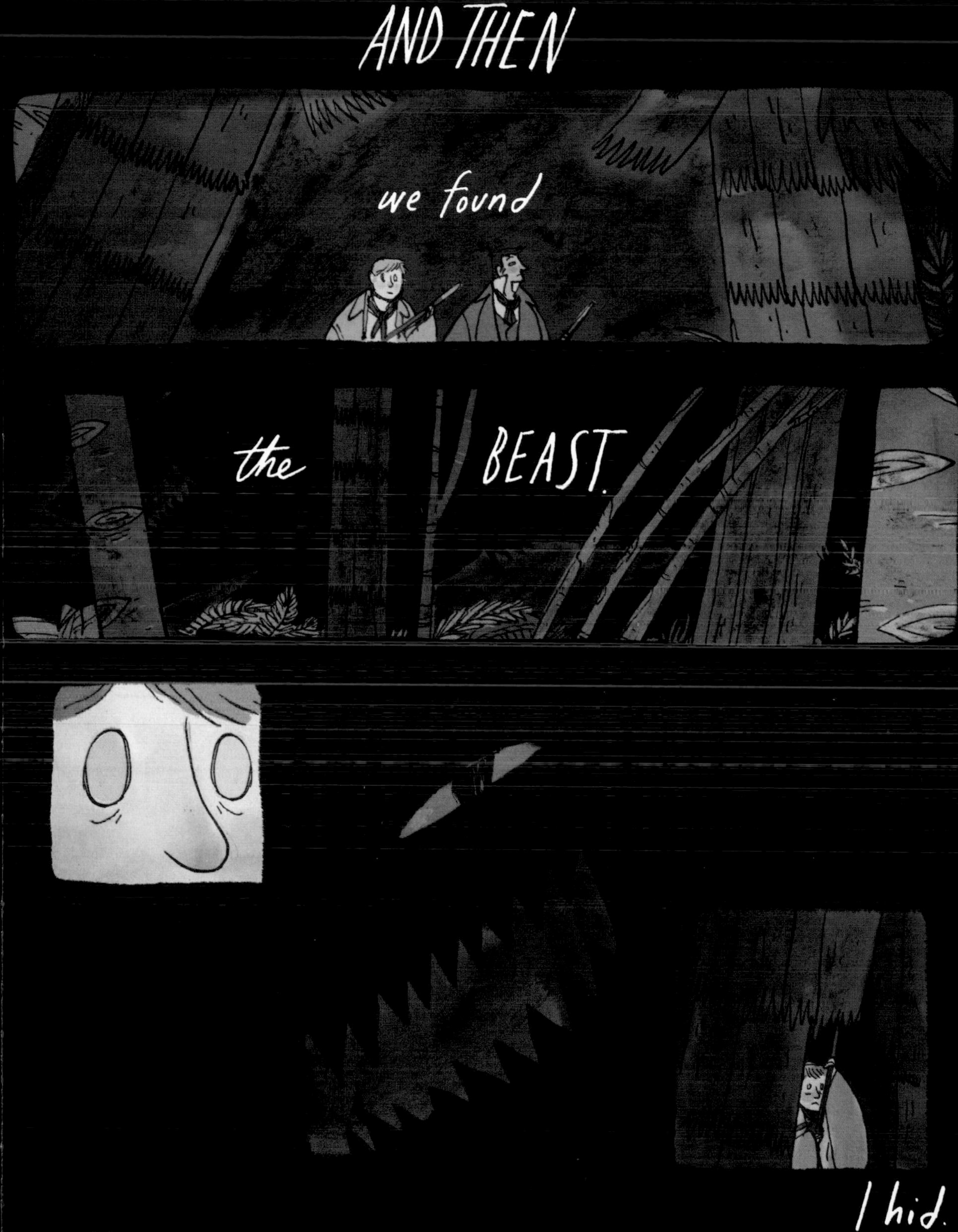
AND THEN
we found
the
BEAST.
I hid.

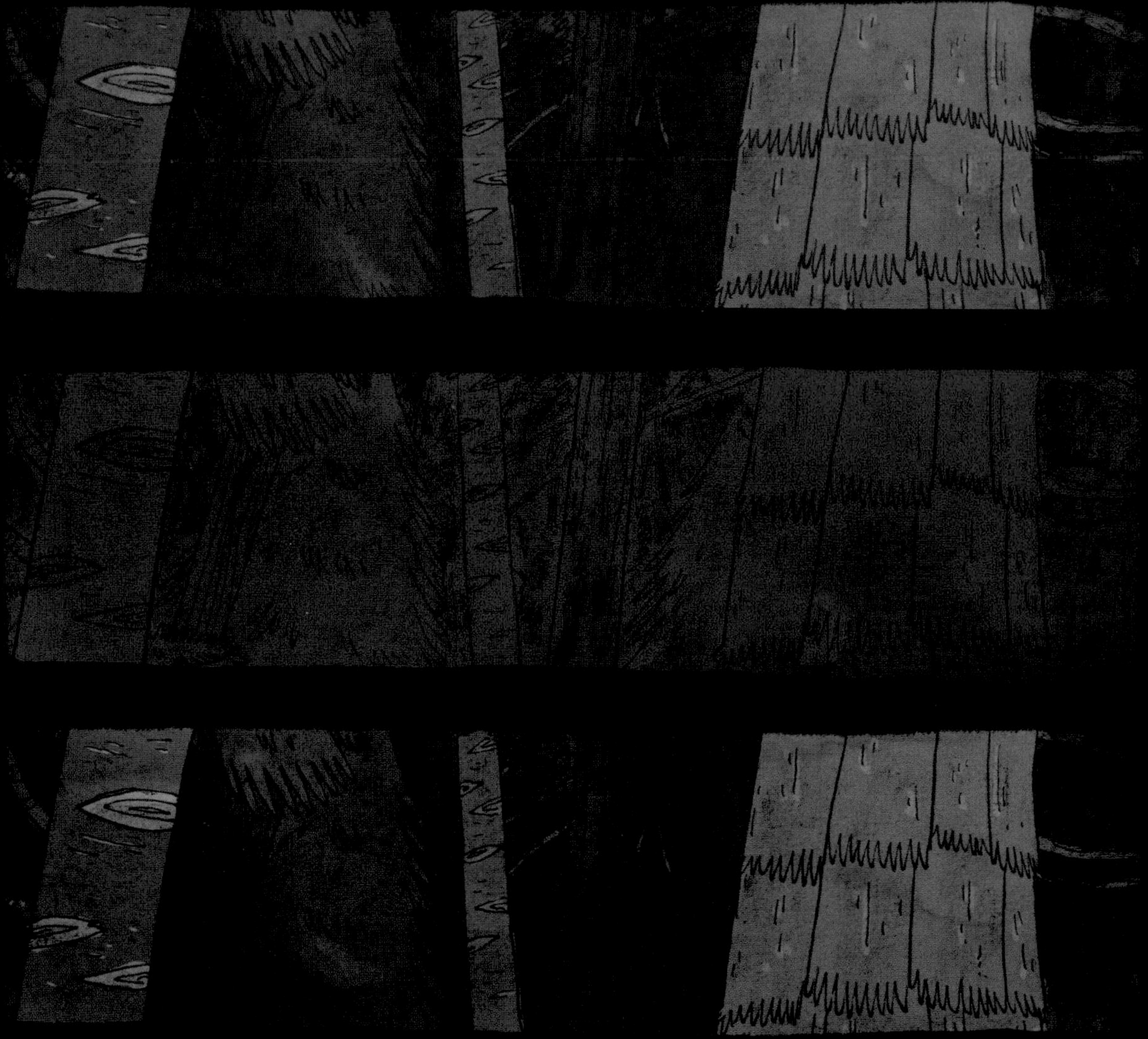

When I crawled from my hiding place
and found my brother...

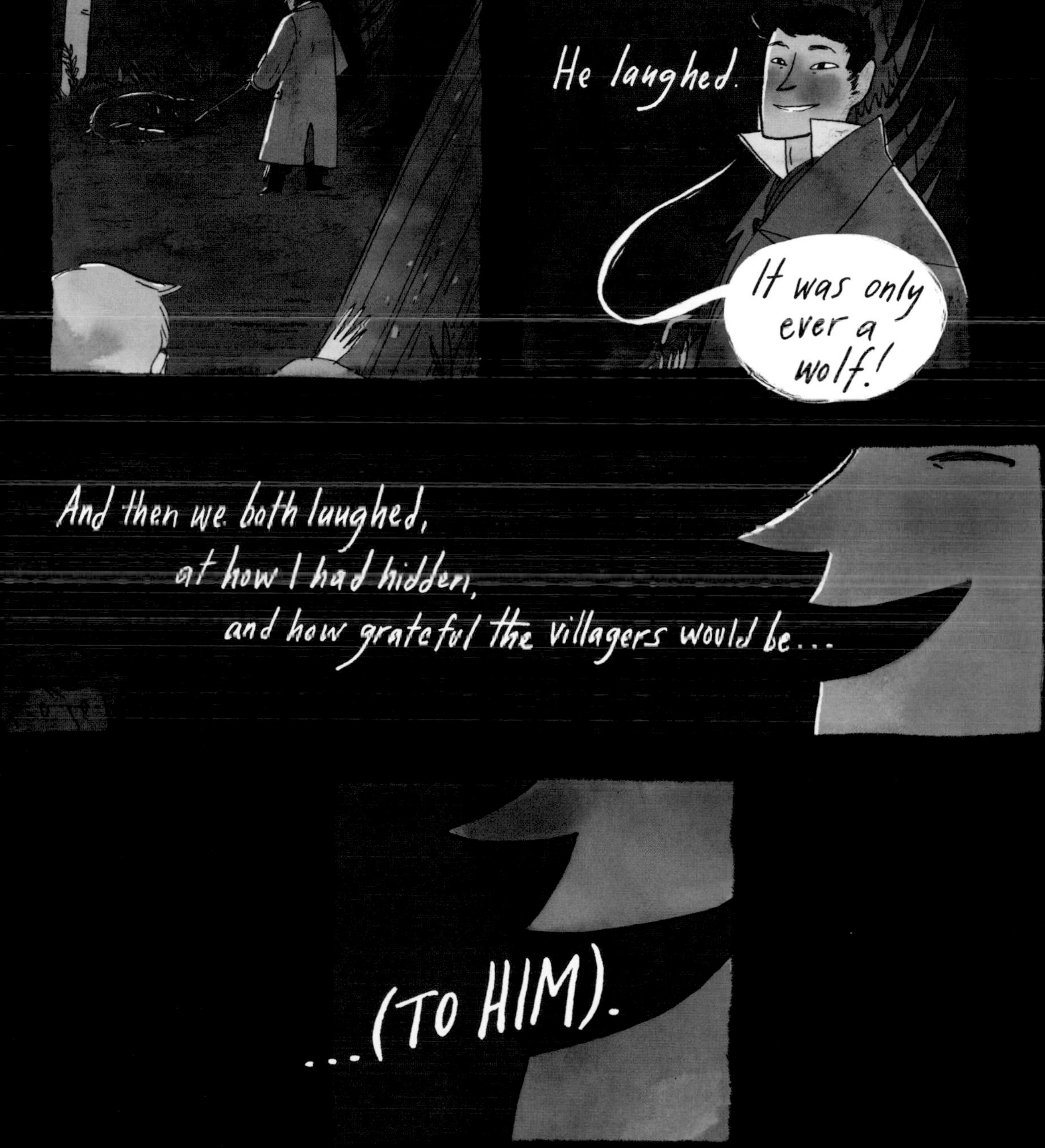
He laughed.
It was only ever a wolf!
And then we both laughed,
at how I had hidden,
and how grateful the villagers would be...
...(TO HIM).

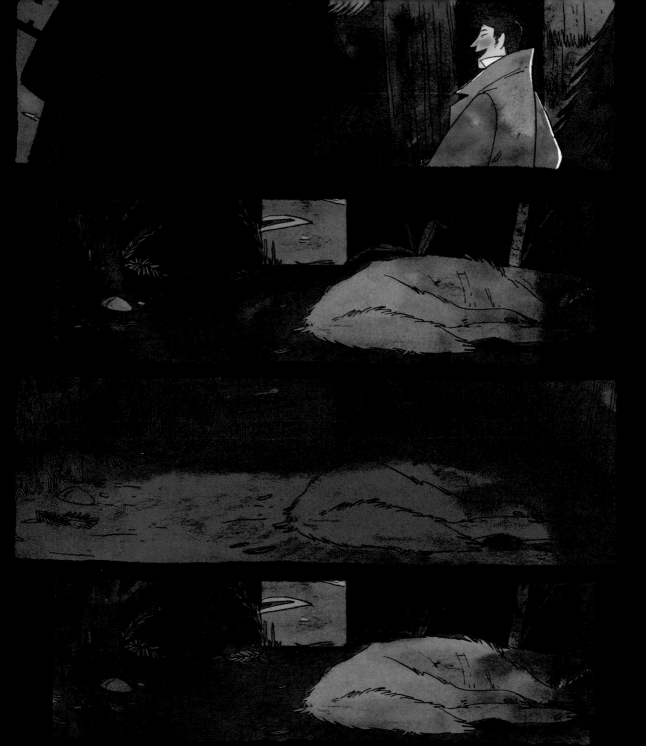

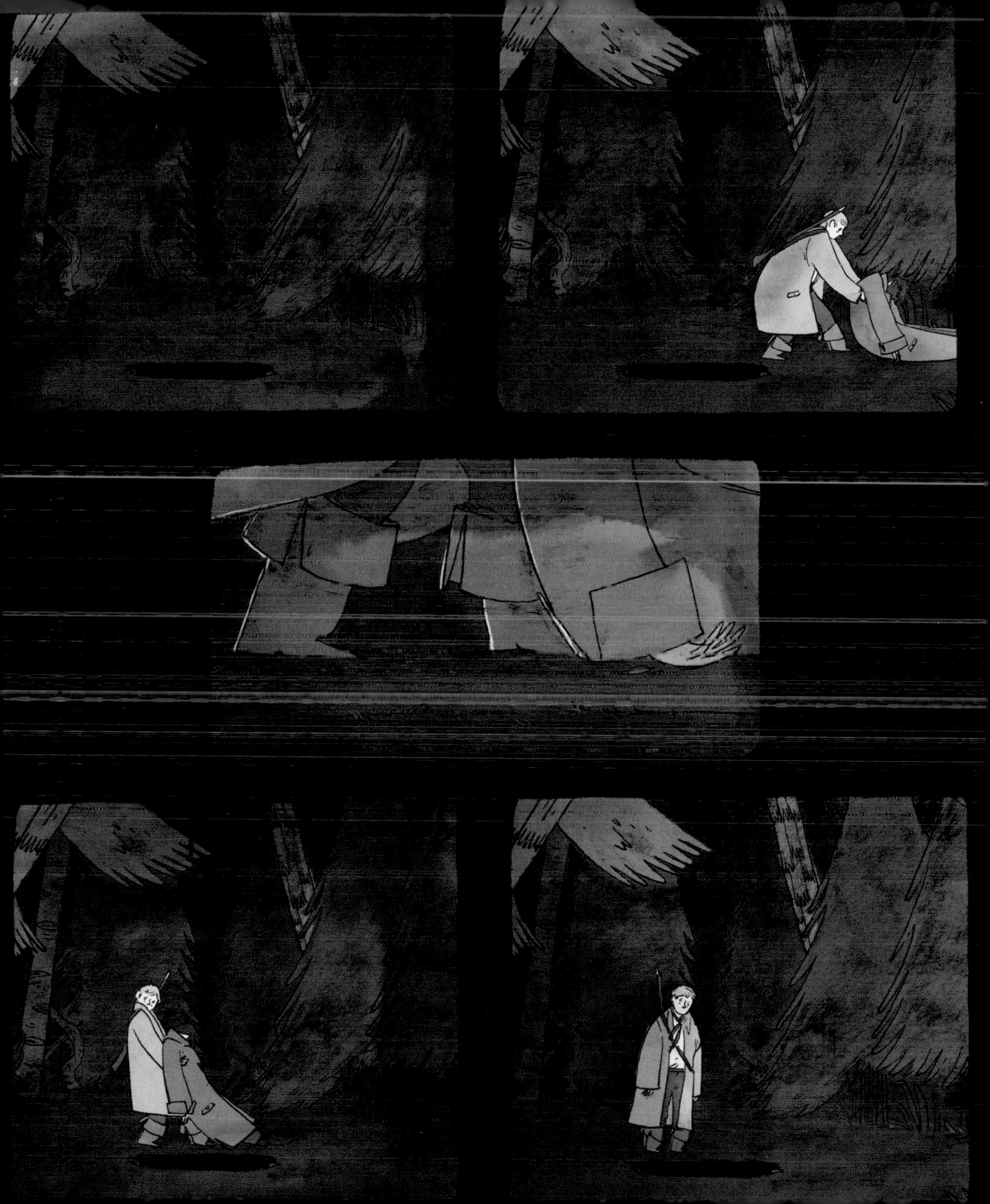

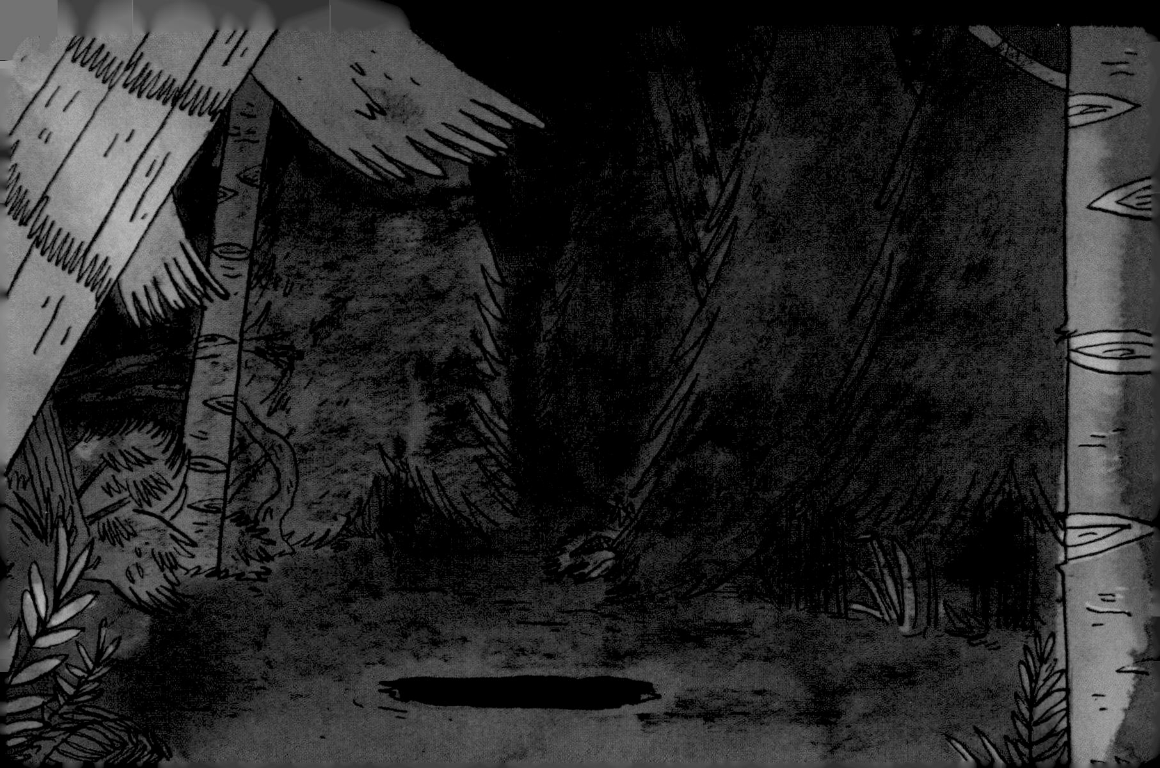

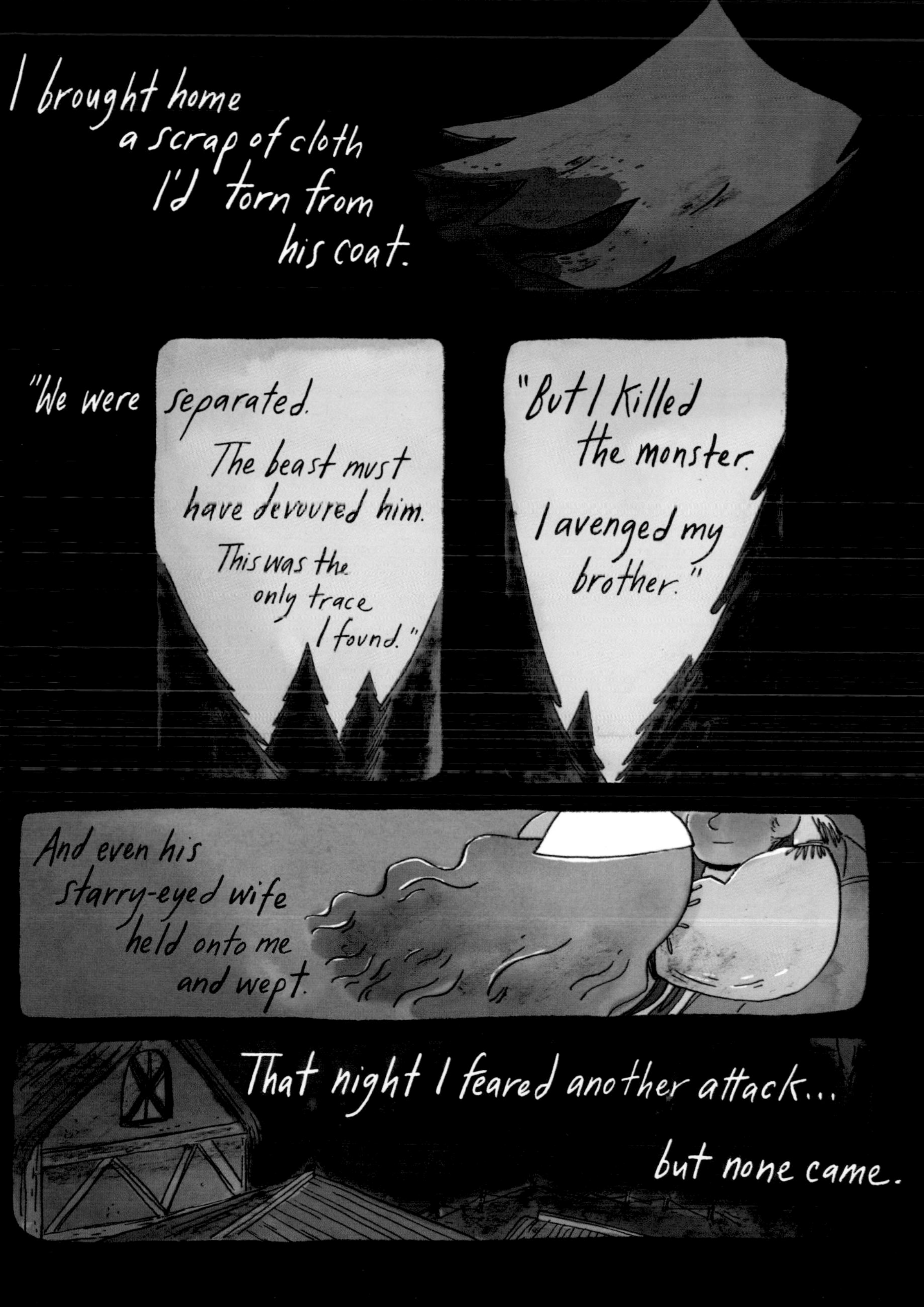
I brought home a scrap of cloth I'd torn from his coat.
"We were separated.
The beast must have devoured him.
This was the only trace I found."
"But I killed the monster.
I avenged my brother."
And even his starry-eyed wife held onto me and wept.
That night I feared another attack...
but none came.

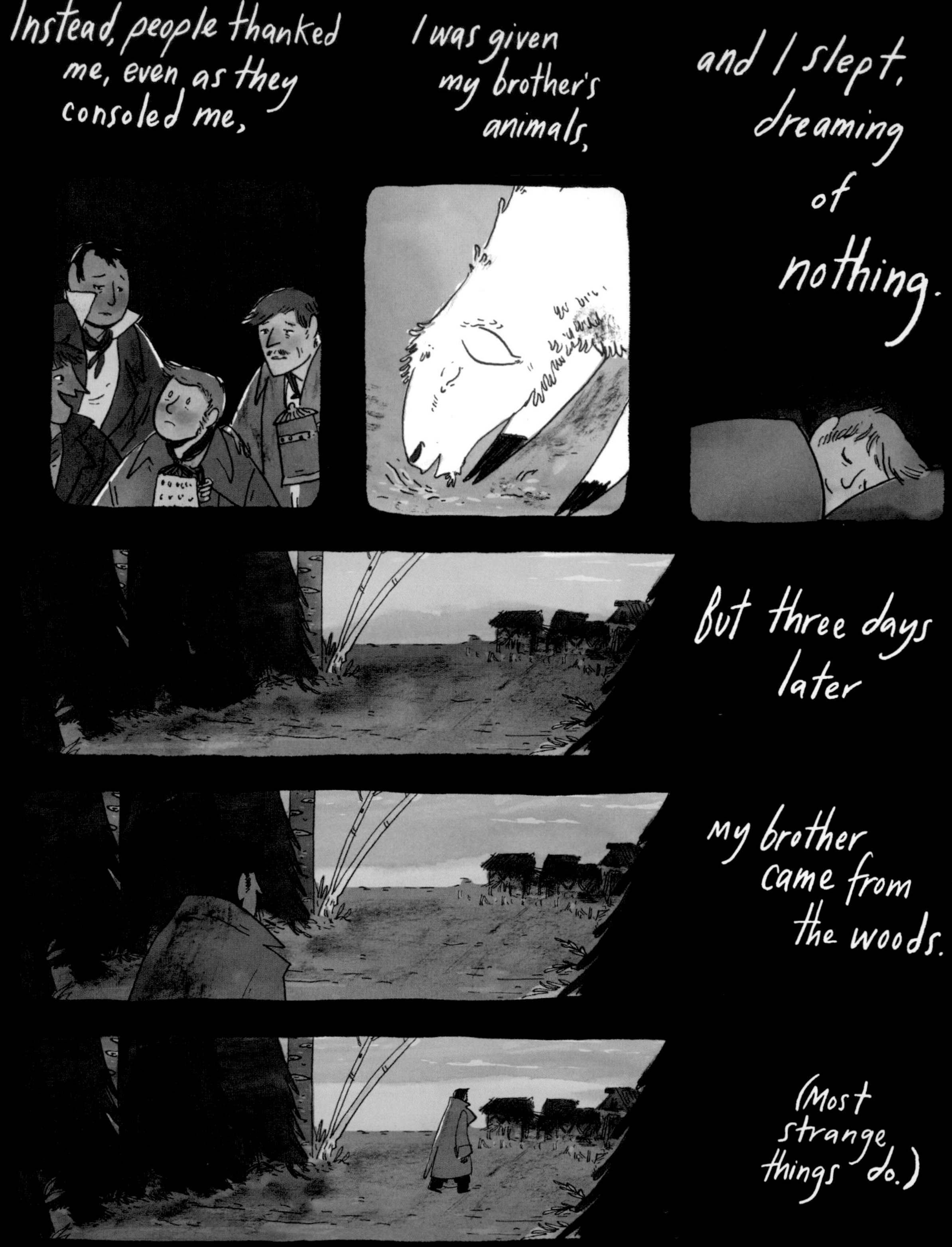

Instead, people thanked me, even as they consoled me,
I was given my brother's animals,
and I slept, dreaming of nothing.
But three days later
my brother came from the woods.
(Most strange things do.)

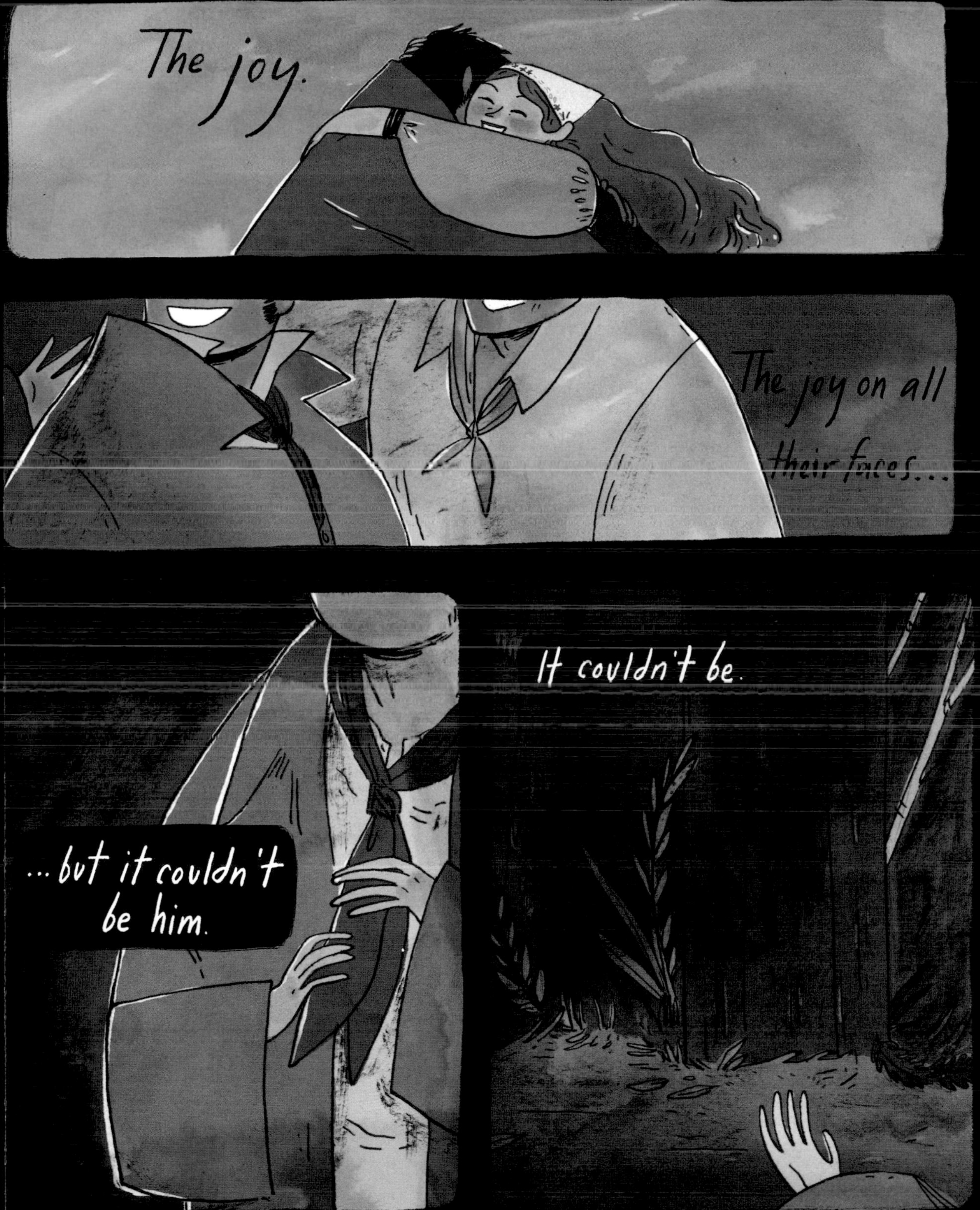
The joy.
The joy on all their faces...
It couldn't be.
...but it couldn't be him.

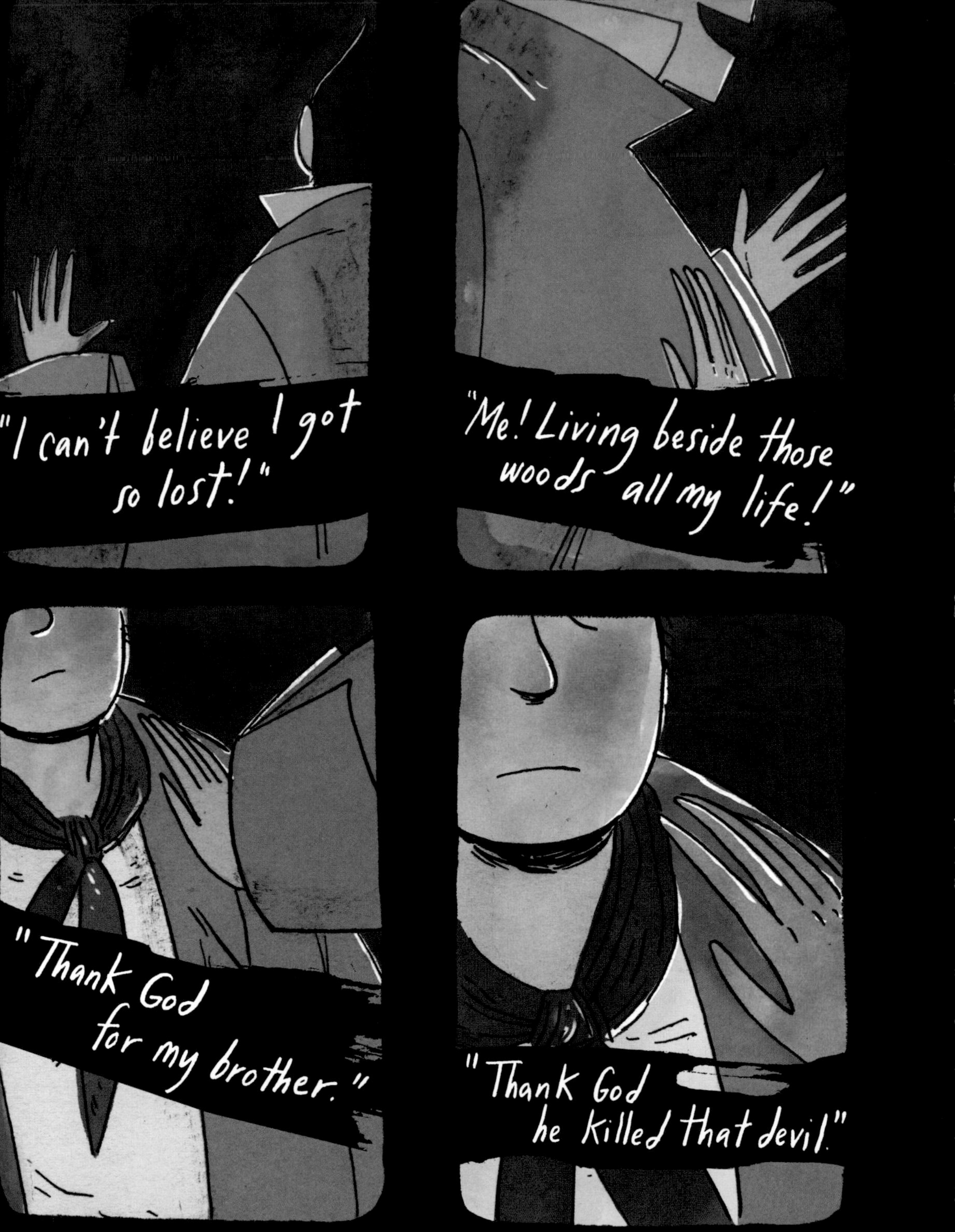
"I can't believe I got so lost!"
"Me! Living beside those woods all my life!"
"Thank God for my brother."
"Thank God he killed that devil."

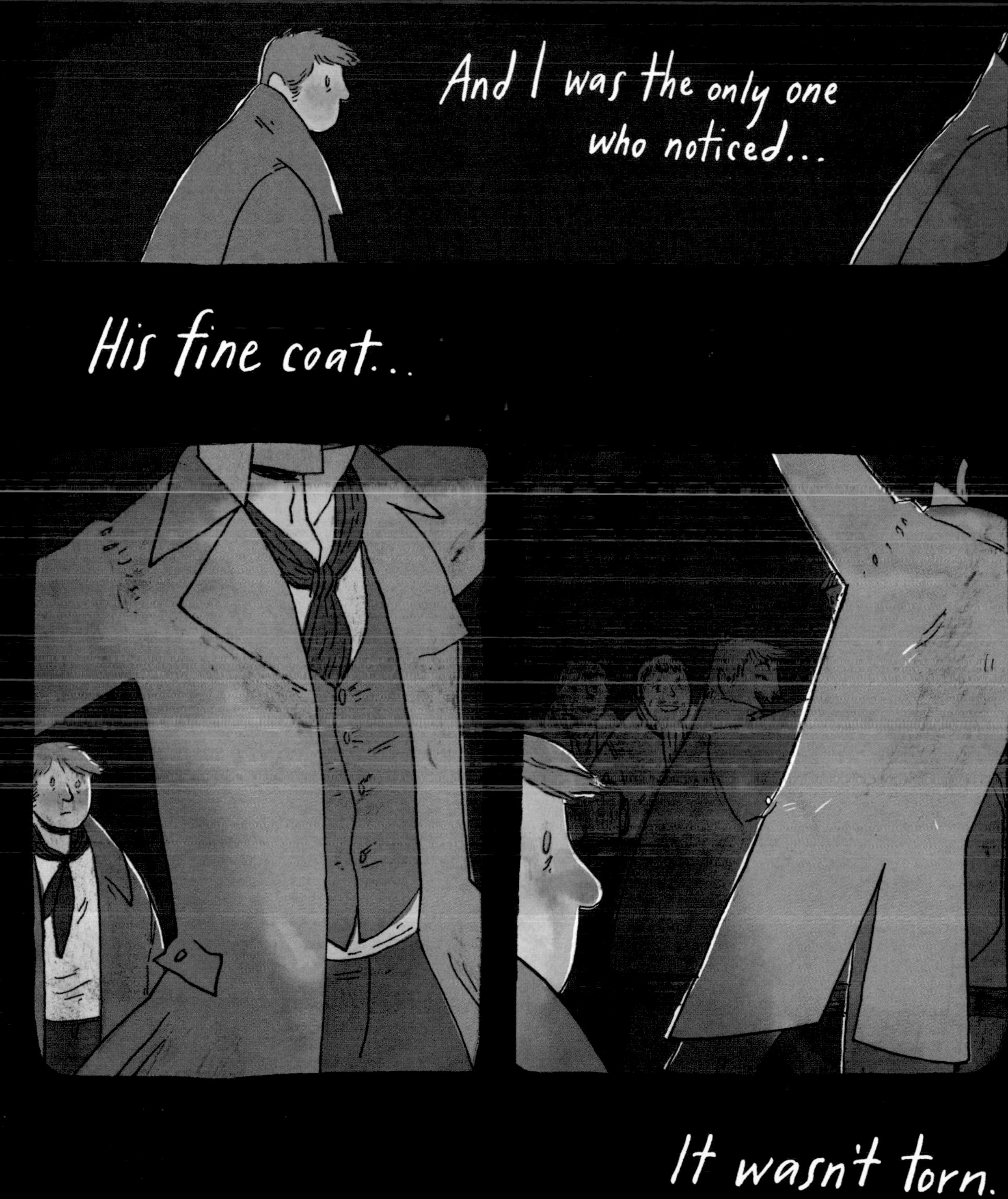
And I was the only one
who noticed...
His fine coat...
It wasn't torn.

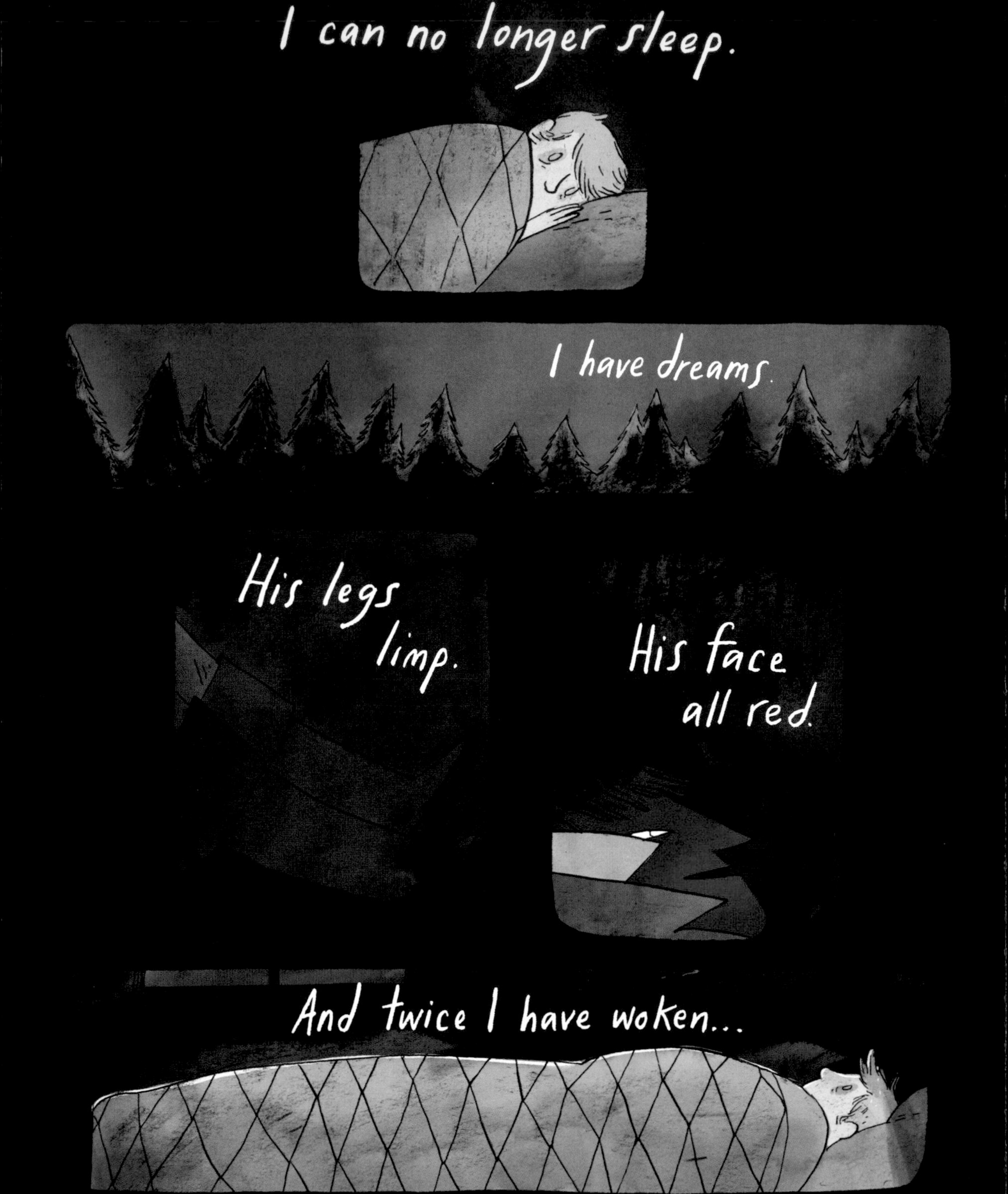
I can no longer sleep.
I have dreams.
His legs limp.
His face all red.
And twice I have woken...

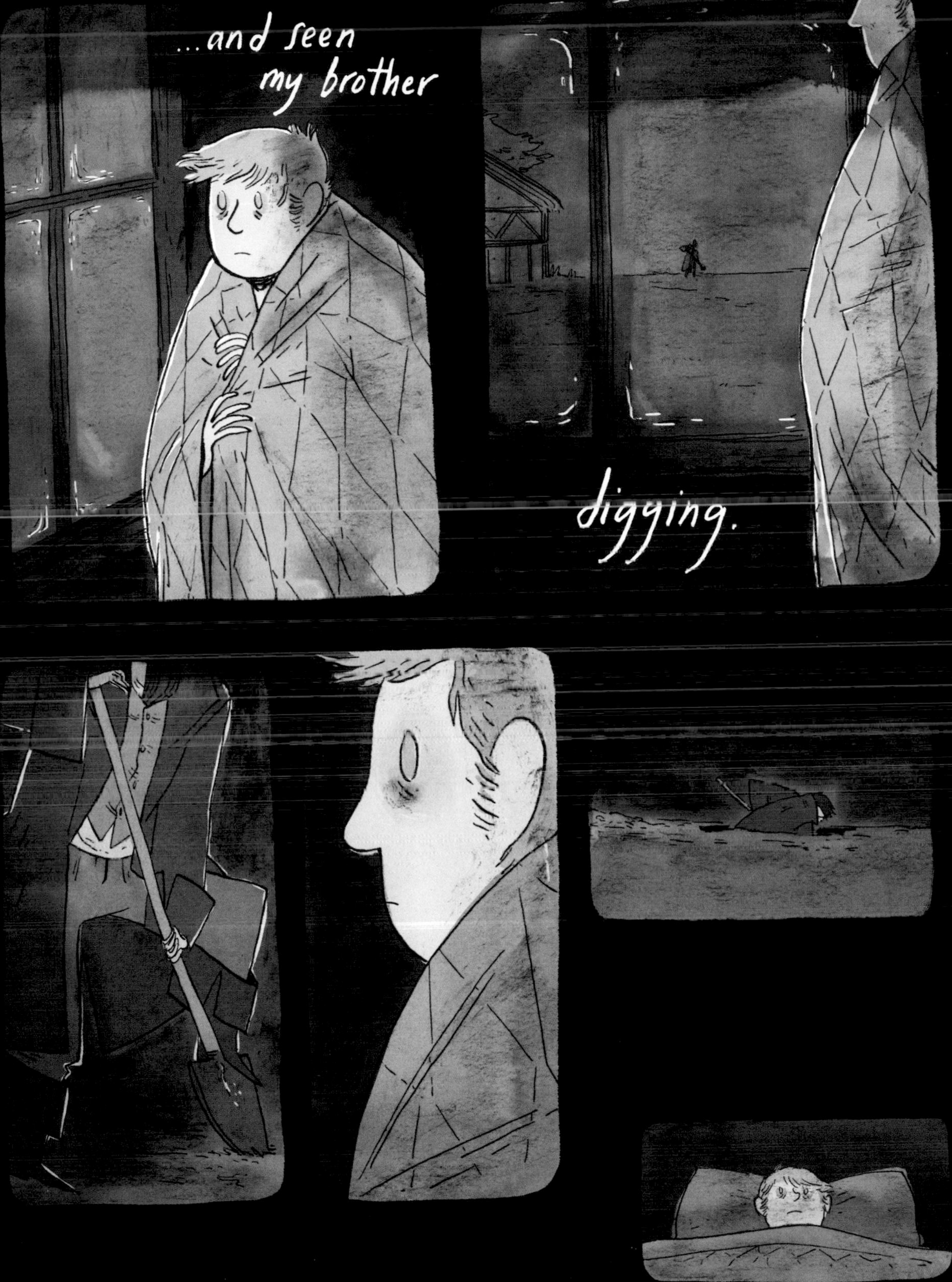
...and seen my brother
digging.

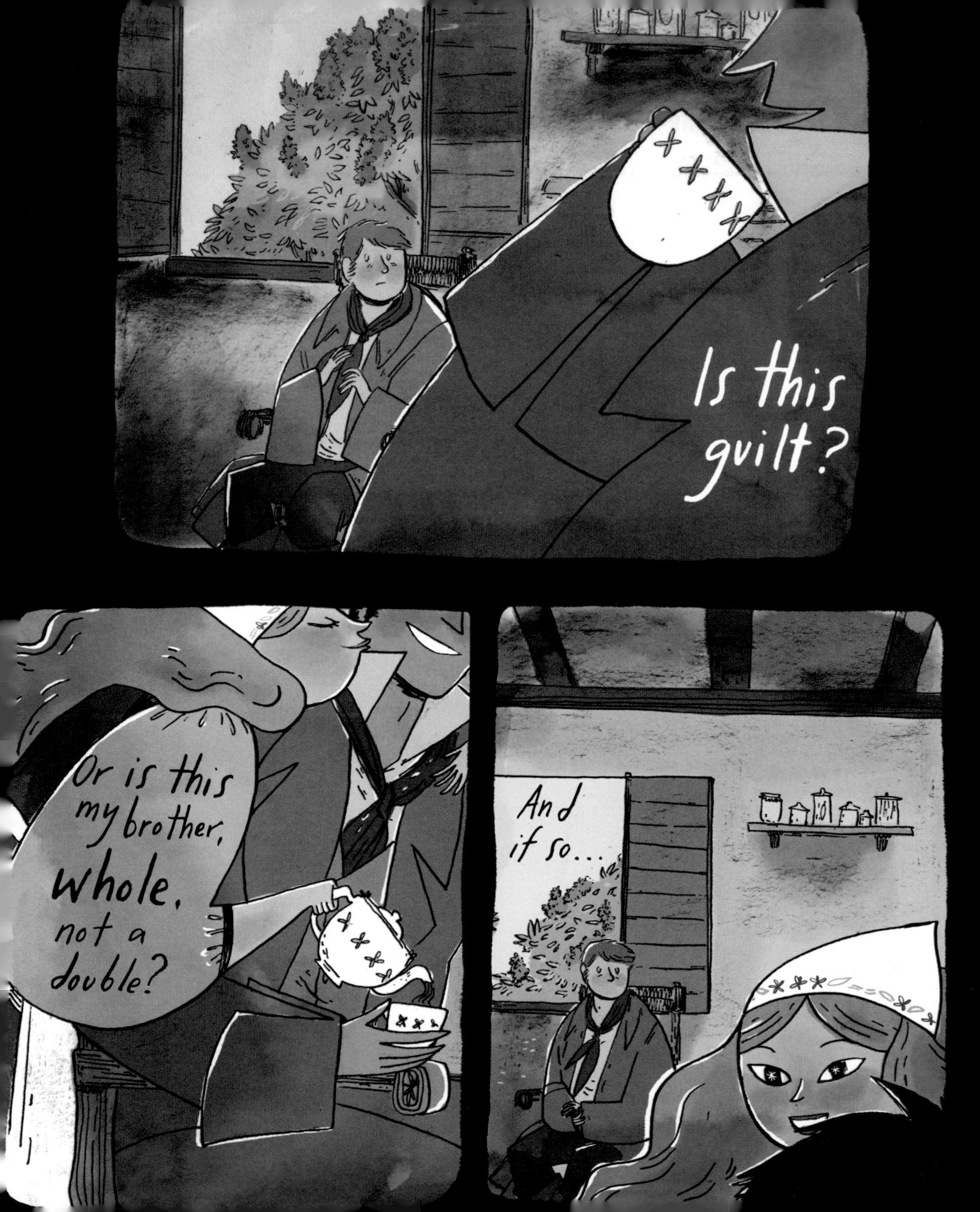
Is this guilt?
Or is this my brother, whole, not a double?
And if so...

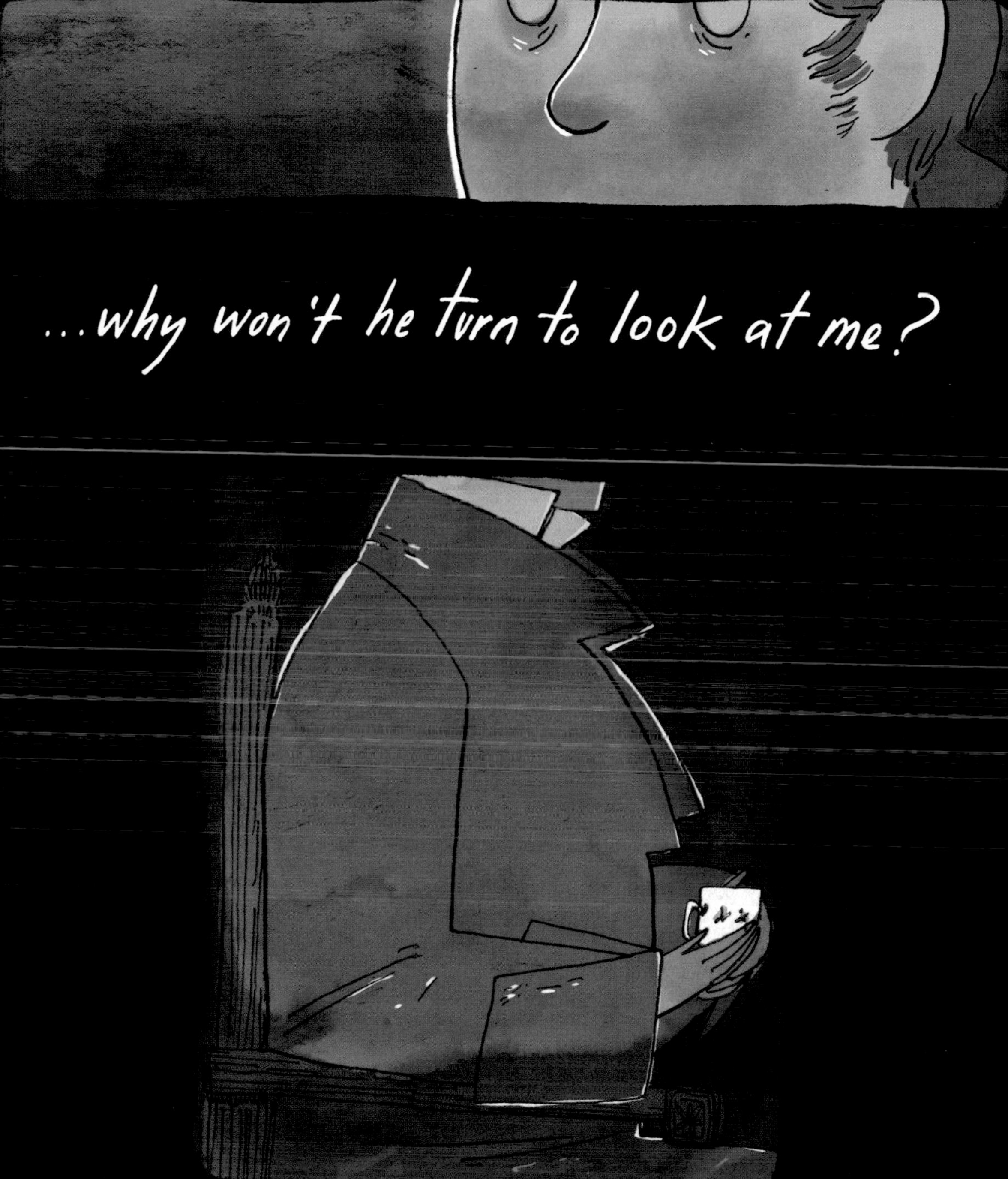
...why won't he turn to look at me?

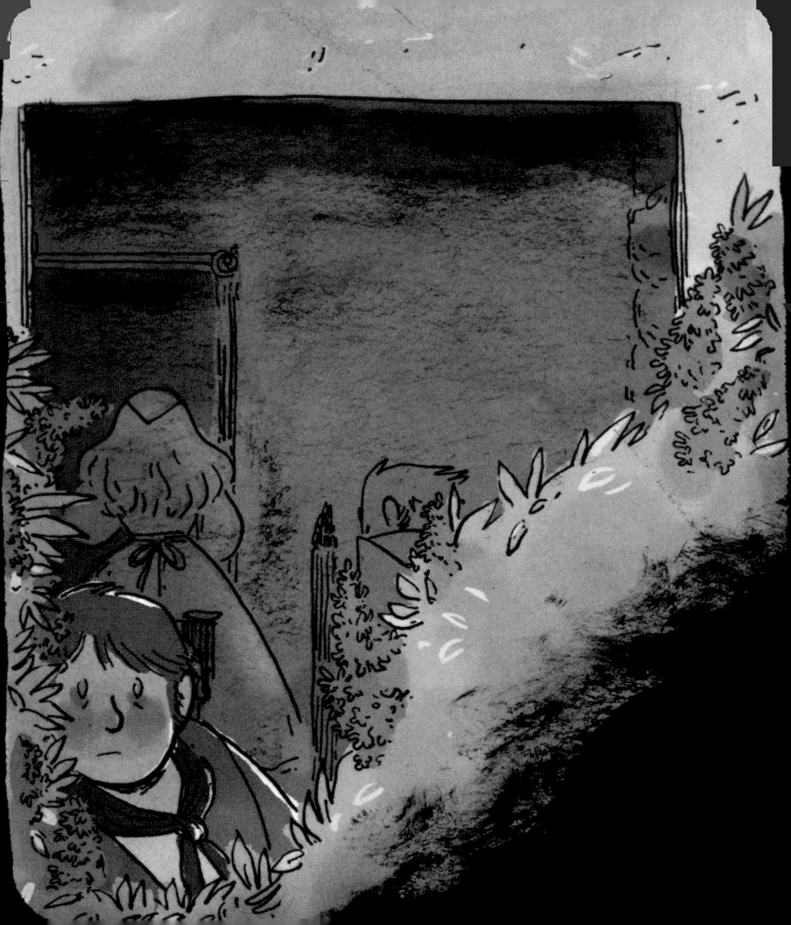

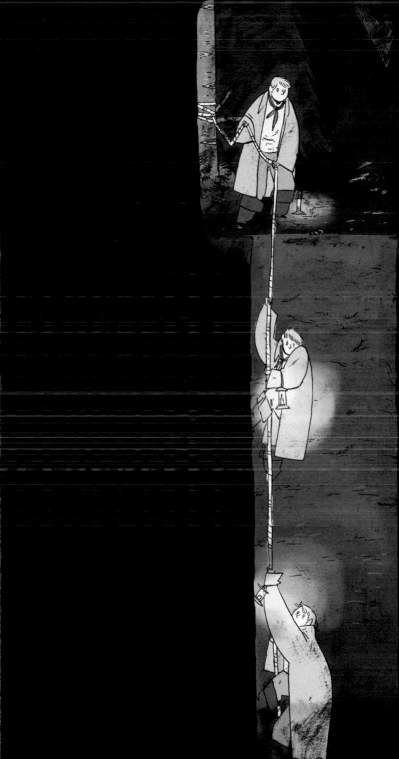

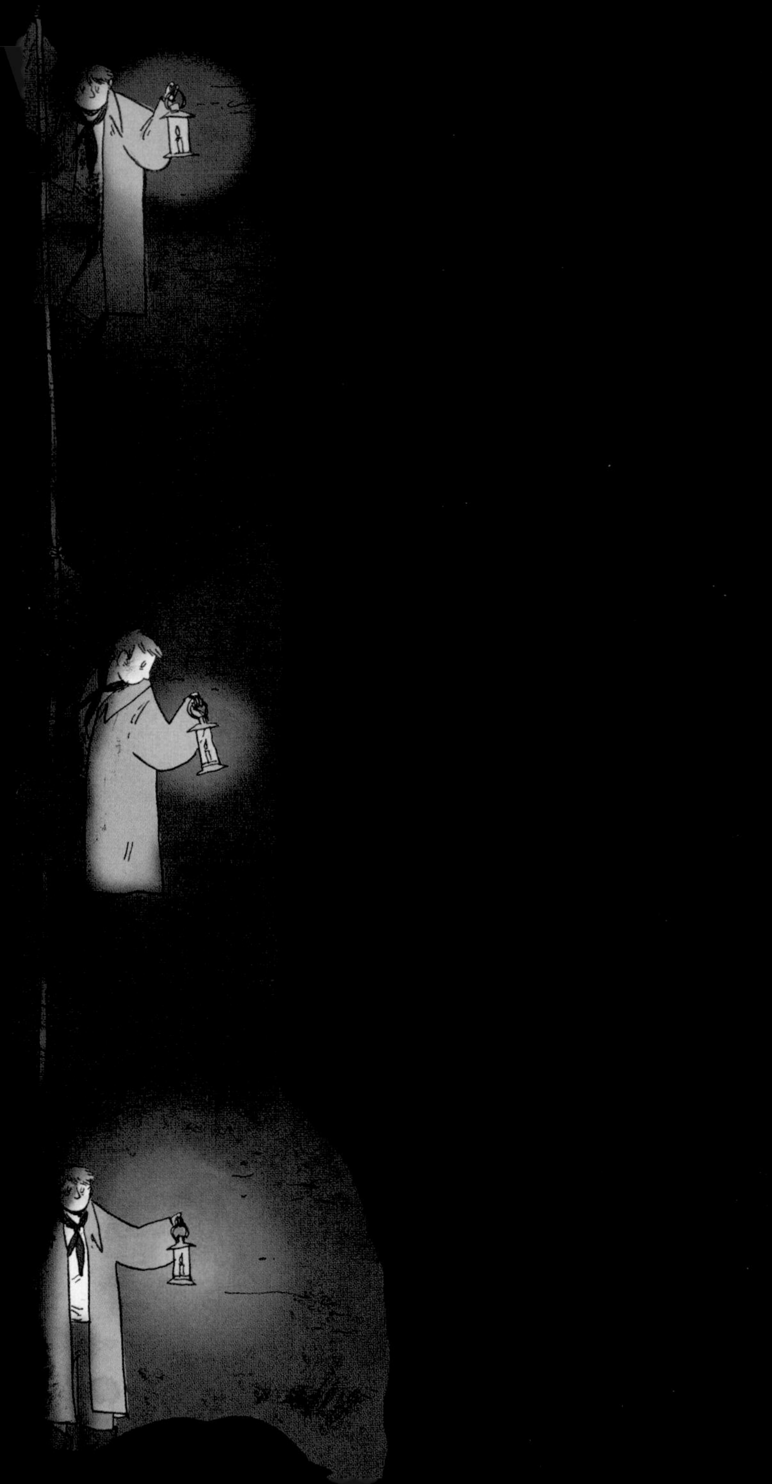

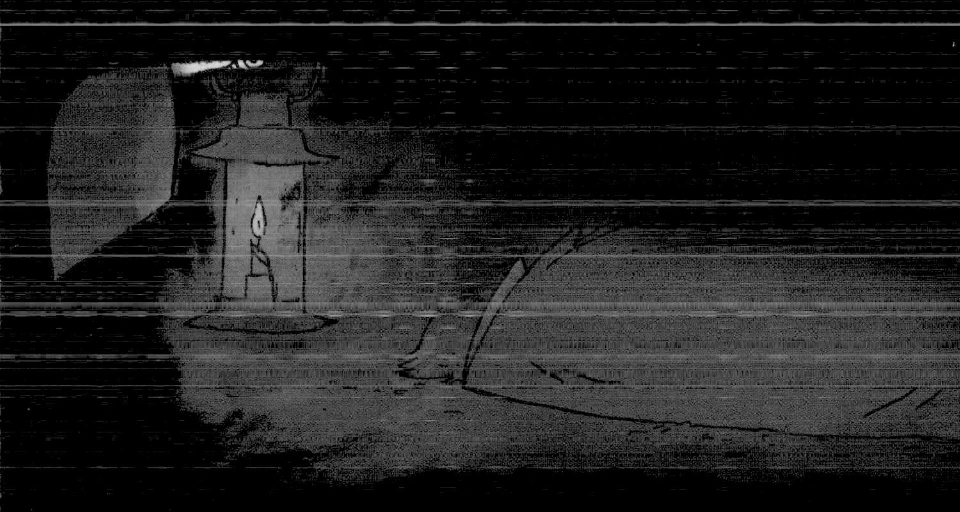

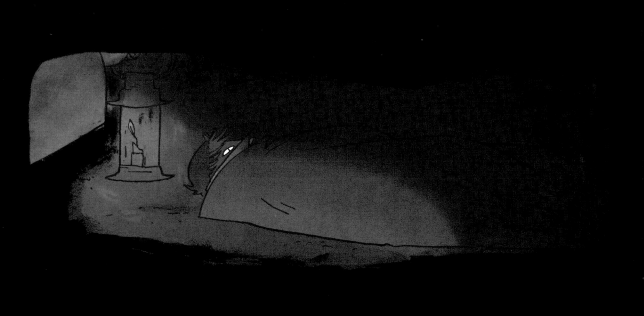

MY FRIEND JANNA

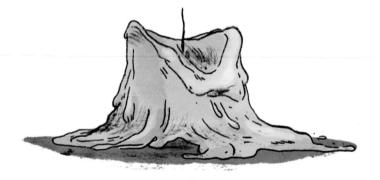

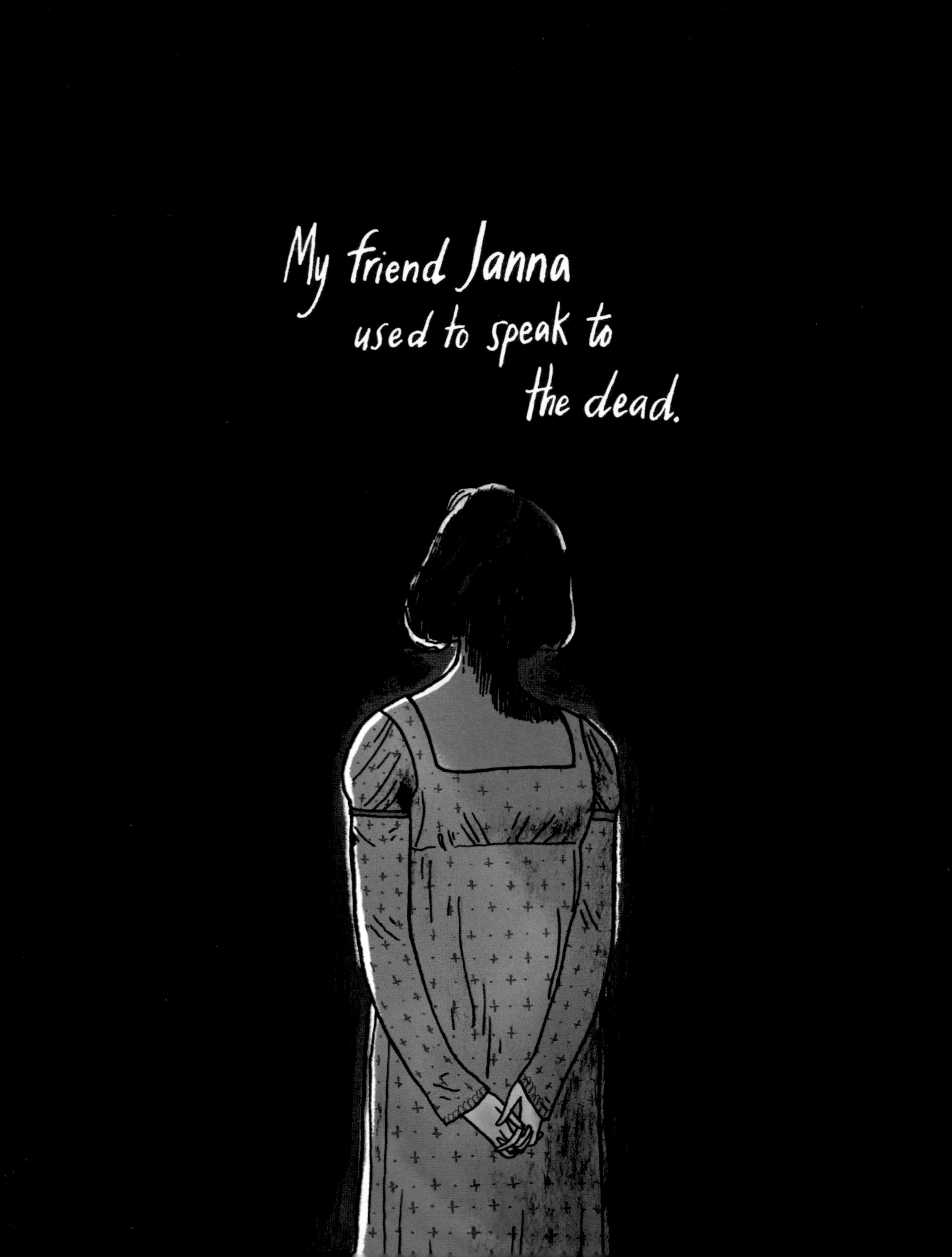
My friend Janna
used to speak to
the dead.

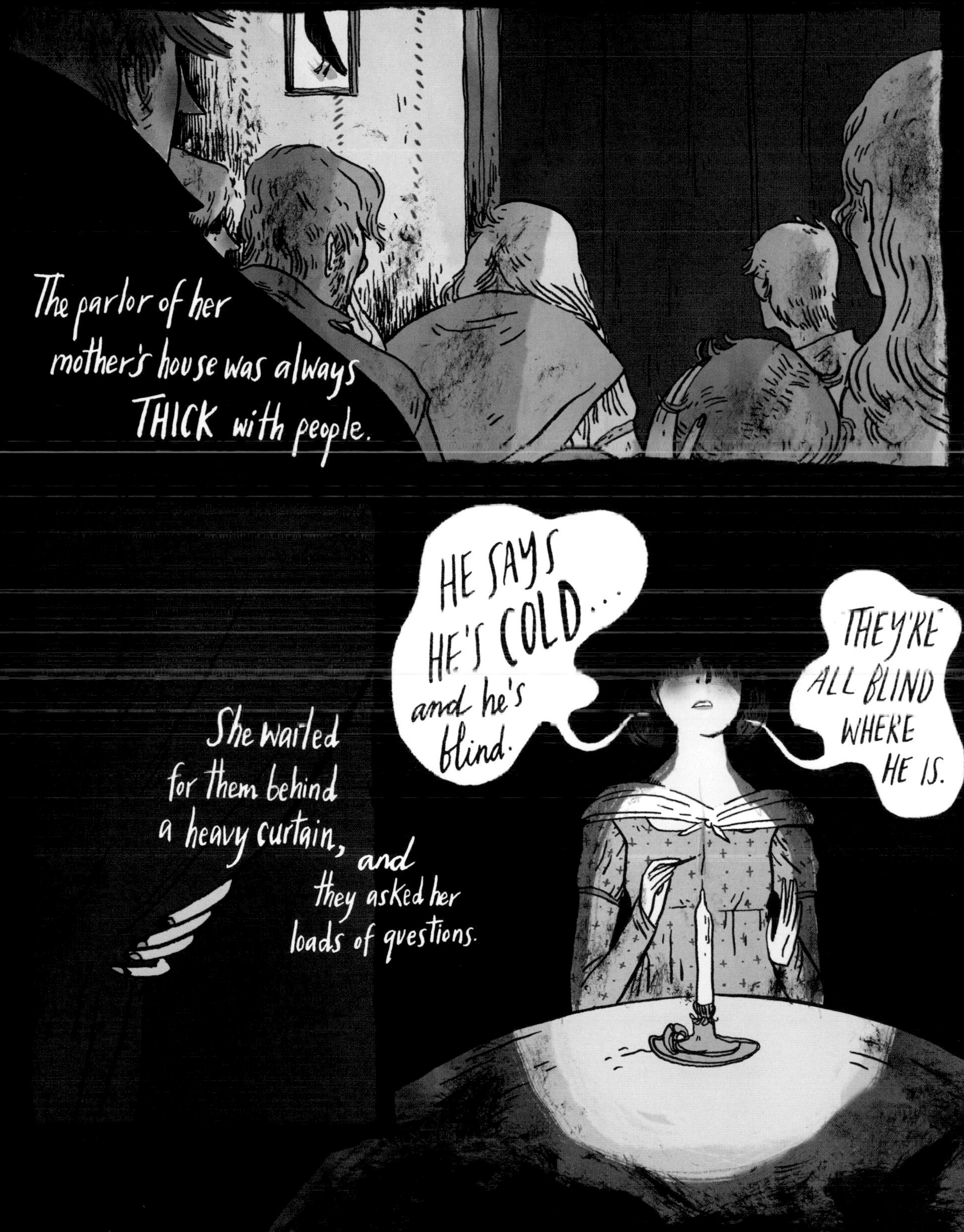

The parlor of her mother's house was always THICK with people.
She wailed for them behind a heavy curtain, and they asked her loads of questions.
HE SAYS HE'S COLD... and he's blind.
THEY'RE ALL BLIND WHERE HE IS.

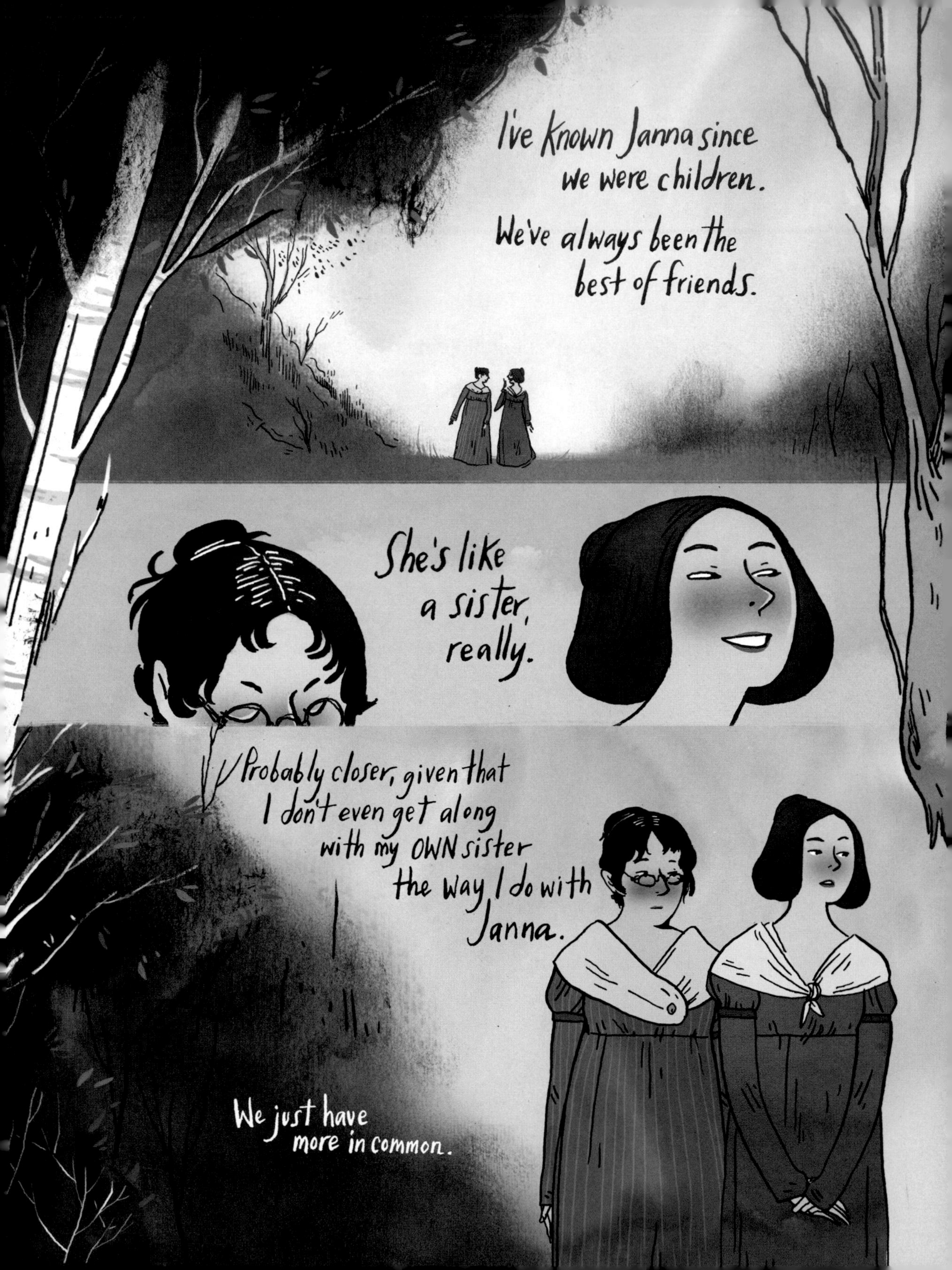
I've known Janna since we were children.
We've always been the best of friends.
She's like a sister, really.
Probably closer, given that I don't even get along with my OWN sister the way I do with Janna.
We just have more in common.

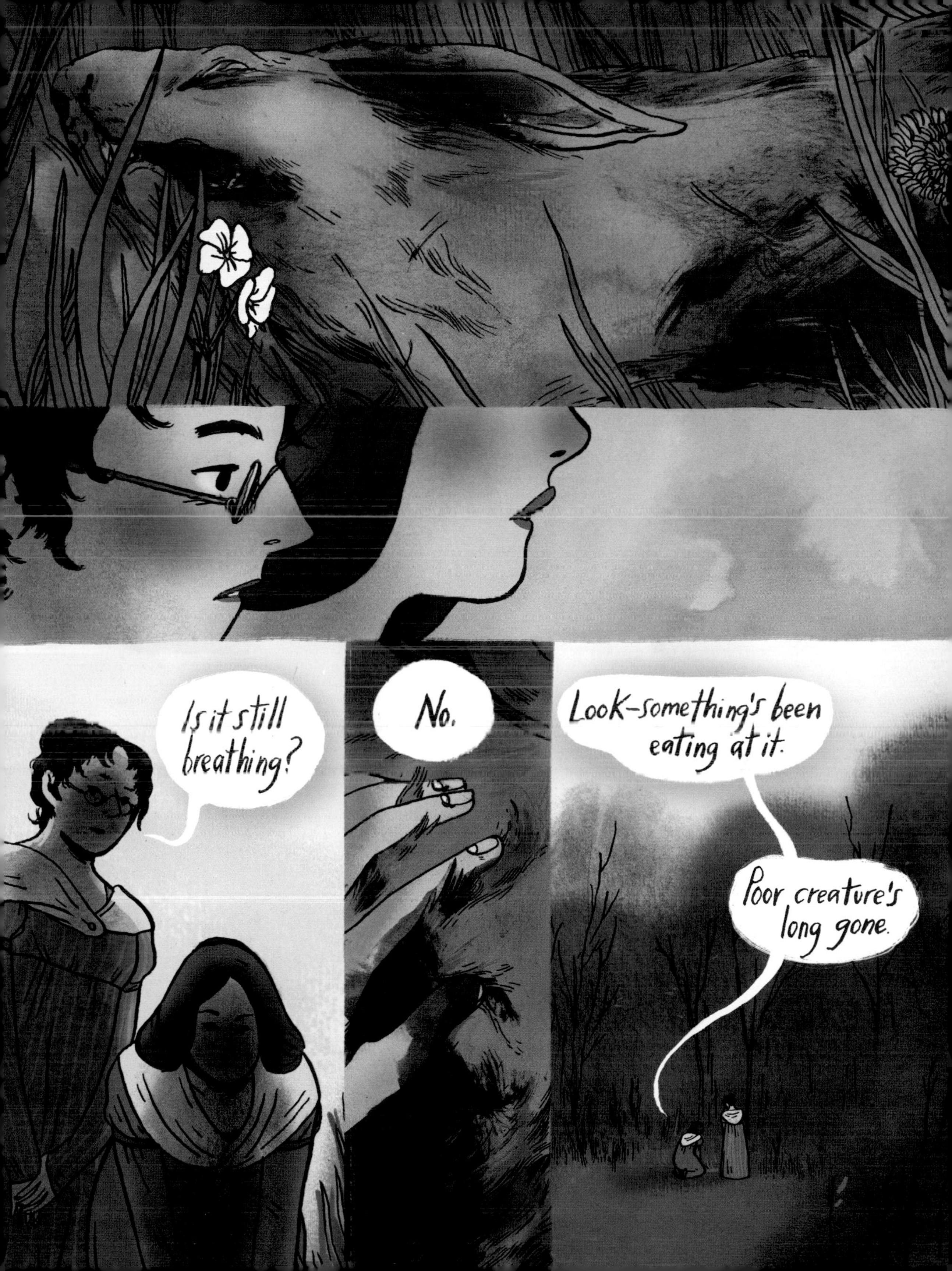
Is it still breathing?
No.
Look–something's been eating at it.
Poor creature's long gone.

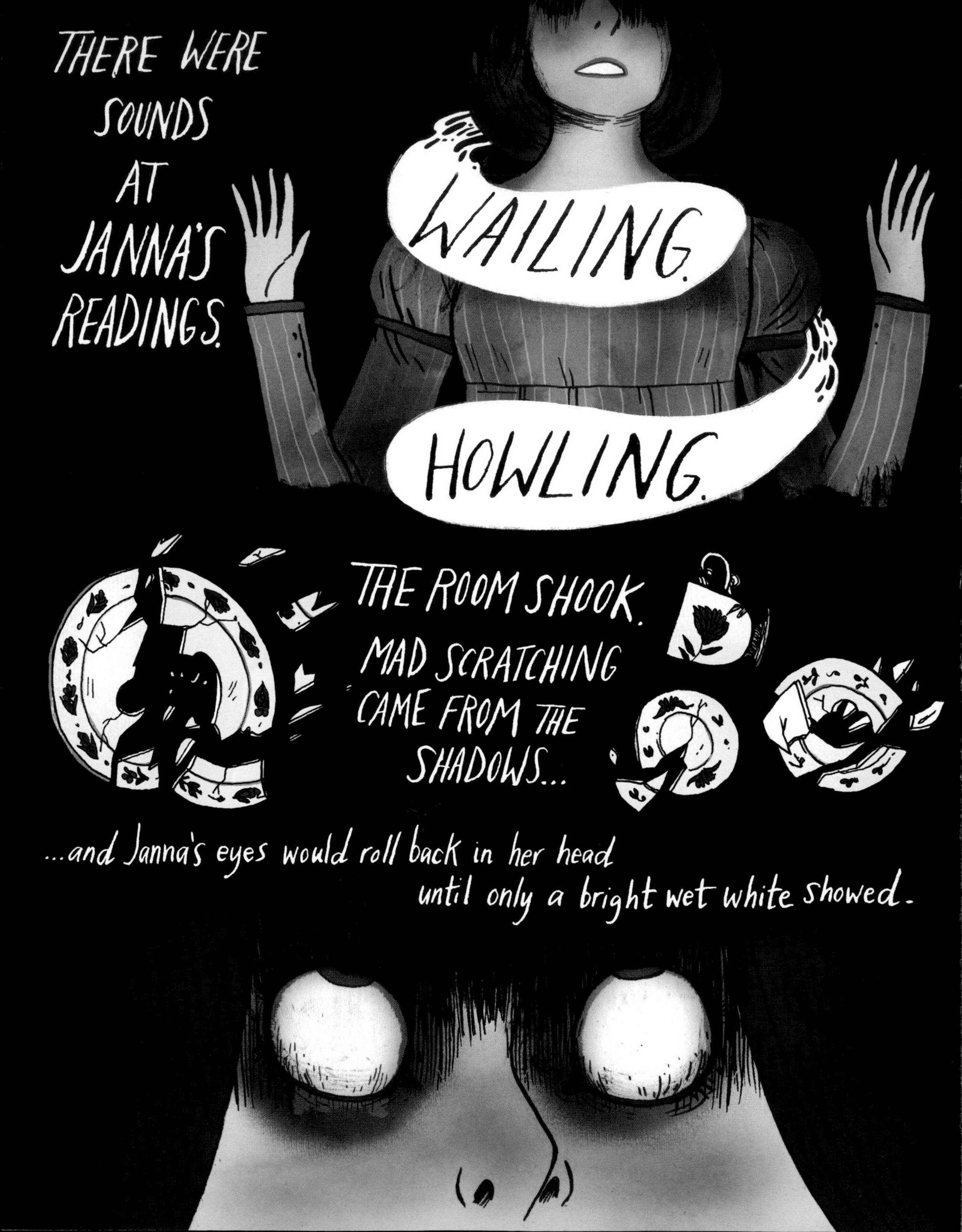
THERE WERE SOUNDS AT JANNA'S READINGS.
WAILING.
HOWLING.
THE ROOM SHOOK.
MAD SCRATCHING CAME FROM THE SHADOWS...
...and Janna's eyes would roll back in her head until only a bright wet white showed.

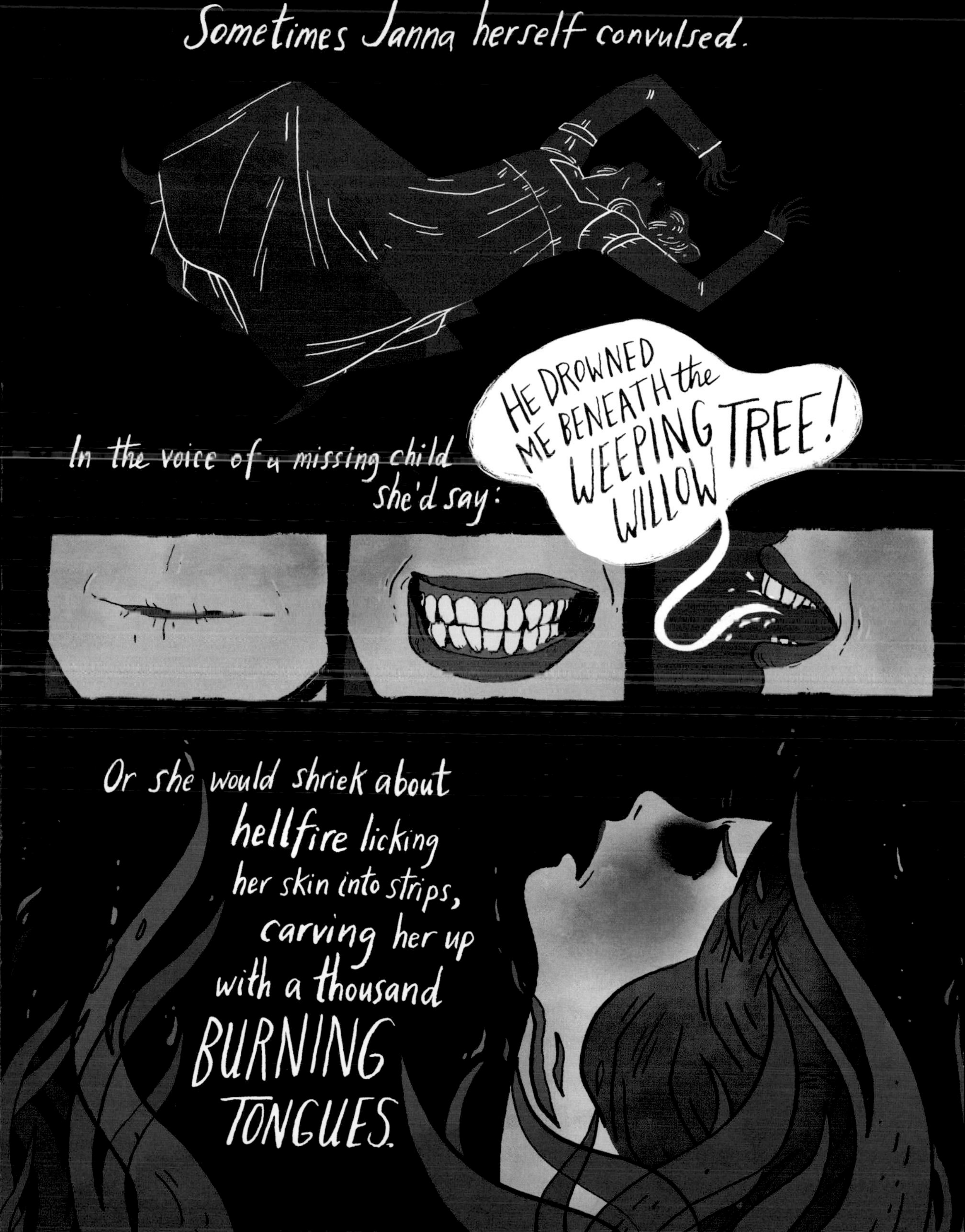
Sometimes Janna herself convulsed.
In the voice of a missing child she'd say:
HE DROWNED ME BENEATH the WEEPING WILLOW TREE!
Or she would shriek about hellfire licking her skin into strips, carving her up with a thousand BURNING TONGUES.

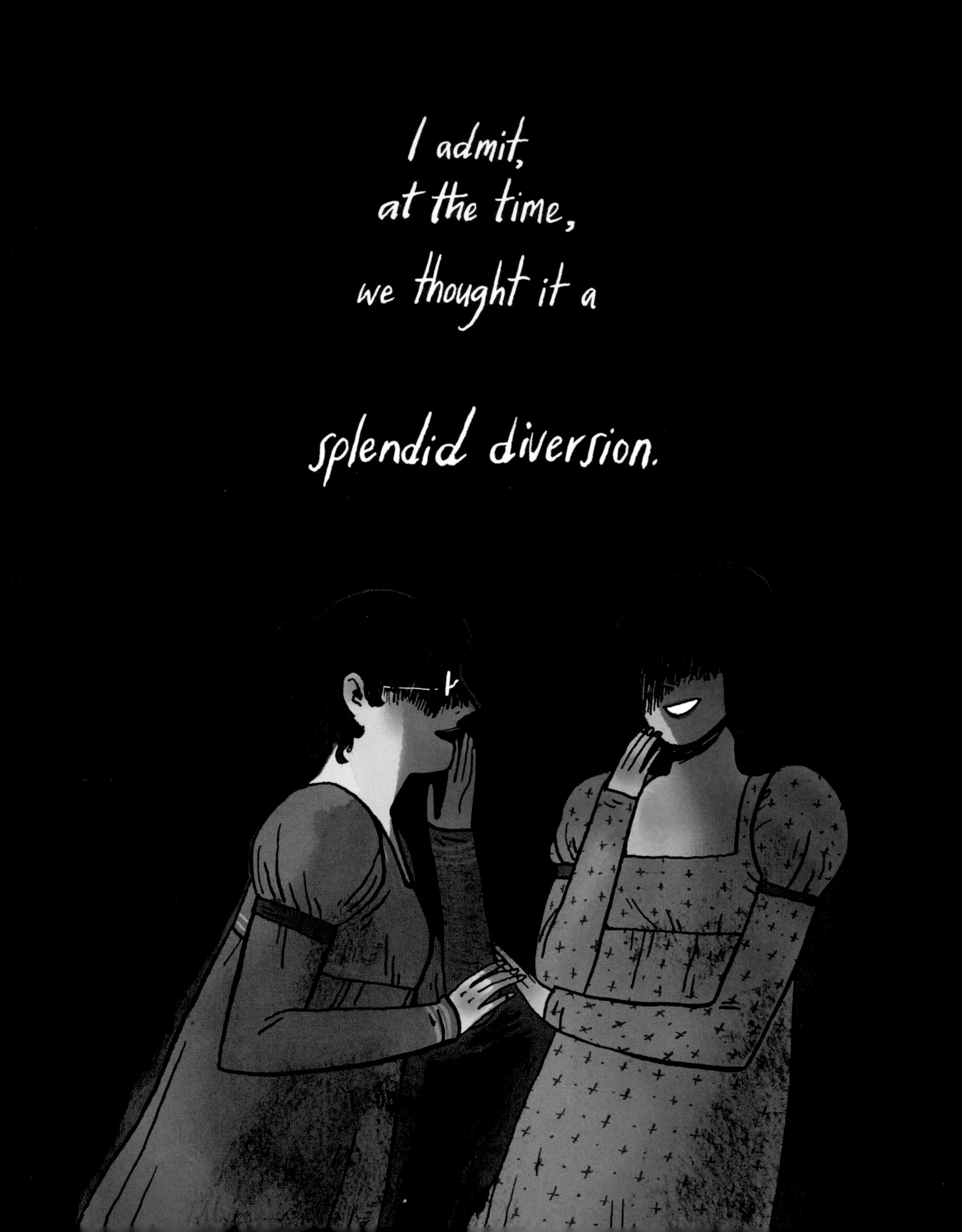
I admit,
at the time,
we thought it a
splendid diversion.

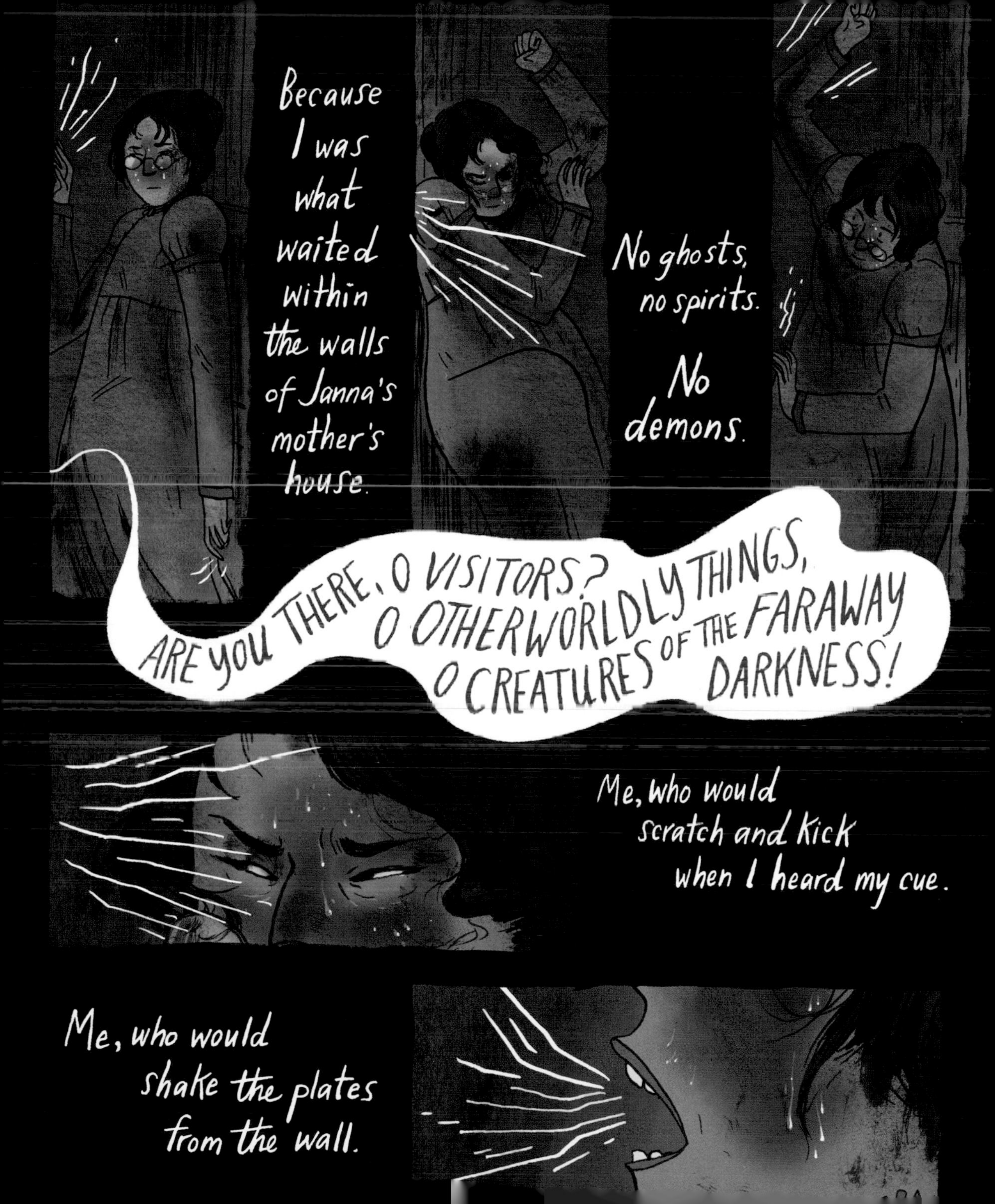
Because I was what waited within the walls of Janna's mother's house.
No ghosts, no spirits.
No demons.
ARE YOU THERE, O VISITORS? O OTHERWORLDLY THINGS, O CREATURES OF THE FARAWAY DARKNESS!
Me, who would scratch and kick when I heard my cue.
Me, who would shake the plates from the wall.

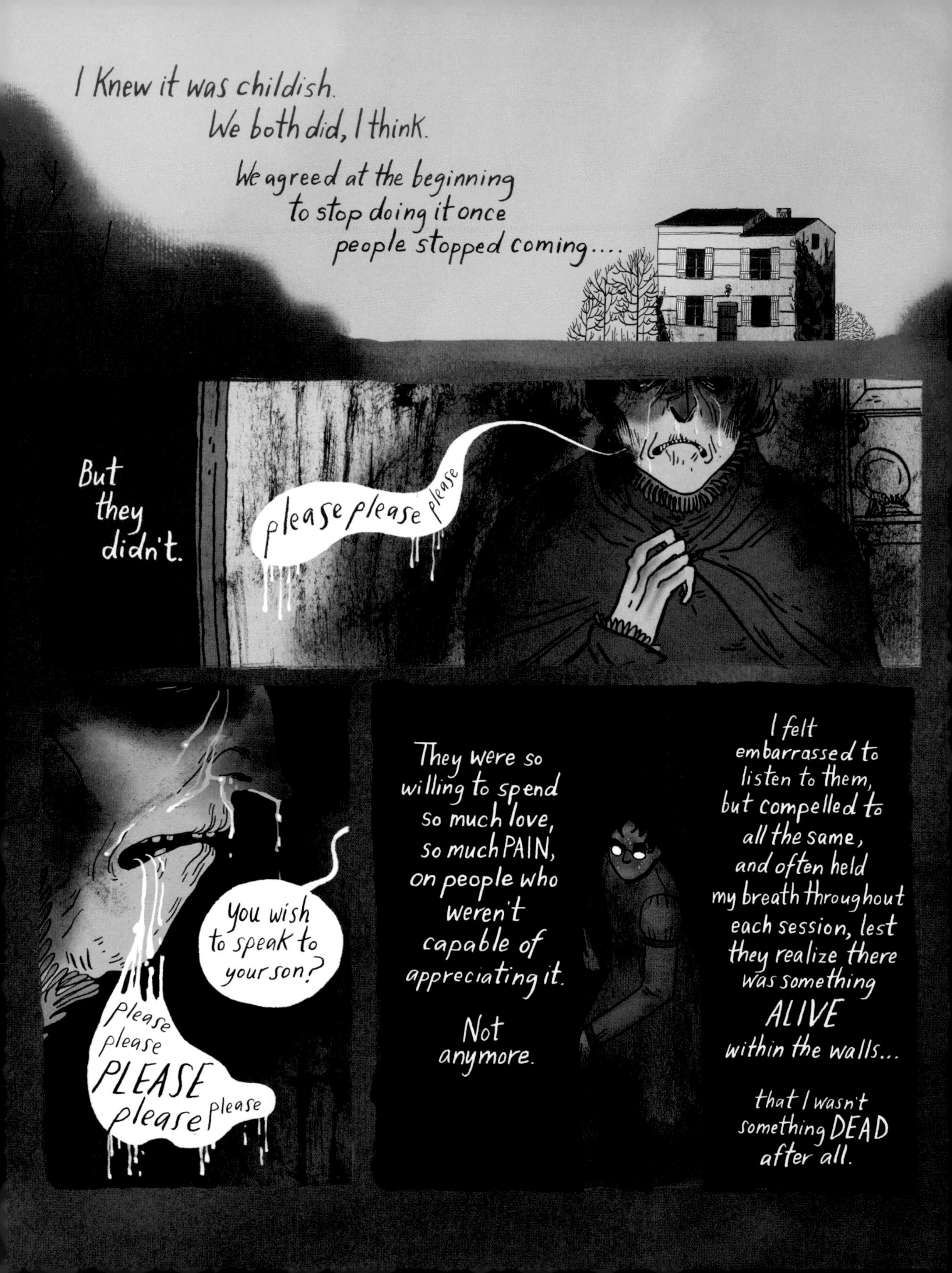

I Knew it was childish.
We both did, I think.
We agreed at the beginning to stop doing it once people stopped coming....
But they didn't.
please please please
You wish to speak to your son?
Please please PLEASE please please
They were so willing to spend so much love, so much PAIN, on people who weren't capable of appreciating it.
Not anymore.
I felt embarrassed to listen to them, but compelled to all the same, and often held my breath throughout each session, lest they realize there was something ALIVE within the walls...
that I wasn't something DEAD after all.

We did TRY to think of ways for Janna to cease the sessions....
We could pretend you've had an accident? You've hit your head and knocked all the spirits out.
Wouldn't a brush with death put me even CLOSER in touch with the other side?
"Brush with DEATH"! I wasn't proposing we crack your SKULL open! I just thought a bump might—
If there was ONE person on earth who could hear you when you spoke...
...would you let them go because of a bump on the noggin?
And ultimately we just left it. We went back to the sessions. We stopped talking about quitting altogether, like we'd never brought it up at all.

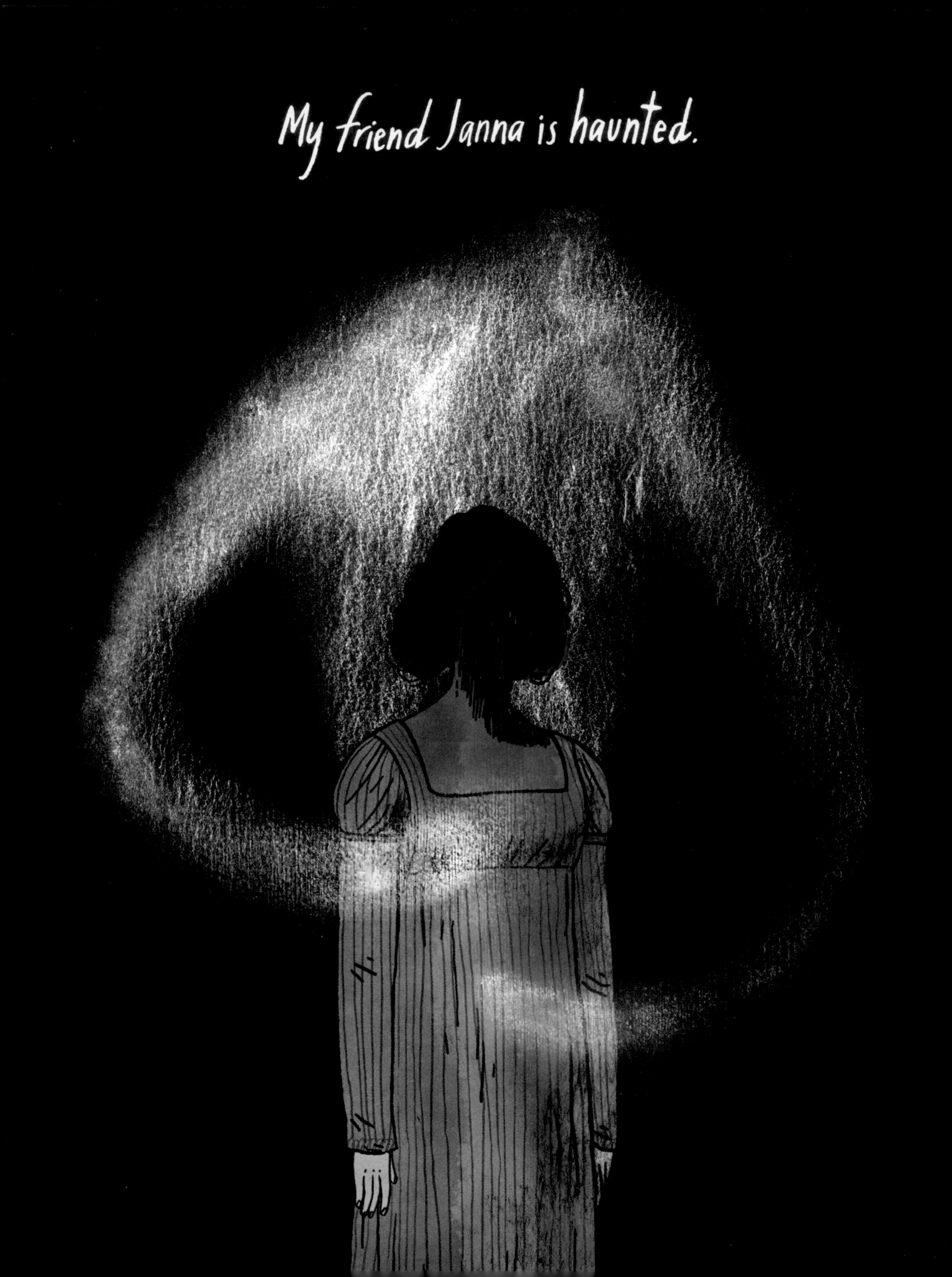
My friend Janna is haunted.

I'm not sure it's by a ghost.

I've never seen a ghost before.

But this thing I see...

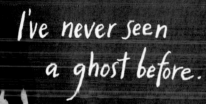

and Janna doesn't.

Never even claimed to.

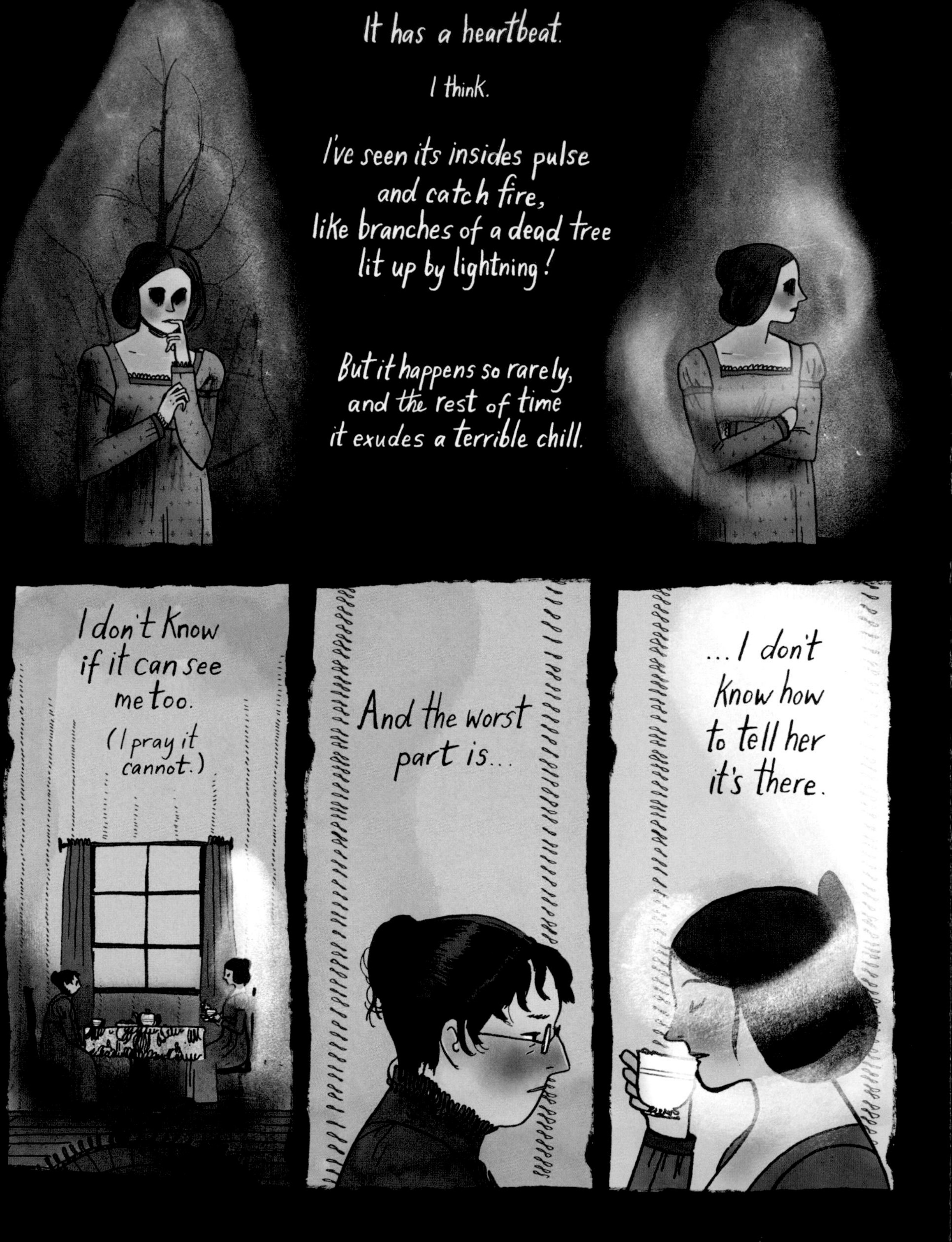
It has a heartbeat.
I think.
I've seen its insides pulse and catch fire, like branches of a dead tree lit up by lightning!
But it happens so rarely, and the rest of time it exudes a terrible chill.
I don't Know if it can see me too.
(I pray it cannot.)
And the worst part is...
...I don't Know how to tell her it's there.

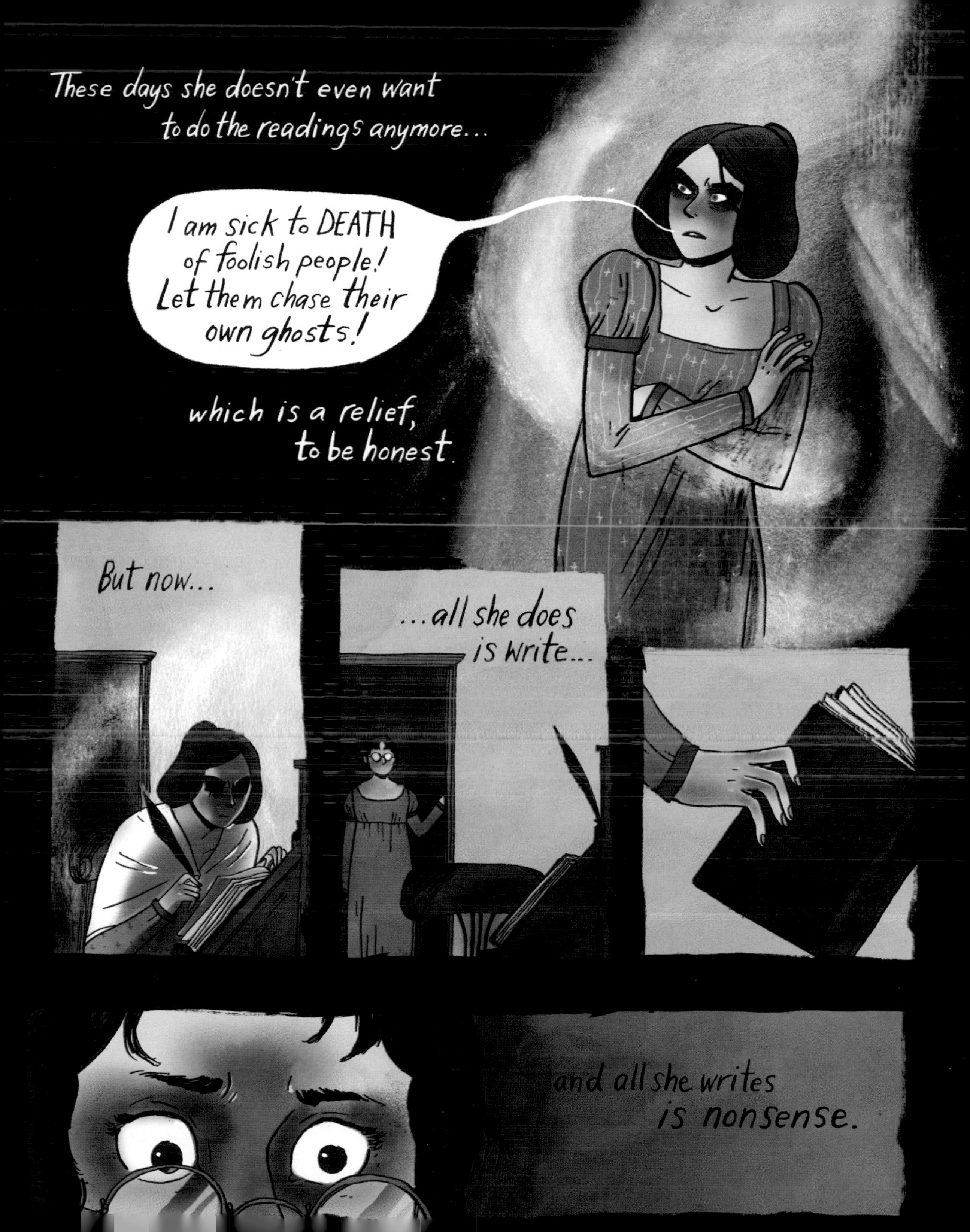
These days she doesn't even want to do the readings anymore...
I am sick to DEATH of foolish people! Let them chase their own ghosts!
which is a relief, to be honest.
But now...
...all she does is write...
and all she writes is nonsense.

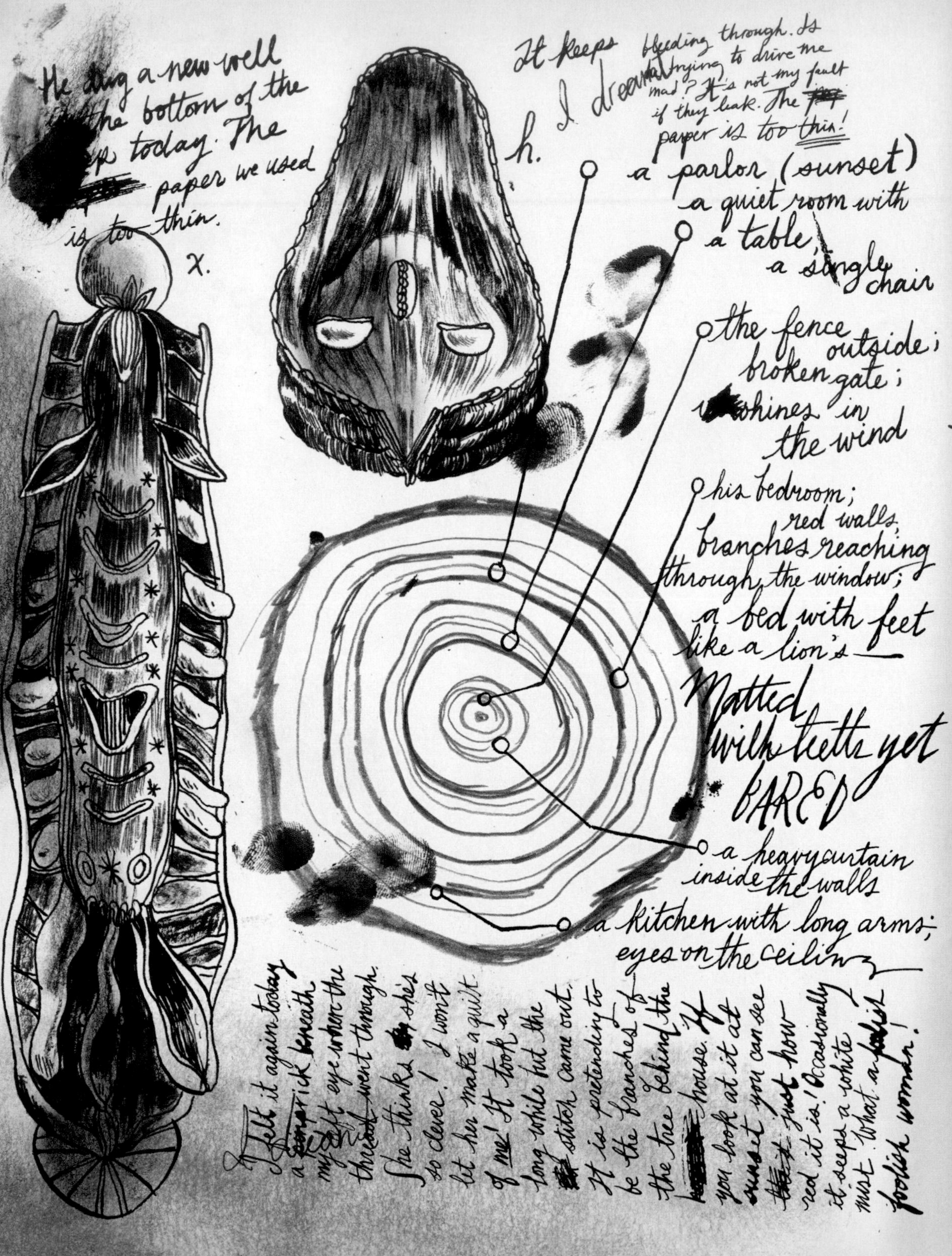

He dug a new well
the bottom of the
p today. The
paper we used
is too thin.
X.
It keeps
h. I dream
bleeding through. Is
trying to drive me
mad? It's not my fault
if they leak. The
paper is too thin!
a parlor (sunset)
a quiet room with
a table,
a single chair
the fence outside;
broken gate;
whines in
the wind
his bedroom;
red walls,
branches reaching
through the window;
a bed with feet
like a lion's
Matted
with teeth yet
BARED
a heavy curtain
inside the walls
a kitchen with long arms;
eyes on the ceiling
I felt it again today
a prick beneath
my left eye when the
thread went through.
She thinks she's
so clever! I won't
let her make a quilt
of me! It took a
long while but the
stitch came out.
It is pretending to
be the branches of
the tree behind the
house. If
you look at it at
sunset you can see
just how
red it is! Occasionally
it seeps a white
mist. What a
foolish woman!

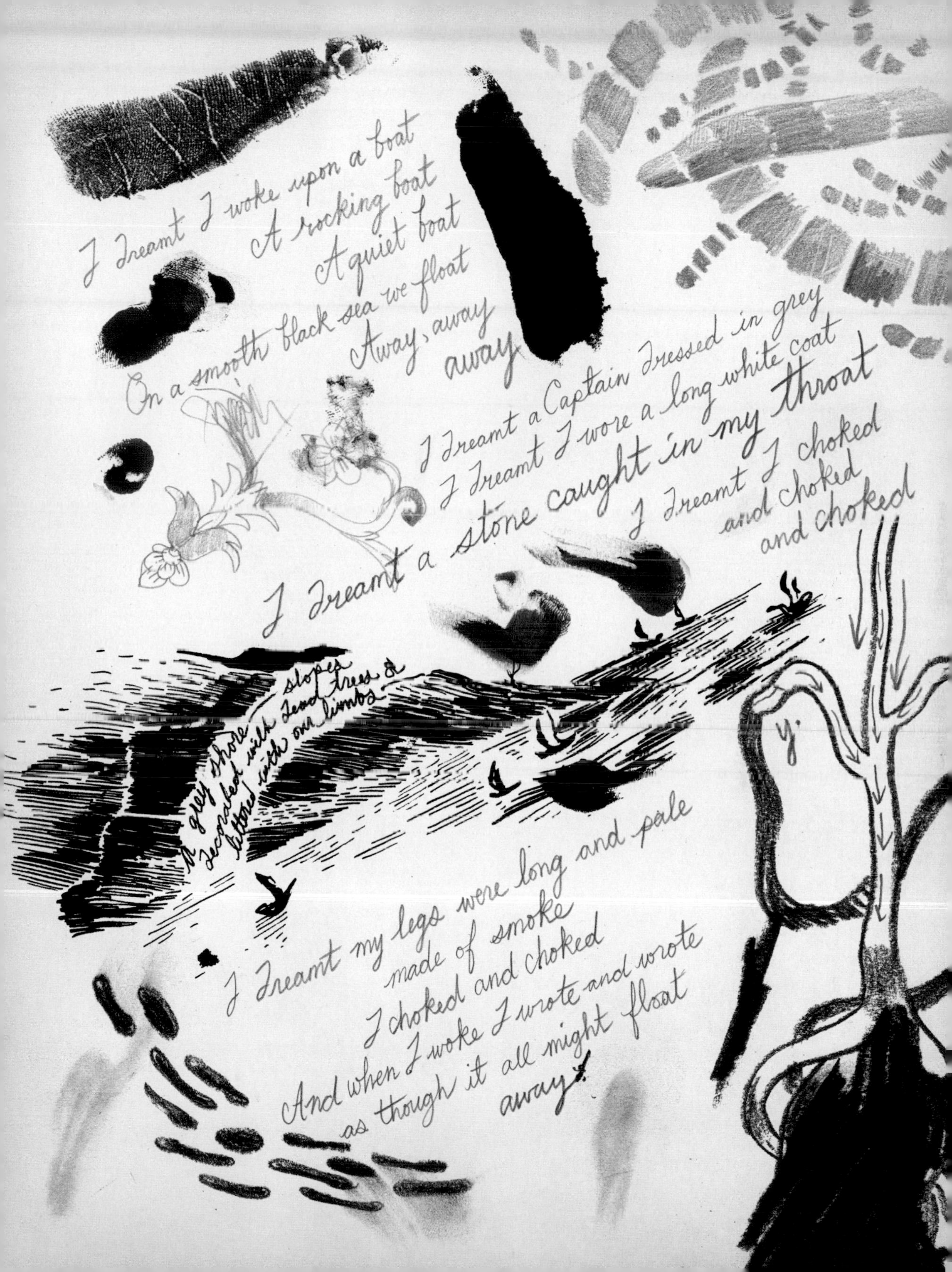
I dreamt I woke upon a boat
A rocking boat
A quiet boat
On a smooth black sea we float
Away, away
away
I dreamt a Captain dressed in grey
I dreamt I wore a long white coat
I dreamt a stone caught in my throat
I dreamt I choked
and choked
and choked
A grey shore slopes
decorated with dead trees &
littered with our limbs.
I dreamt my legs were long and pale
made of smoke
I choked and choked
And when I woke I wrote and wrote
as though it all might float
away.

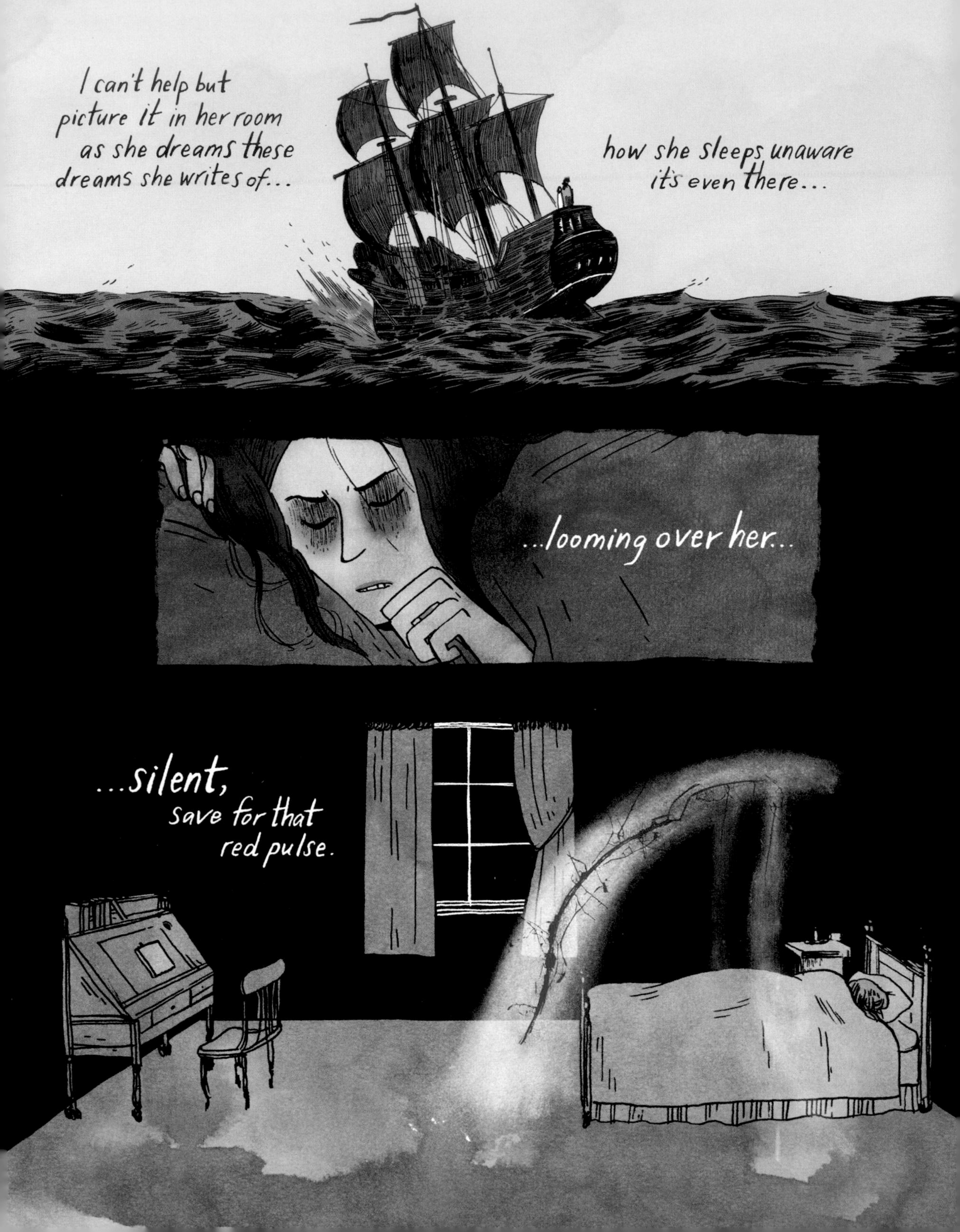
I can't help but picture it in her room as she dreams these dreams she writes of...
how she sleeps unaware it's even there...
...looming over her...
...silent, save for that red pulse.

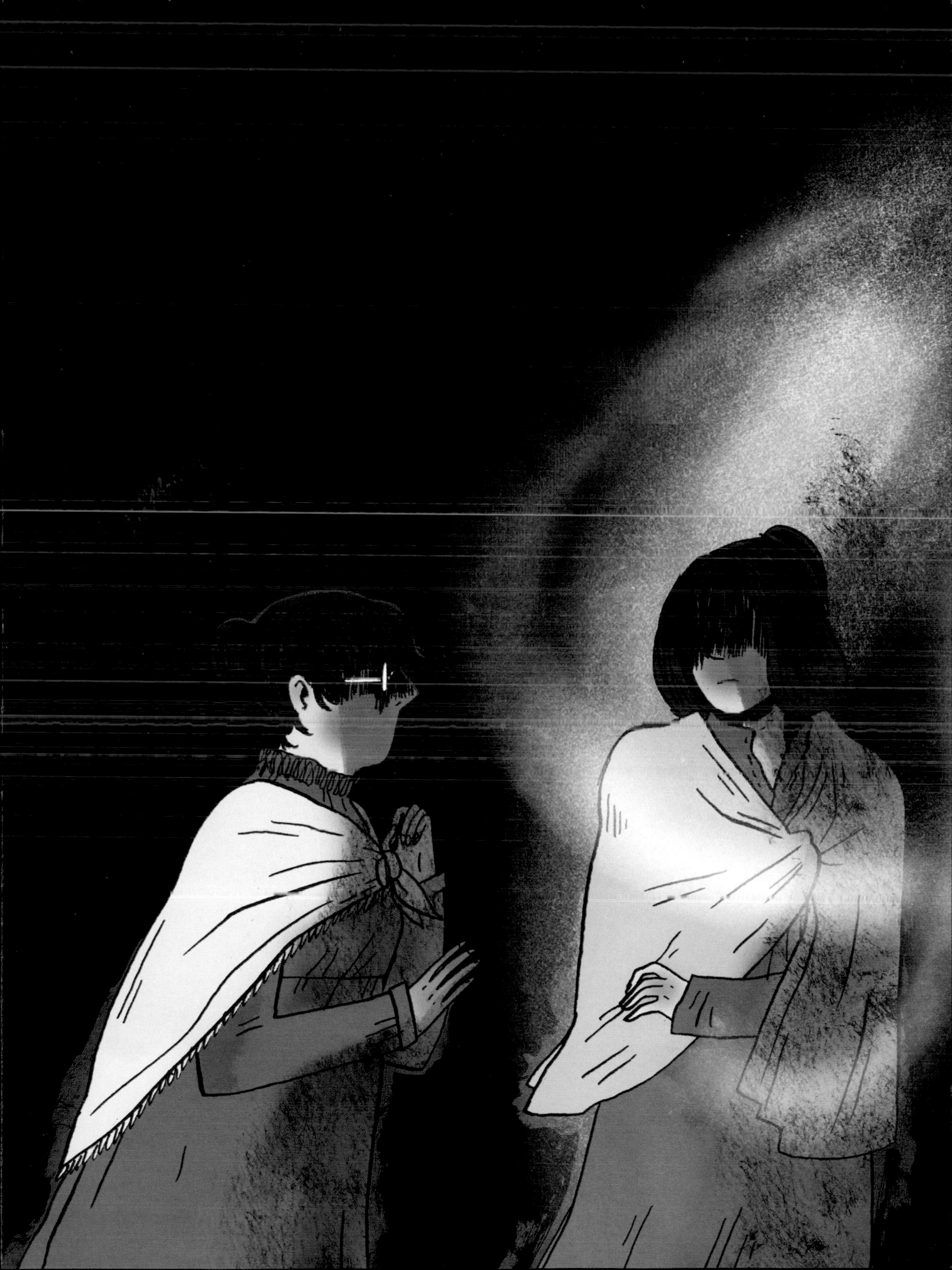

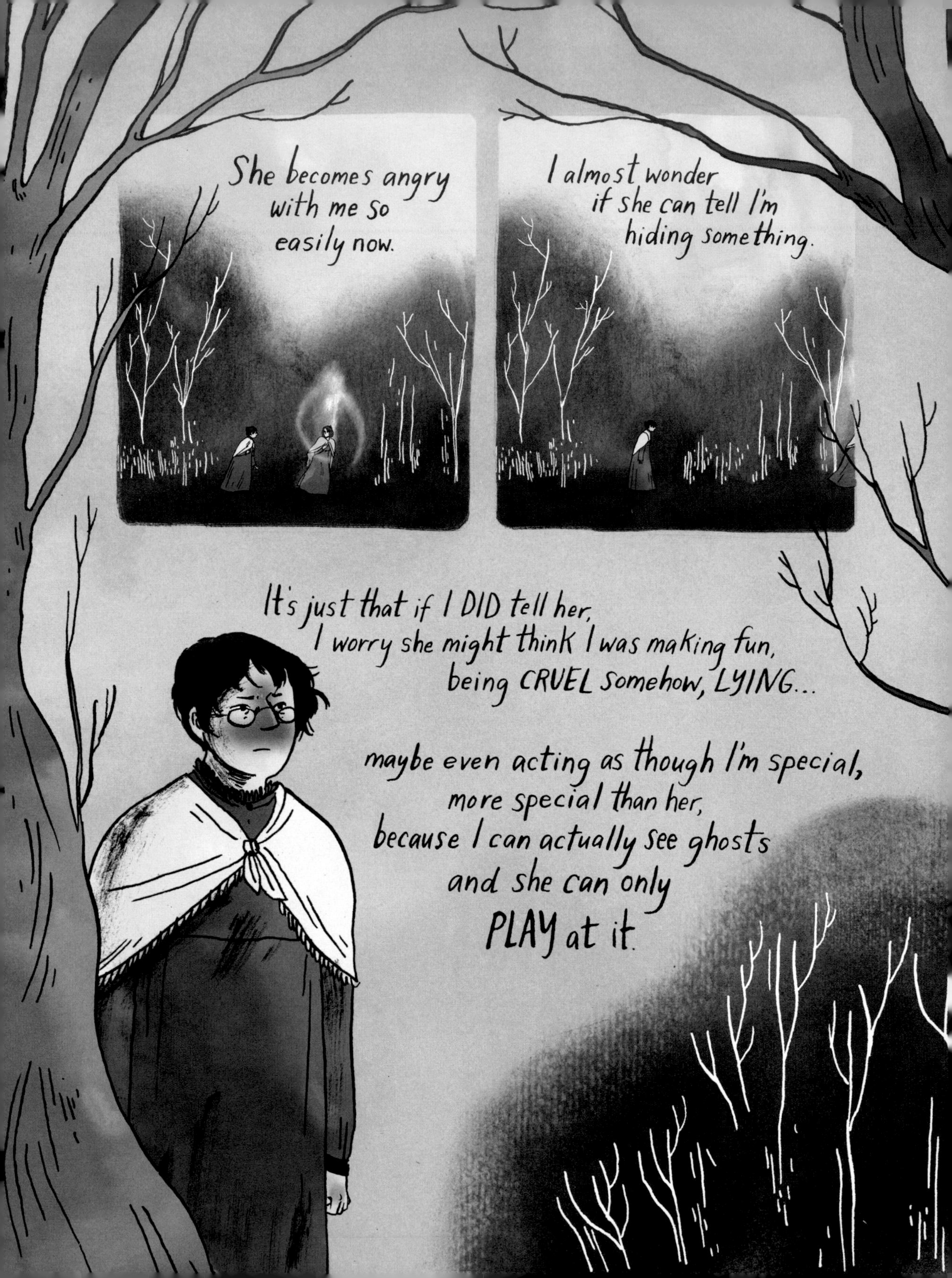
She becomes angry with me so easily now.
I almost wonder if she can tell I'm hiding something.
It's just that if I DID tell her, I worry she might think I was making fun, being CRUEL somehow, LYING...
maybe even acting as though I'm special, more special than her, because I can actually see ghosts and she can only PLAY at it.

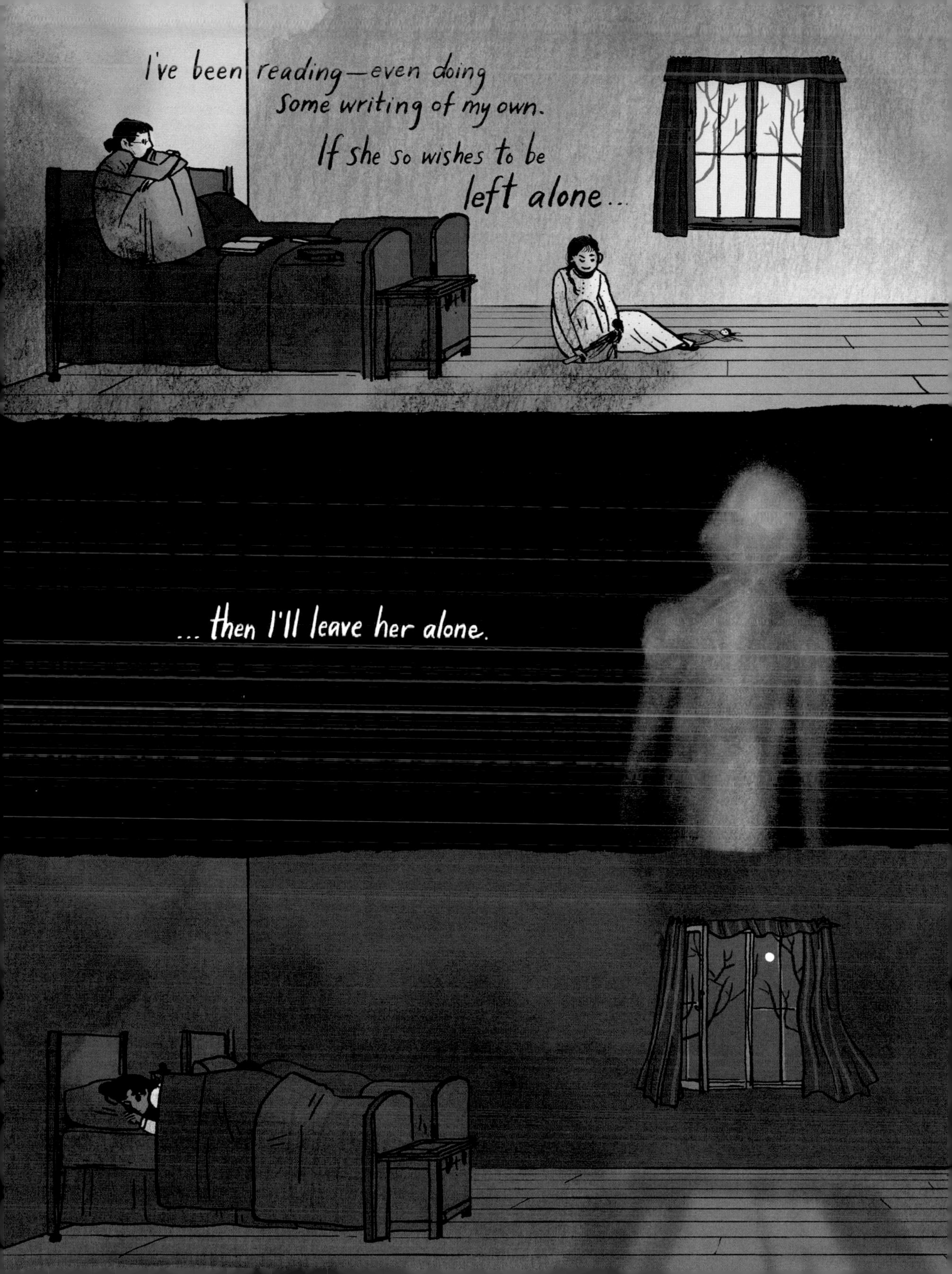
I've been reading—even doing some writing of my own.
If she so wishes to be left alone...
... then I'll leave her alone.

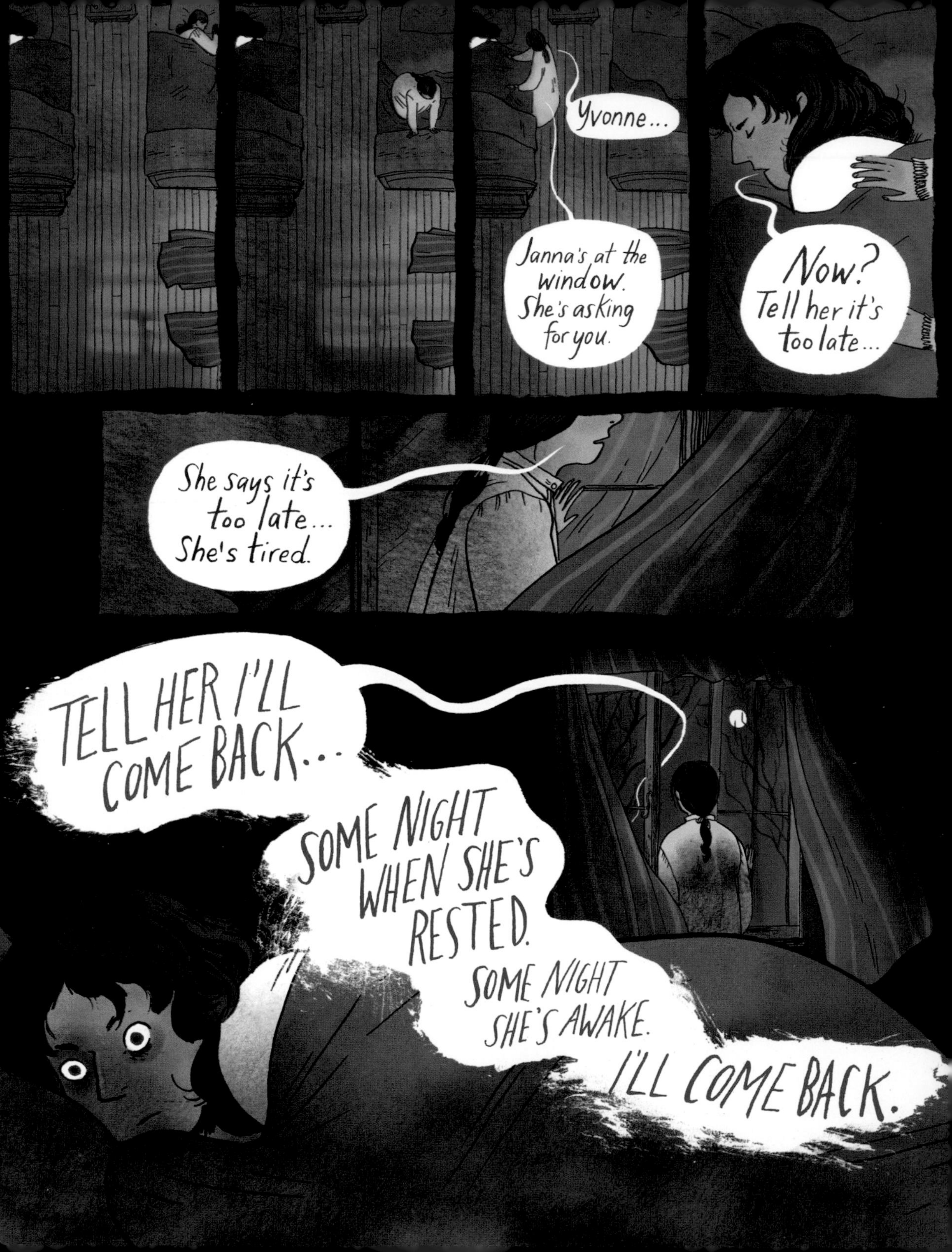
Yvonne...
Janna's at the window. She's asking for you.
Now? Tell her it's too late...
She says it's too late... She's tired.
TELL HER I'LL COME BACK...
SOME NIGHT WHEN SHE'S RESTED.
SOME NIGHT SHE'S AWAKE.
I'LL COME BACK.

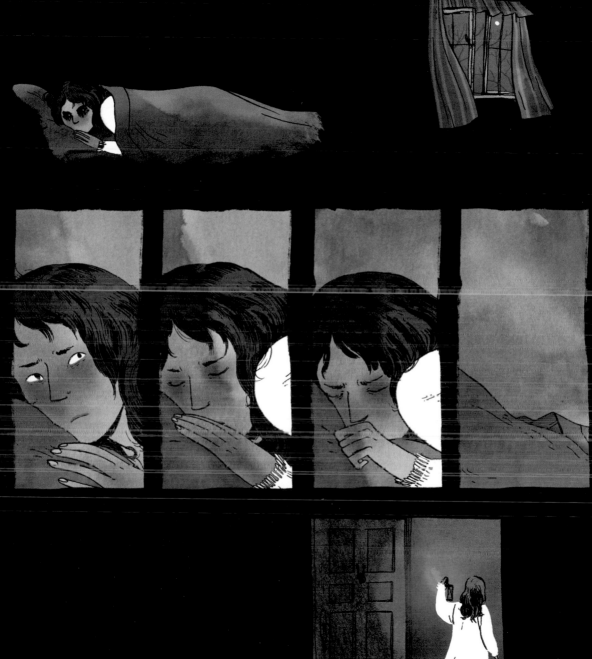

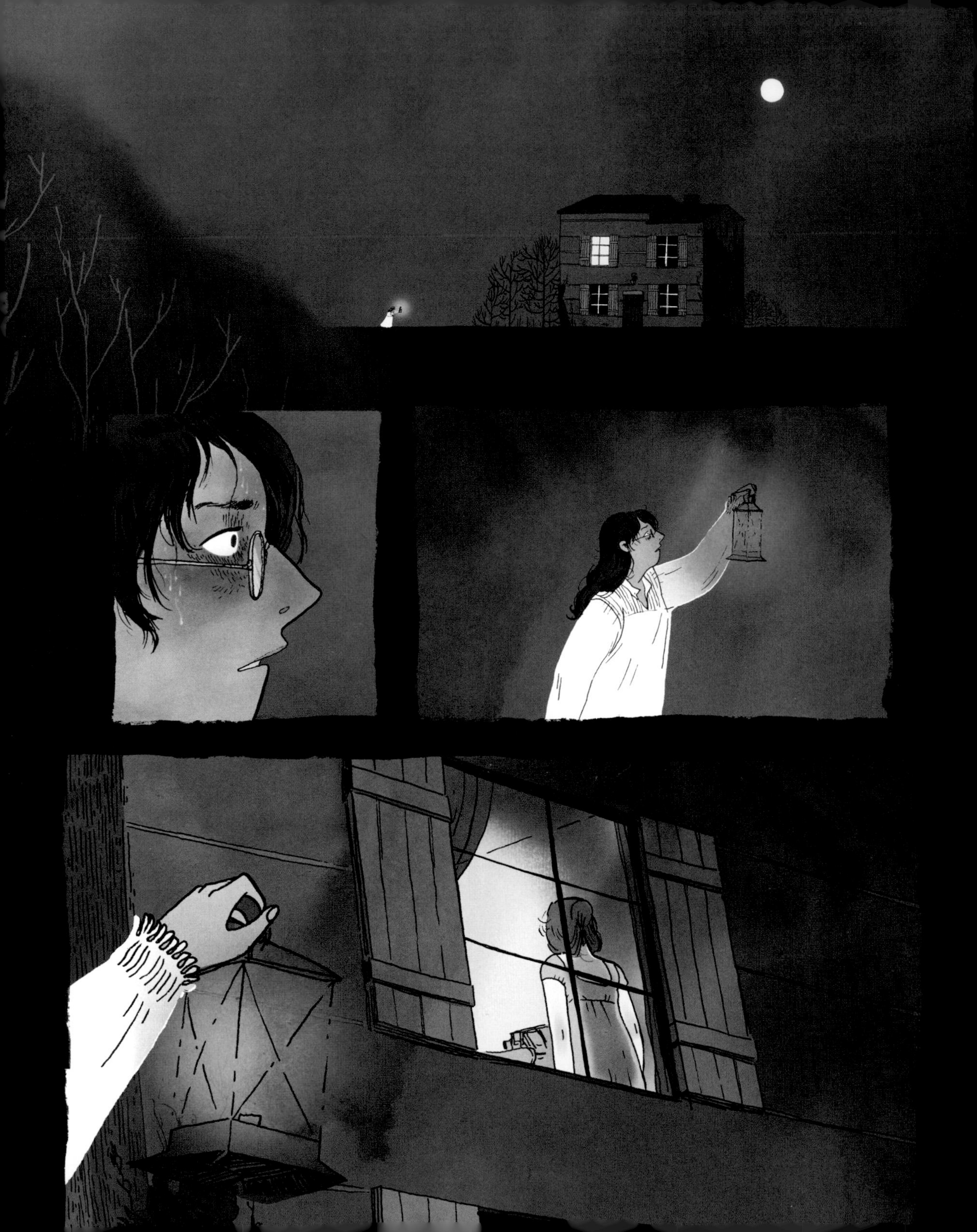

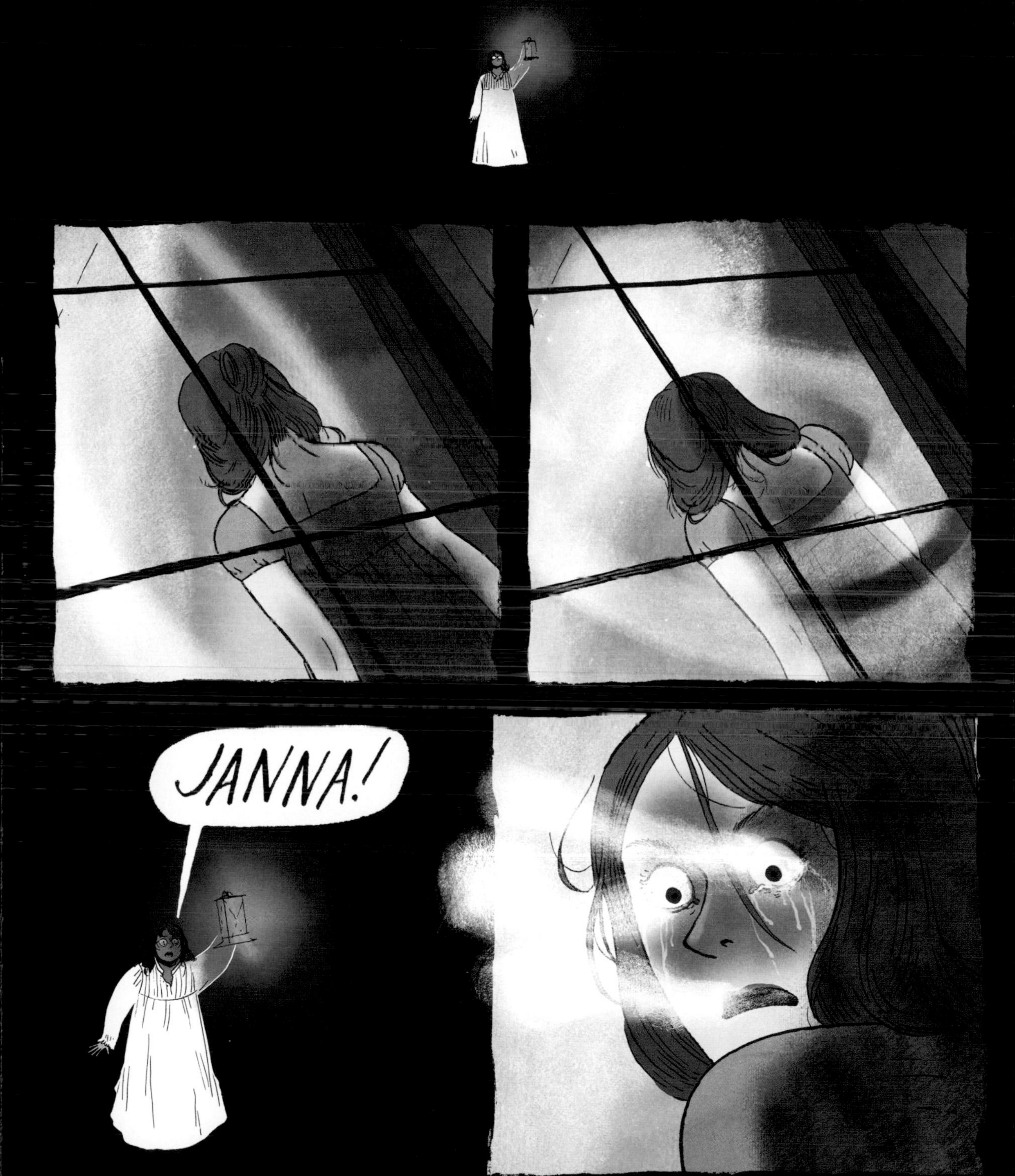
JANNA!

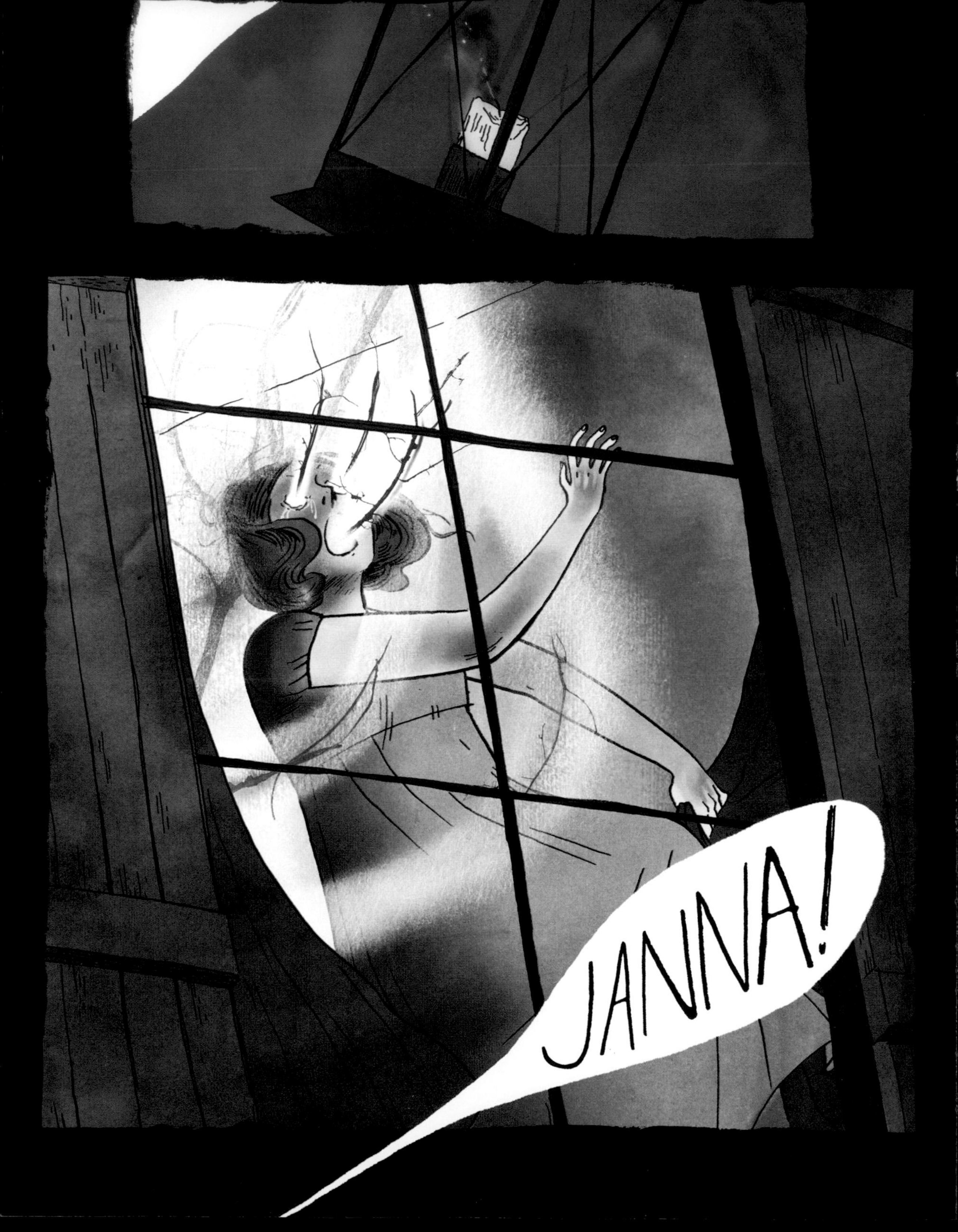
JANNA!

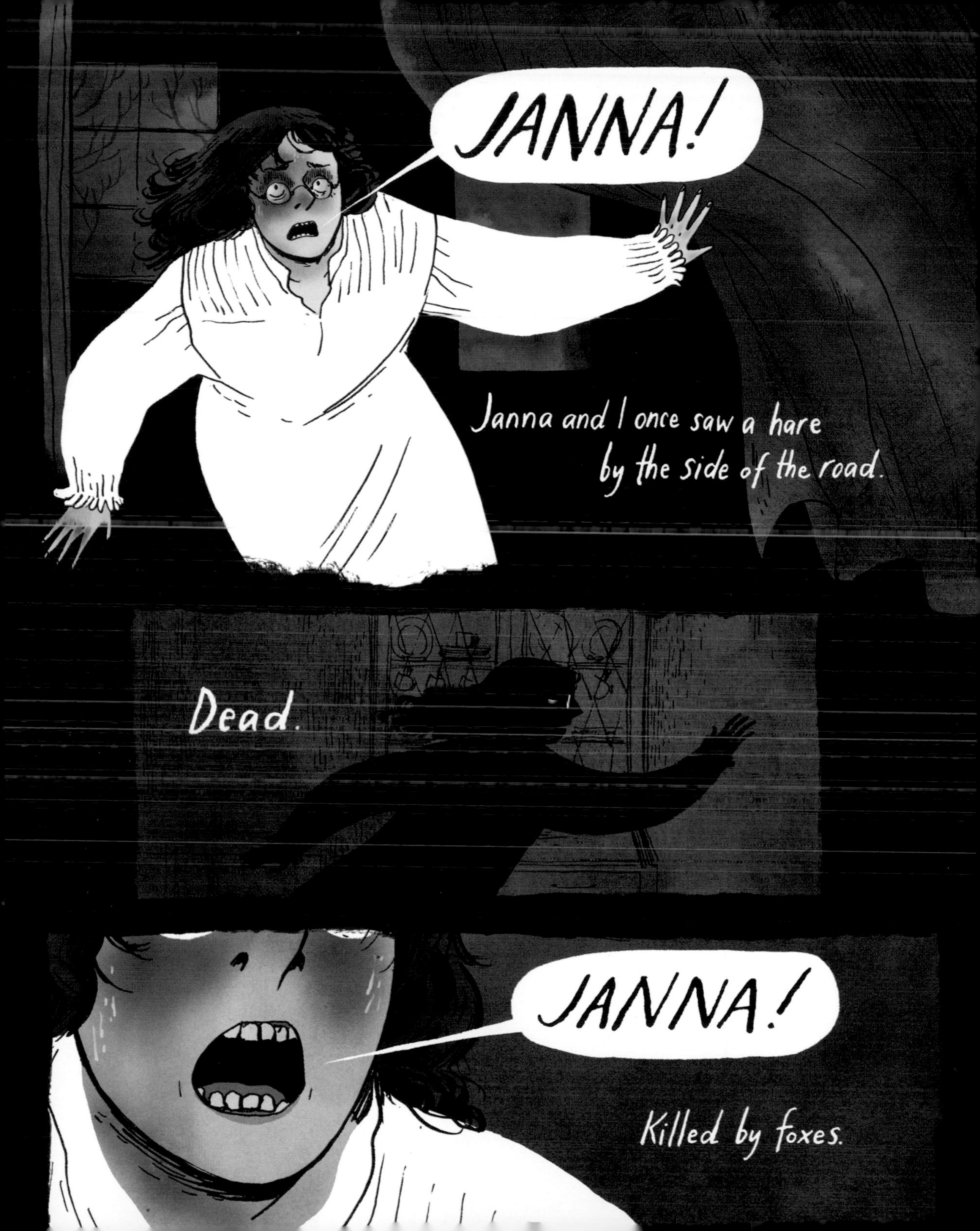
JANNA!
Janna and I once saw a hare by the side of the road.
Dead.
JANNA!
Killed by foxes.

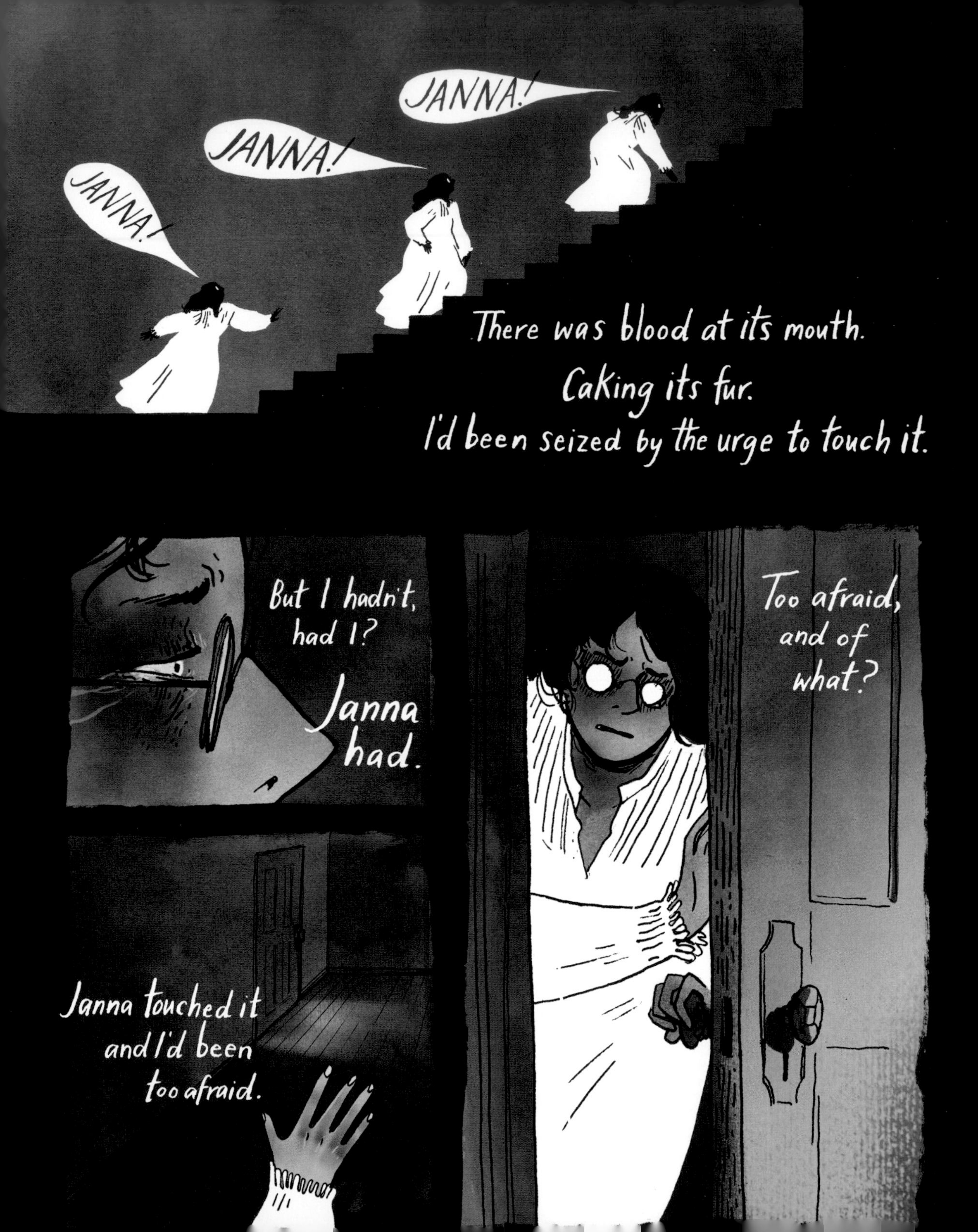

JANNA!
JANNA!
JANNA!
There was blood at its mouth.
Caking its fur.
I'd been seized by the urge to touch it.
But I hadn't, had I?
Janna had.
Too afraid, and of what?
Janna touched it and I'd been too afraid.

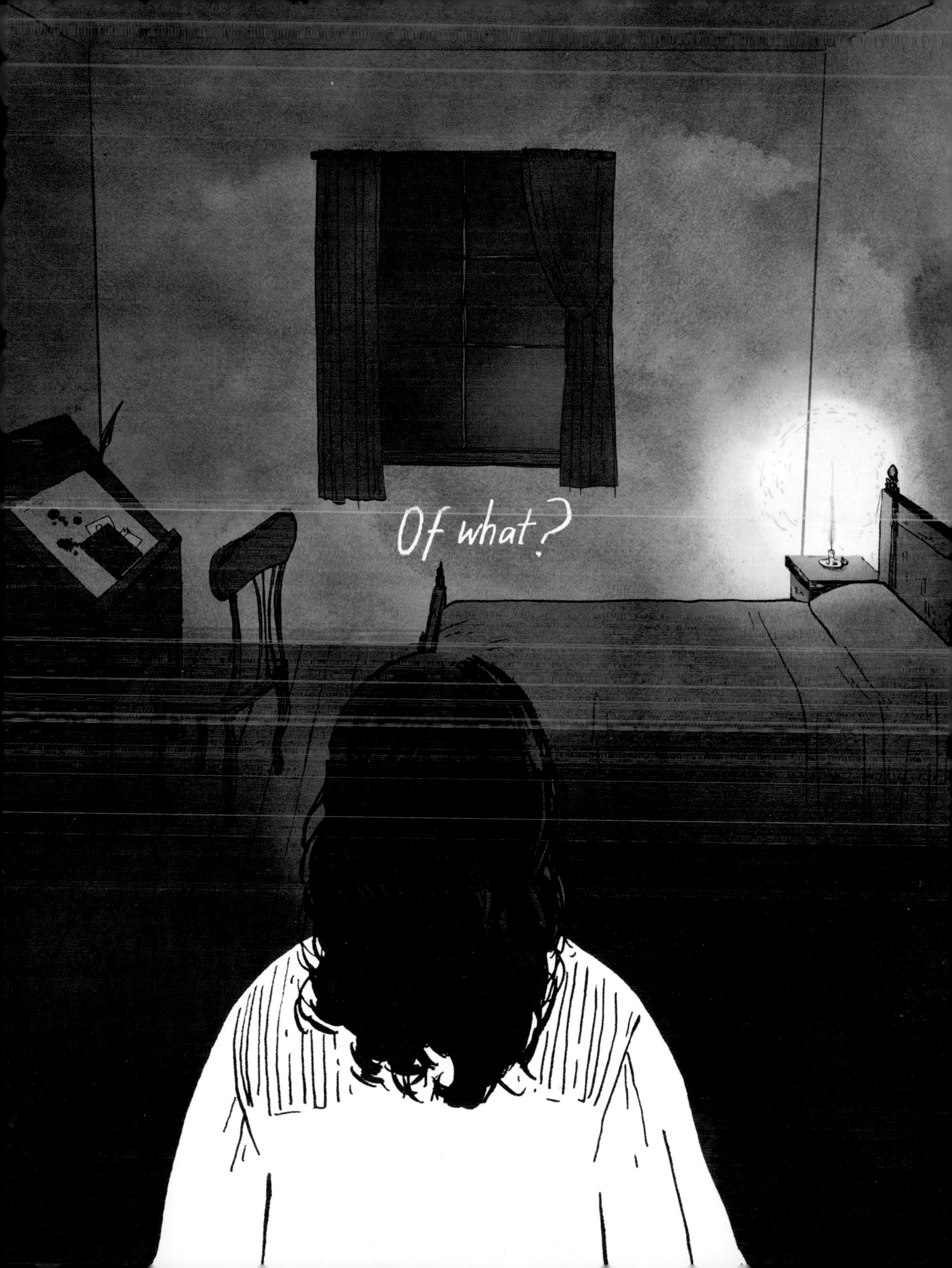
Of what?

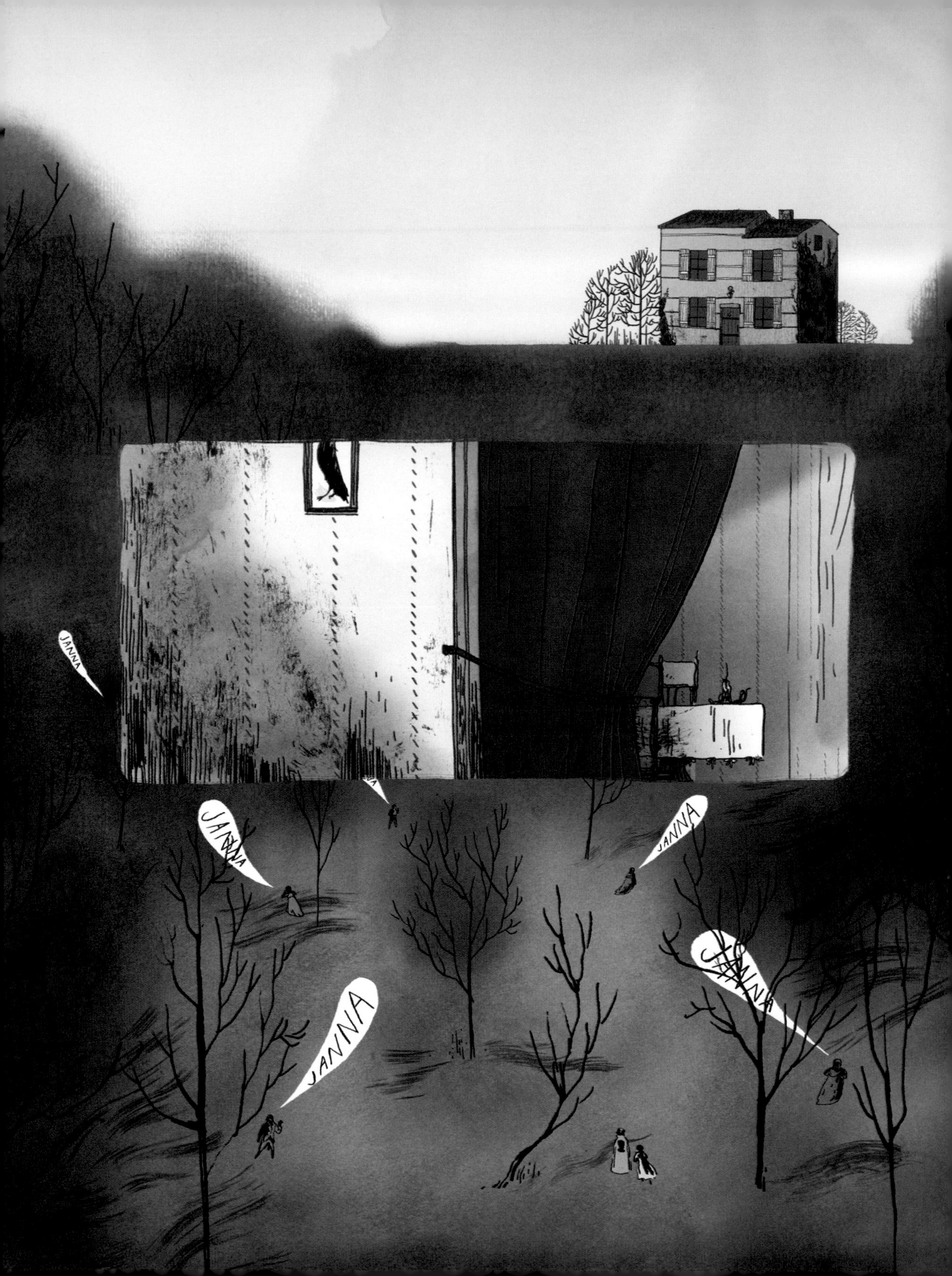
JANNA
JANNA
JANNA
JANNA
JANNA

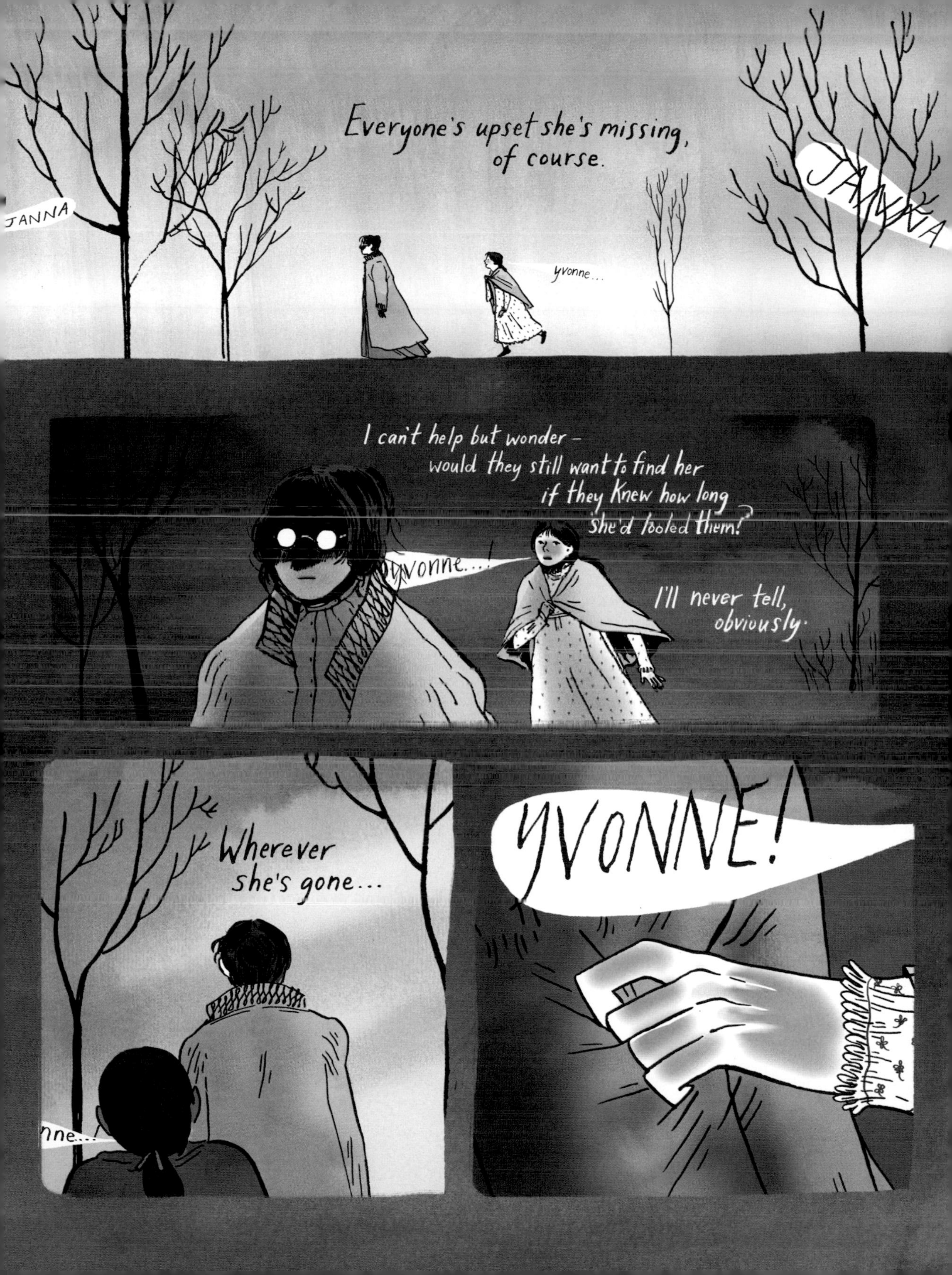
Everyone's upset she's missing, of course.
JANNA
yvonne...
JANNA
I can't help but wonder – would they still want to find her if they knew how long she'd fooled them?
yvonne...!
I'll never tell, obviously.
Wherever she's gone...
nne...!
YVONNE!

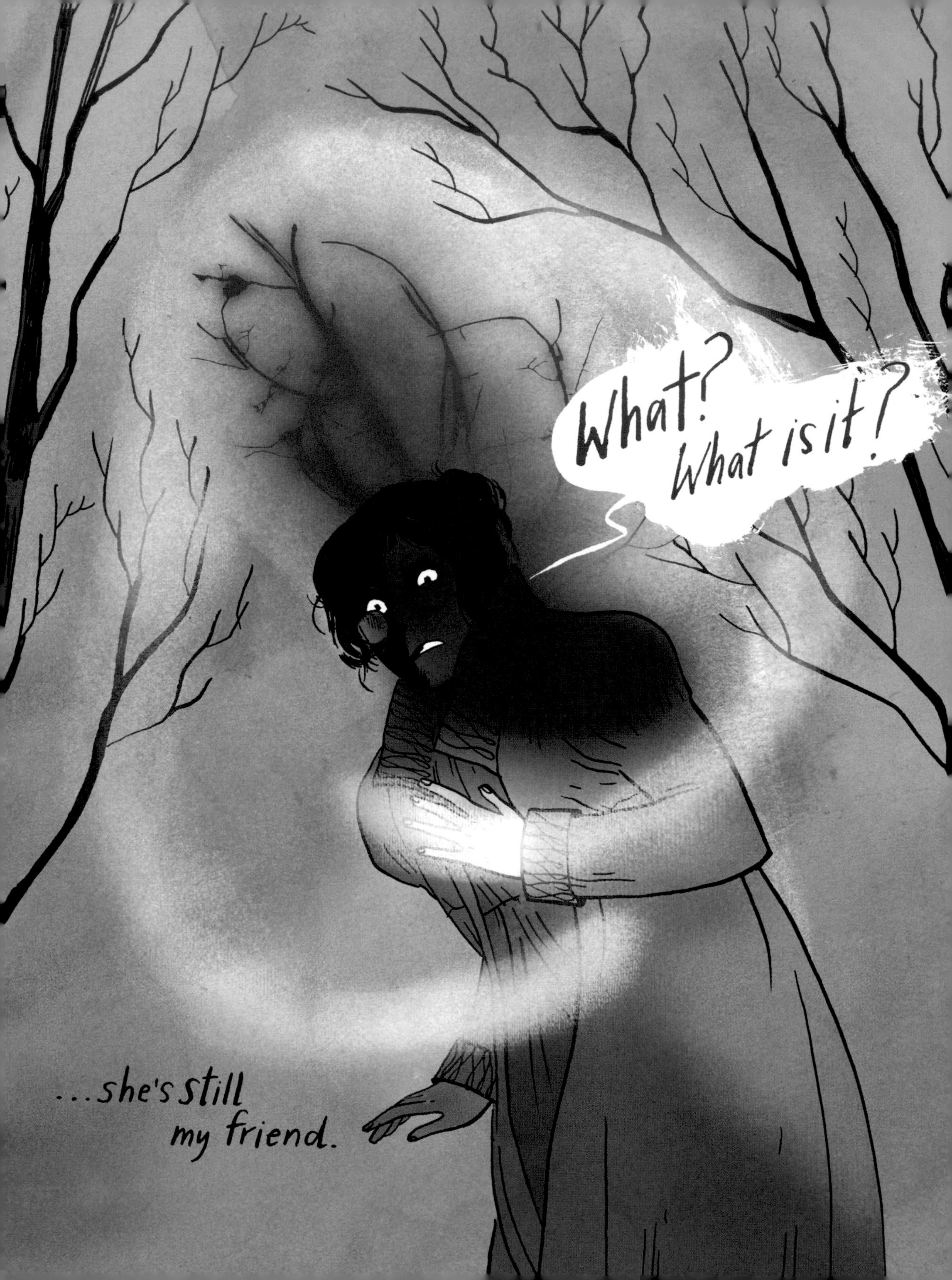
What? What is it?
...she's still my friend.

THE NESTING PLACE

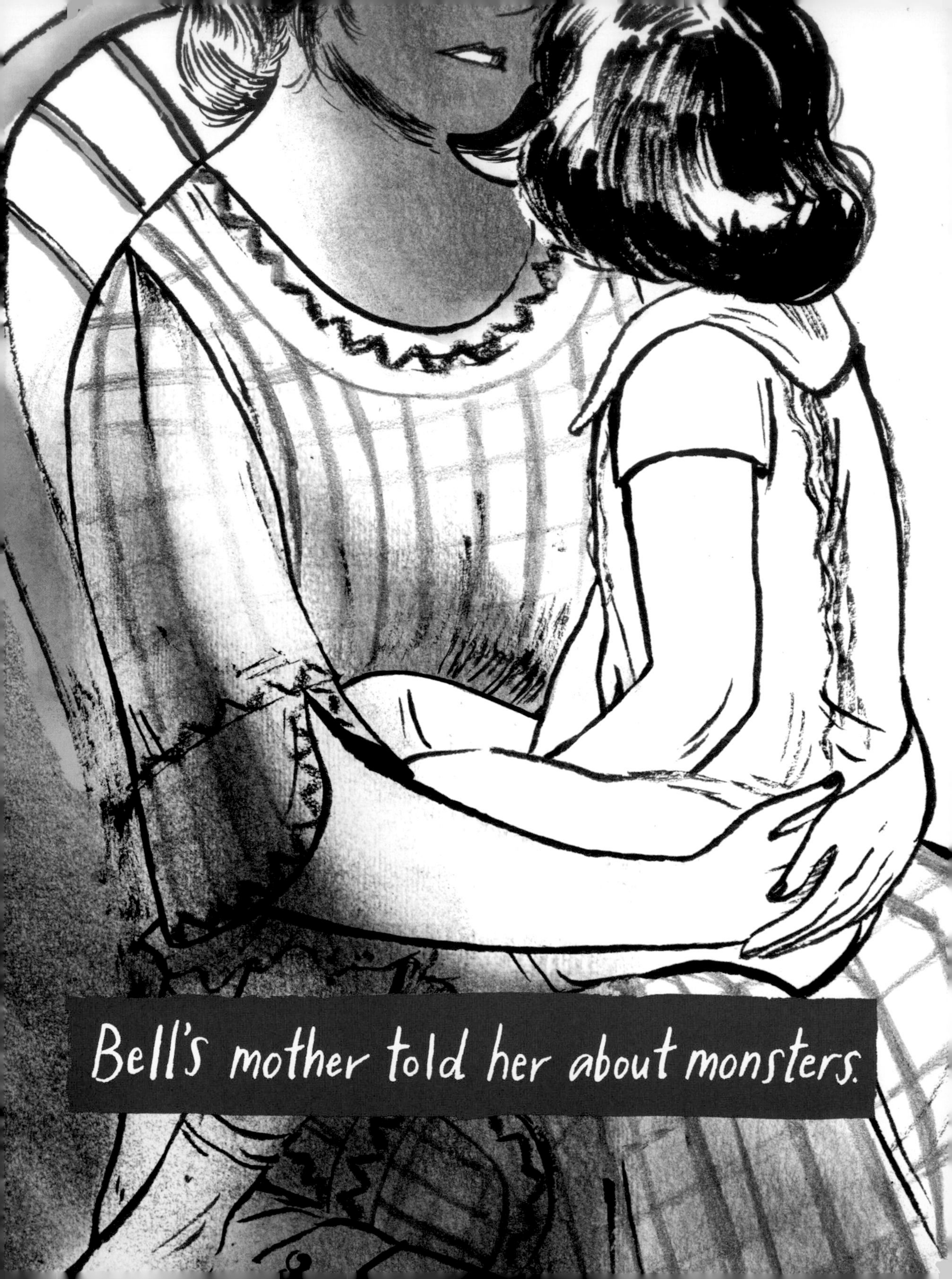
Bell's mother told her about monsters.

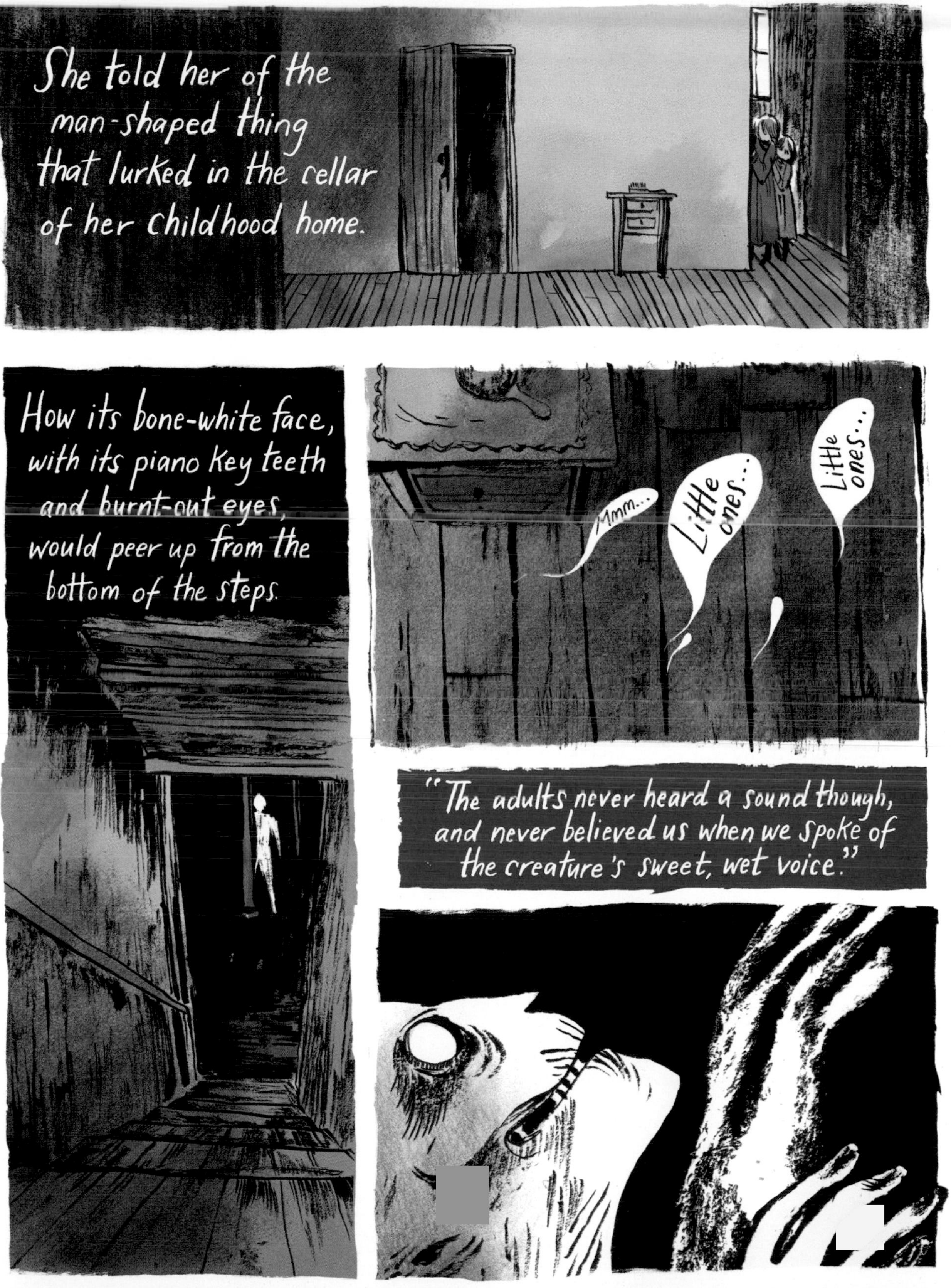
She told her of the man-shaped thing that lurked in the cellar of her childhood home.
How its bone-white face, with its piano key teeth and burnt-out eyes, would peer up from the bottom of the steps.
Mmm...
Little ones...
Little ones...
"The adults never heard a sound though, and never believed us when we spoke of the creature's sweet, wet voice."

She spoke of the dark fog that seeped
over their town years ago...

...and of the thousand mouths it hid.

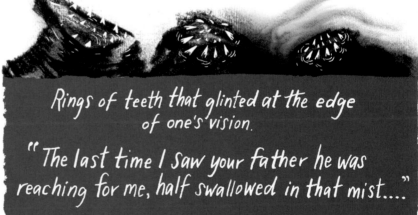

Rings of teeth that glinted at the edge
of one's vision.

"The last time I saw your father he was
reaching for me, half swallowed in that mist...."

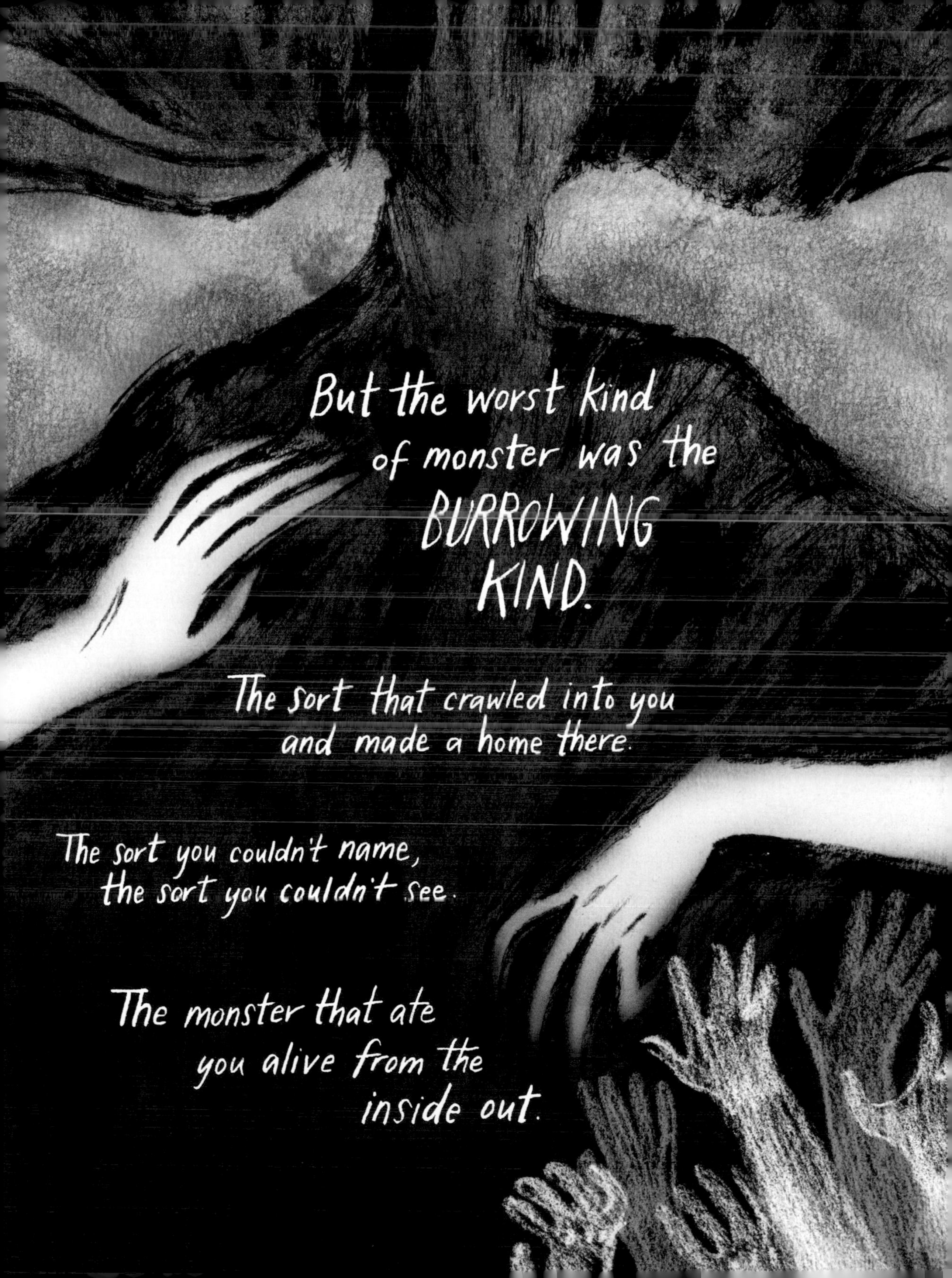
But the worst kind of monster was the BURROWING KIND.
The sort that crawled into you and made a home there.
The sort you couldn't name, the sort you couldn't see.
The monster that ate you alive from the inside out.

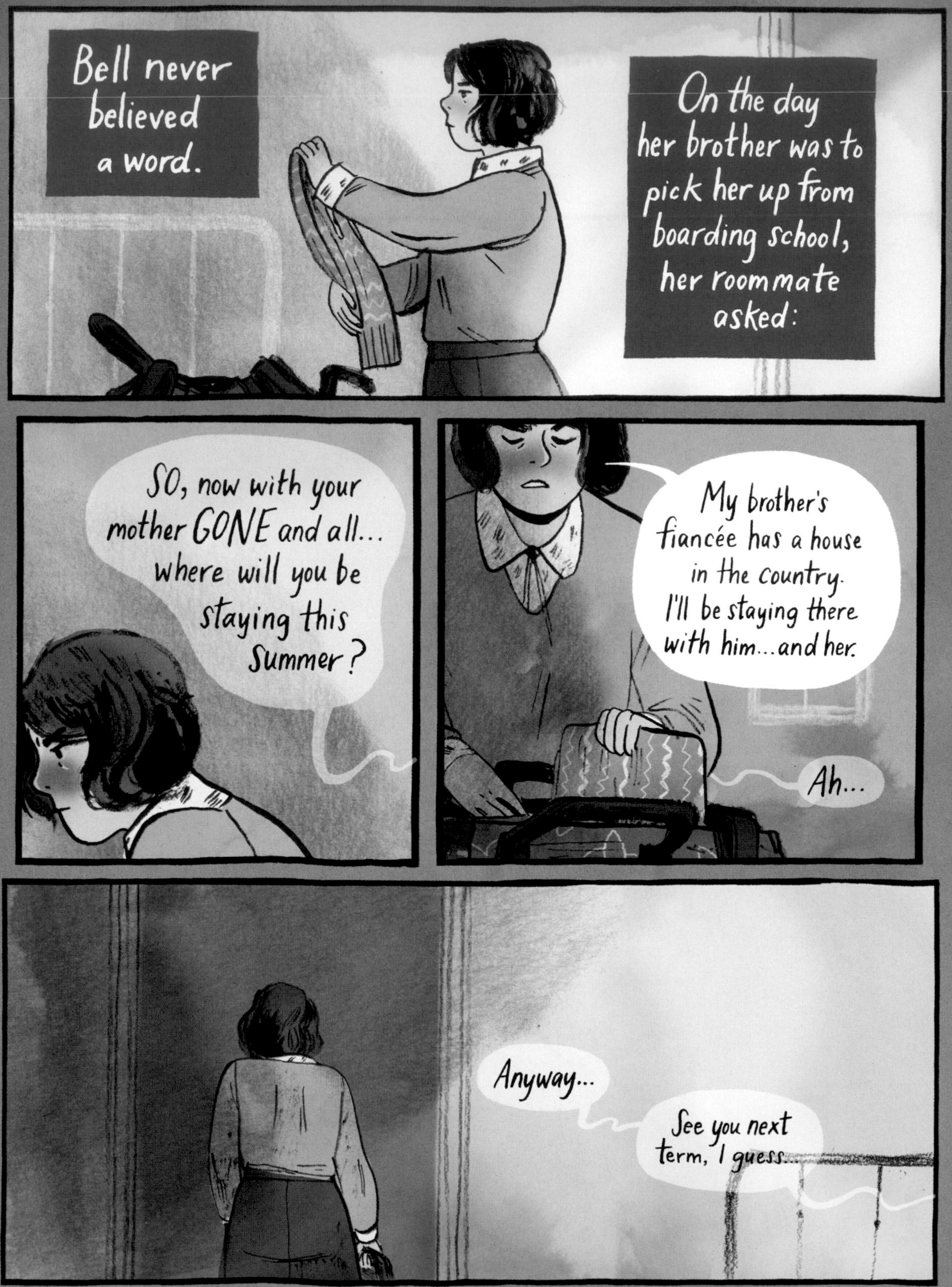
Bell never believed a word.
On the day her brother was to pick her up from boarding school, her roommate asked:
SO, now with your mother GONE and all... where will you be staying this summer?
My brother's fiancée has a house in the country. I'll be staying there with him...and her.
Ah...
Anyway...
See you next term, I guess...

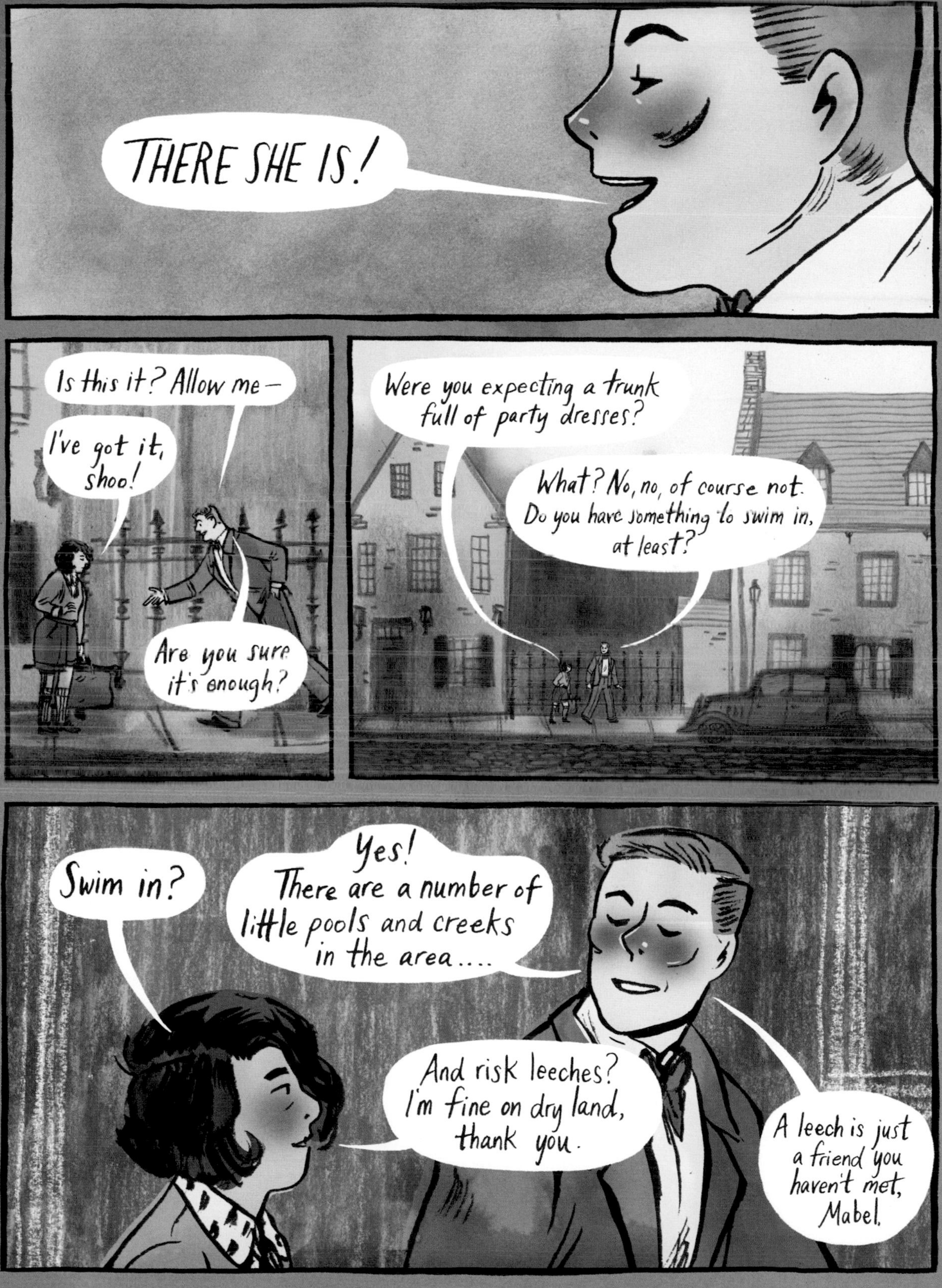
THERE SHE IS!
Is this it? Allow me—
I've got it, shoo!
Are you sure it's enough?
Were you expecting a trunk full of party dresses?
What? No, no, of course not. Do you have something to swim in, at least?
Swim in?
Yes! There are a number of little pools and creeks in the area....
And risk leeches? I'm fine on dry land, thank you.
A leech is just a friend you haven't met, Mabel.

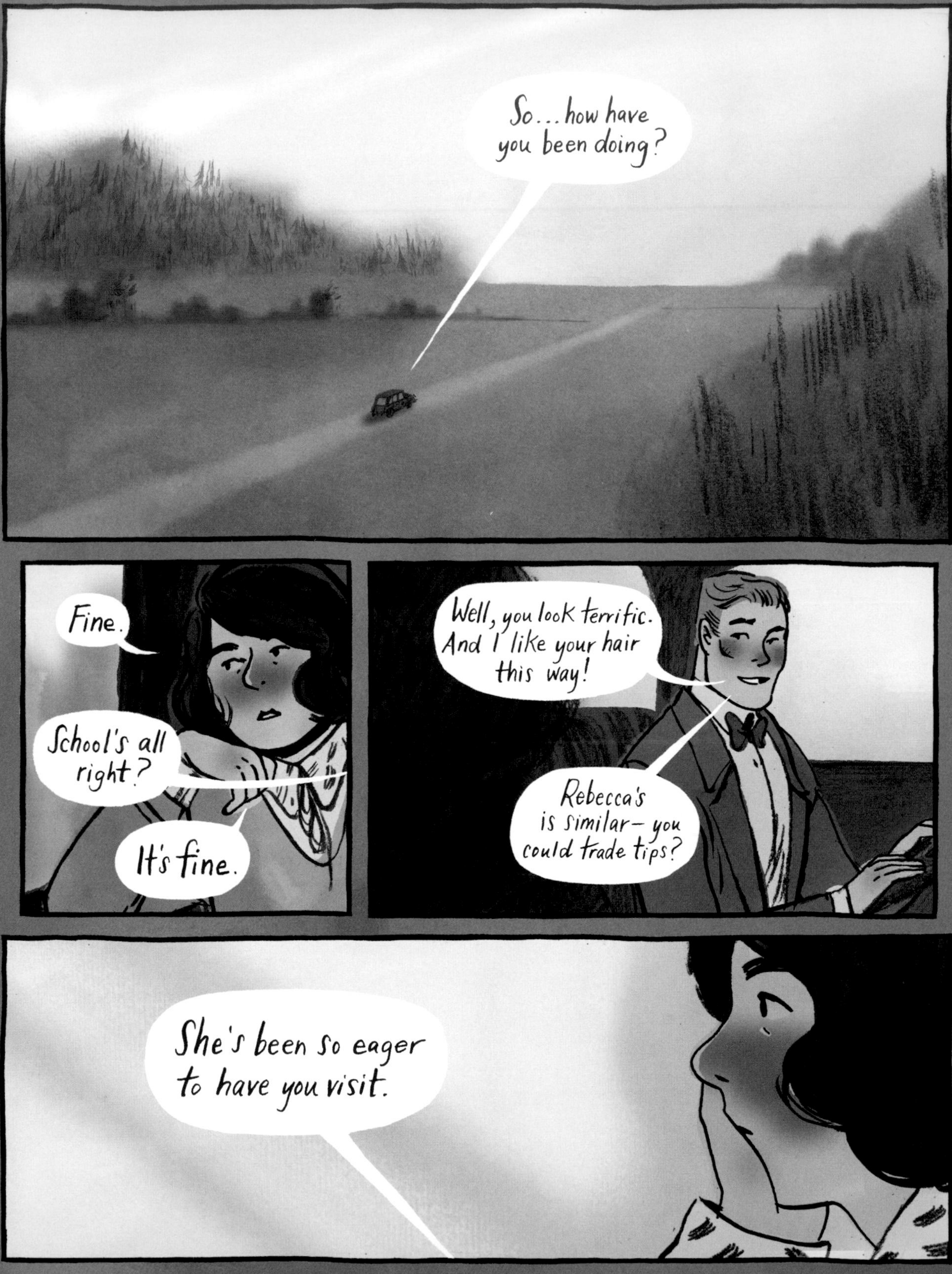
So... how have you been doing?
Fine.
School's all right?
It's fine.
Well, you look terrific. And I like your hair this way!
Rebecca's is similar— you could trade tips?
She's been so eager to have you visit.

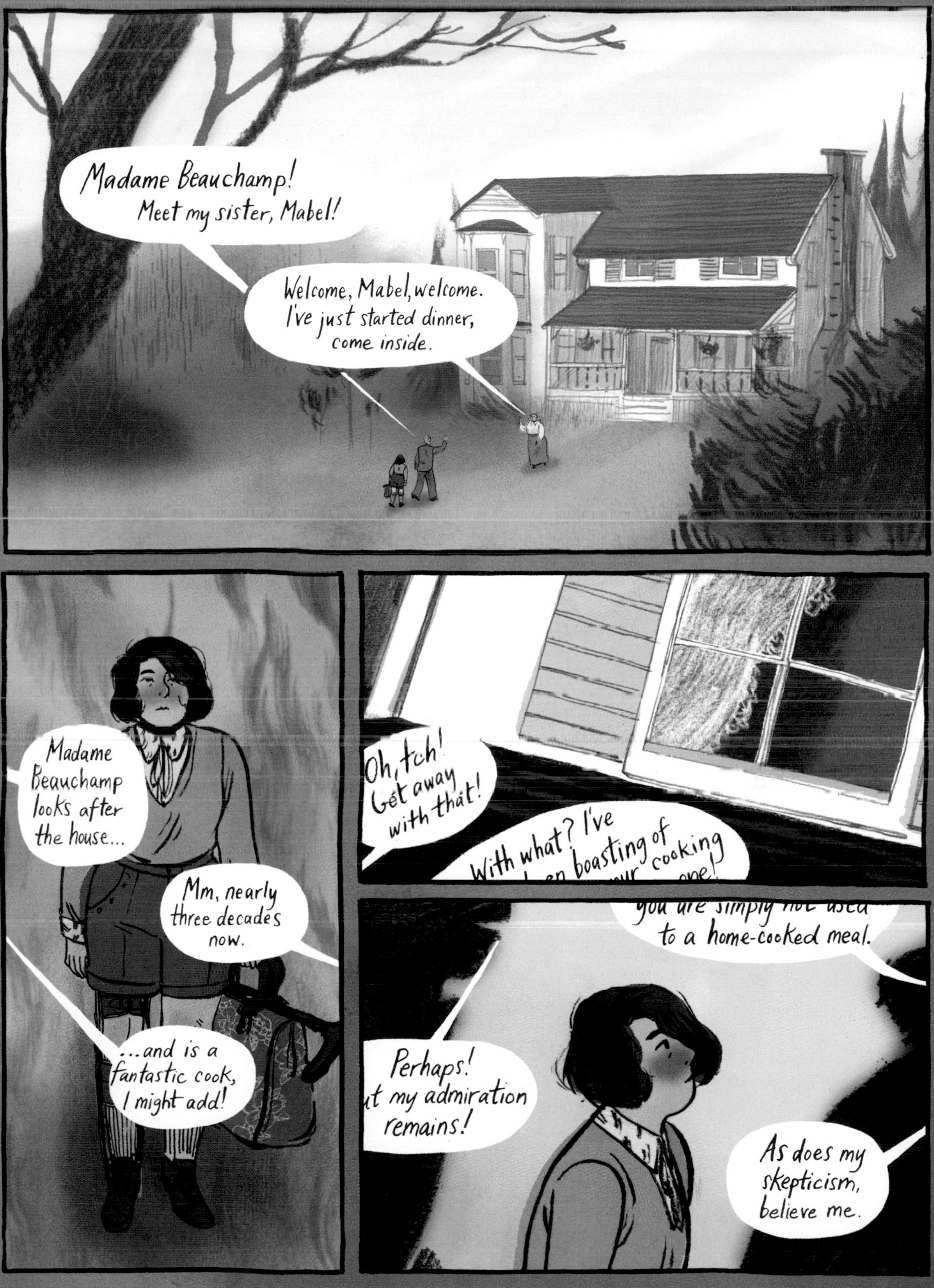
Madame Beauchamp! Meet my sister, Mabel!
Welcome, Mabel, welcome. I've just started dinner, come inside.
Madame Beauchamp looks after the house...
Mm, nearly three decades now.
...and is a fantastic cook, I might add!
Oh, tch! Get away with that!
With what? I've
to a home-cooked meal.
Perhaps!
t my admiration remains!
As does my skepticism, believe me.

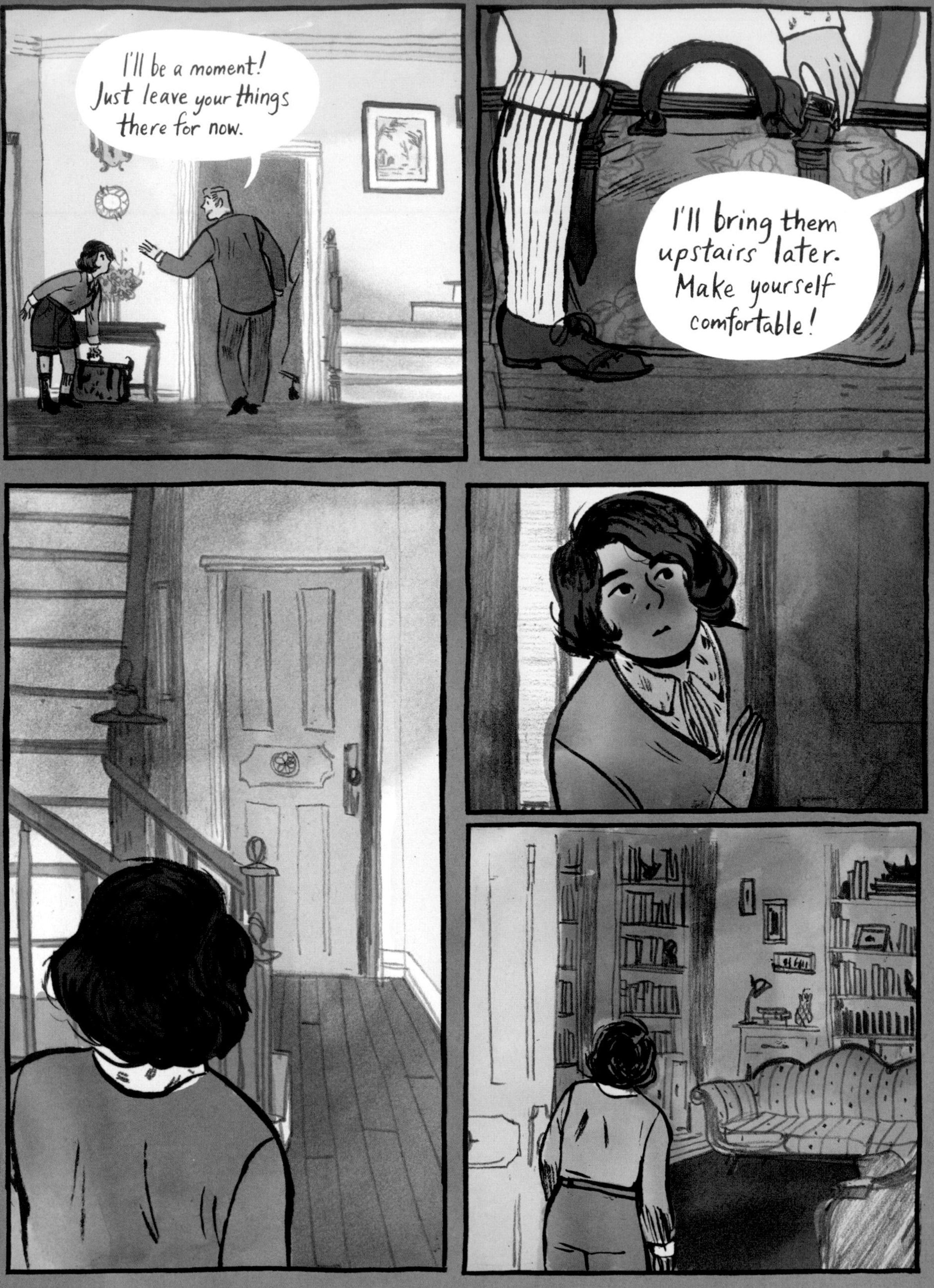
I'll be a moment! Just leave your things there for now.
I'll bring them upstairs later. Make yourself comfortable!

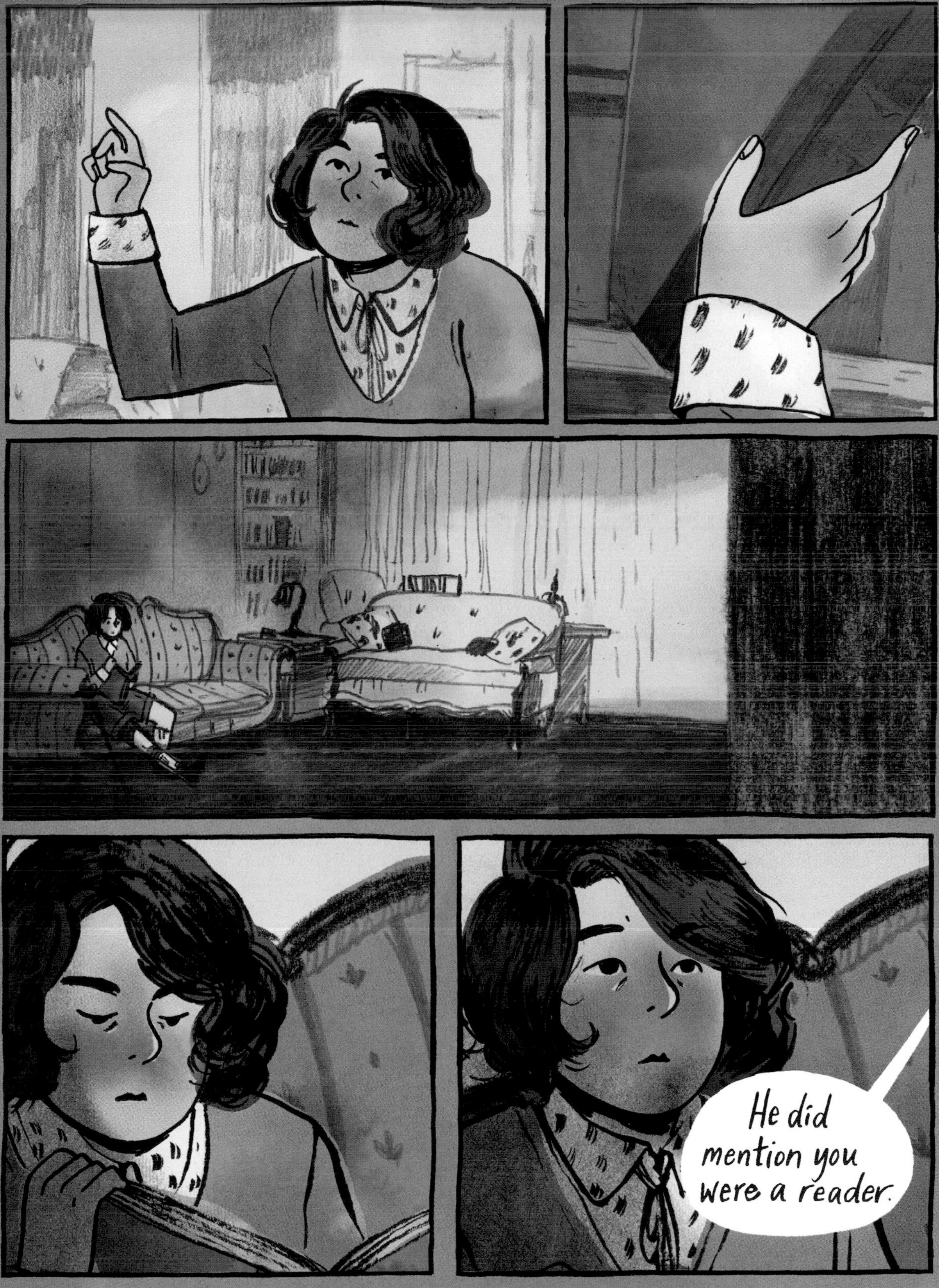
He did mention you were a reader.

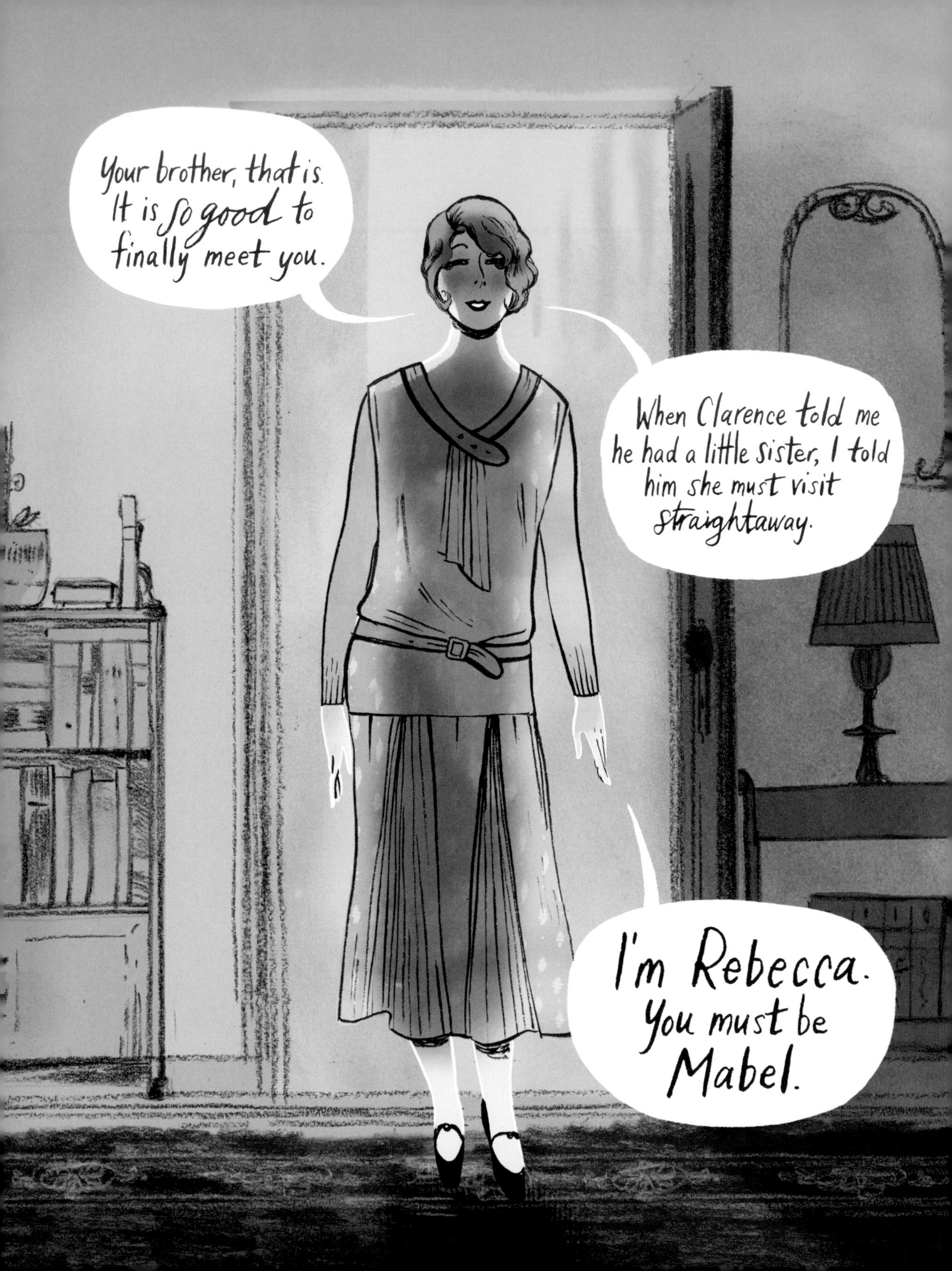
Your brother, that is. It is so good to finally meet you.
When Clarence told me he had a little sister, I told him she must visit straightaway.
I'm Rebecca. You must be Mabel.

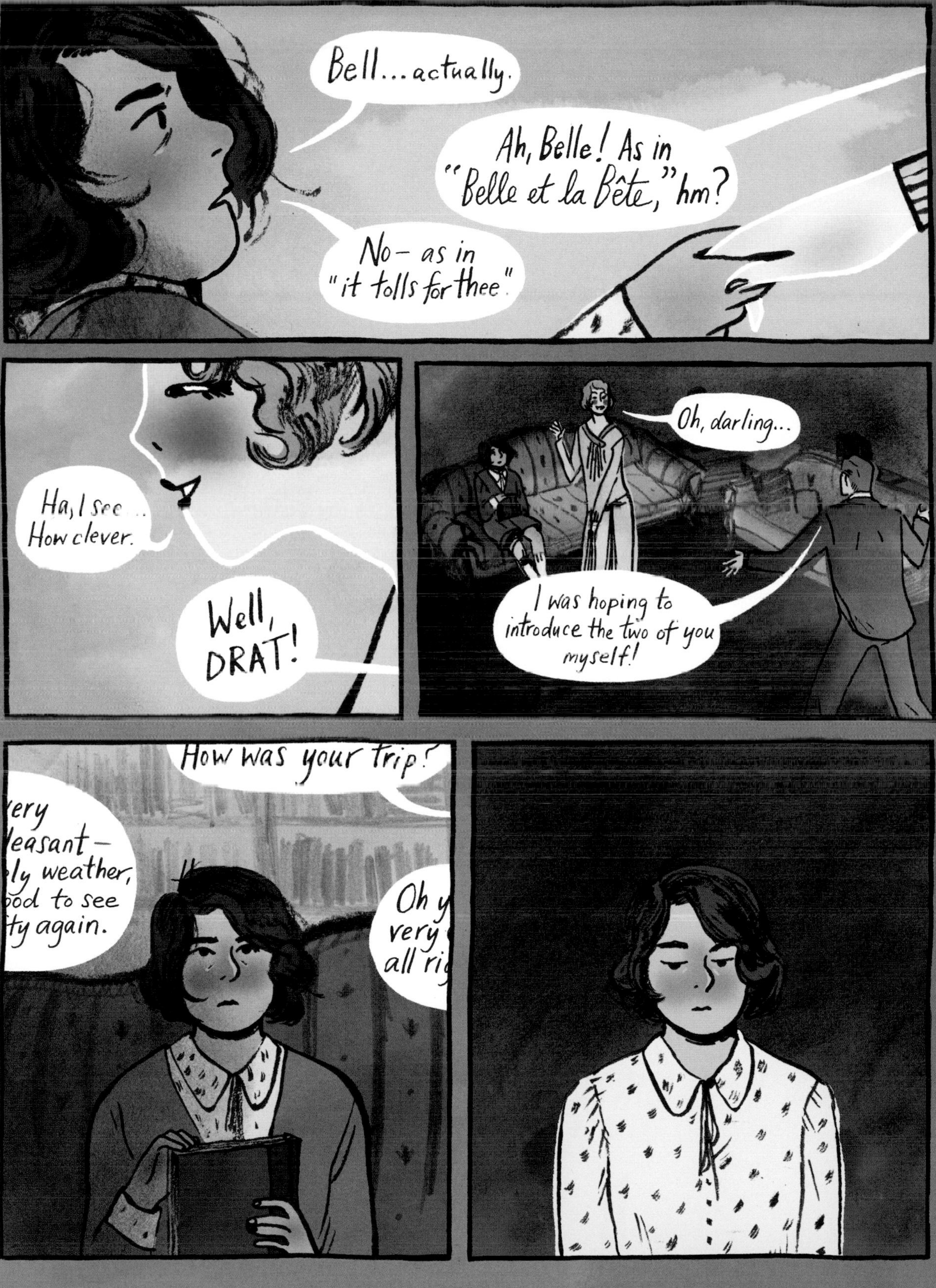
Bell... actually.
Ah, Belle! As in "Belle et la Bête," hm?
No– as in "it tolls for thee".
Ha, I see... How clever.
Well, DRAT!
Oh, darling...
I was hoping to introduce the two of you myself!
How was your trip?

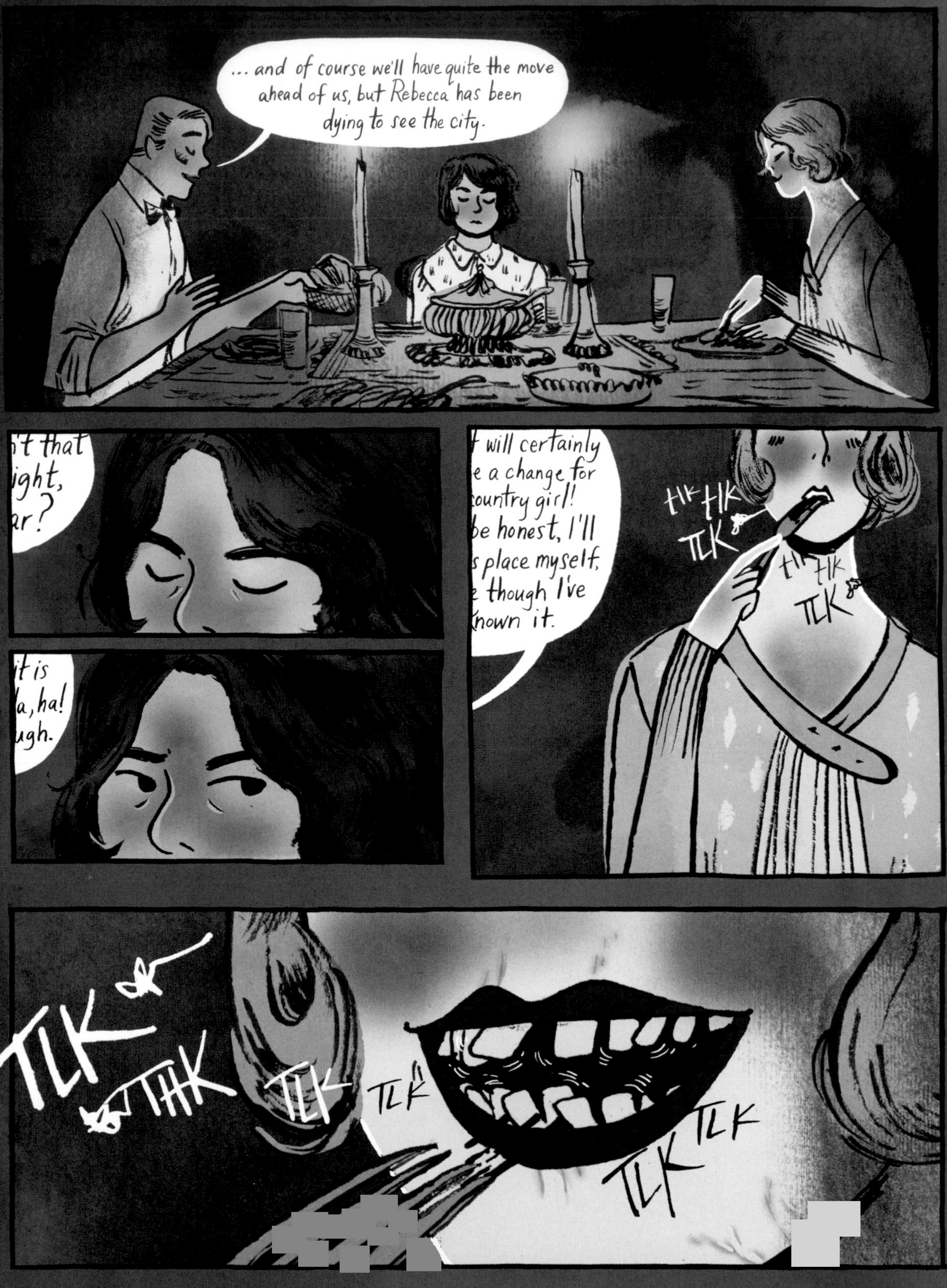

... and of course we'll have quite the move ahead of us, but Rebecca has been dying to see the city.
t that ight, ar?
it is a, ha! ugh.
will certainly e a change for country girl! be honest, I'll s place myself, though I've known it.
tlk tlk TLK
tlk tlk TLK
TLK
THK
TLK
TLK
TLK
TLK

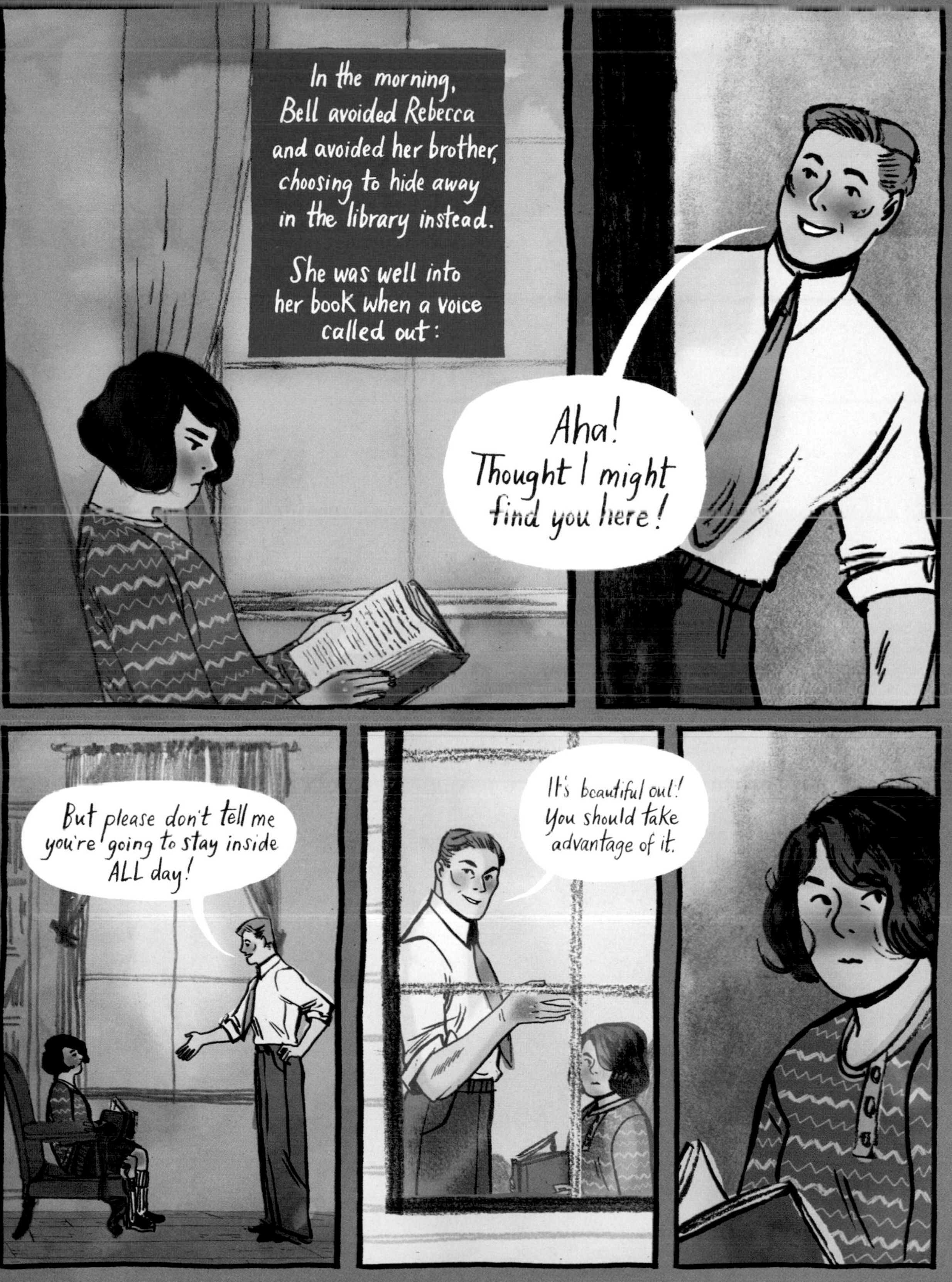
In the morning, Bell avoided Rebecca and avoided her brother, choosing to hide away in the library instead.
She was well into her book when a voice called out:
Aha! Thought I might find you here!
But please don't tell me you're going to stay inside ALL day!
It's beautiful out! You should take advantage of it.

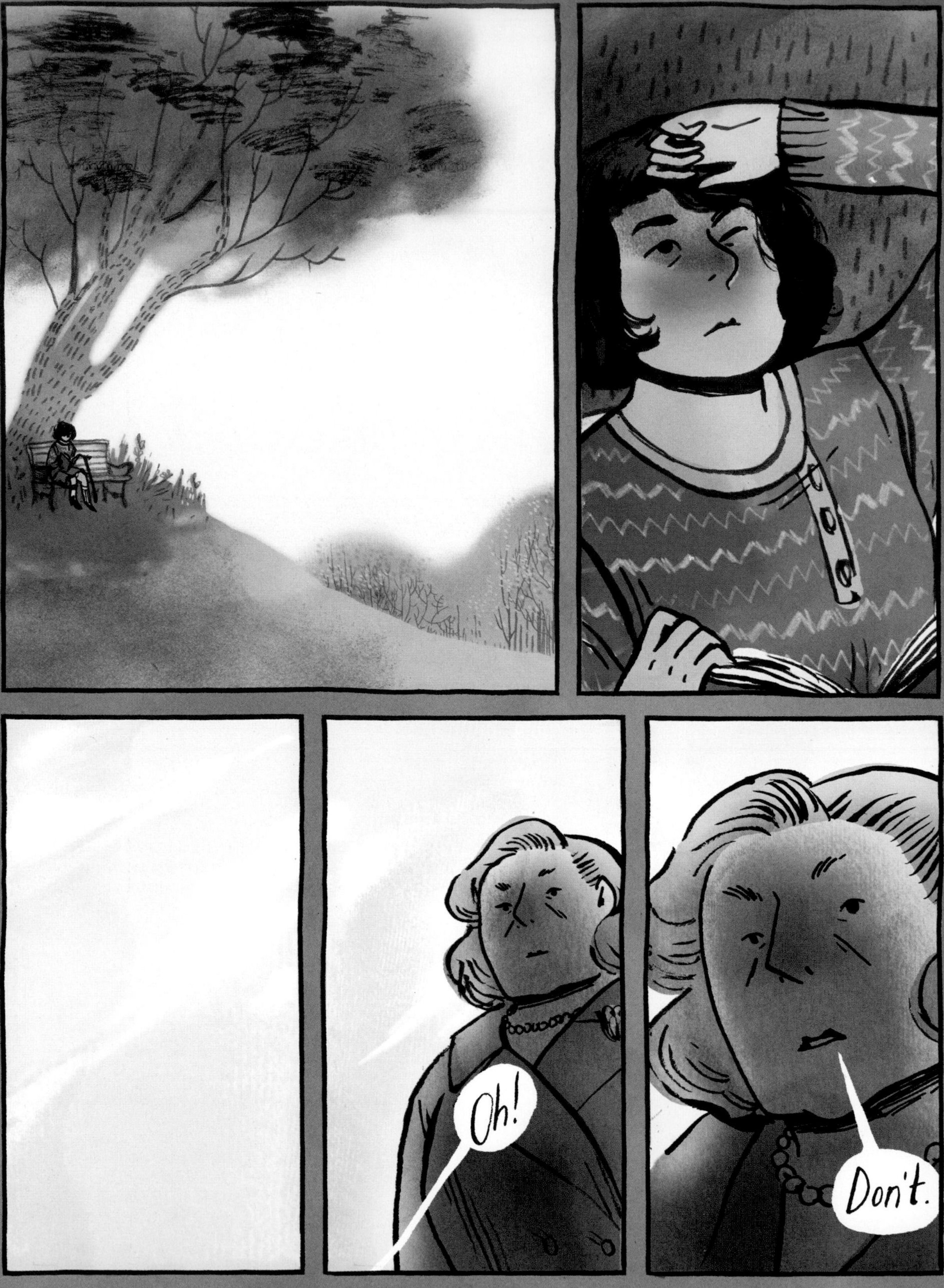
Oh!
Don't.

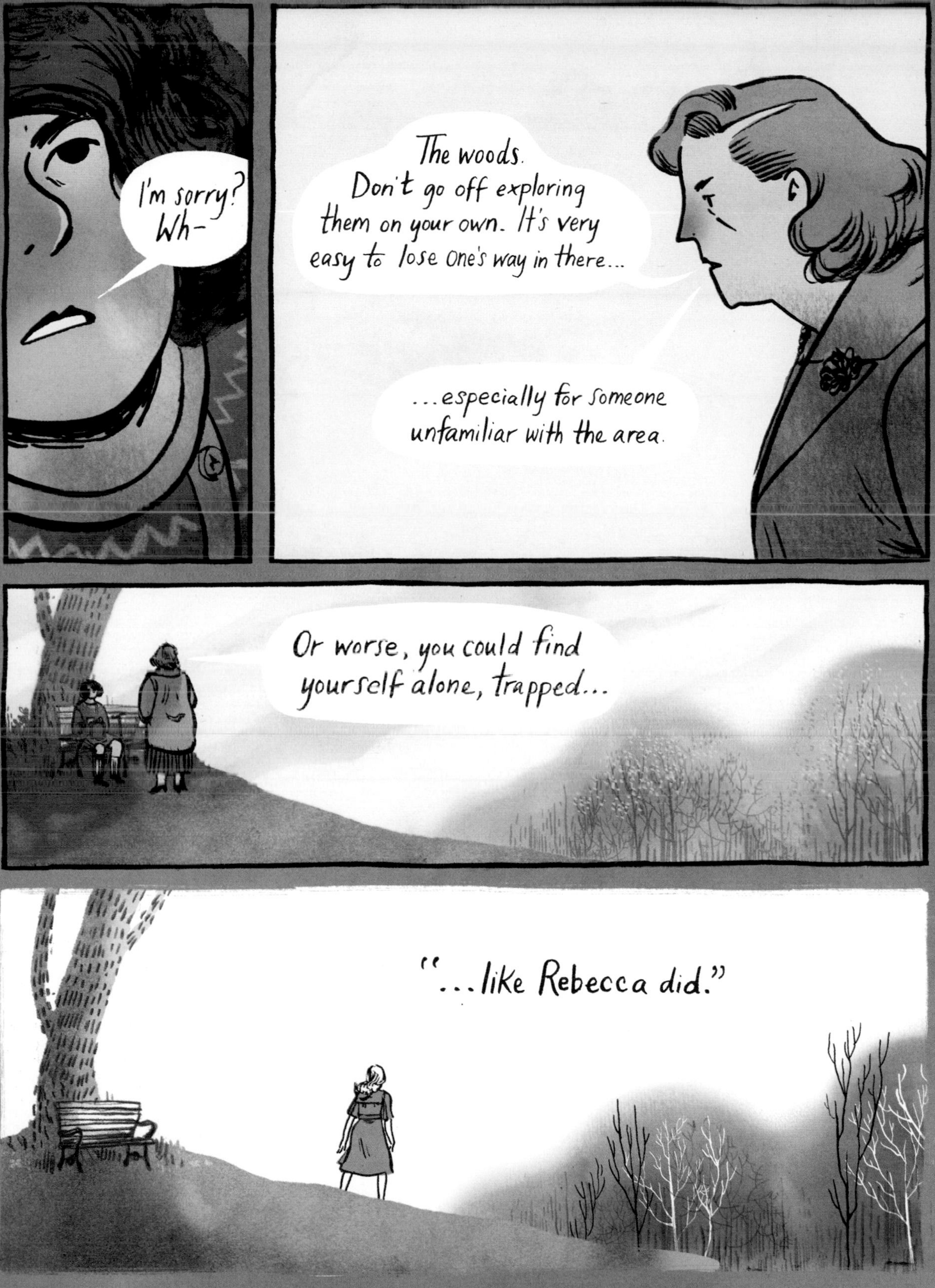
I'm sorry? Wh-
The woods. Don't go off exploring them on your own. It's very easy to lose one's way in there...
...especially for someone unfamiliar with the area.
Or worse, you could find yourself alone, trapped...
"...like Rebecca did."

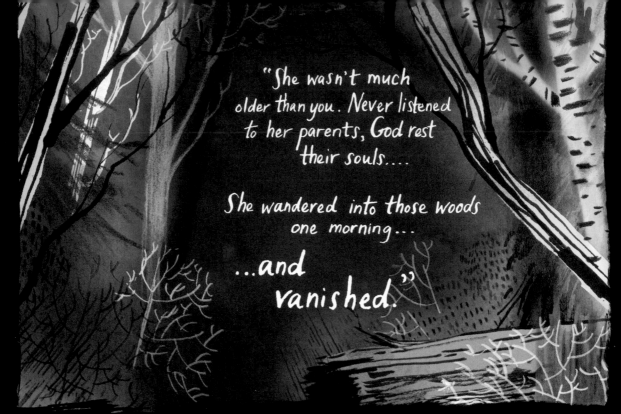

"She wasn't much older than you. Never listened to her parents, God rest their souls....

She wandered into those woods one morning...

...and vanished."

"We found her three days later, at the bottom of a cave.

She'd fallen and been unable to climb out."

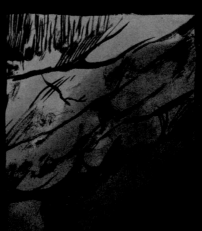

"THREE days all alone in the dark...

drinking water out of a fetid pool to stay alive.

All alone."

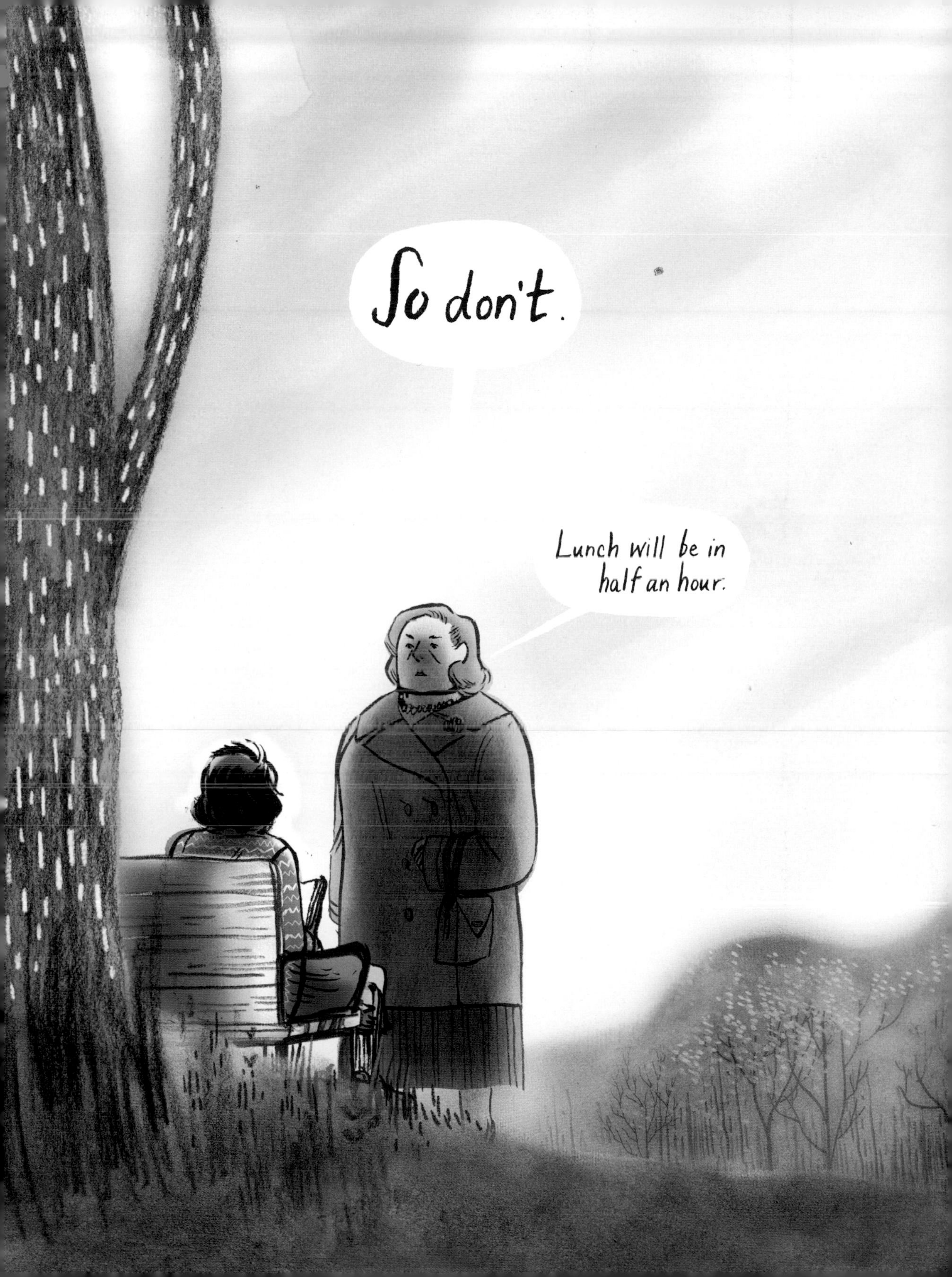
So don't.
Lunch will be in half an hour.

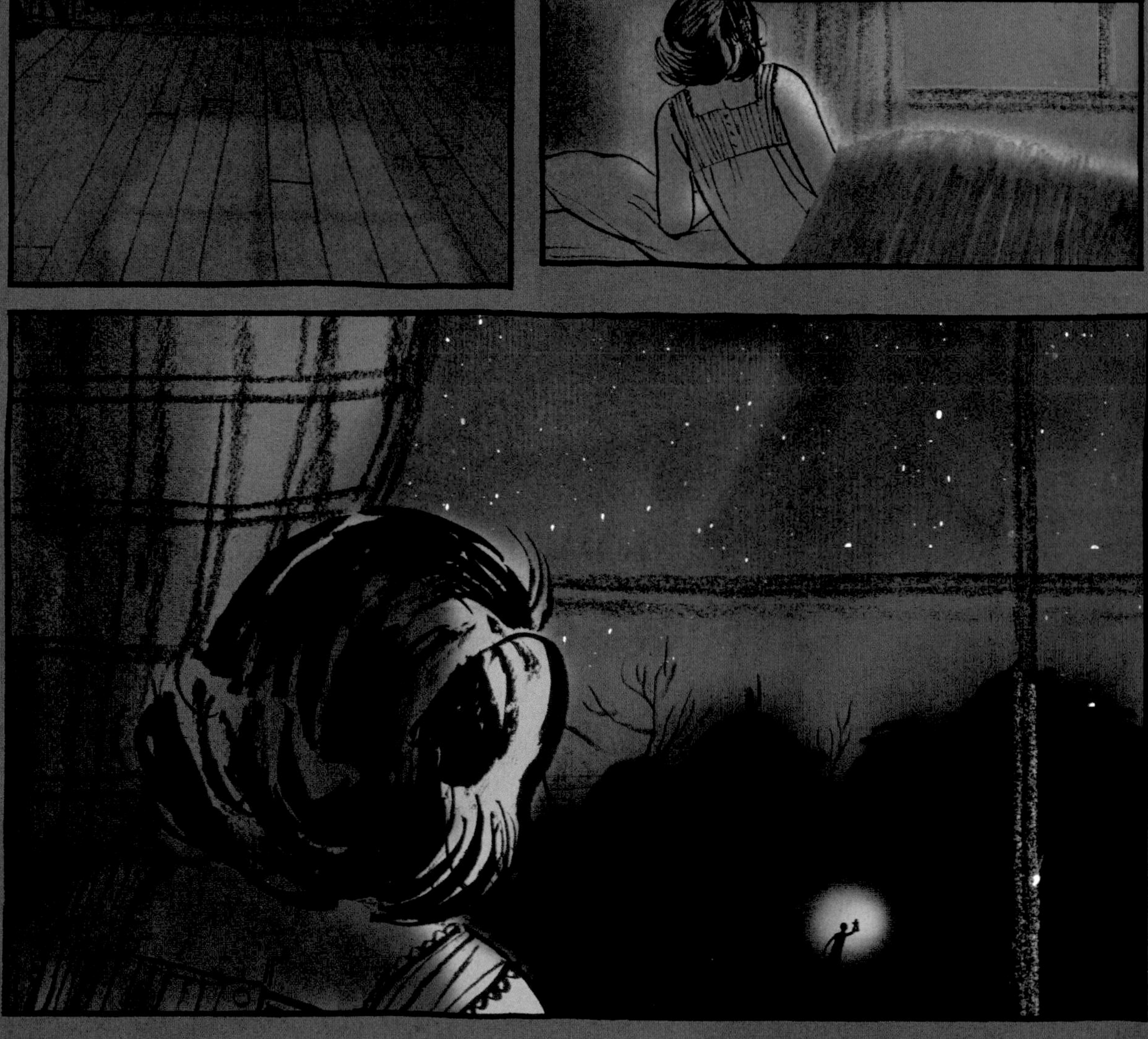

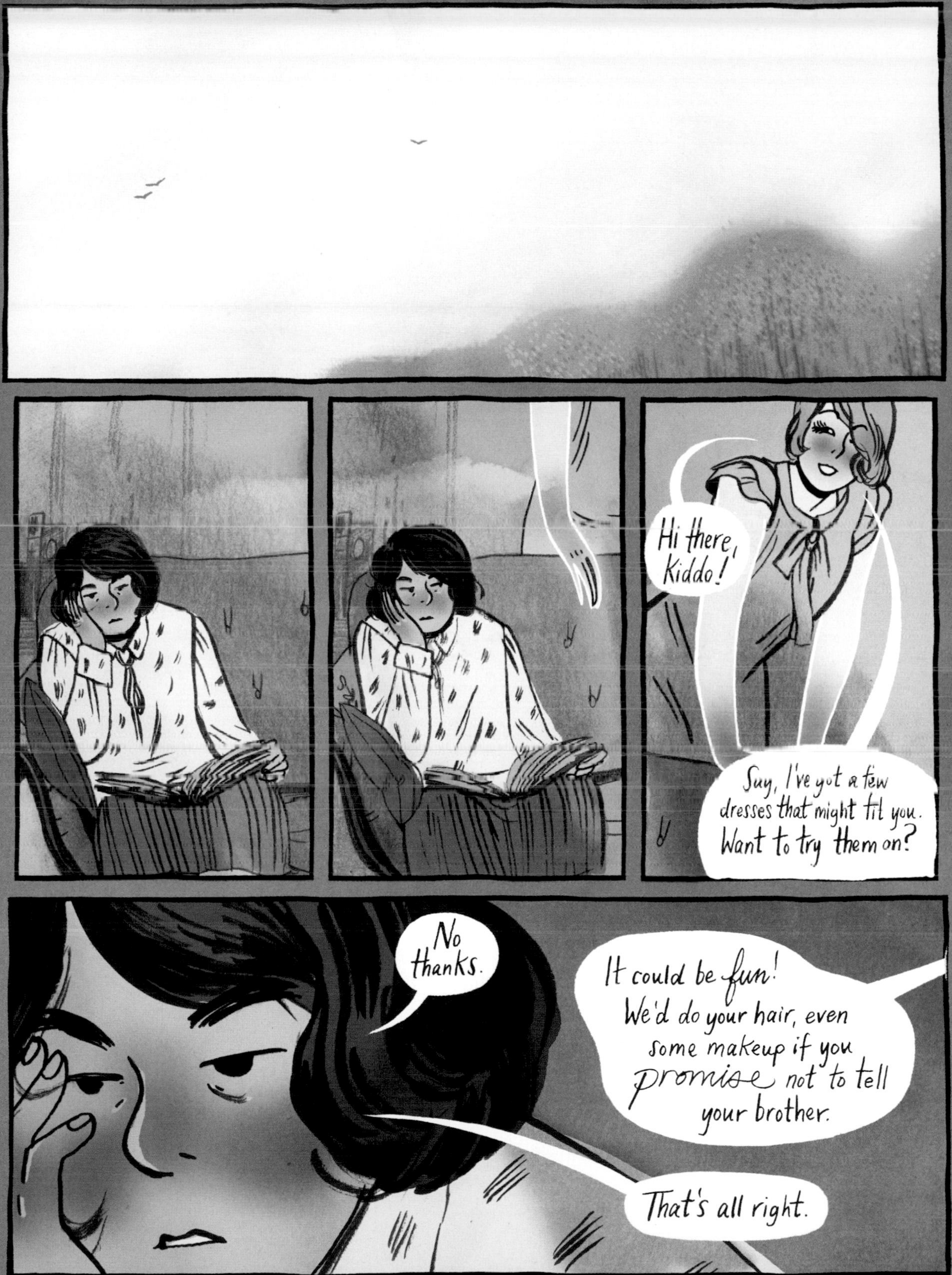
Hi there, Kiddo!
Say, I've got a few dresses that might fit you. Want to try them on?
No thanks.
It could be fun! We'd do your hair, even some makeup if you promise not to tell your brother.
That's all right.

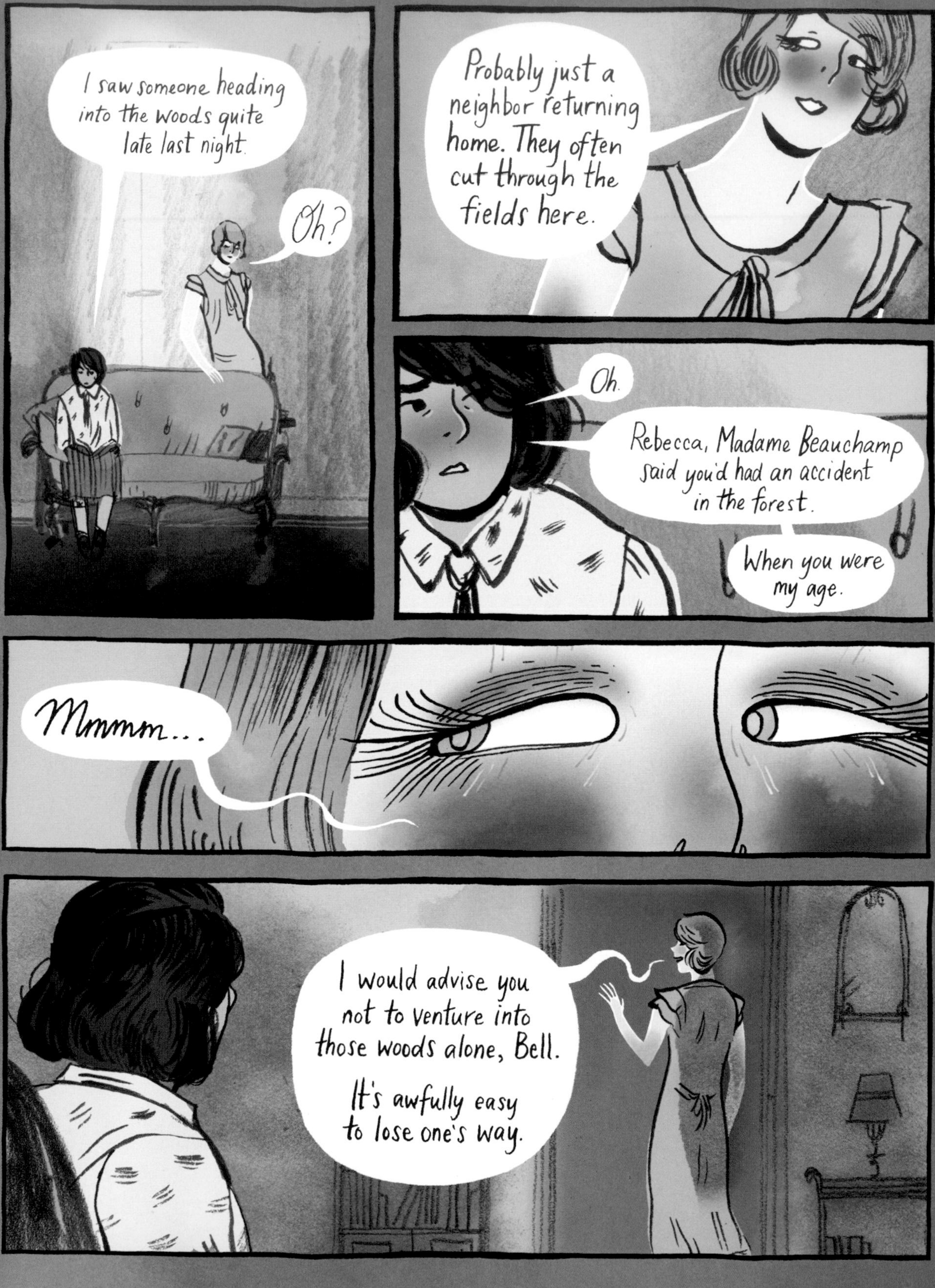
I saw someone heading into the woods quite late last night.
Oh?
Probably just a neighbor returning home. They often cut through the fields here.
Oh.
Rebecca, Madame Beauchamp said you'd had an accident in the forest.
When you were my age.
Mmmm...
I would advise you not to venture into those woods alone, Bell.
It's awfully easy to lose one's way.

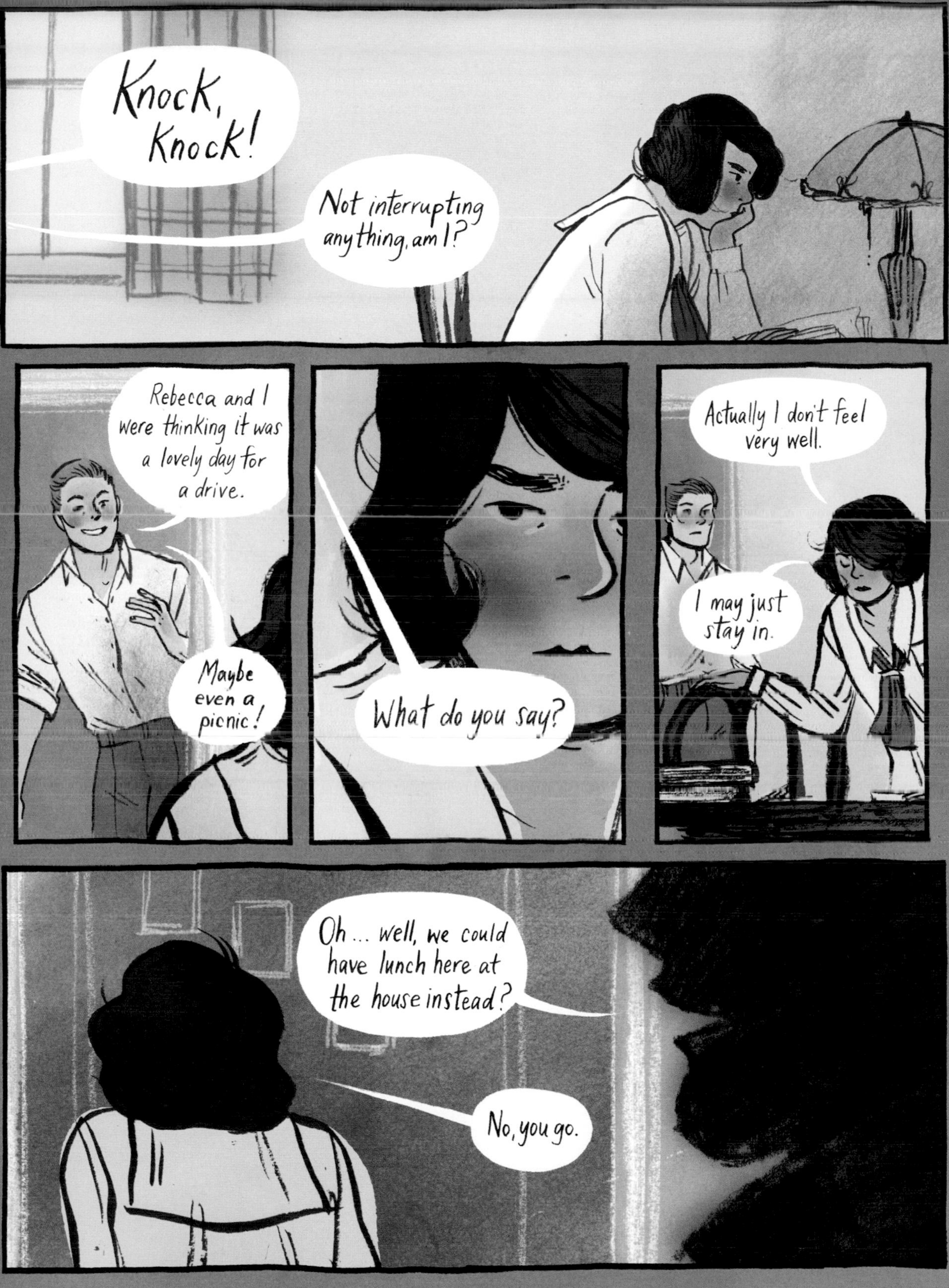
Knock, Knock!
Not interrupting anything, am I?
Rebecca and I were thinking it was a lovely day for a drive.
Maybe even a picnic!
What do you say?
Actually I don't feel very well.
I may just stay in.
Oh... well, we could have lunch here at the house instead?
No, you go.

Suit yourself. I'll be outside, getting the car ready, if you change your mind.

SKKlchSSS

SSS

Rebecca...it's not working...

sskklchsss

Quiet.

ssKklchsssKss

W-wait... Tonight, try again tonight...

Bell refused to go down for dinner that night.

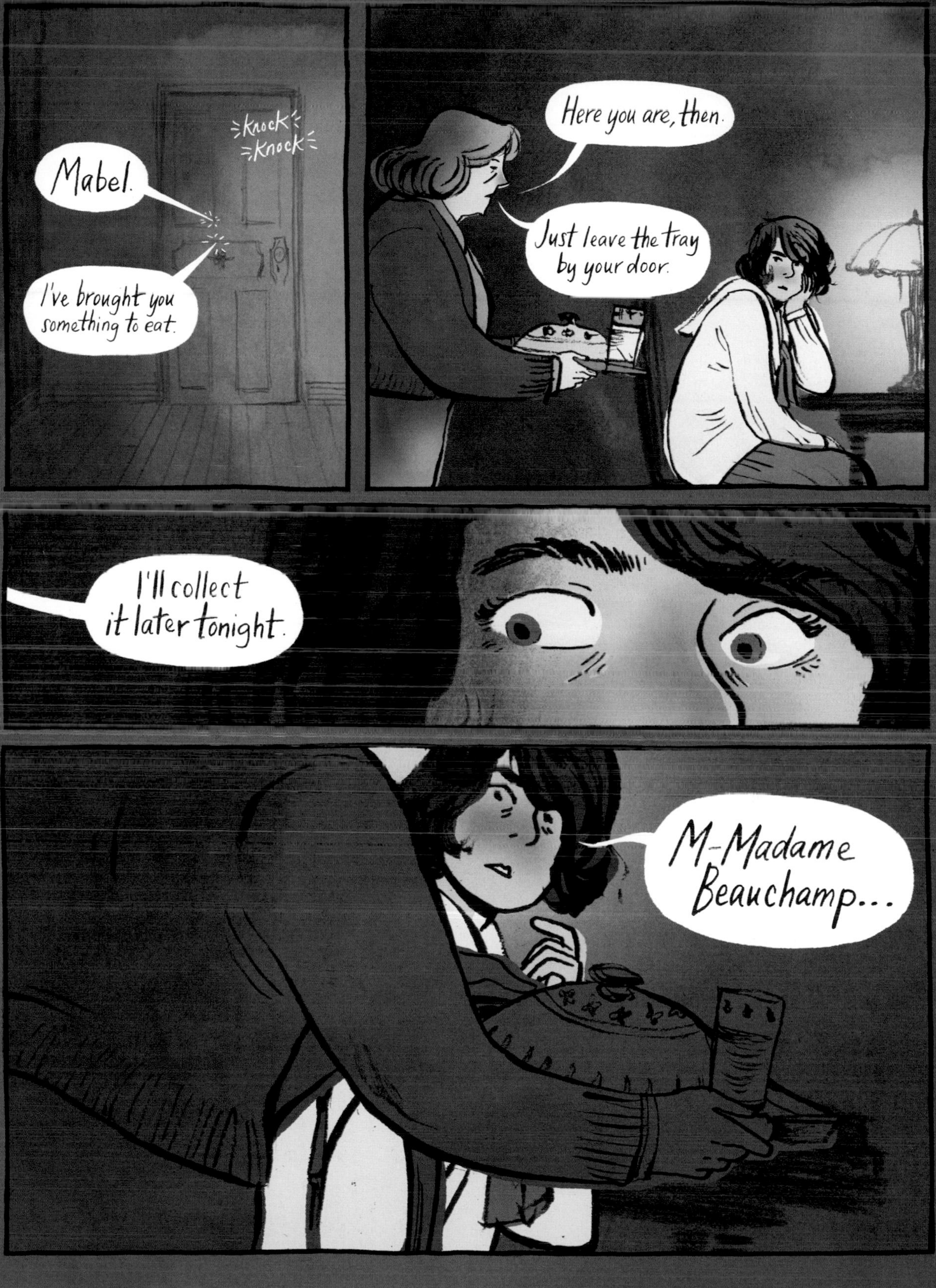
knock knock
Mabel.
I've brought you something to eat.
Here you are, then.
Just leave the tray by your door.
I'll collect it later tonight.
M-Madame Beauchamp...

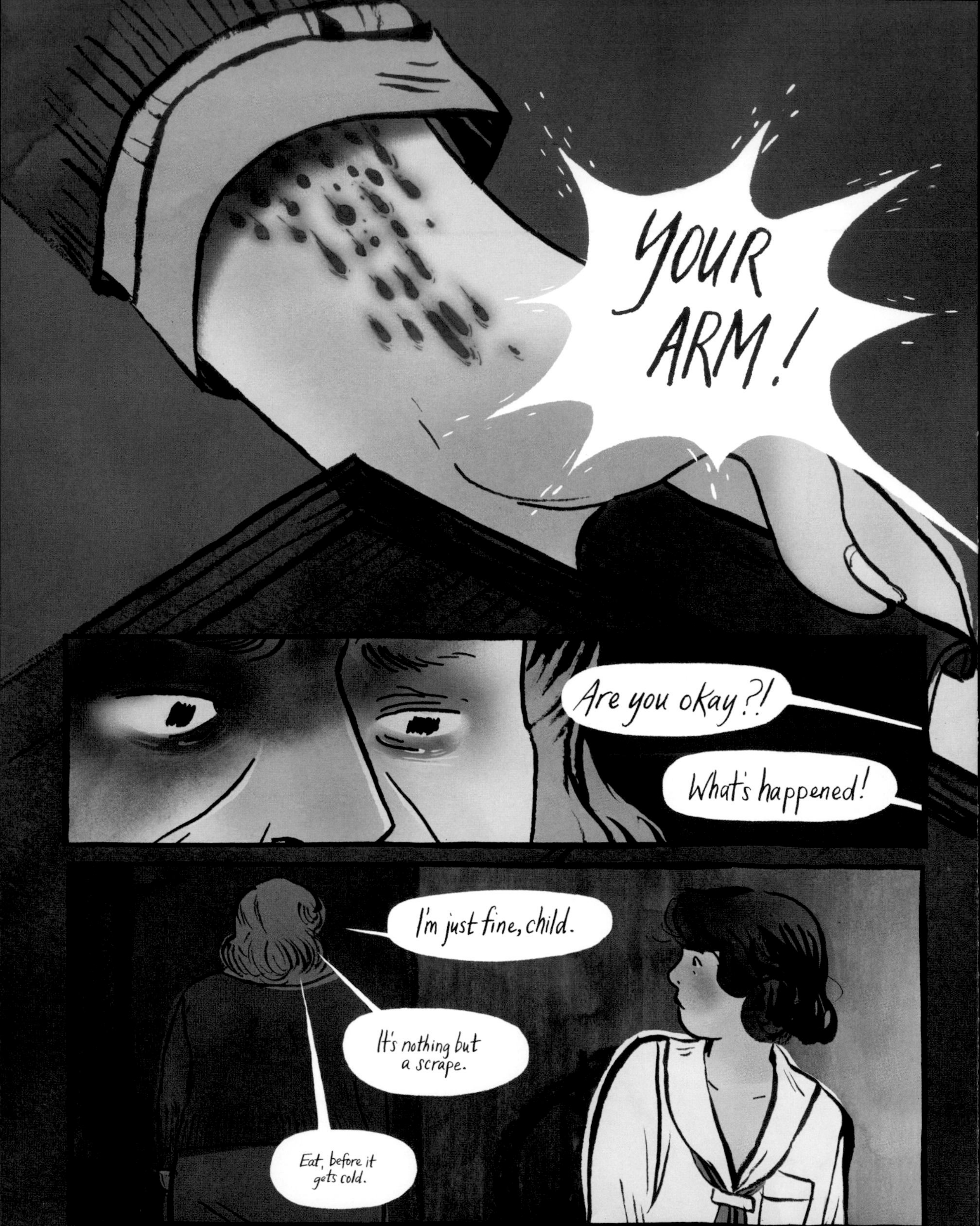
YOUR ARM!
Are you okay?!
What's happened!
I'm just fine, child.
It's nothing but a scrape.
Eat, before it gets cold.

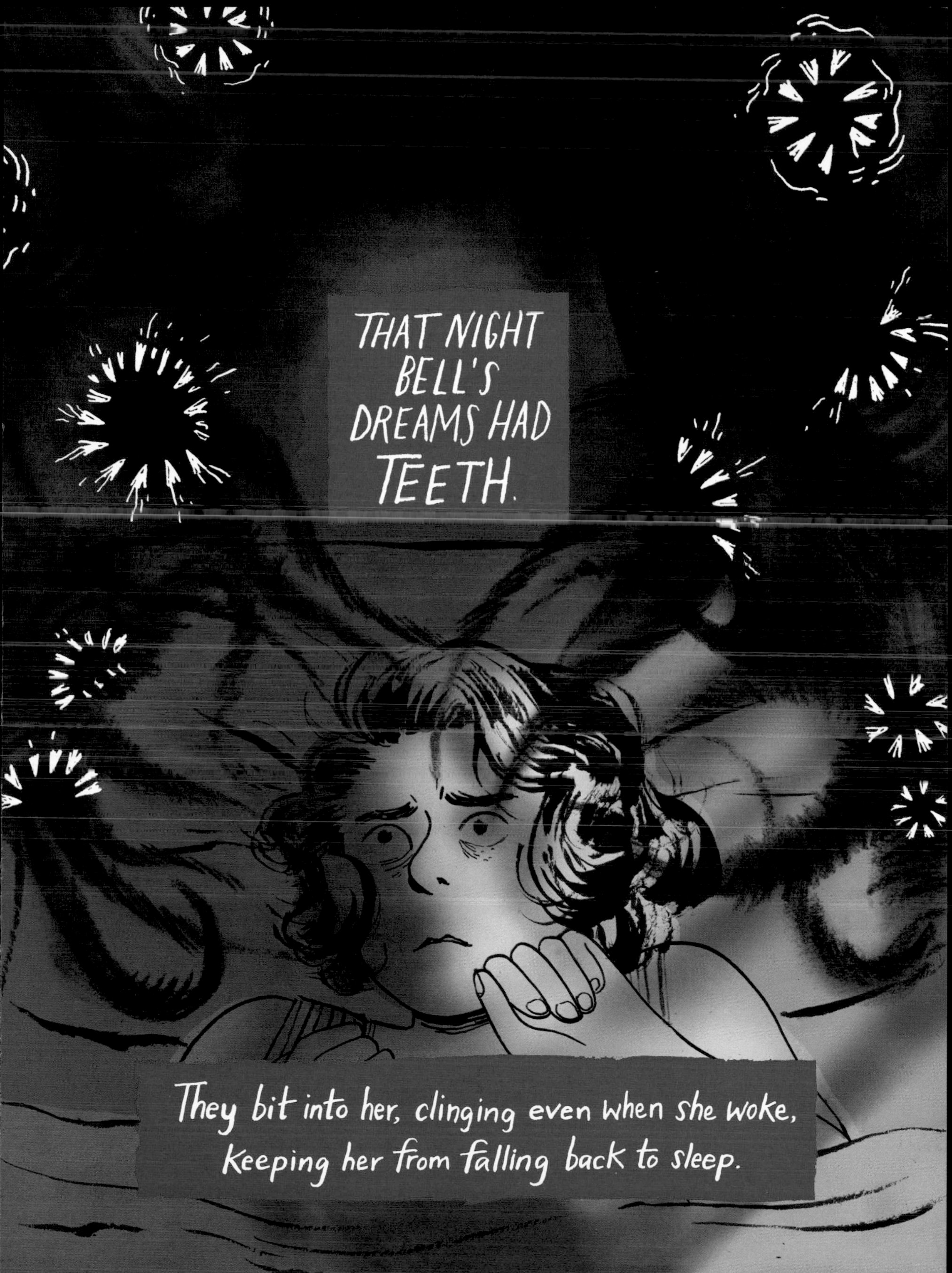
THAT NIGHT BELL'S DREAMS HAD TEETH.
They bit into her, clinging even when she woke, keeping her from falling back to sleep.

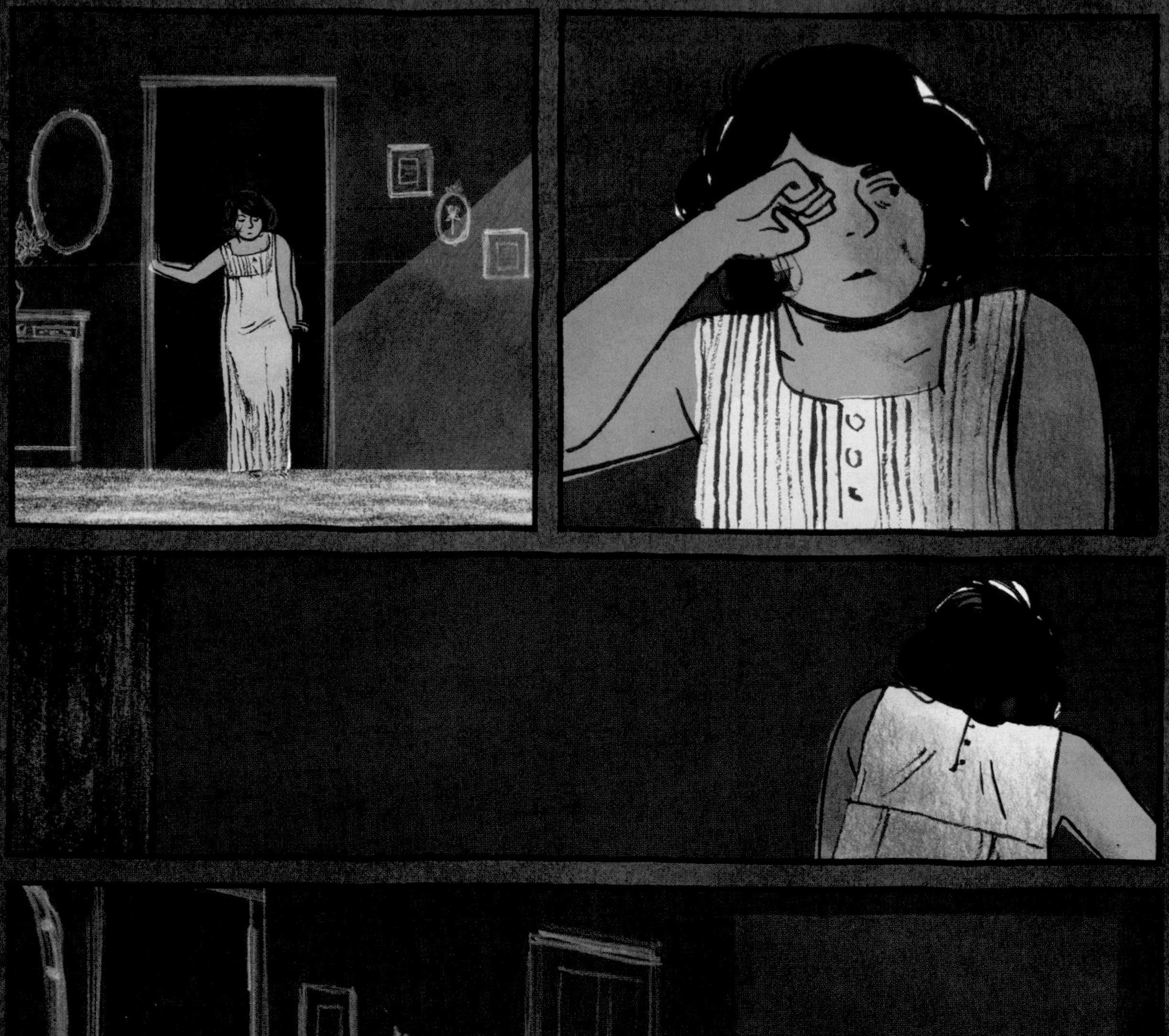

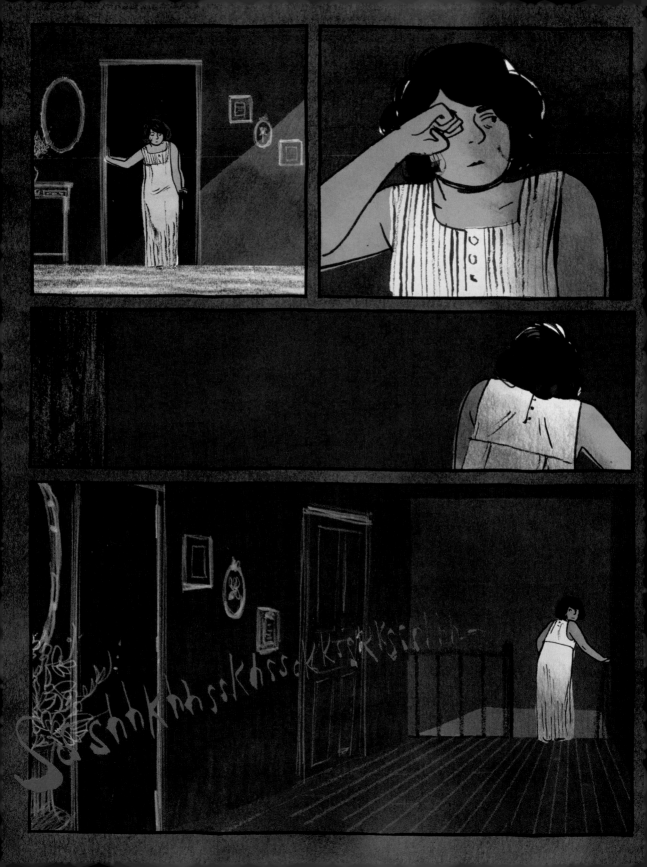

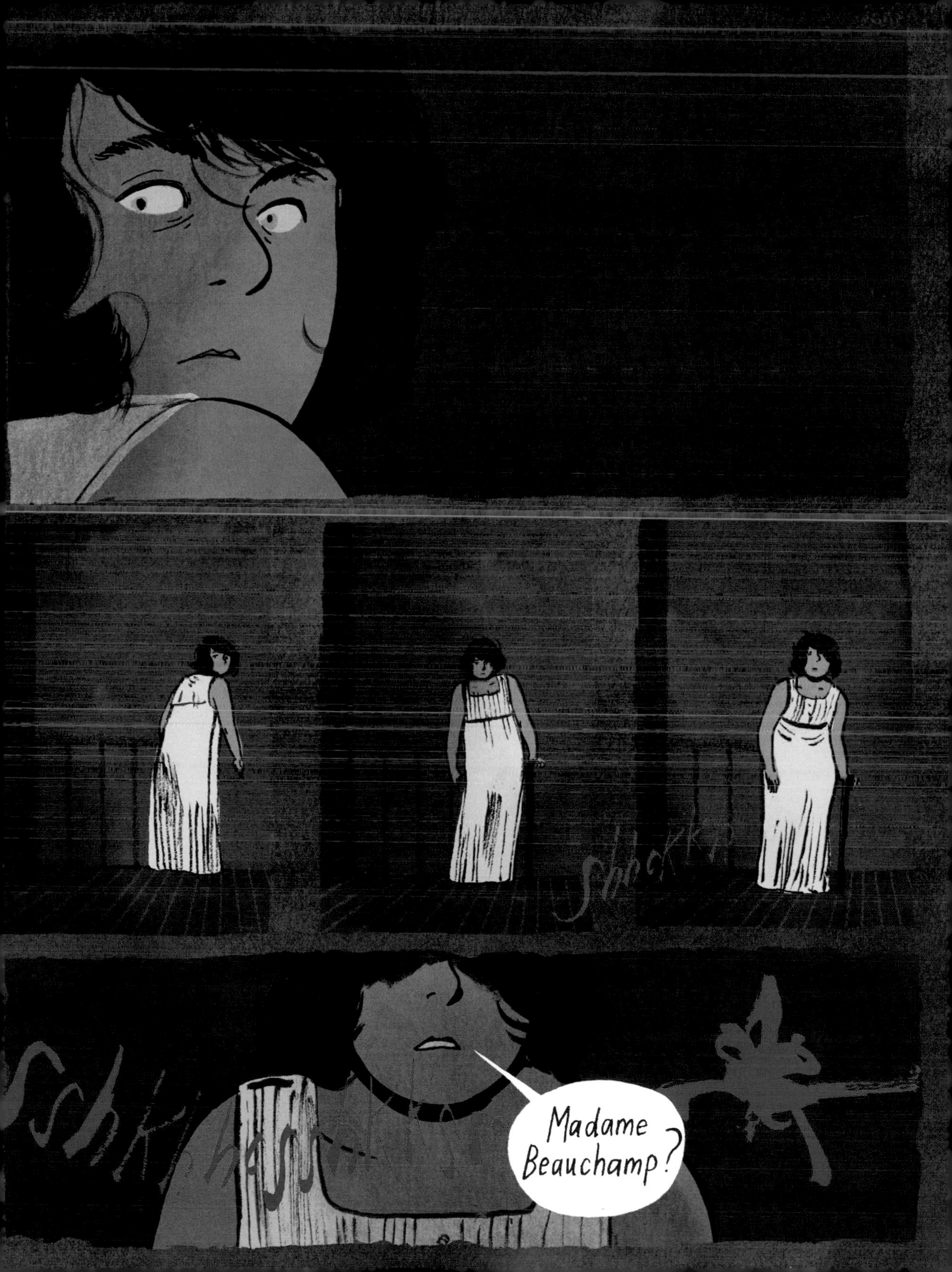
Madame Beauchamp?

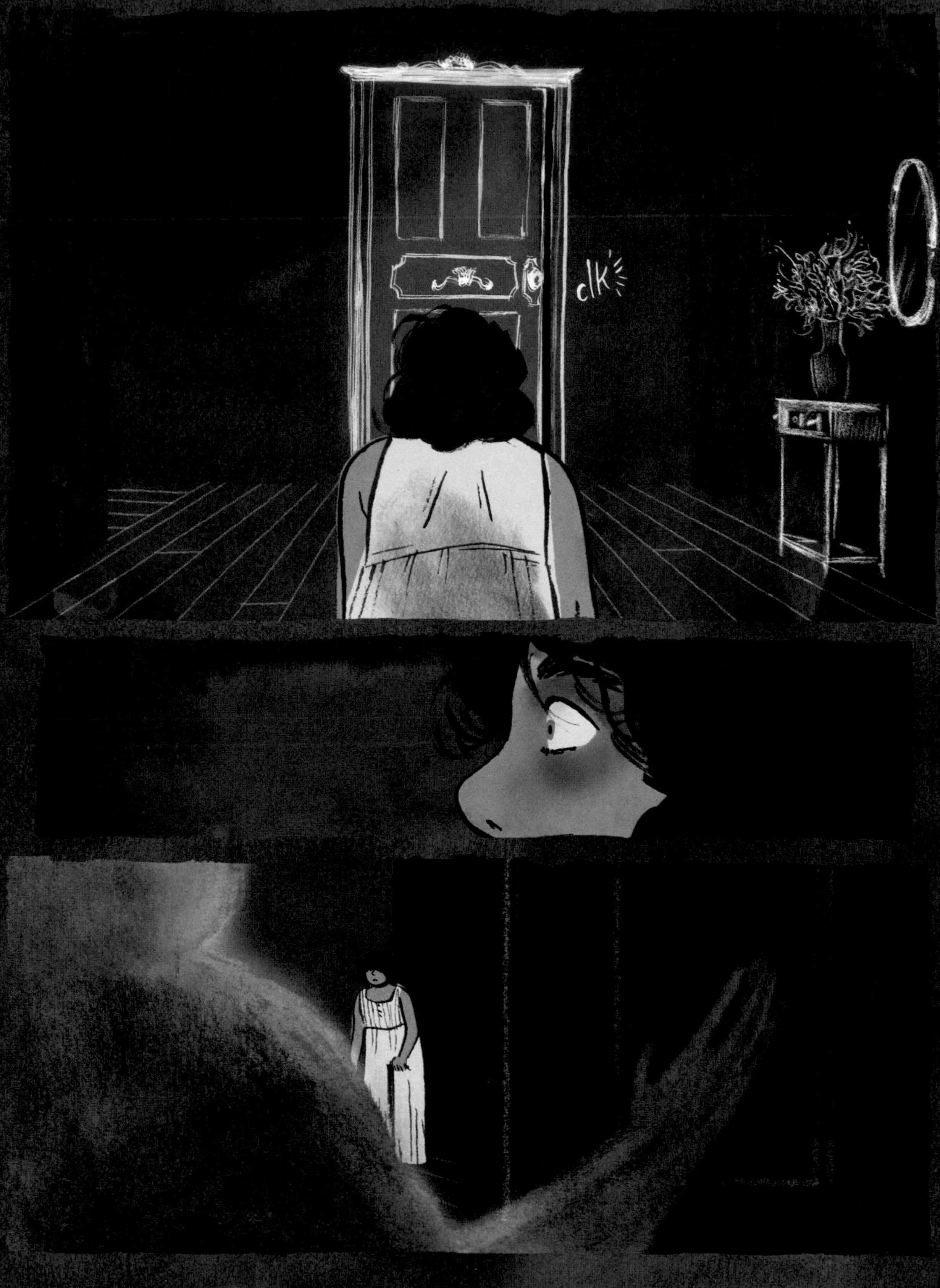
clk

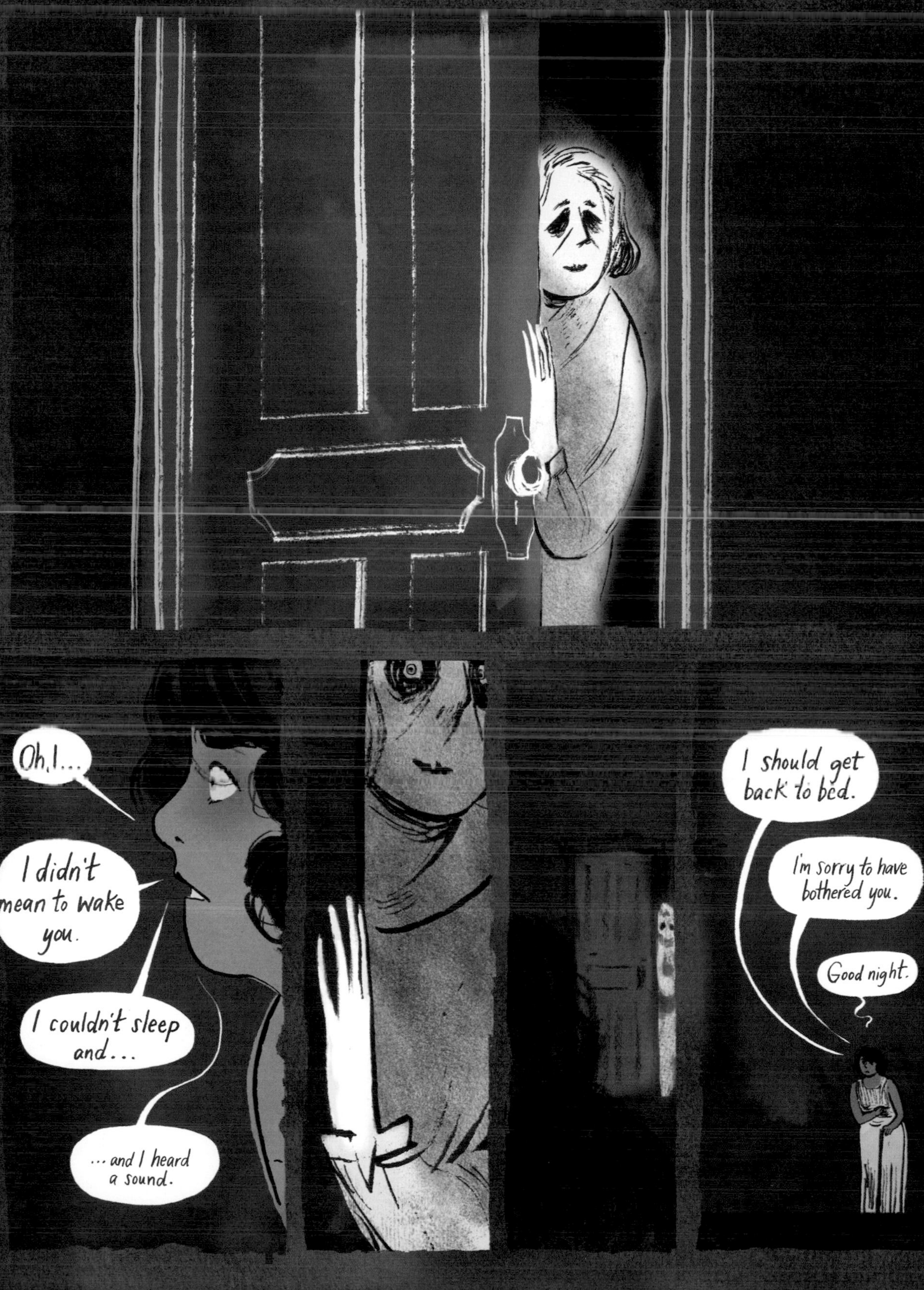
Oh, I...
I didn't mean to wake you.
I couldn't sleep and...
... and I heard a sound.
I should get back to bed.
I'm sorry to have bothered you.
Good night.

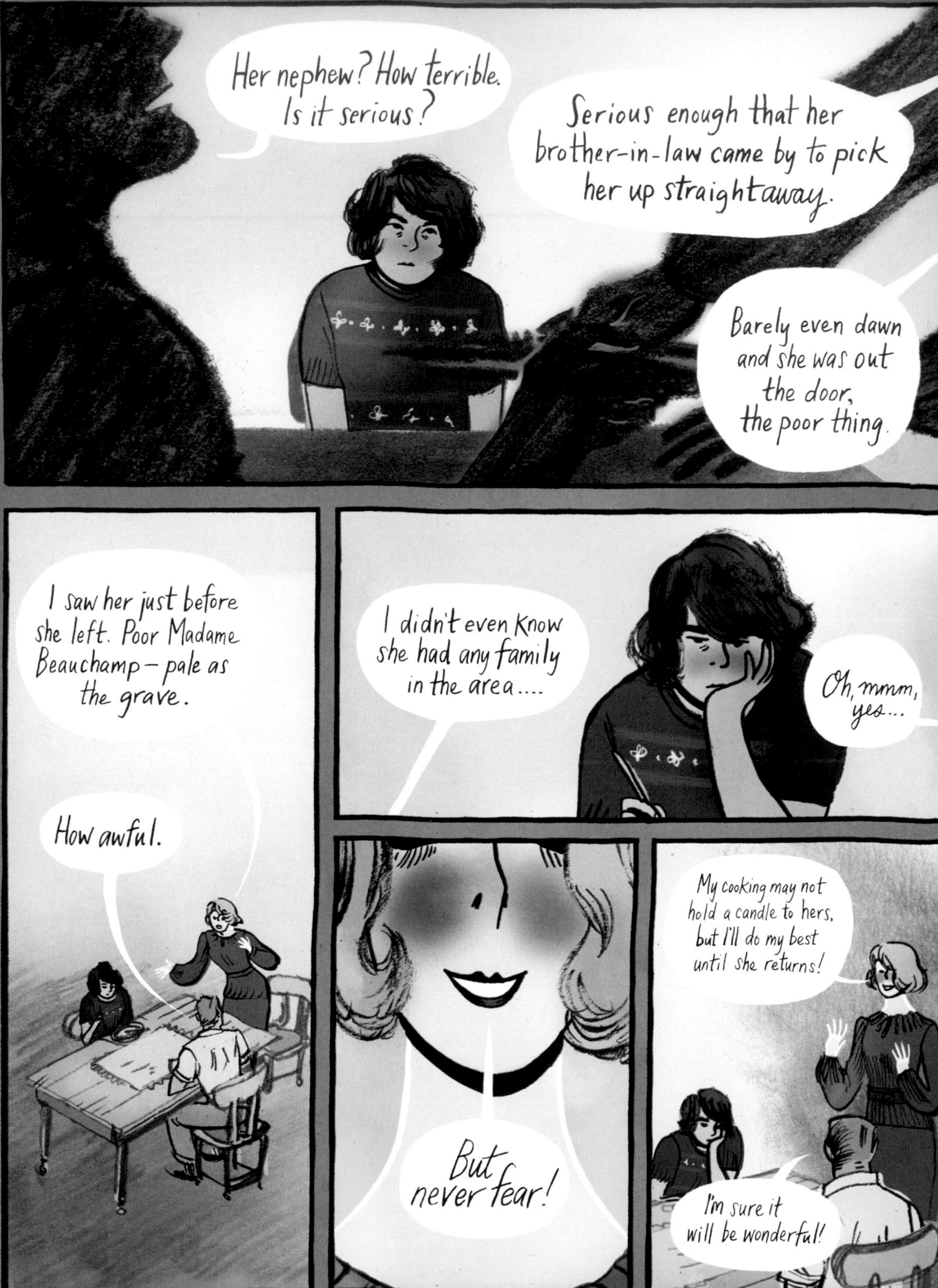
Her nephew? How terrible. Is it serious?
Serious enough that her brother-in-law came by to pick her up straightaway.
Barely even dawn and she was out the door, the poor thing.
I saw her just before she left. Poor Madame Beauchamp—pale as the grave.
How awful.
I didn't even know she had any family in the area....
Oh, mmm, yes...
But never fear!
My cooking may not hold a candle to hers, but I'll do my best until she returns!
I'm sure it will be wonderful!

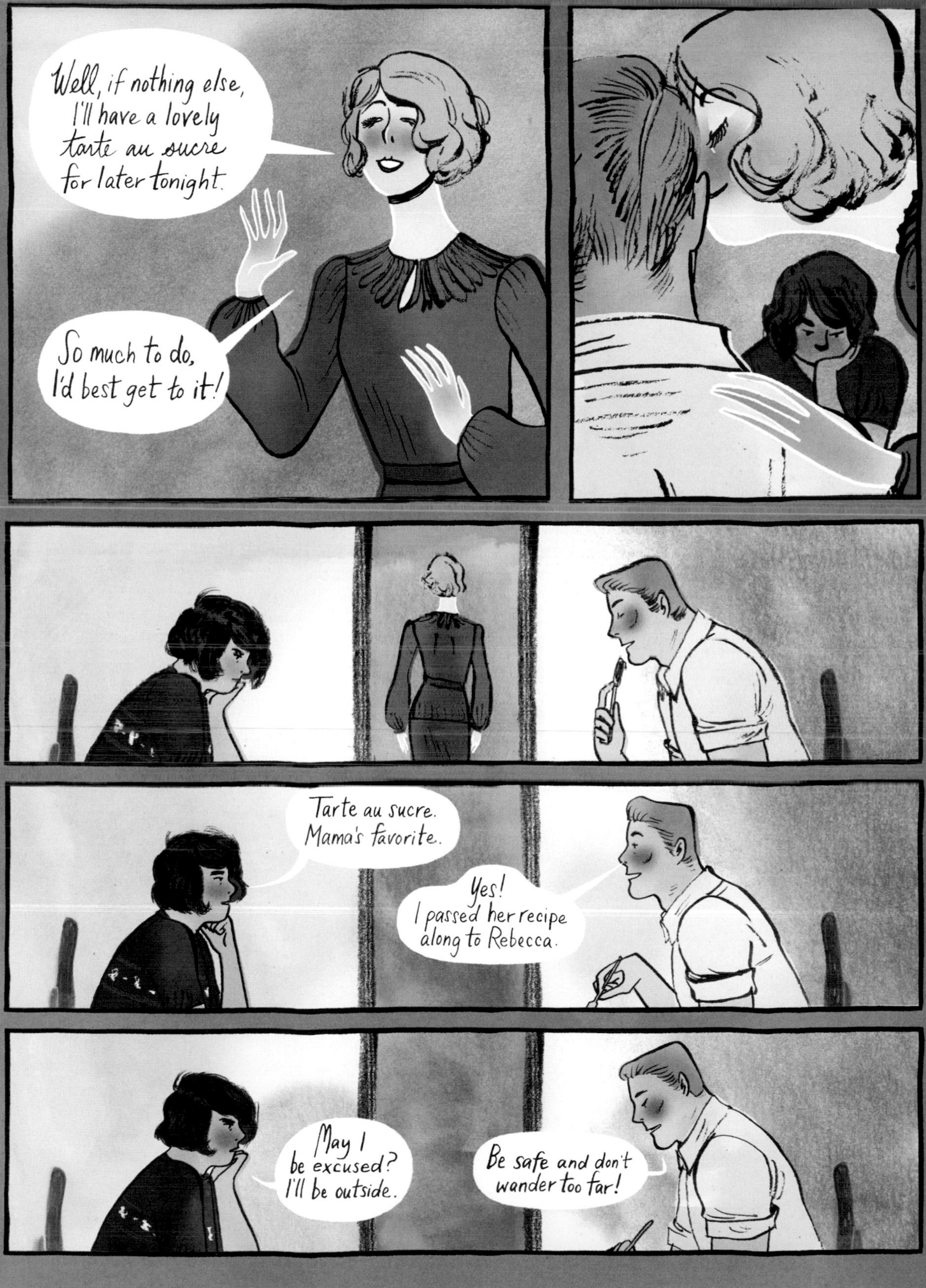
Well, if nothing else, I'll have a lovely tarte au sucre for later tonight.
So much to do, I'd best get to it!
Tarte au sucre. Mama's favorite.
Yes! I passed her recipe along to Rebecca.
May I be excused? I'll be outside.
Be safe and don't wander too far!

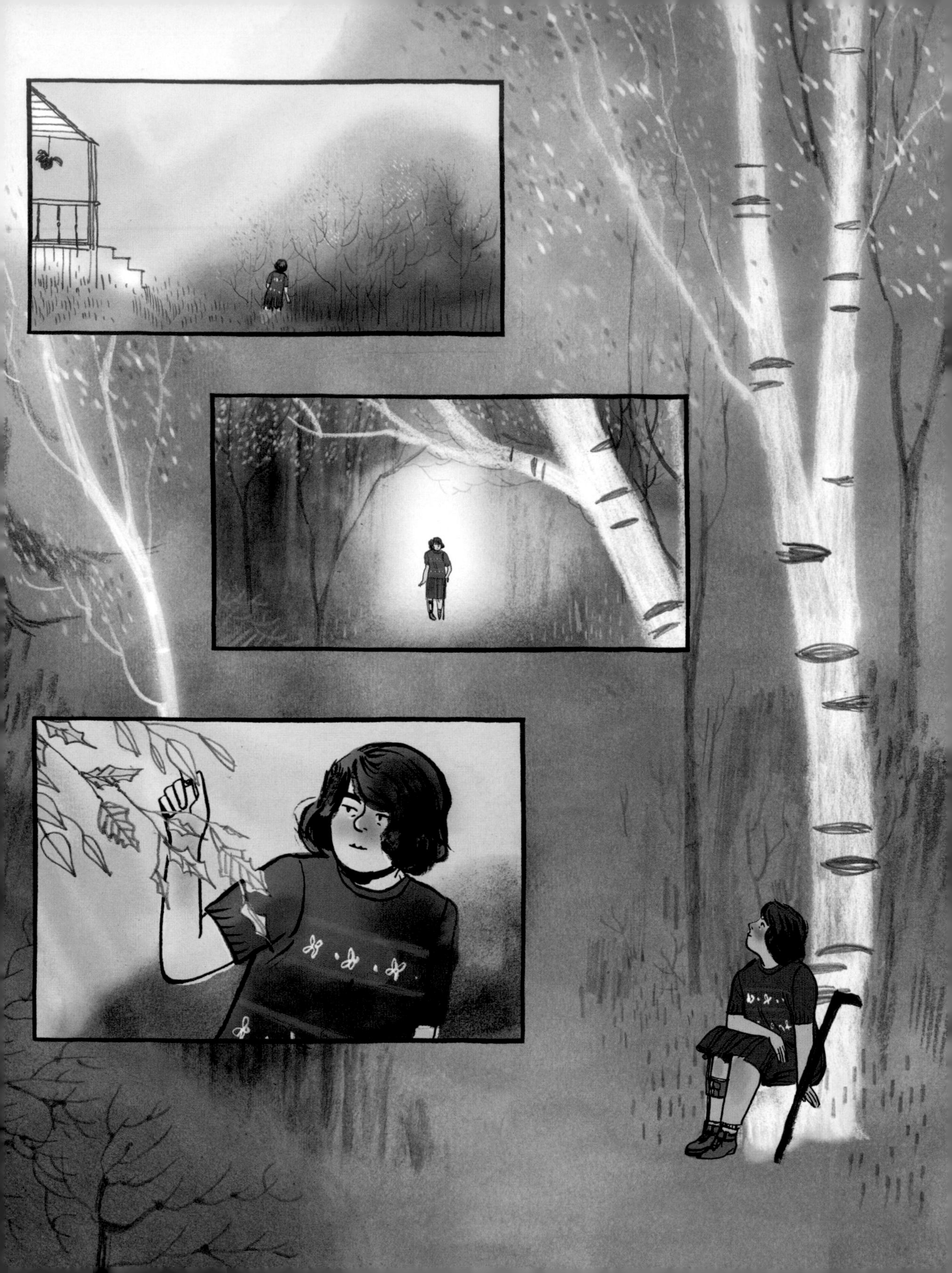

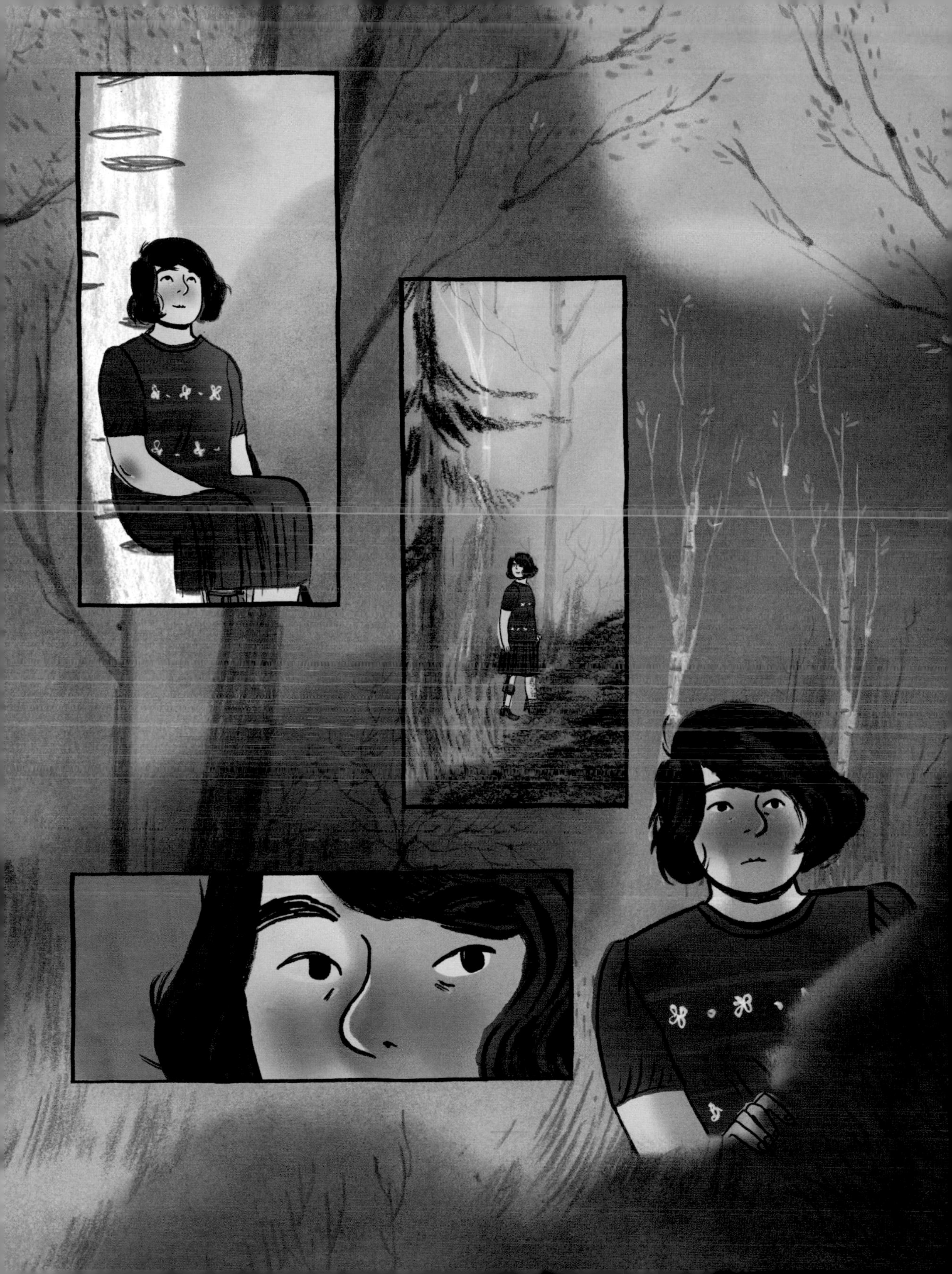

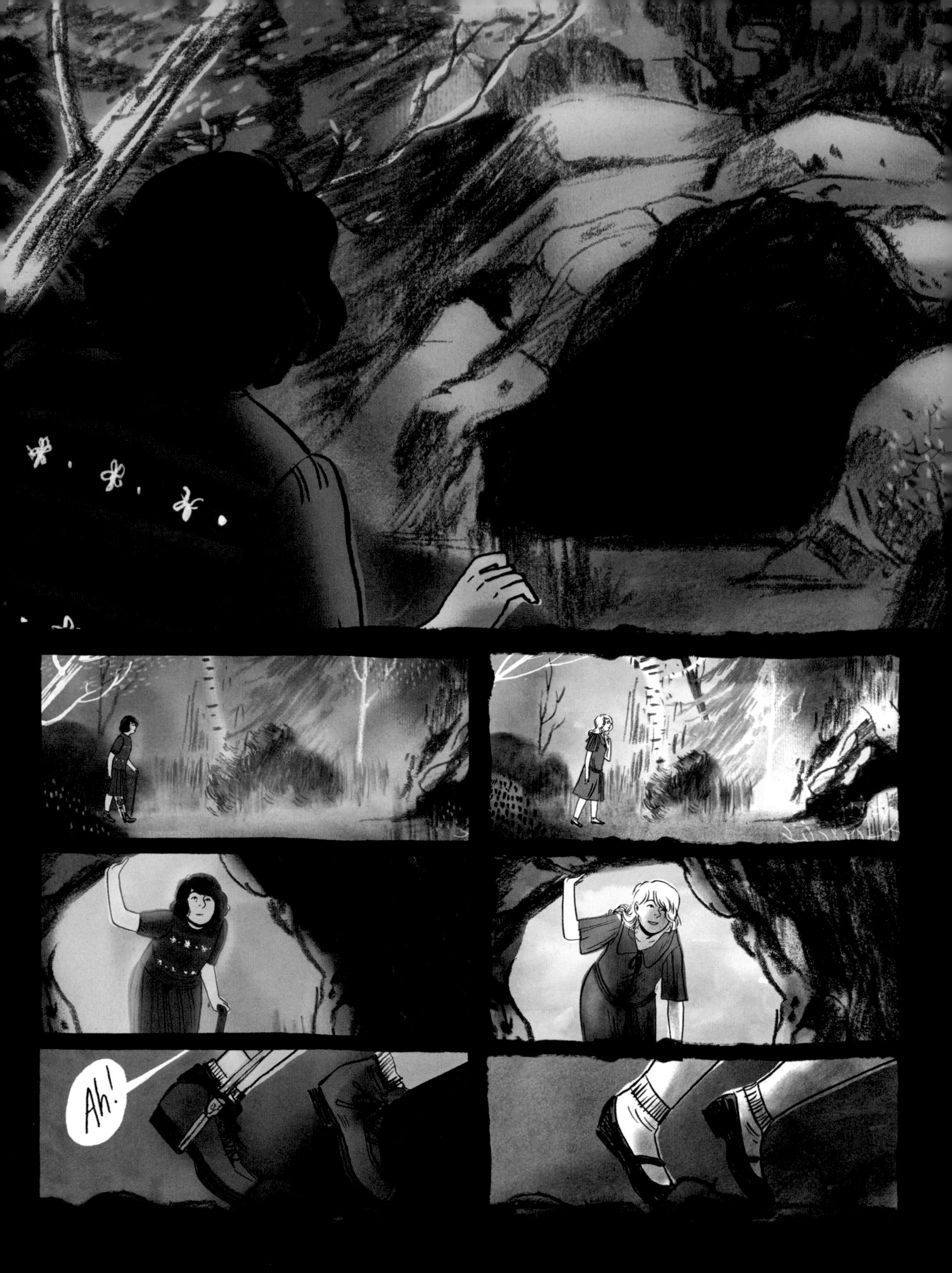
Ah!

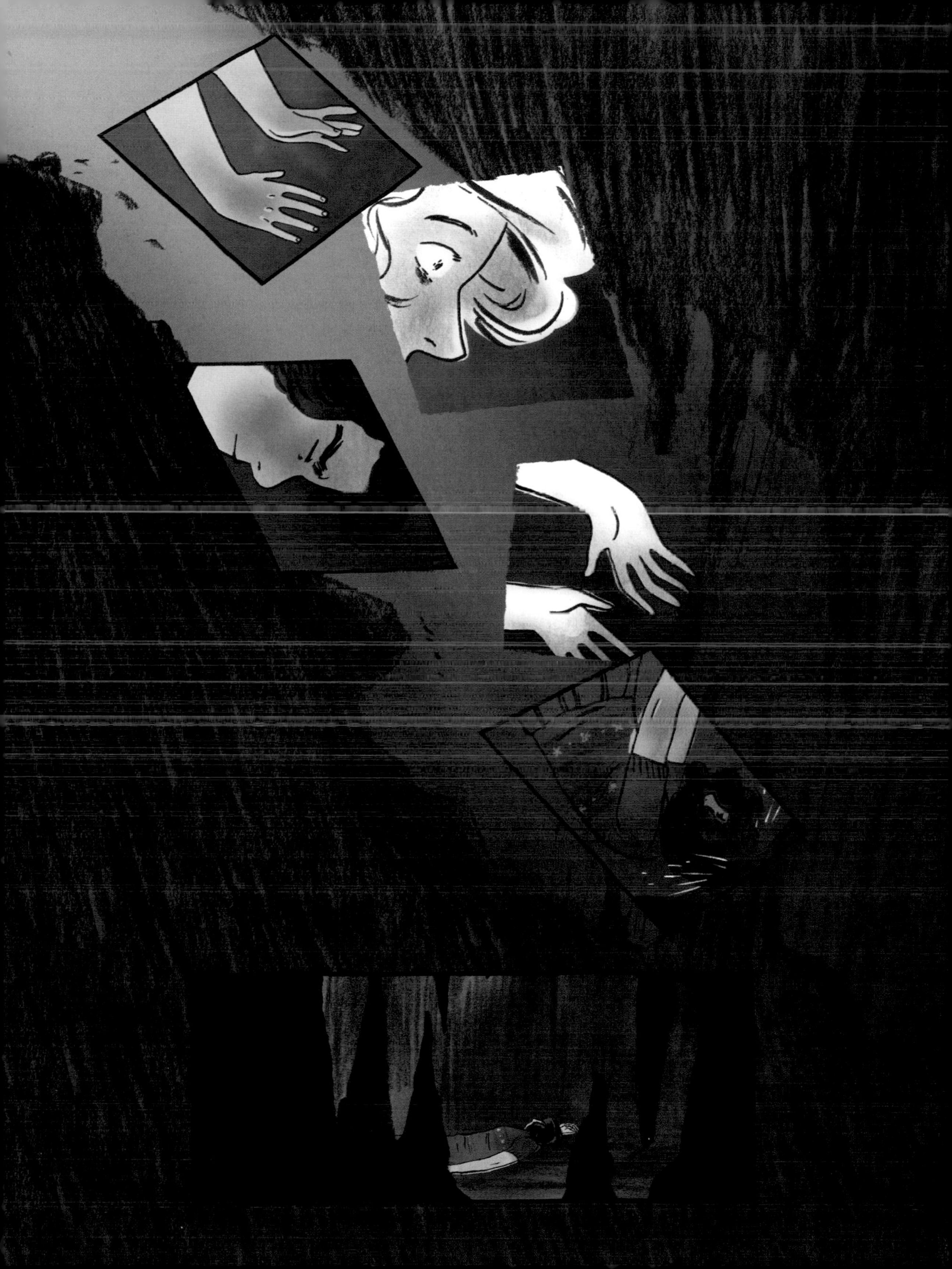

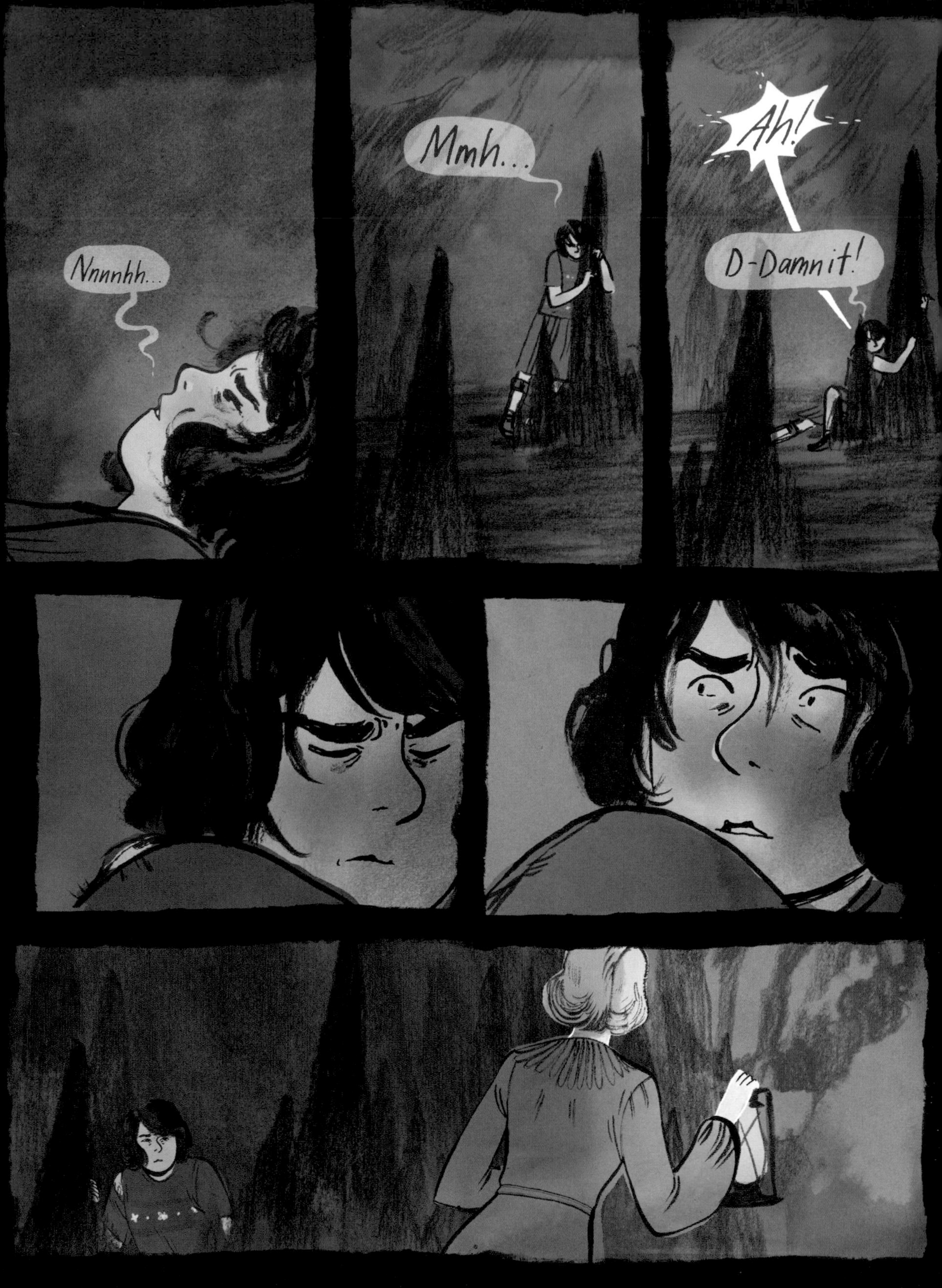
Nnnnhh...
Mmh...
Ah!
D-Damnit!

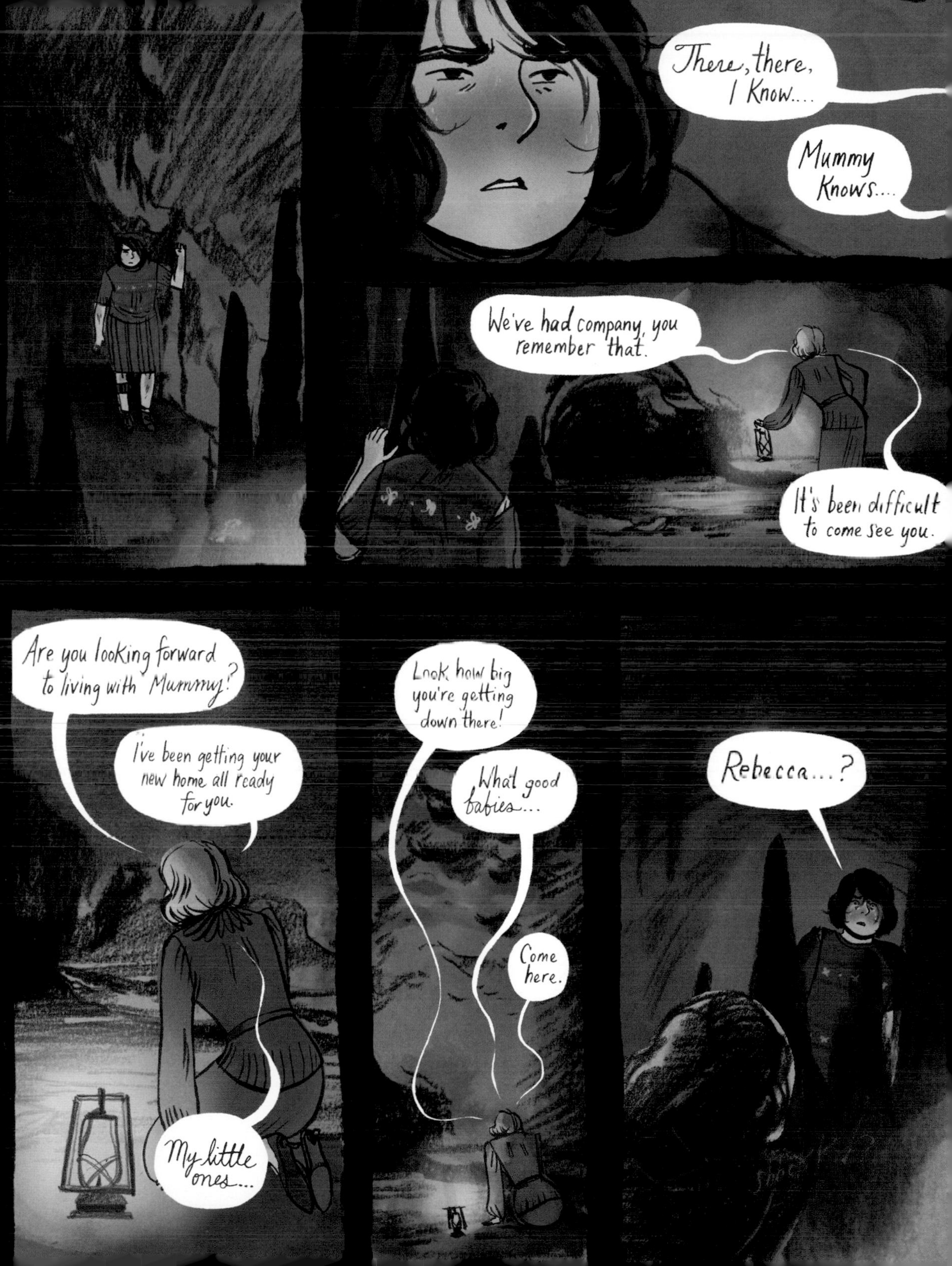
There, there, I Know....
Mummy Knows....
We've had company, you remember that.
It's been difficult to come see you.
Are you looking forward to living with Mummy?
I've been getting your new home all ready for you.
My little ones...
Look, how big you're getting down there!
What good babies...
Come here.
Rebecca...?

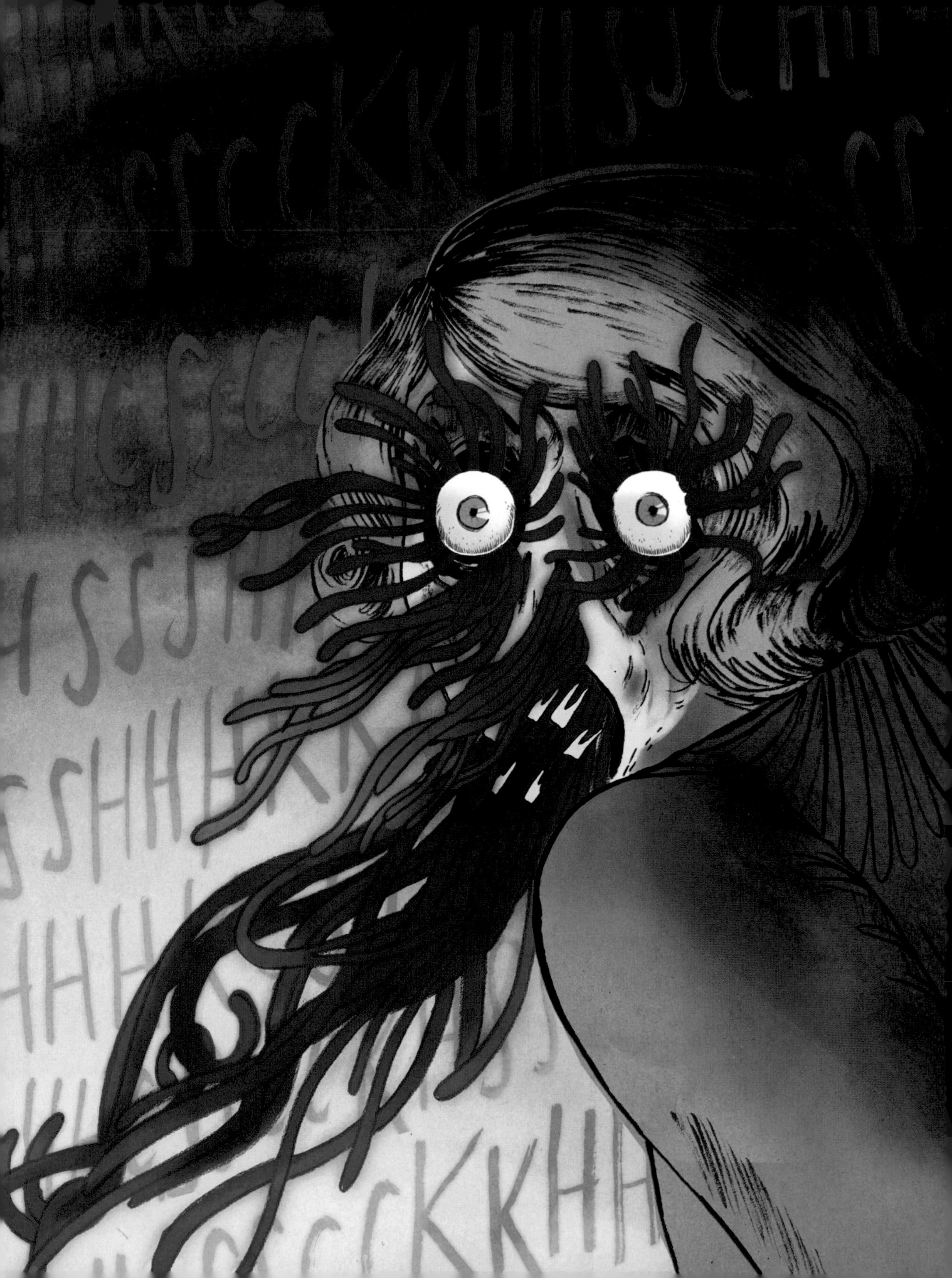
SSCCKHH

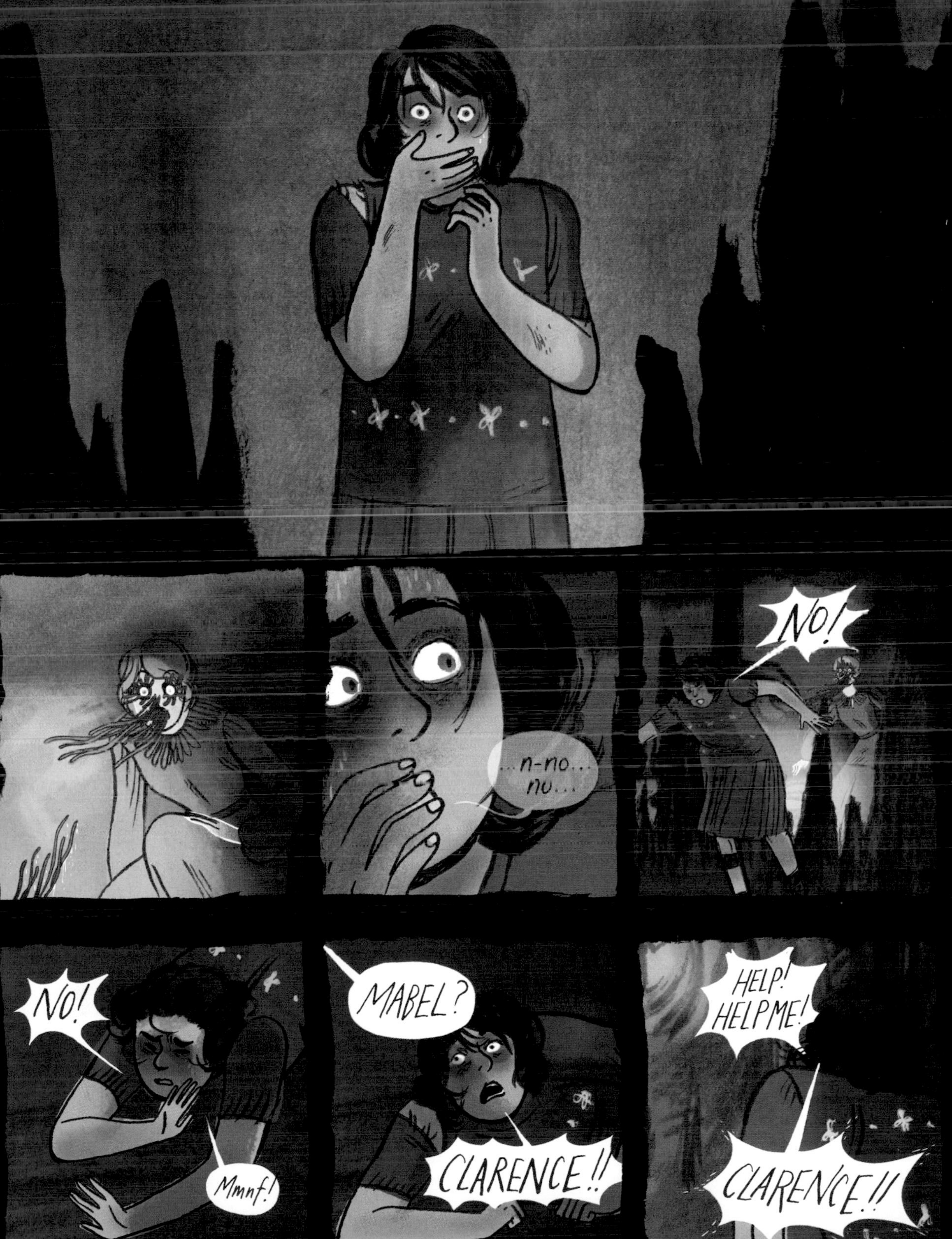
...n-no...
no...
NO!
NO!
Mmnf!
MABEL?
CLARENCE!!
HELP!
HELP ME!
CLARENCE!!

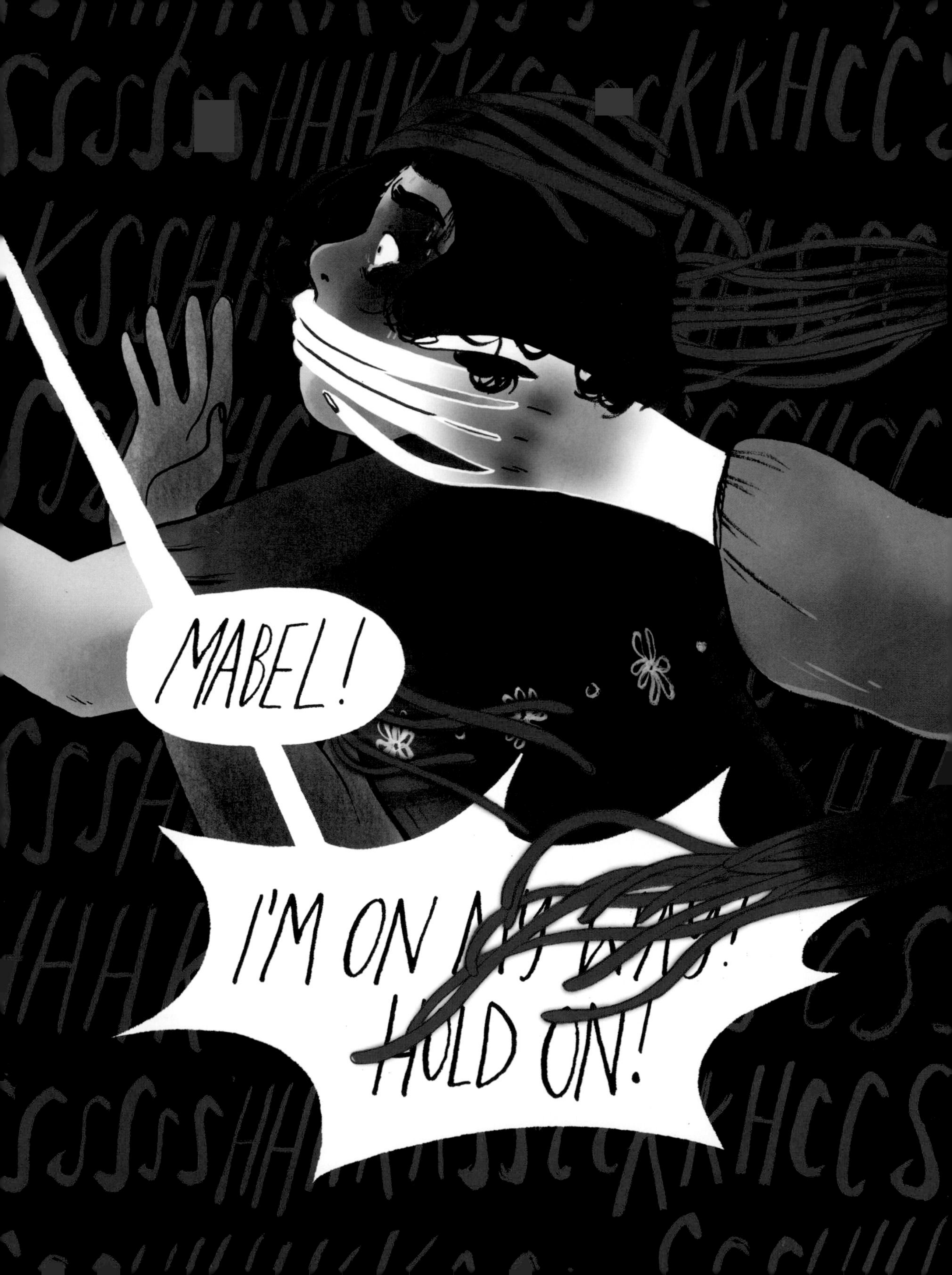
MABEL!
I'M ON
HOLD ON!

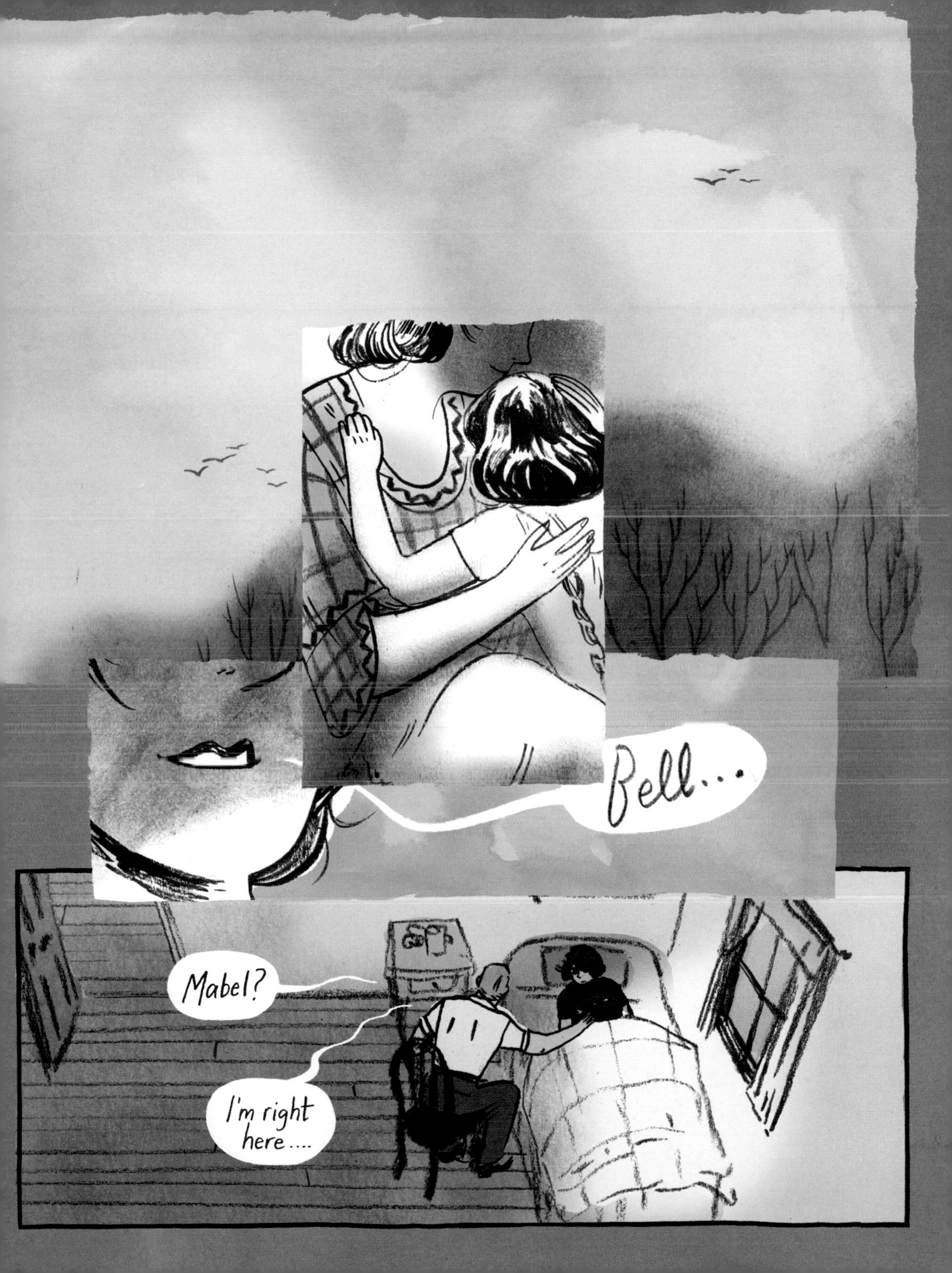
Bell...
Mabel?
I'm right here....

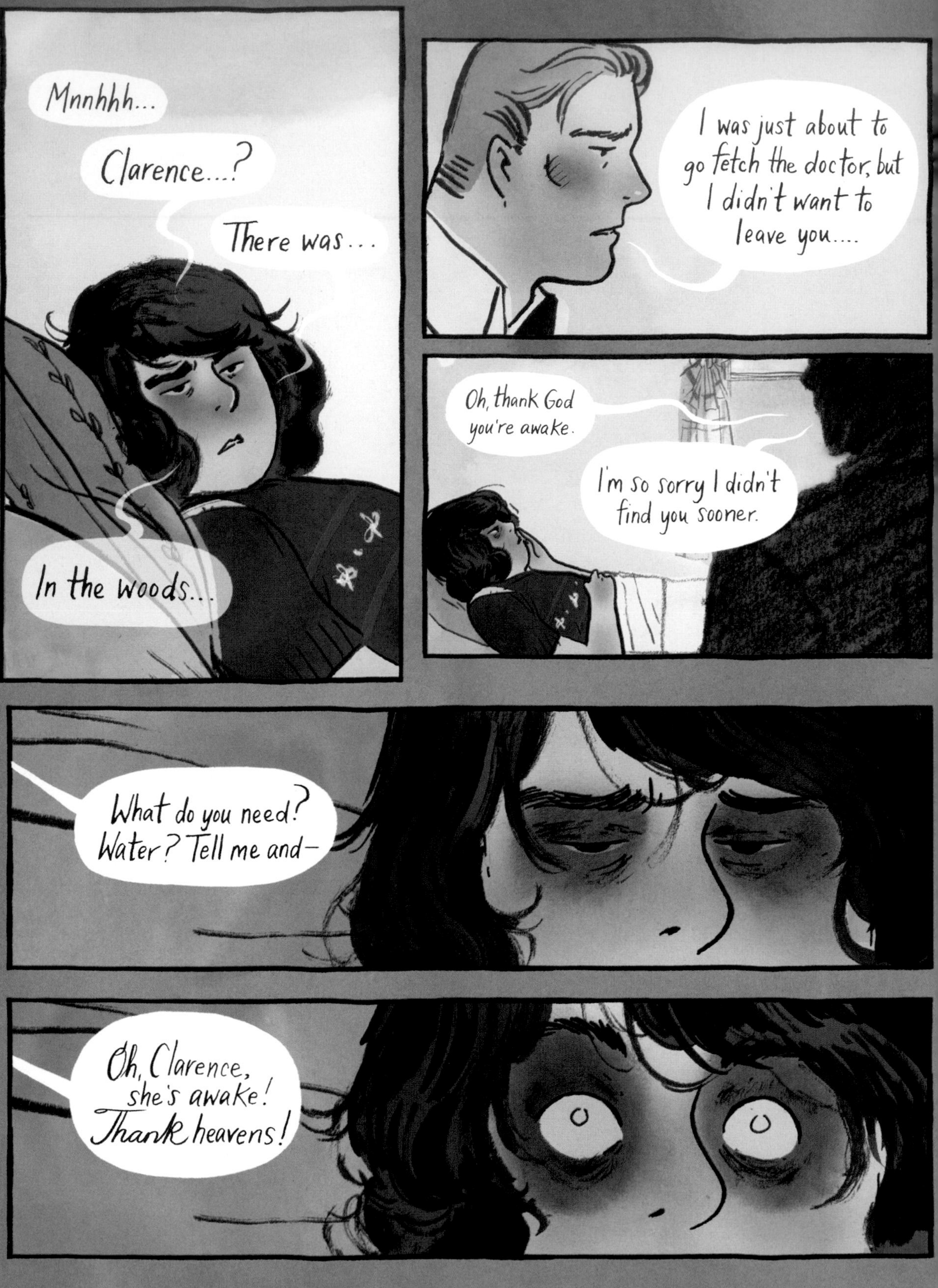
Mnnhhh...
Clarence...?
There was...
In the woods...
I was just about to go fetch the doctor, but I didn't want to leave you....
Oh, thank God you're awake.
I'm so sorry I didn't find you sooner.
What do you need? Water? Tell me and–
Oh, Clarence, she's awake! Thank heavens!

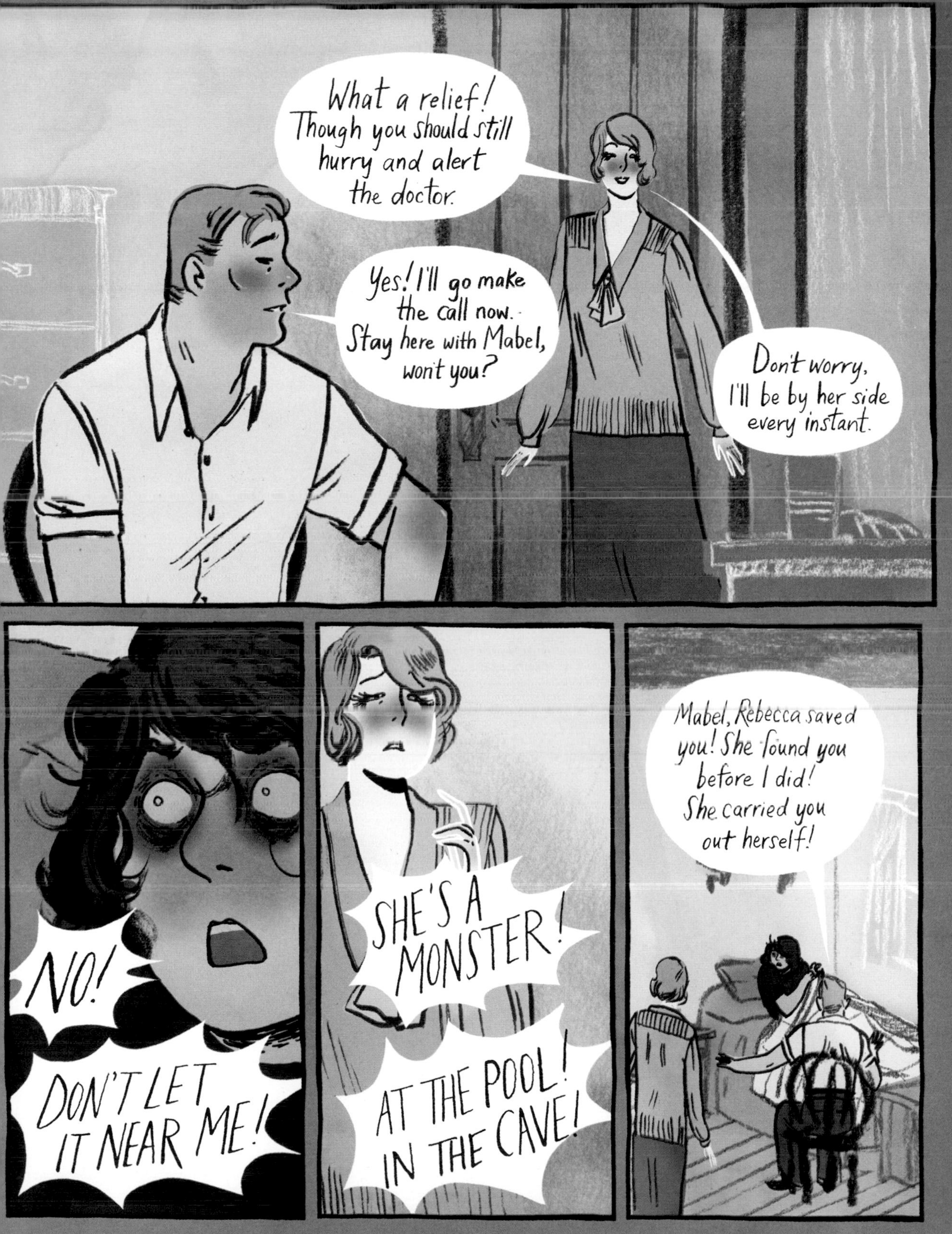
What a relief! Though you should still hurry and alert the doctor.
Yes! I'll go make the call now. Stay here with Mabel, won't you?
Don't worry, I'll be by her side every instant.
NO!
DON'T LET IT NEAR ME!
SHE'S A MONSTER!
AT THE POOL! IN THE CAVE!
Mabel, Rebecca saved you! She found you before I did! She carried you out herself!

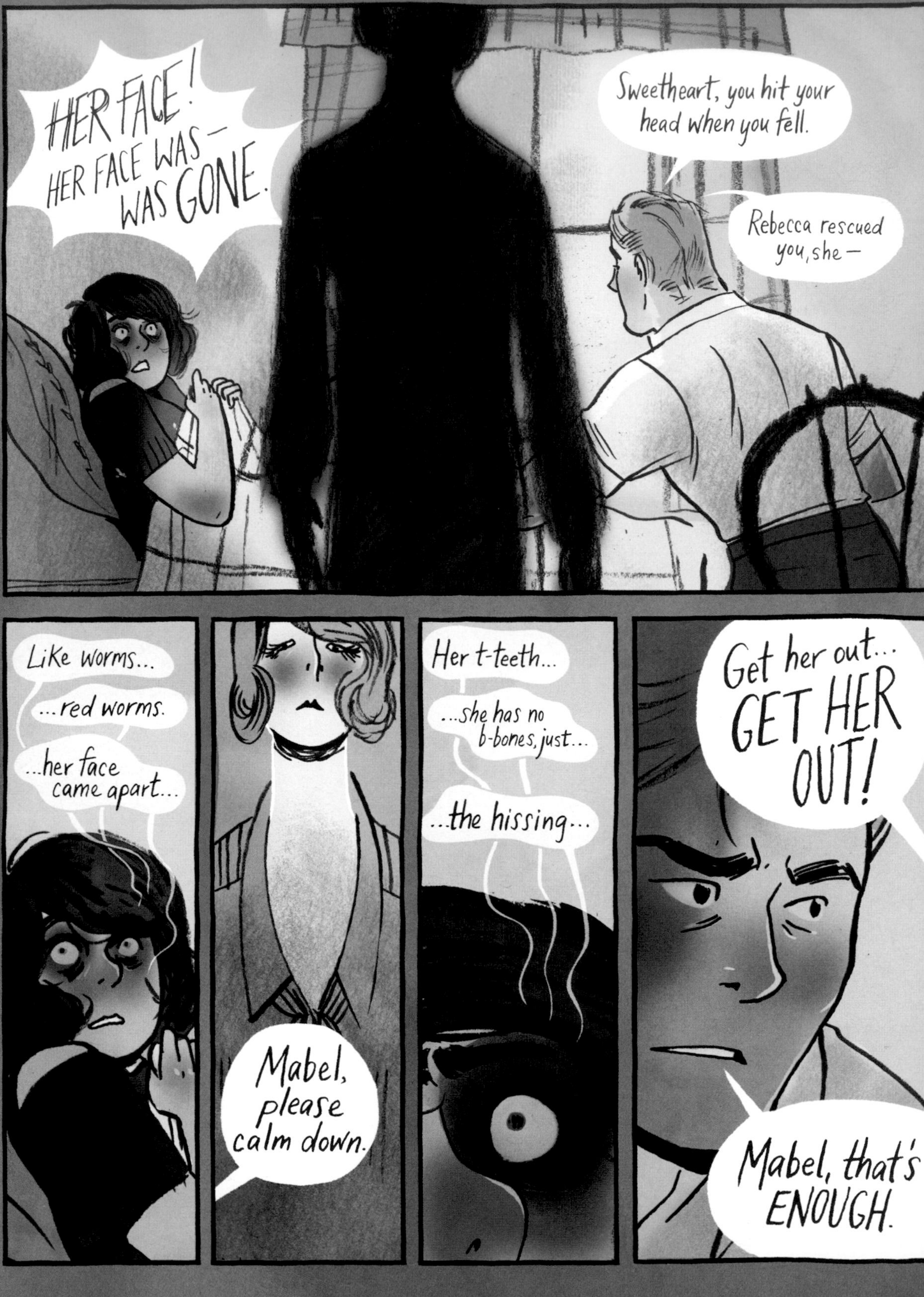
HER FACE! HER FACE WAS— WAS GONE.
Sweetheart, you hit your head when you fell.
Rebecca rescued you, she—
Like worms...
...red worms.
...her face came apart...
Mabel, please calm down.
Her t-teeth...
...she has no b-bones, just...
...the hissing...
Get her out... GET HER OUT!
Mabel, that's ENOUGH.

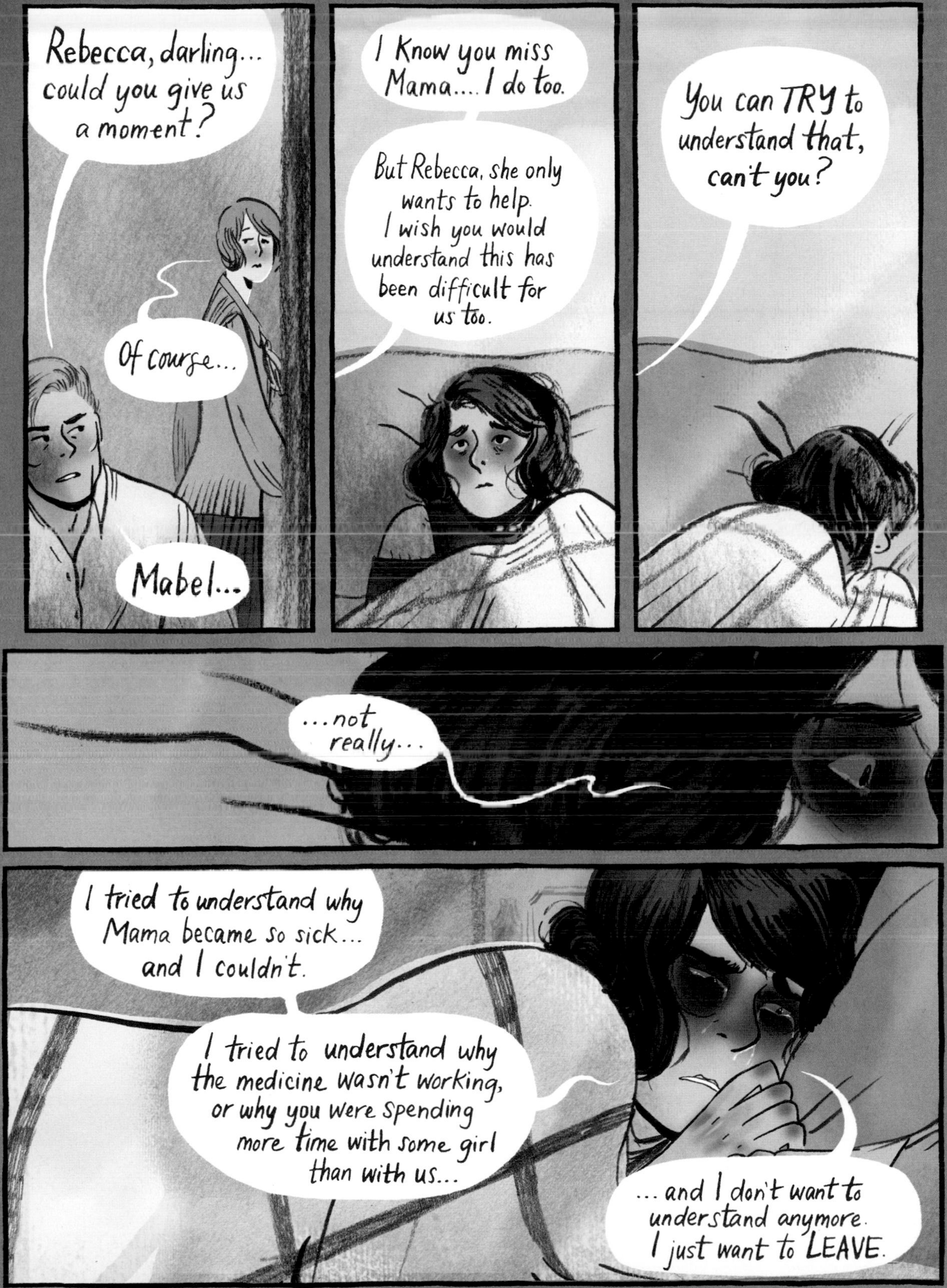
Rebecca, darling... could you give us a moment?
Of course...
Mabel...
I Know you miss Mama.... I do too.
But Rebecca, she only wants to help. I wish you would understand this has been difficult for us too.
You can TRY to understand that, can't you?
...not really...
I tried to understand why Mama became so sick... and I couldn't.
I tried to understand why the medicine wasn't working, or why you were spending more time with some girl than with us...
...and I don't want to understand anymore. I just want to LEAVE.

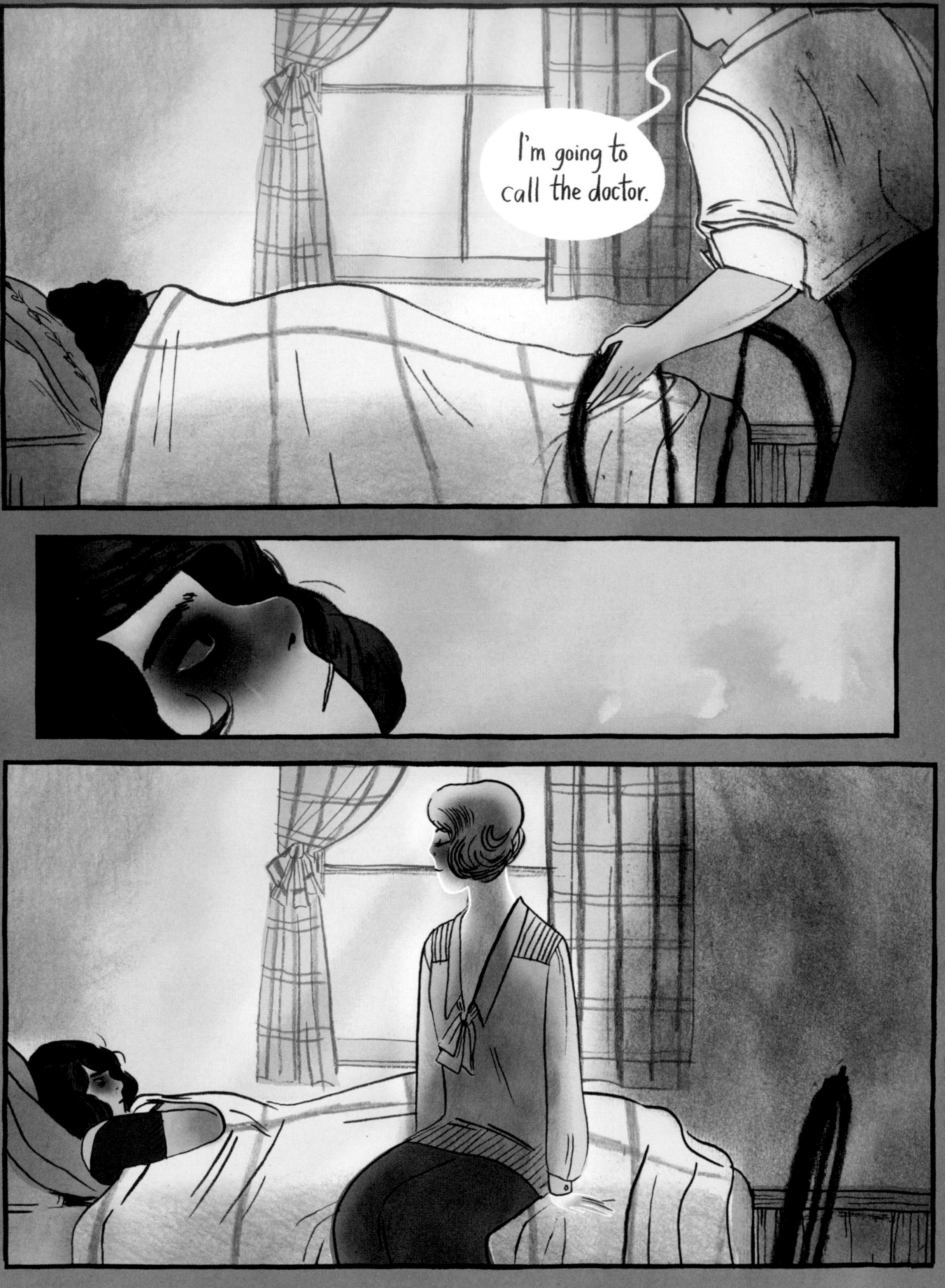
I'm going to call the doctor.

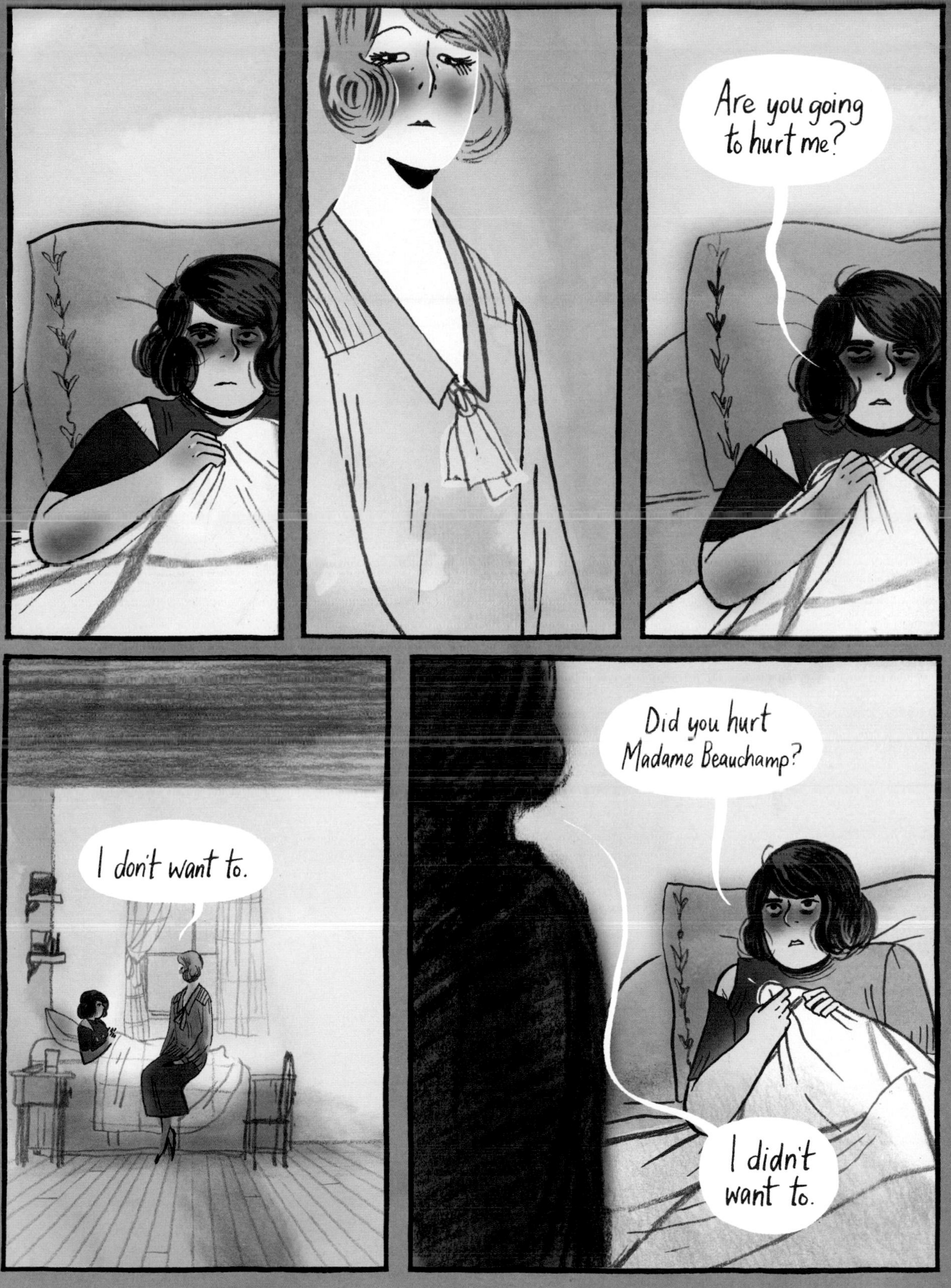
Are you going to hurt me?
I don't want to.
Did you hurt Madame Beauchamp?
I didn't want to.

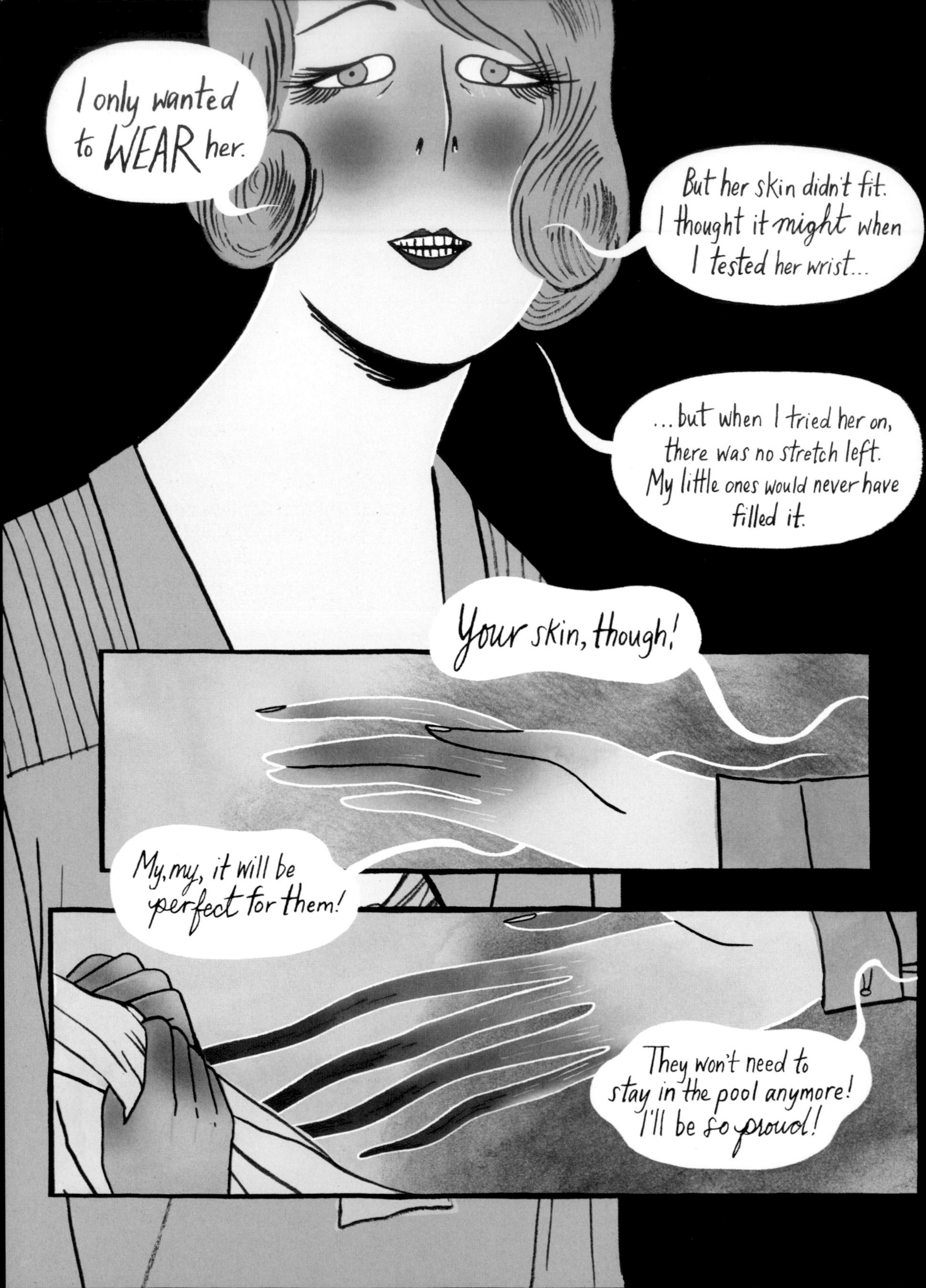
I only wanted to WEAR her.
But her skin didn't fit. I thought it might when I tested her wrist...
...but when I tried her on, there was no stretch left. My little ones would never have filled it.
Your skin, though!
My, my, it will be perfect for them!
They won't need to stay in the pool anymore! I'll be so proud!

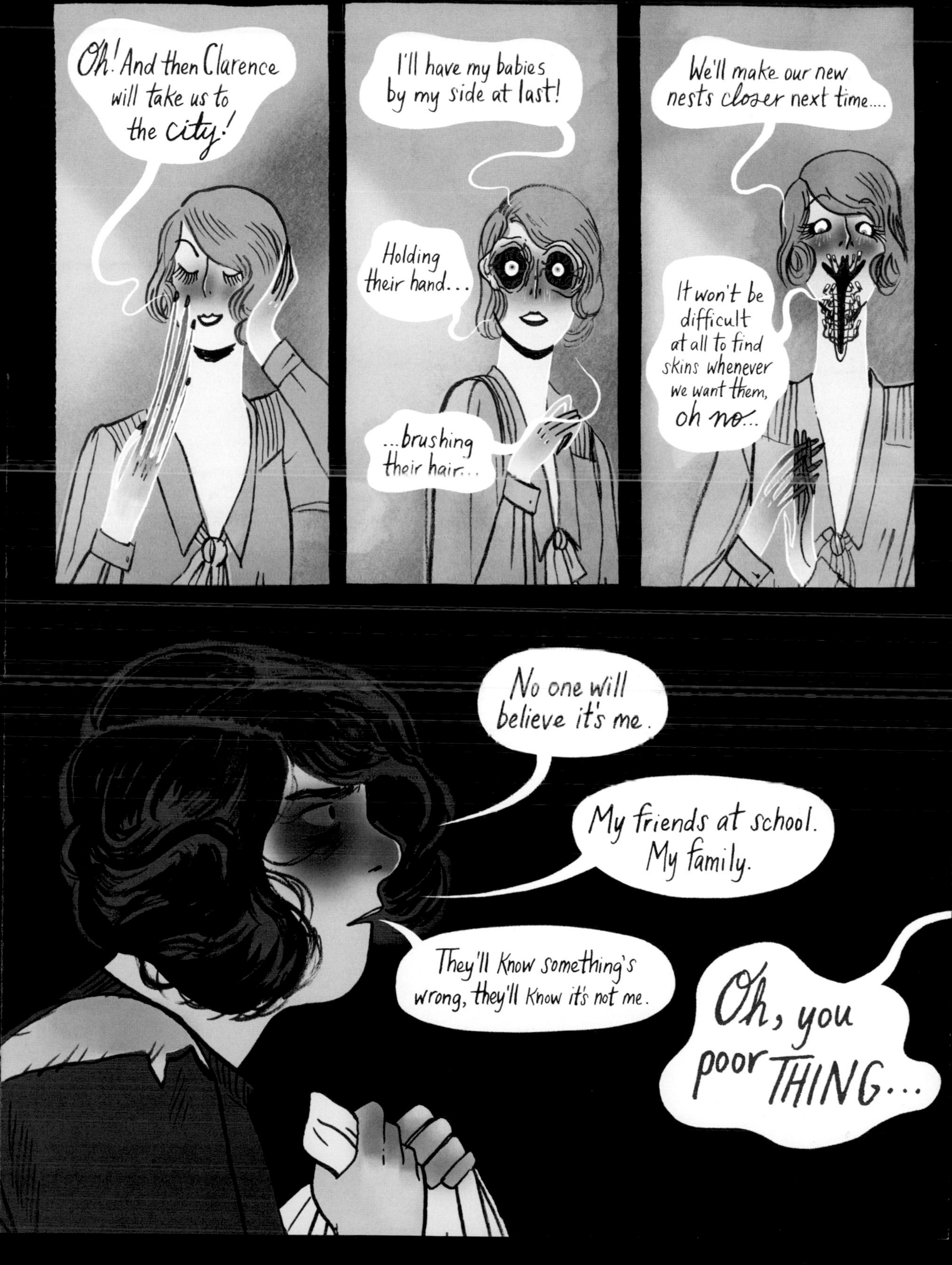

Oh! And then Clarence will take us to the city!
I'll have my babies by my side at last!
Holding their hand...
...brushing their hair...
We'll make our new nests closer next time....
It won't be difficult at all to find skins whenever we want them, oh no...
No one will believe it's me.
My friends at school. My family.
They'll know something's wrong, they'll know it's not me.
Oh, you poor THING...

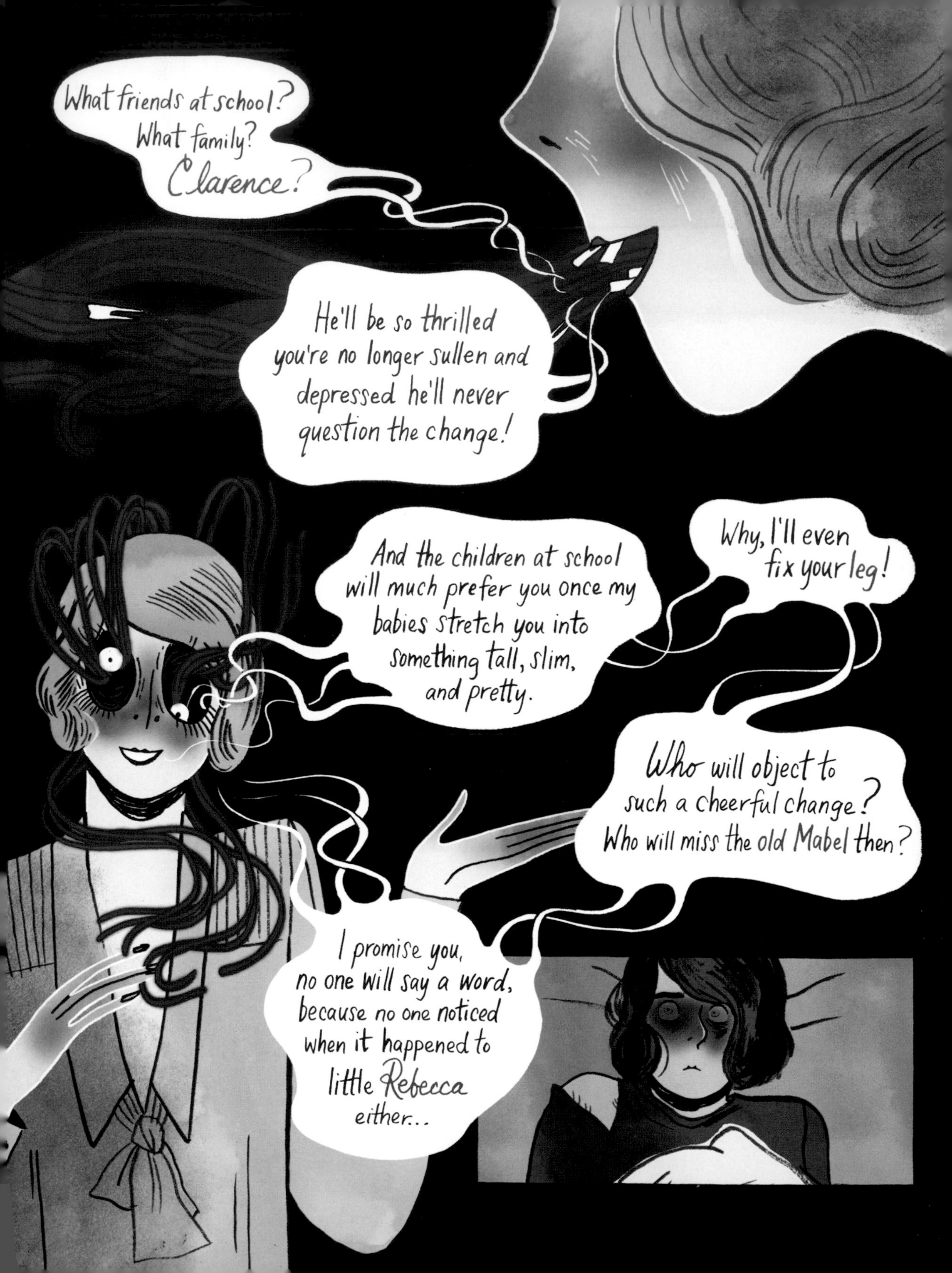
What friends at school? What family? Clarence?
He'll be so thrilled you're no longer sullen and depressed he'll never question the change!
And the children at school will much prefer you once my babies stretch you into something tall, slim, and pretty.
Why, I'll even fix your leg!
Who will object to such a cheerful change? Who will miss the old Mabel then?
I promise you, no one will say a word, because no one noticed when it happened to little Rebecca either...

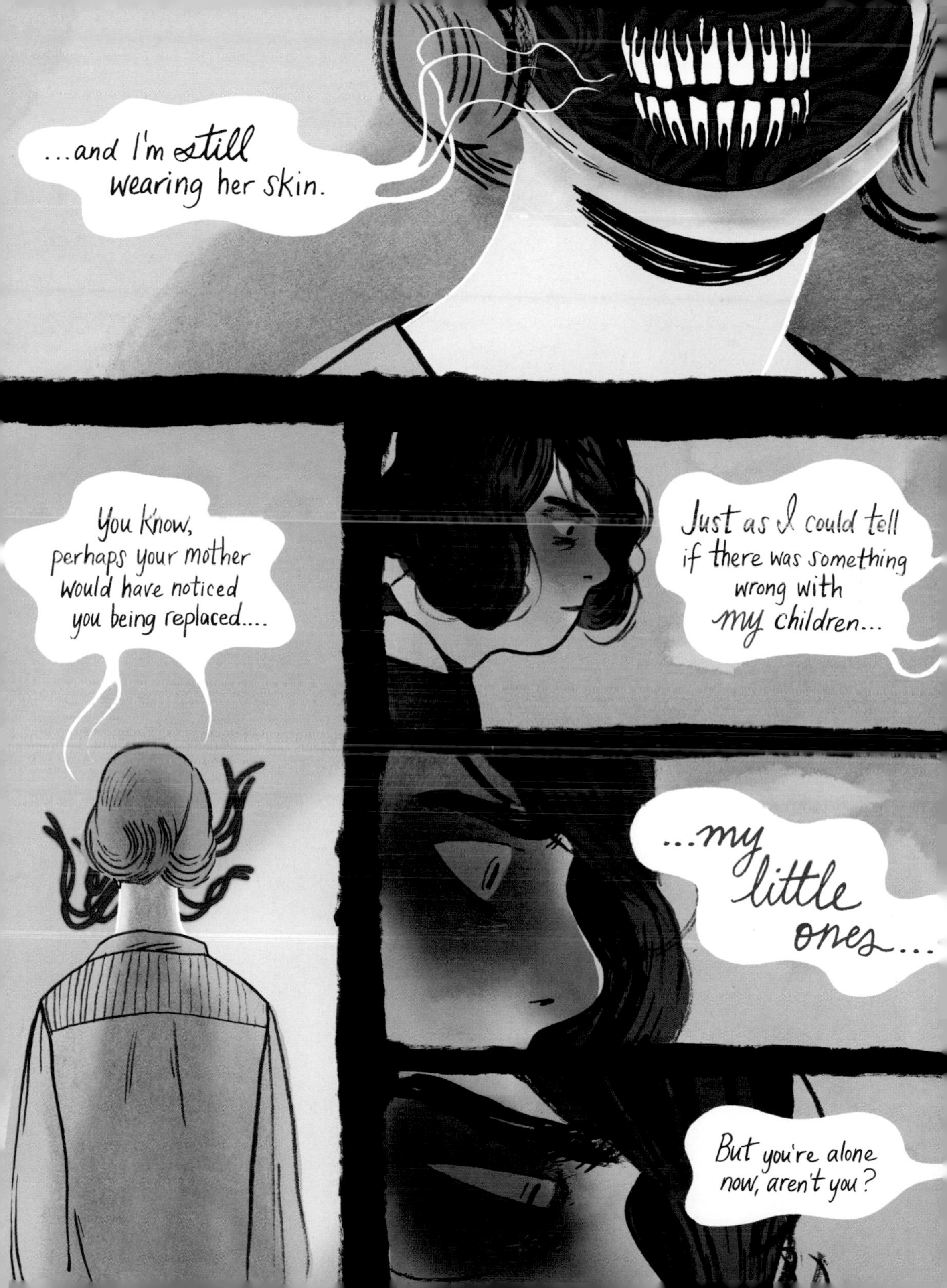
...and I'm still wearing her skin.
You know, perhaps your mother would have noticed you being replaced....
Just as I could tell if there was something wrong with my children...
...my little ones...
But you're alone now, aren't you?

And they still have me.

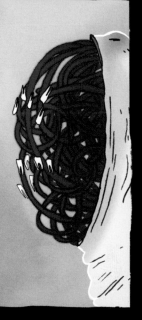

WAIT!

BELL TOLD THE MONSTER:

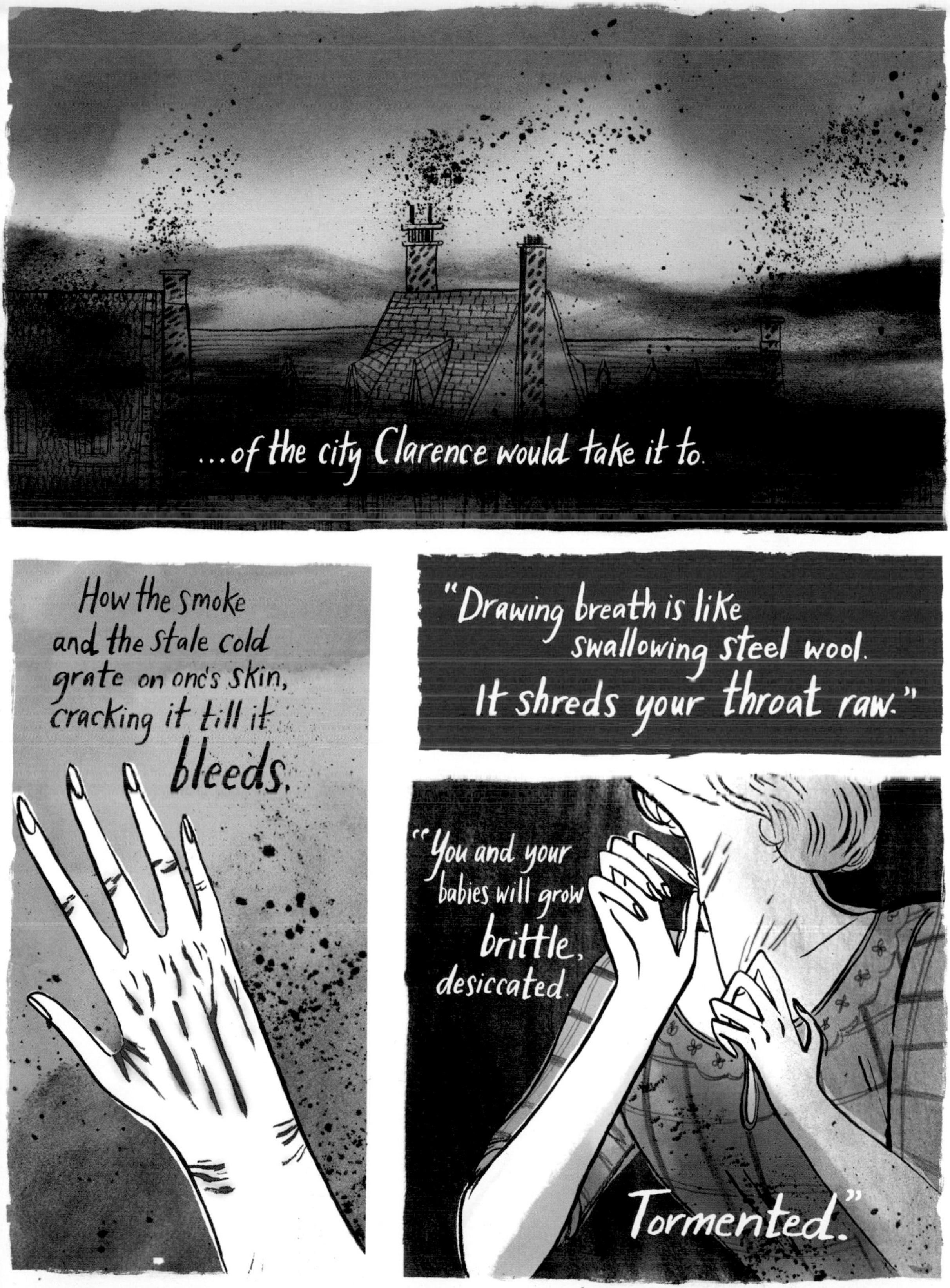

...of the city Clarence would take it to.
How the smoke and the stale cold grate on one's skin, cracking it till it bleeds.
"Drawing breath is like swallowing steel wool. It shreds your throat raw."
"You and your babies will grow brittle, desiccated.
Tormented."

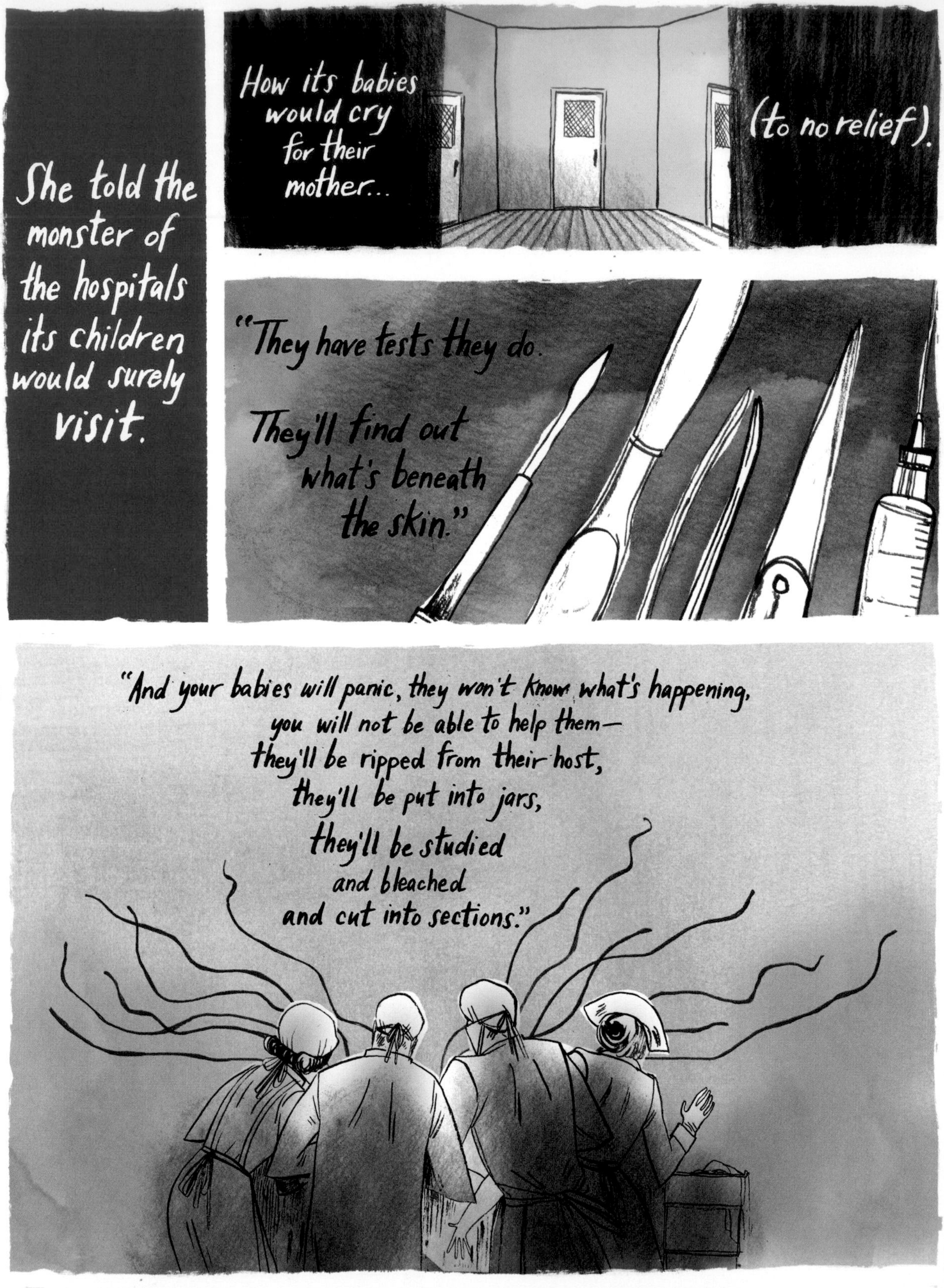
She told the monster of the hospitals its children would surely visit.
How its babies would cry for their mother...
(to no relief).
"They have tests they do.
They'll find out what's beneath the skin."
"And your babies will panic, they won't know what's happening, you will not be able to help them— they'll be ripped from their host, they'll be put into jars, they'll be studied and bleached and cut into sections."

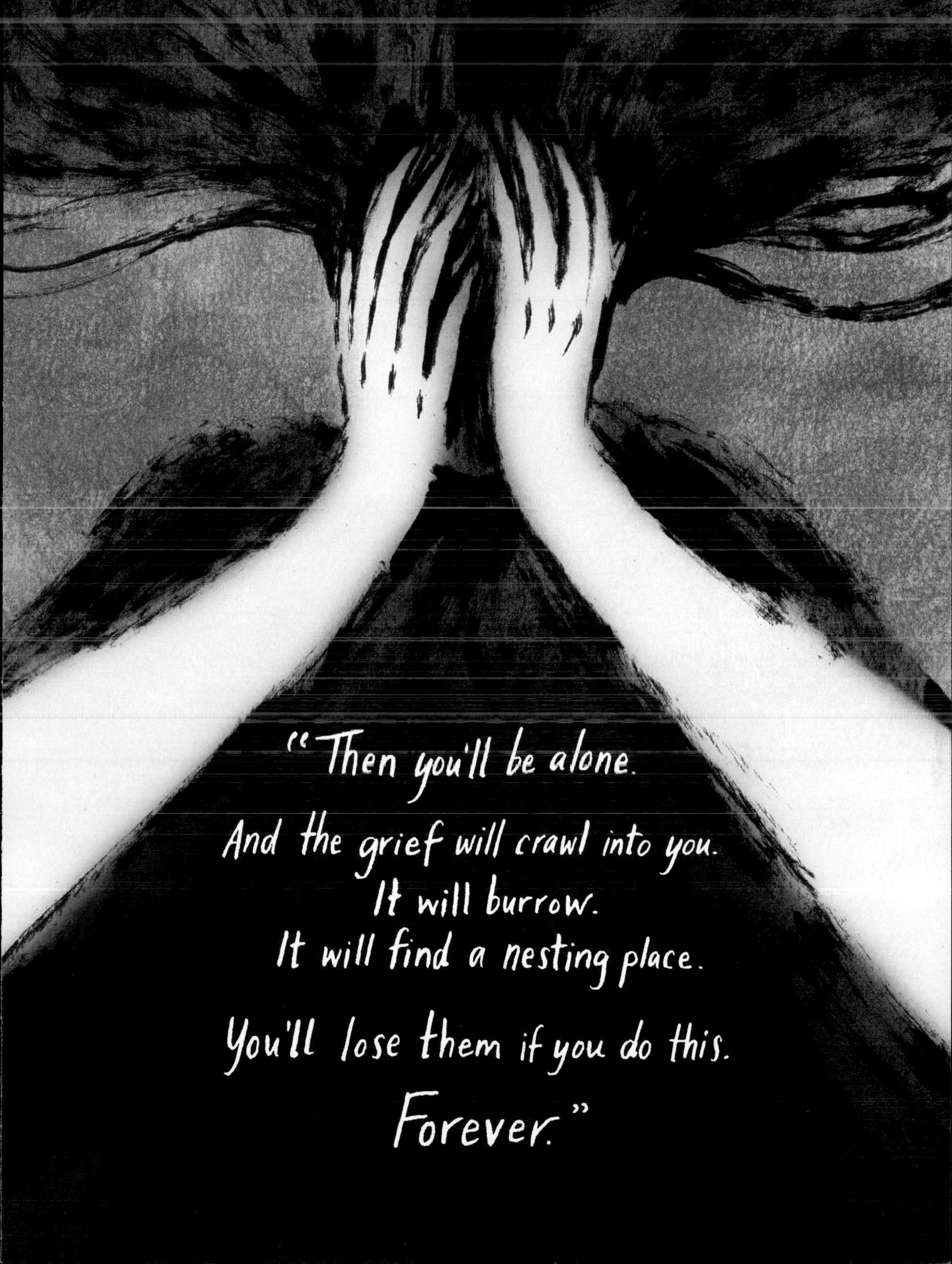
"Then you'll be alone.
And the grief will crawl into you.
It will burrow.
It will find a nesting place.
You'll lose them if you do this.
Forever."

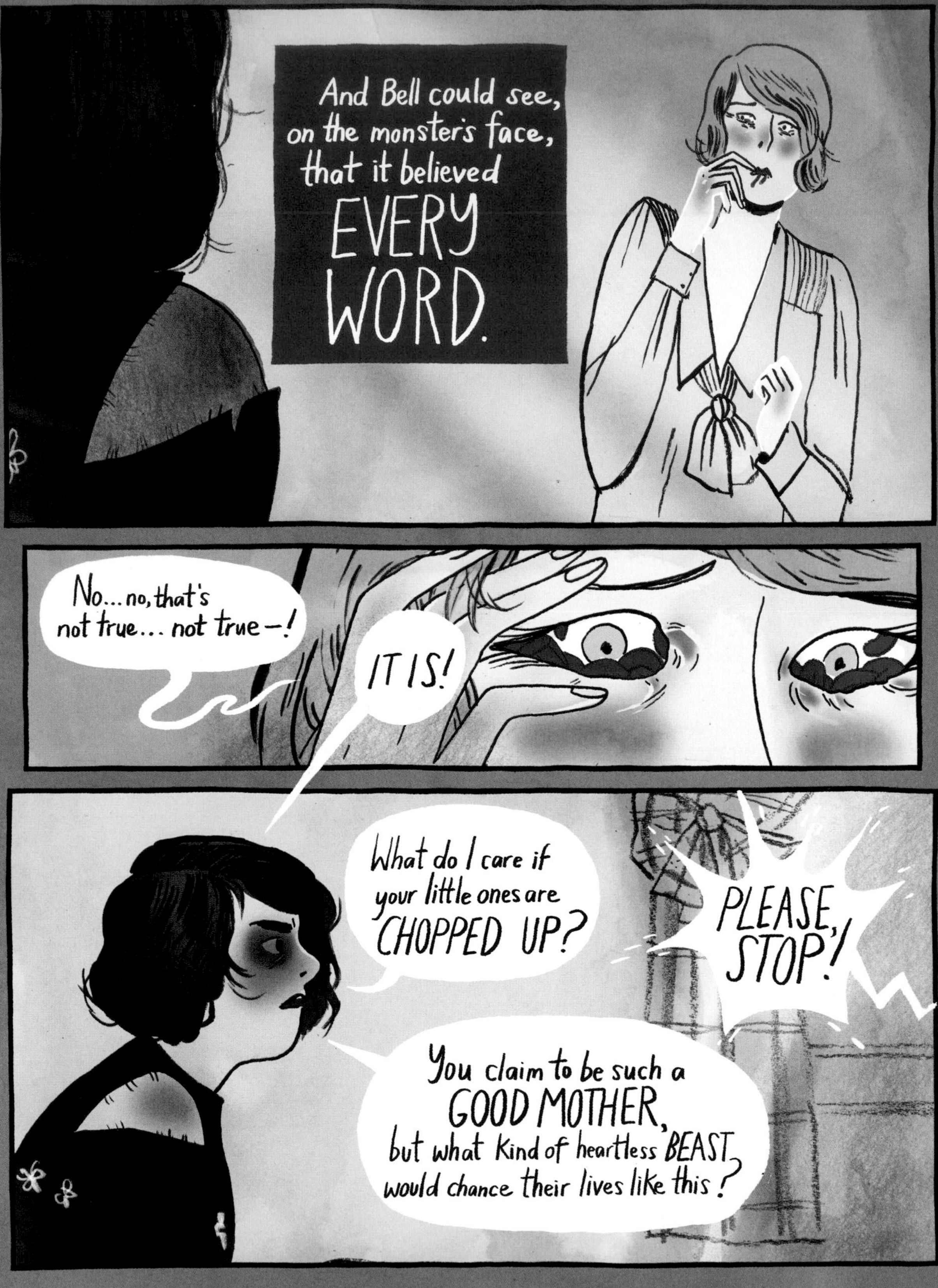

And Bell could see, on the monster's face, that it believed EVERY WORD.
No... no, that's not true... not true-!
IT IS!
What do I care if your little ones are CHOPPED UP?
PLEASE, STOP!
You claim to be such a GOOD MOTHER, but what kind of heartless BEAST would chance their lives like this?

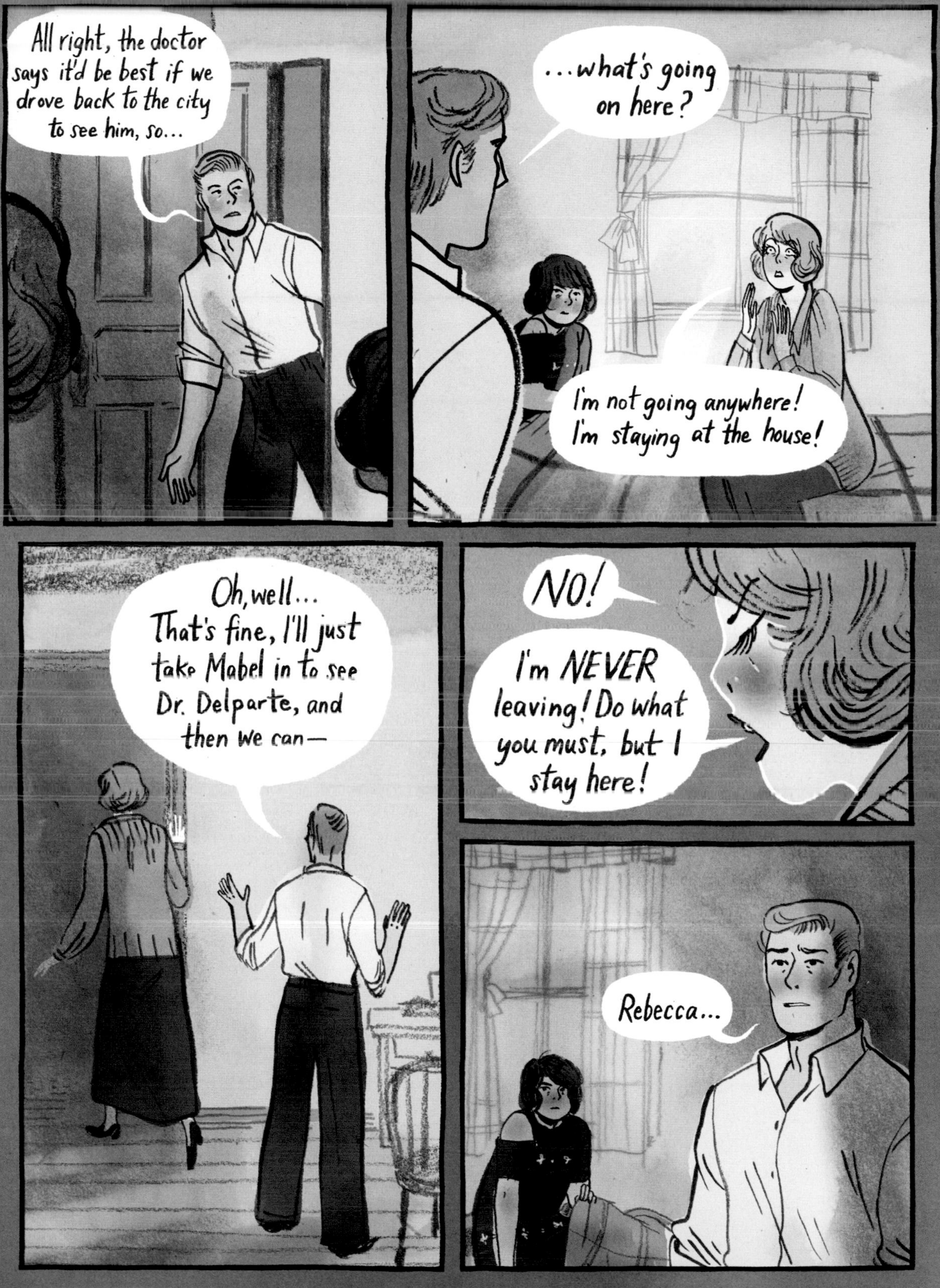
All right, the doctor says it'd be best if we drove back to the city to see him, so...
...what's going on here?
I'm not going anywhere! I'm staying at the house!
Oh, well... That's fine, I'll just take Mabel in to see Dr. Delparte, and then we can—
NO!
I'm NEVER leaving! Do what you must, but I stay here!
Rebecca...

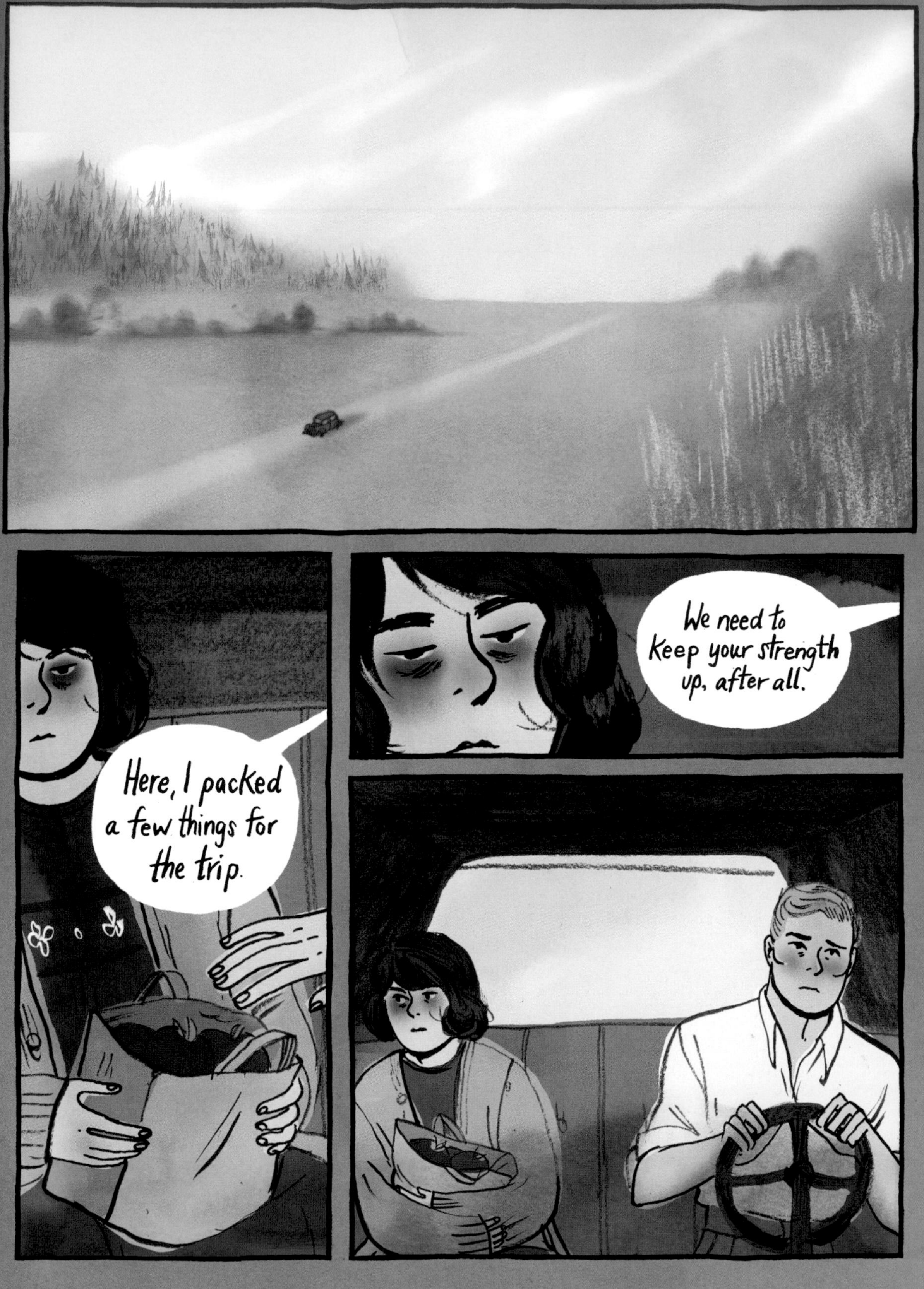
Here, I packed a few things for the trip.
We need to keep your strength up, after all.

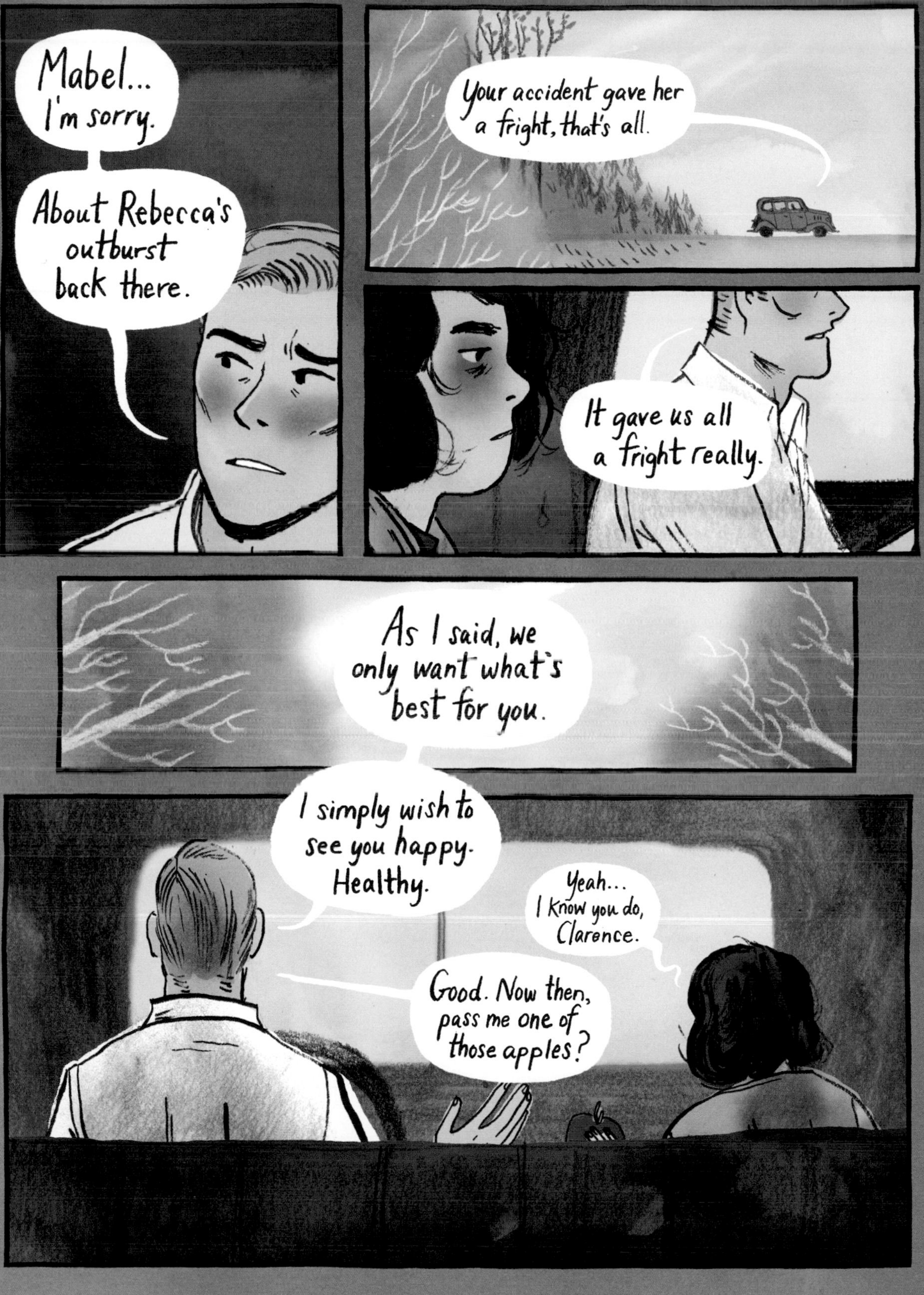
Mabel... I'm sorry.
About Rebecca's outburst back there.
Your accident gave her a fright, that's all.
It gave us all a fright really.
As I said, we only want what's best for you.
I simply wish to see you happy. Healthy.
Yeah... I know you do, Clarence.
Good. Now then, pass me one of those apples?

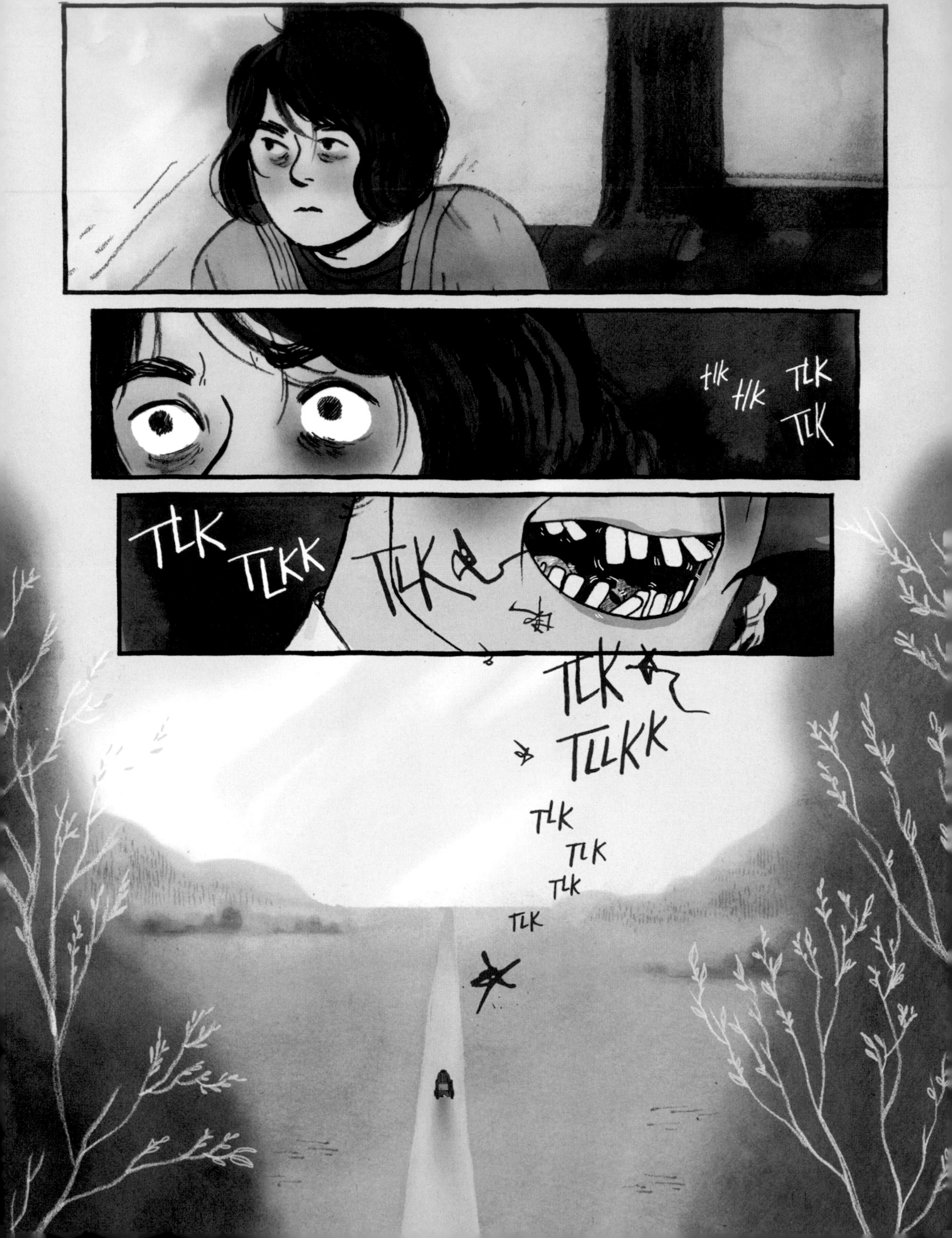
tlk tlk TLK
TLK
TLK
TLKK
TLK
TLK
TLLKK
TLK
TLK
TLK
TLK

IN CONCLUSION

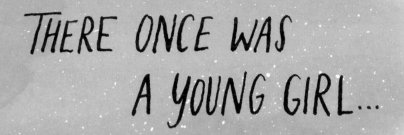

THERE ONCE WAS
A YOUNG GIRL...

...who lived at the edge
of a deep, dense forest.

Before she left for her mother's house, her father told her:
DON'T LINGER in the WOODS.
TRAVEL SWIFT and SAFE.
THERE ARE WOLVES circling in the DARK.
Yes, Papa.

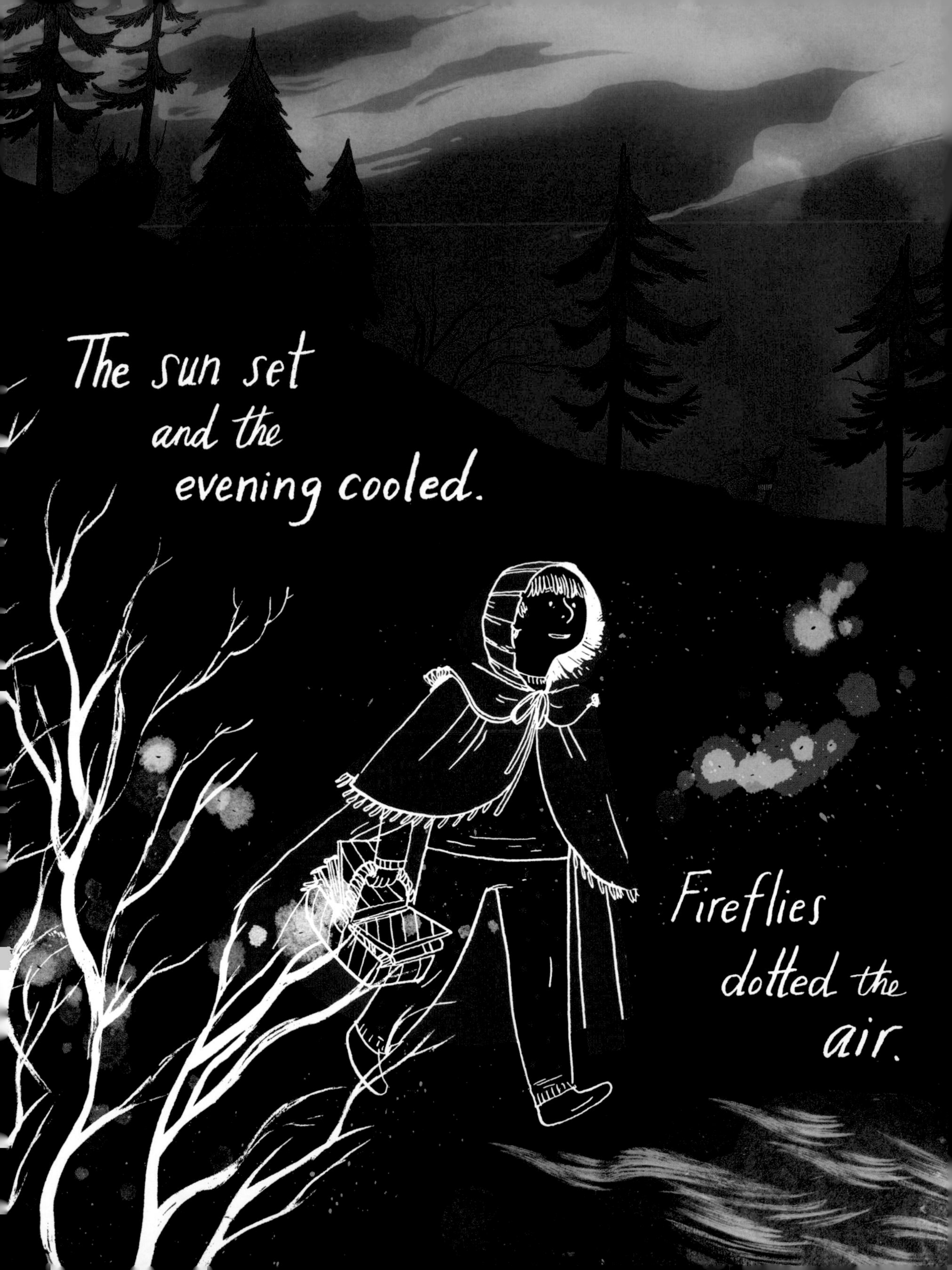
The sun set and the evening cooled.
Fireflies dotted the air.

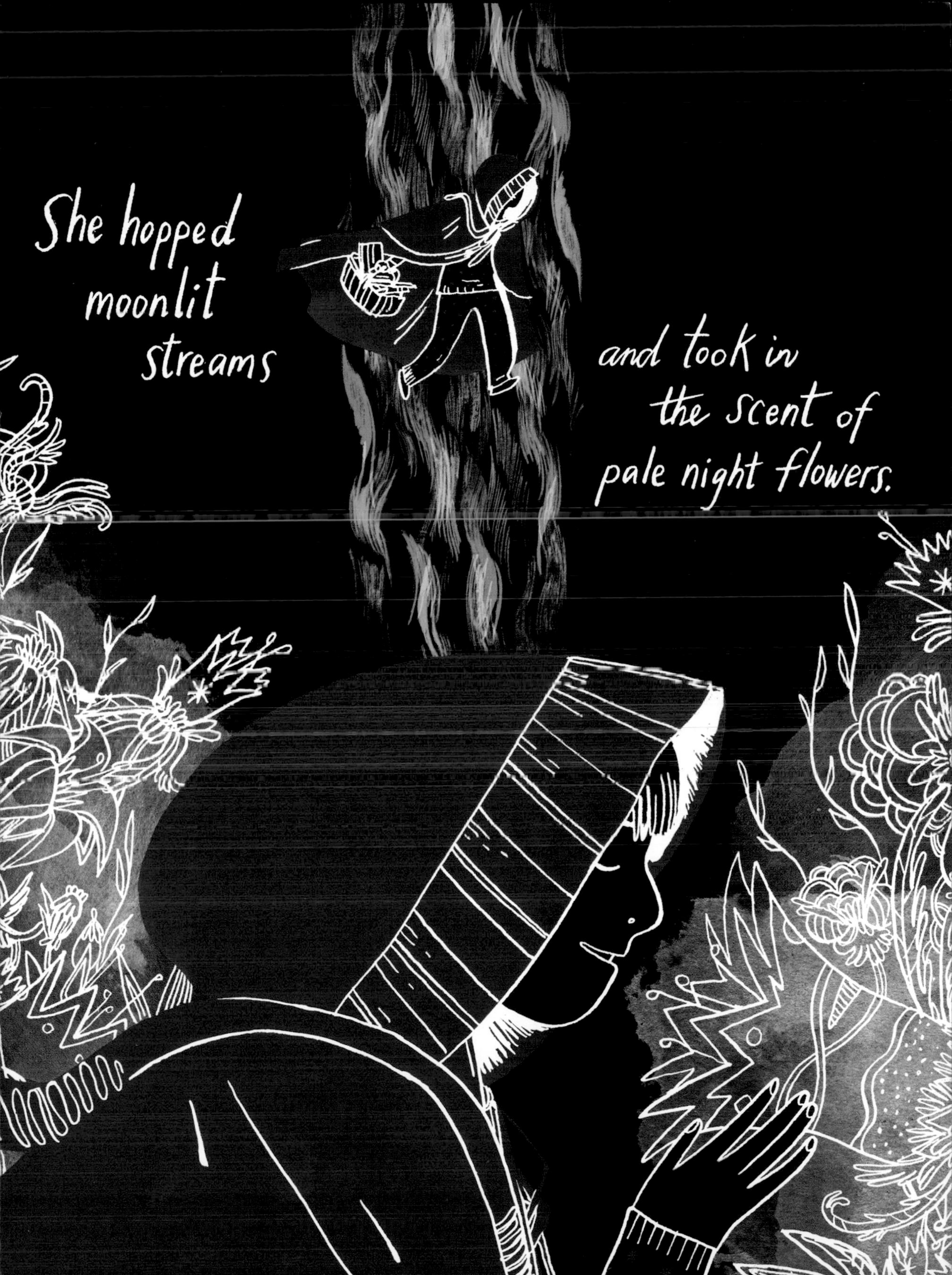
She hopped moonlit streams
and took in the scent of pale night flowers.

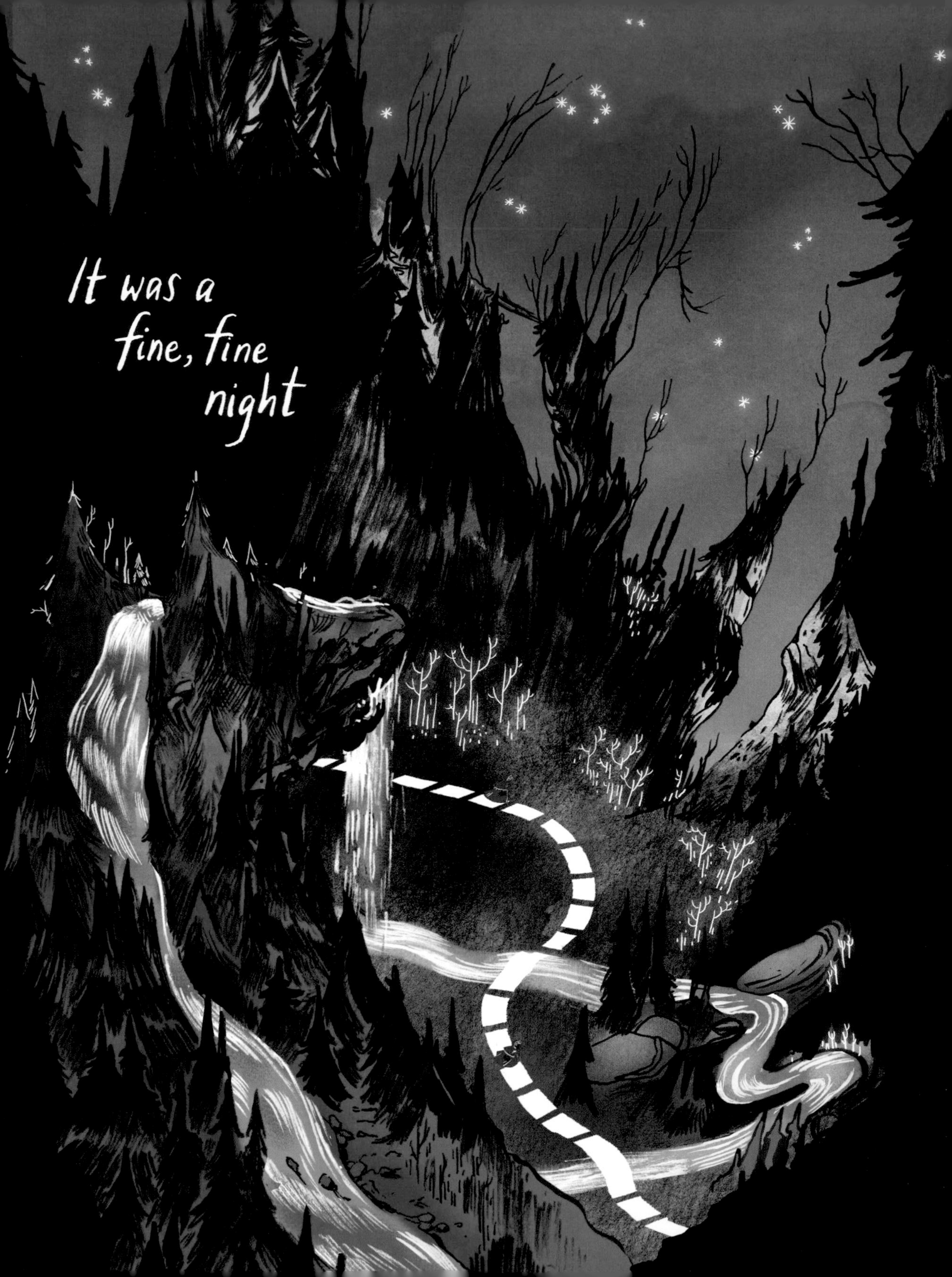
It was a
fine, fine
night

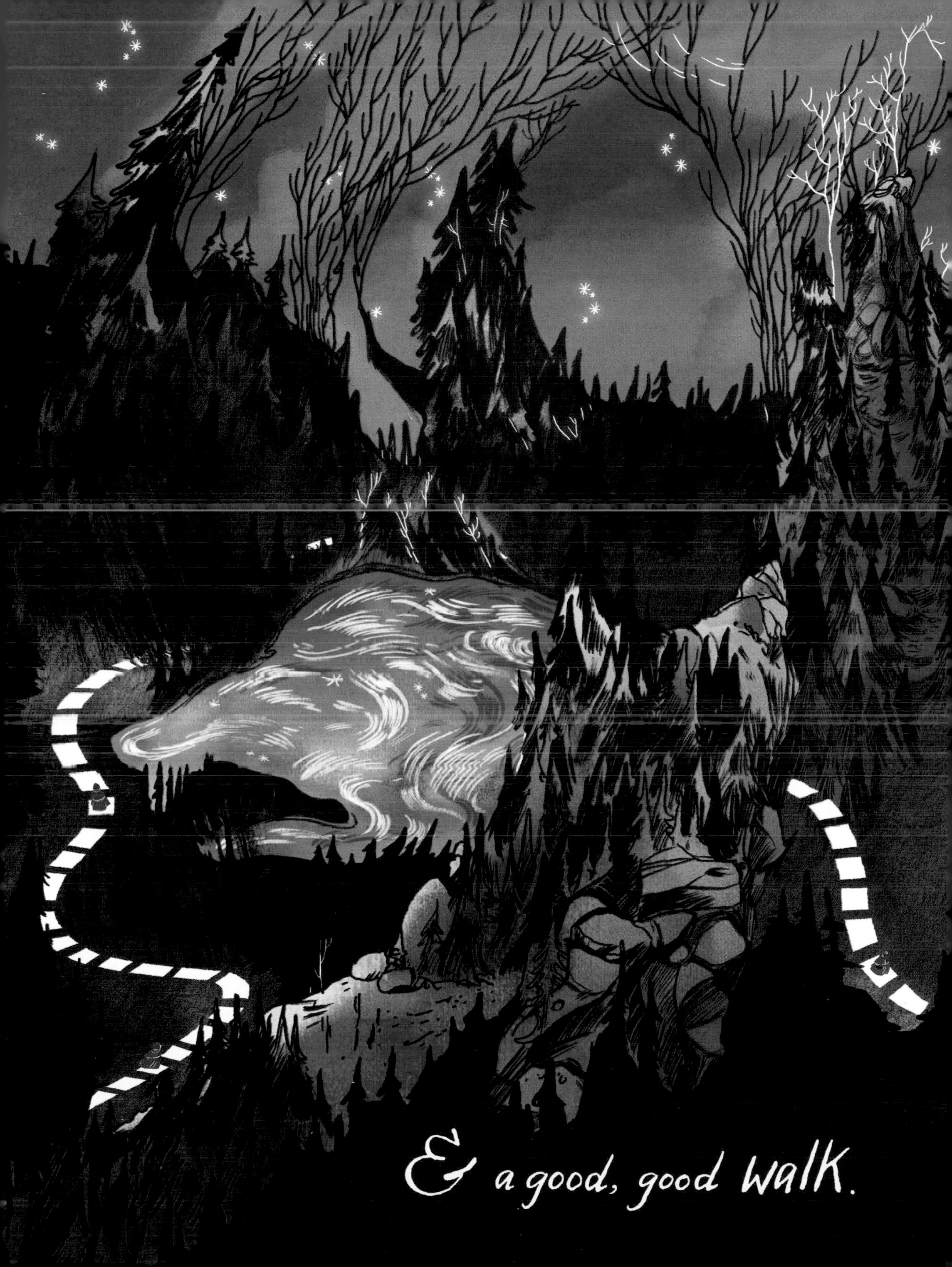
& a good, good walk.

After she arrived at her mother's house,

her mother embraced her,
Kissed her,

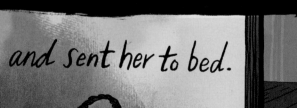

and sent her to bed.

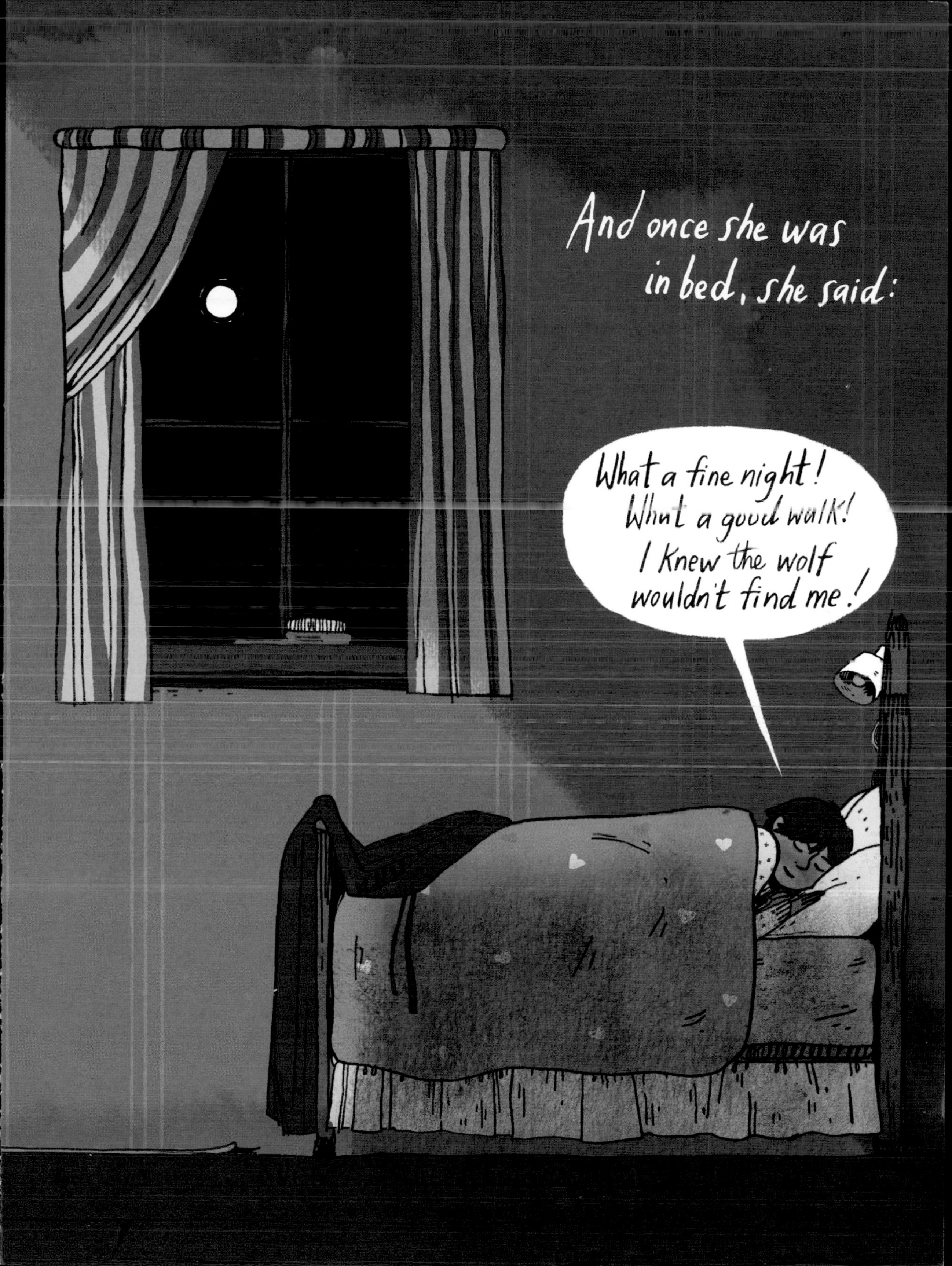
And once she was in bed, she said:
What a fine night! What a good walk! I knew the wolf wouldn't find me!

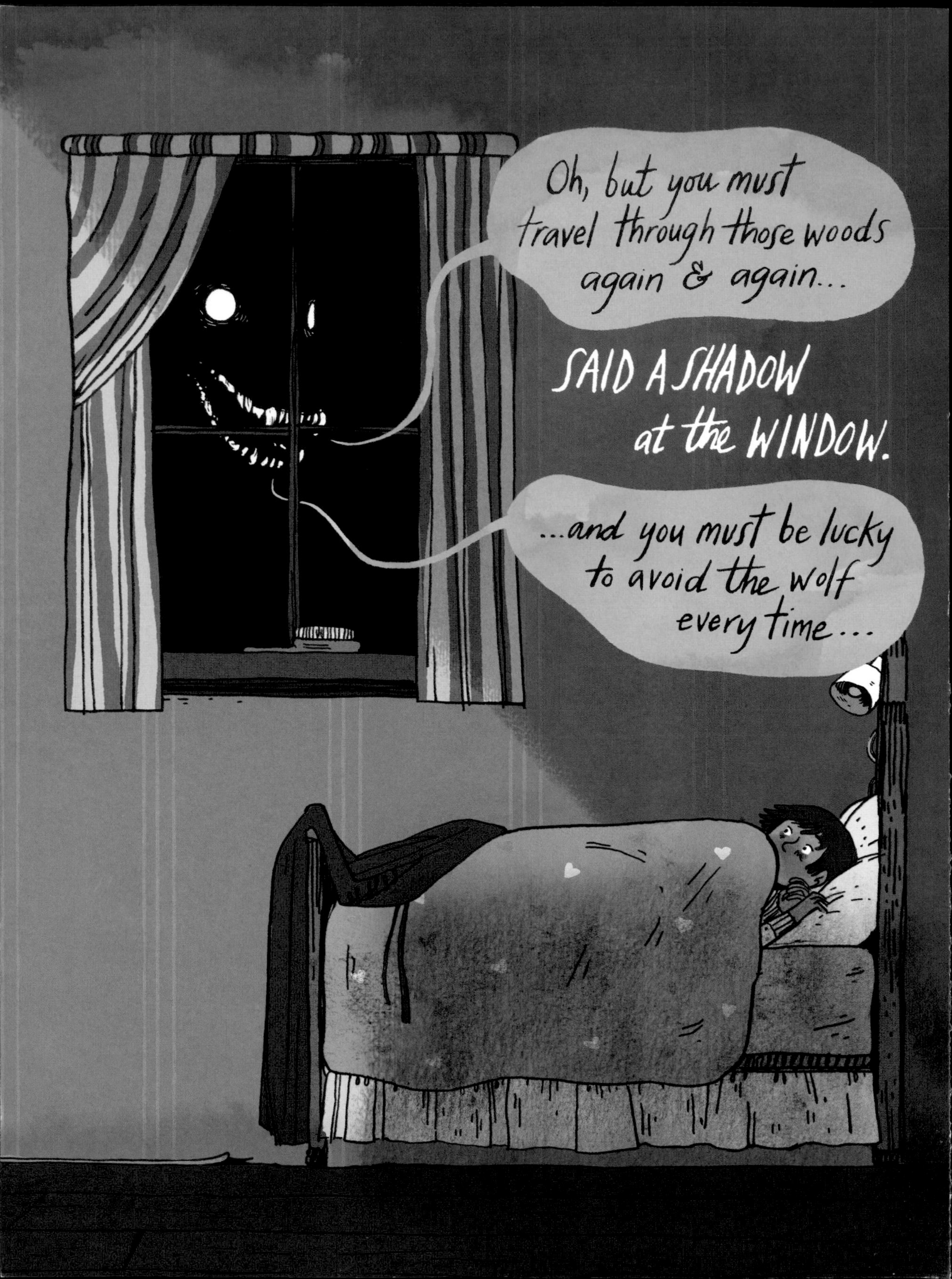
Oh, but you must travel through those woods again & again...
SAID A SHADOW at the WINDOW.
...and you must be lucky to avoid the wolf every time...

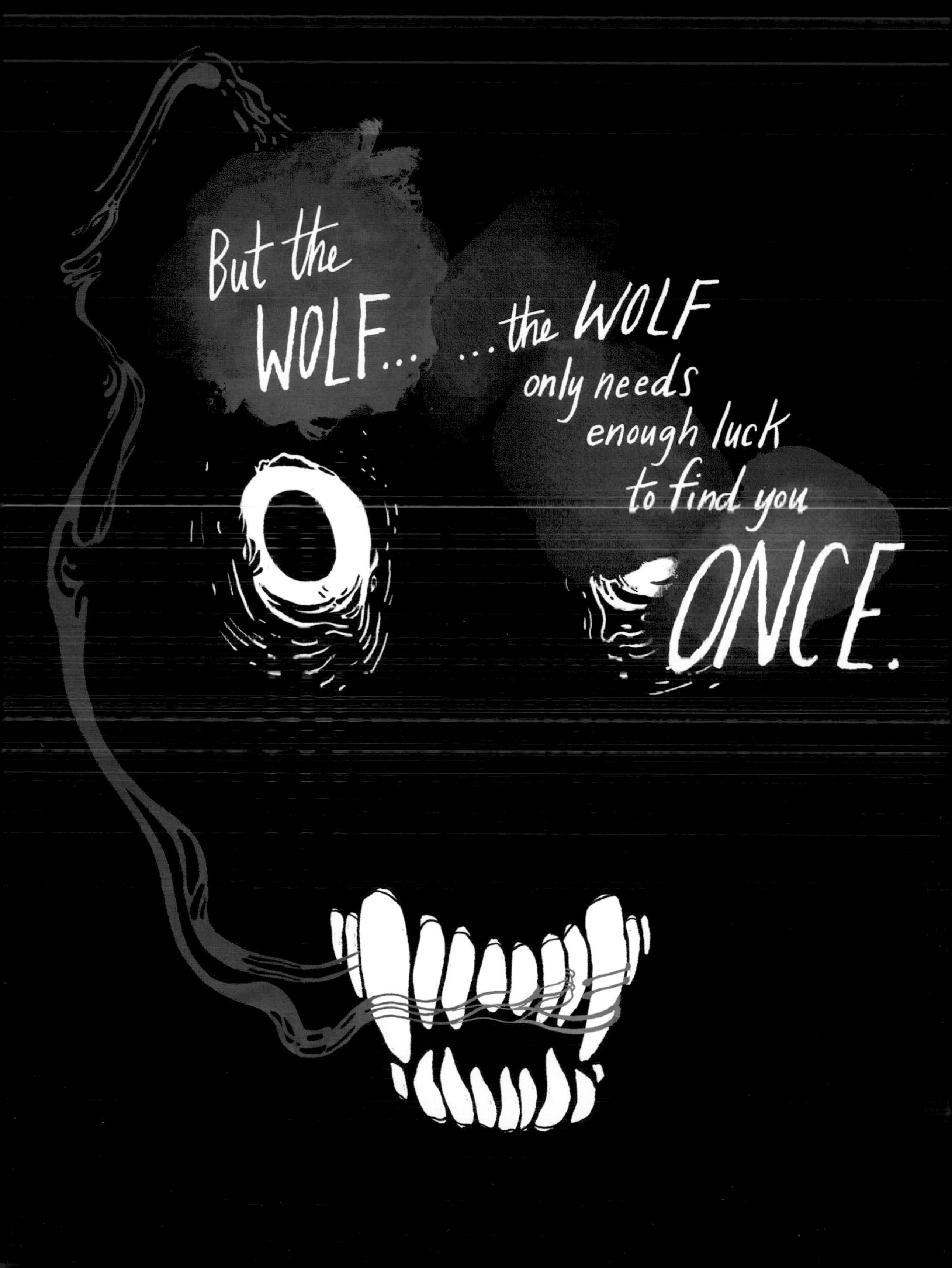
But the WOLF...
...the WOLF only needs enough luck to find you ONCE.

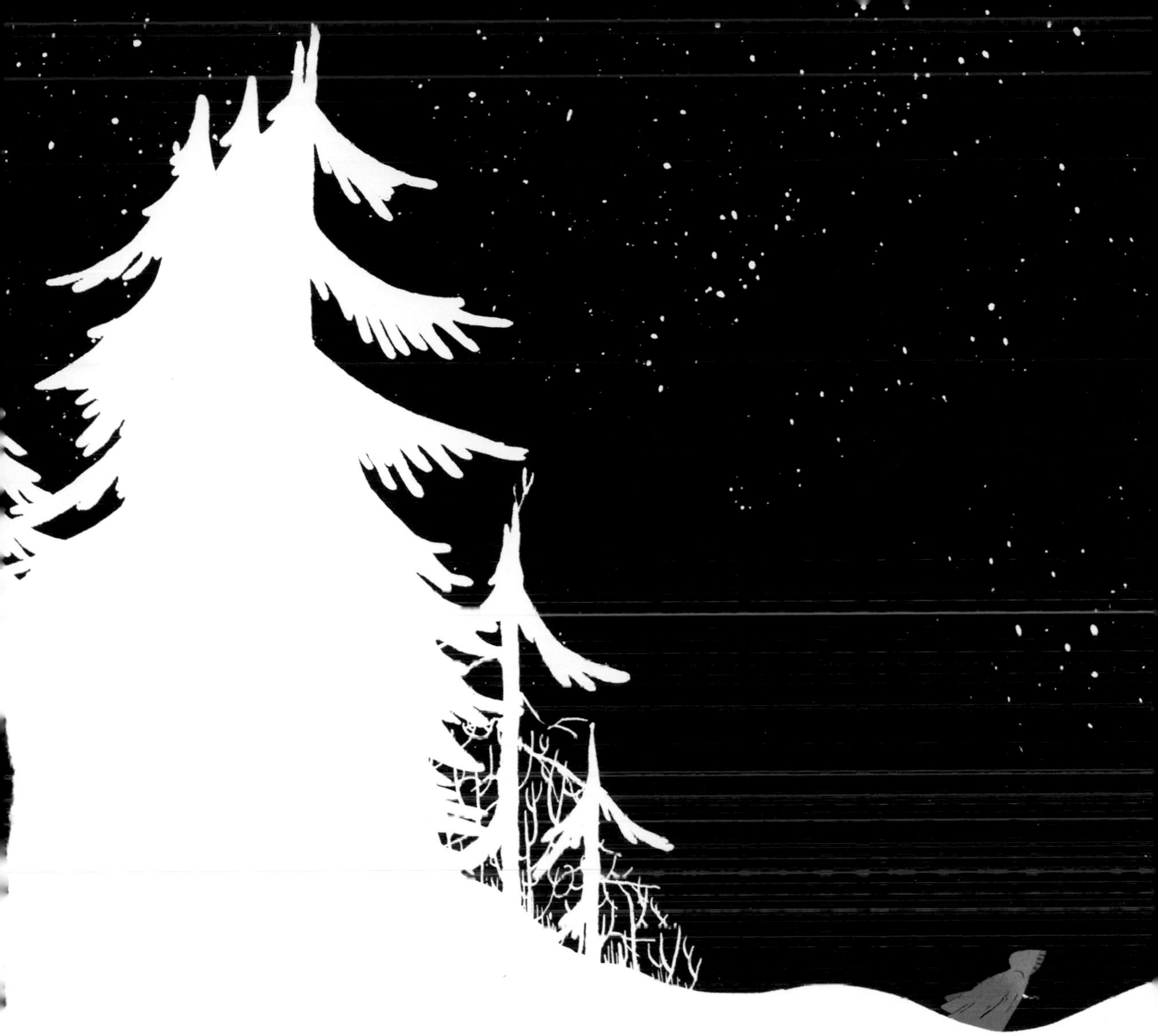

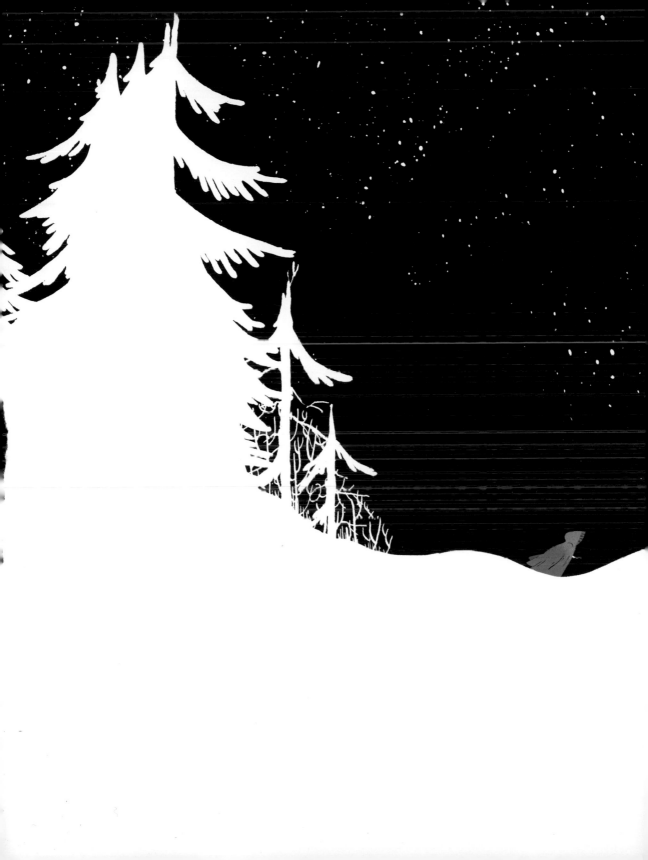

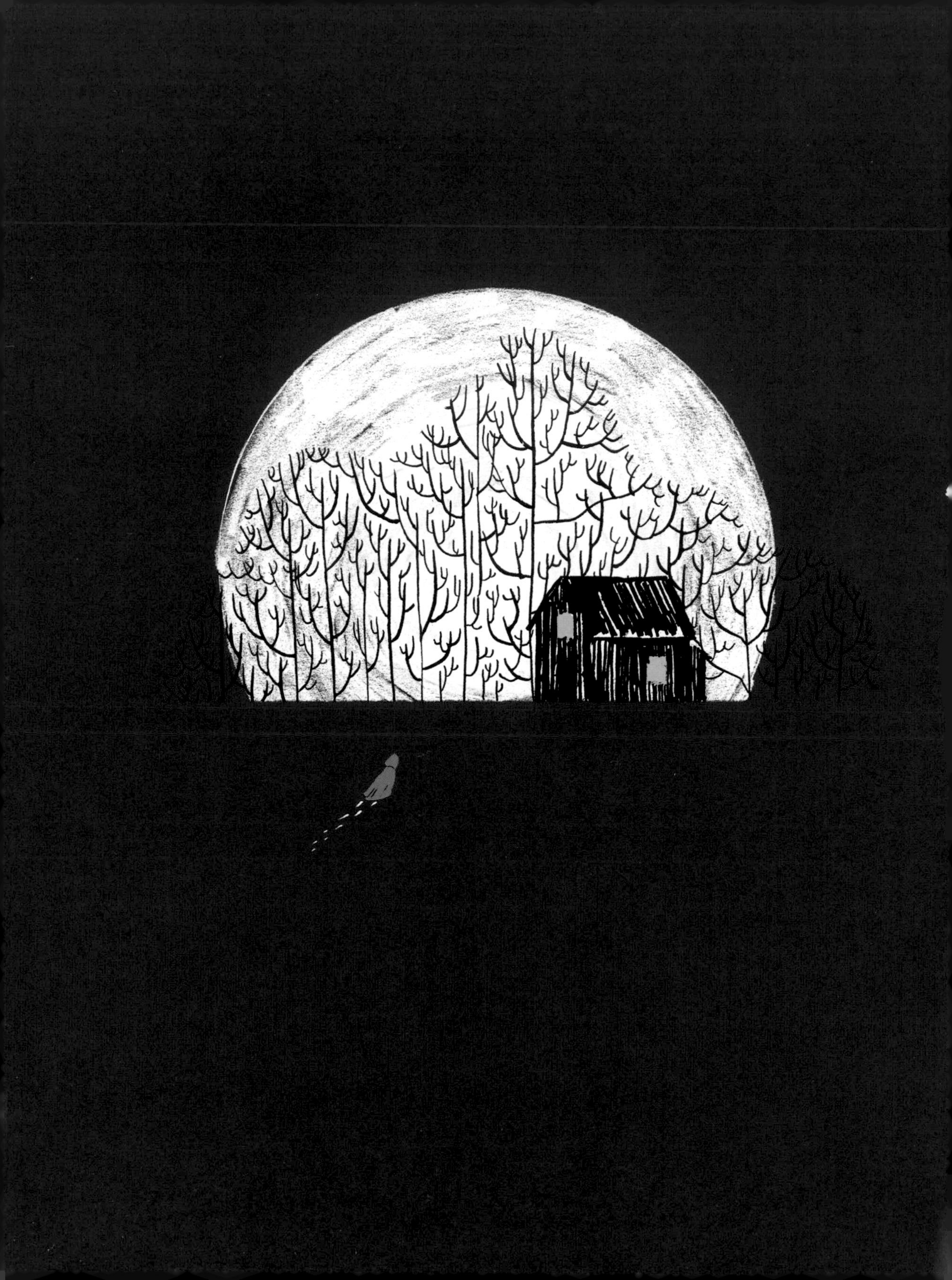